W9-CEW-385

Loss of Innocence

Dear Norie,
Dear, dear friend —
Thank you for all your
enthusiasm!
fondly,
Anne

LOSS
of
INNOCENCE

A NOVEL OF THE FRENCH REVOLUTION

by
Anne Newton Walther

TAPESTRIES PUBLISHING
SAN FRANCISCO

Published in the United States by
Tapestries Publishing
www.tapestriespublishing.com
Distributed by IPM, 800-758-3756

Jacket design: George Mattingly Design/Berkeley
Text design: George Mattingly Design,
adapted from a design by David Bullen

PUBLISHER'S CATALOGING-IN-PUBLICATION DATA

Walther, Anne N.
Loss of innocence: a novel of the French Revolution / by Anne Newton Walther.
   p.   cm.
  ISBN-13: 978-0-9676703-4-8
  ISBN-10: 0-9676703-4-9
  1. France—History—Revolution, 1789–1799—Fiction.   I. Title.
PS3573.A47265L67   2007
813.54 dc

LIBRARY OF CONGRESS CONTROL NUMBER: 2007901287

Printed in Canada on acid-free paper

ISBN 978-0-9676703-4-8

5 4 3 2 1

To the French,
without whom the American Revolution
would not have succeeded,
and to the Americans
who landed on the French beaches
and liberated France,
completing the circle.

Acknowledgments

Writing is a lonely business. Perhaps that is why the people who come and go during the process, lending their expertise, knowledge, and in some cases simple and much needed encouragement, are more deeply appreciated than might be the case in other professions or endeavors.

I am deeply indebted to Zipporah Collins, George Mattingly, Mark Woodworth, and Anita Halton, the professionals, who I also count as my friends. I owe a debt of gratitude to Beau Kealy, Lucy Shaw Beatty, and Anne Lawrence, the readers, who painstakingly soldiered through the early stages of the manuscript, offering valuable suggestions and corrections. I owe a special thanks, again, to Katherine Neville, a comrade in arms, who, among other things, never fails to refer me to just the right person, in this case Ann La Farge, whose generous gift of time and professional editing polished the rough diamond and made it shine. Thank you, Ann.

On every project there are special angels: Nonie de Limur, the memoir of Lucy de la Tour du Pin and your constant enthusiasm for this project were invaluable; Béatrice Gomory, the French resources you generously supplied filled essential gaps in my knowledge of the revolutionary period. I thank you both.

To my special friends—you know who you are—who are always

in my corner lending your enthusiastic support, you are the wind beneath my wings.

As always, in all my endeavors, dear family, near and far, I couldn't have done it without you. To my husband, Roger, before, during, and forever, thank you for your staunch support, your enduring patience, and your love.

LOSS
of
INNOCENCE

PROLOGUE

OCTOBER 16, 1793
Paris — Place de la Révolution

The figure of the man was little more than a dark shadow in the deep recess of the doorway. His was not the coarse blue wool of the peasants or the popular red stripe of the *sans-culottes*. His drab jacket and trousers blended with the stone of the building, the wooden staff he gripped loosely in his hand, and the dim, gray light. His hat drawn low on his brow was not the people's *bonnet rouge*, nor did it sport the blue and red cockade of the revolution. He was invisible. The doorway in which he lurked stood in the shadow of the guillotine. He was oblivious to the stench of the place, to the dark stains that spread in all directions from the base of the scaffold.

He had come early to position himself. He had watched through the drizzle as the people of Paris, wearing a rainbow of color once denied them, moved into the Place de la Révolution — mothers with infants suckling at their breasts, young boys atop their fathers' shoulders, old men and women tottering forward into the square supported by younger arms. He had watched as the soldiers positioned themselves strategically amongst the growing throng.

3

The drizzle continued through the long hours as the multitude waited with an air of expectancy. He looked out over the silent crowd. Where was the circus atmosphere that accompanied other executions, the ribald jokes and bantering amongst the spectators, the pushing and shoving of children jockeying for position? This scene seemed almost planned, orchestrated.

Then, in the distance, the clatter of a tumbrel's wheels struck like thunder in the stillness. The crowd as one turned towards the sound. He could follow the progress of the wagon as the crowd parted, making way for it. Finally, into his view appeared a head in a plain bonnet floating forward above the mass of people. As if by a silent command, the populace fell back, making a path. The tumbrel moved slowly across the final distance to the scaffold.

The figure standing erect in the cart was gaunt to the point of emaciation. She looked neither left nor right, but gazed above the heads of the throng at an invisible horizon. As the wagon drew nearer, he could see the milky surface of the one sightless eye, barely visible beneath the bonnet's brim. Her dingy white gown hung limply, swaying with the movement of the wagon. One ringless hand rested lightly on the cart.

Finally, the tumbrel came to a halt at the foot of the scaffold. For the first time the woman seemed aware of her surroundings. Her gaze traveled slowly from the scaffold platform that stood six feet above the ground, up the looming structure of the guillotine to the large, angled blade that hung cocked into position. She closed her eyes and lowered her head, swaying as a shudder passed through her. Then, opening her eyes, she tightened her grip on the side of the cart and stared ahead as before. Rough hands pulled her down from the wagon. It was then that the man in the shadows saw the tattered, plum-colored slippers, the one touch of color she wore. He watched as she mounted the steep steps, staggered slightly, and stepped on Charles-Henri Sanson's foot. He saw her avert her face from the familiar figure of the public executioner and barely heard her say, *"Pardonnez-moi, monsieur. I didn't mean to."*

Once she was on the scaffold platform, the nearness of the guillotine appeared to catch her off guard. She trembled and stepped back. Sanson caught her arm. It was not clear whether he meant to steady her or move her forward. He reached up and pulled off her bonnet. Reflexively, the woman who once was queen started to reach up as if to smooth her hair, but then dropped her arm to her side. A shocked murmur rose from the people when they saw the woman's raggedly cropped, stark-white hair. The executioner turned her to face the square. She made no move to resist, but stood quietly before them.

A voice cried out, *"L'Autri-Chienne!"* Another shouted, *"Coquine!"* Soon others took up the chant. Angry fists jabbed the air. She made no effort to speak, as her husband had. Now as before, she ignored the people. The executioner motioned her to turn. He awkwardly positioned her on the horizontal plank of the guillotine, strapped her down, and pushed the plank forward, which placed her head into the brace. The crowd fell silent. Sanson pulled the cord of the guillotine. There was a loud swooshing sound as the lethal blade flew down through the grooves. And then, nothing.

As was the custom, the executioner reached into the basket for the head. Gripping a hank of hair, he held the head aloft to the beat of the drums that signified another successful execution. At that moment, the witness slipped from his hiding place. Leaning on his staff to disguise his height, he melted into the crowd.

The Archduchess of Austria, the Queen Consort of France, was dead.

"Courage! I have shown it for years;
think you I shall lose it at the moment
when my sufferings are to end?"

MARIE ANTOINETTE, 1793

I

The young rider urged his mount on, propelled by the thunder-heads building on the distant horizon and by his need to reach the Château de Beaumont to inform its countess, Eugénie Devereux, about what he had learned.

Sitting alone in her sun-drenched garden, Comtesse de Beaumont was unaware of the gathering storm. She was the last in a long and proud lineage dating back to the reign of Charlemagne when the emperor rewarded her ancestor's loyalty with substantial holdings in the Bordeaux valley. Down through the generations, the de Beaumonts' fidelity and political astuteness were invaluable to the reigning powers of France. Groomed from an early age by a doting mother and father, Eugénie Devereux assumed the mantle of responsibility at the time of their premature death and carried it lightly on her young shoulders. Now, no longer a young maid, she is a woman in the prime of life, a person of influence and an active member of the nobility's inner circle.

Enjoying a rare afternoon to herself, Eugénie absently twirled a lock of chestnut hair as she scanned the letter she had just finished writing. She paused, hearing footsteps.

"Ah, Jeremy, you've returned," Eugénie said, smiling at the handsome young black man who walked through the tall hedge, holding a small white dog in his arms. "How did you find Versailles?"

"The same as ever, Madame—the usual gossiping and back-stabbing." Eugénie put her lap desk on the ground and moved the skirt of her yellow gown to make room for him on the stone bench.

Jeremy shook his head. "*Non, merci,* Mistress. It's a relief to stand after so long in the saddle." He put the puppy down on the grass and the little animal immediately scurried over to the hedge and plopped down in the shade of the boxwood.

"Miss Eugénie, the current color becomes you," he said, noticing how the deep shade set off her chestnut hair. "You put the ladies of the court to shame."

"How gallant you are, Jeremy!" she said, then lowered her voice. "But, even this far from court, we must be careful not to give invisible ears grist for the gossip mill. I agree, the queen's choice of yellow this year is a great improvement over that atrocious brownish-green of last season," she said, wrinkling her nose. "The queen may be partial to Rousseau's return-to-nature philosophy, but I say leave the colors of the soil on the Earth as God intended. *D'accord,* tell me about the thoroughbred transaction, and, more importantly, how you found the climate at Versailles since the riots in Paris and the fall of the Bastille."

Jeremy looked at his mistress fondly. It had been fourteen years since the Comtesse de Beaumont brought him as a young boy to France from the island of Bermuda and had drawn up papers securing his freedom. He had quickly endeared himself to all the members of the château household. The countess had seen to it that he received the finest training in France to become a Master of the Horse. He now oversaw her extensive stables, traveling across France and abroad to purchase, sell, and trade bloodstock. Through his efforts, no stable in France surpassed the château's racers and hunters. As the countess's representative, he had become a familiar face at events outside the Thoroughbred world. Acting as the countess's eyes and ears, he also was one of the network of agents who kept her informed of the world beyond the château's walls.

"The court carries on the same as ever, but I felt something disturbing just below the surface," Jeremy replied. "I overheard the queen's confidante, the Austrian ambassador Mercy d'Argenteau, speak of her anger at the developments of the past few weeks and her growing irritation with the Marquis de Lafayette and his reformist views."

"It sounds as if King Louis is caught between a rock and a hard spot," Eugénie murmured, "trying to meet the expectations of the newly formed National Assembly on the one hand and his queen's demands on the other. What he concedes in the morning, she convinces him to reverse by nightfall."

"Yes, that's about the gist of it. Meanwhile, she plans her next ball or amuses herself frolicking with her ladies at the Hamlet."

"It does seem contradictory that she had that quaint peasants' village built as her refuge from the formality of court, and yet she dismisses out of hand the people's woes."

"She's not a friend of the people, nor are they of her," Jeremy said sharply.

"It was not always that way, Jeremy. *Quel dommage!* But who are we to judge her? How easy could it be for that high-spirited young maid of fifteen to leave Austria and her royal family, where she was the cosseted darling, and come to this country to marry the future king and have to conform to the etiquette of a court so different from her own?"

"Madame, you're too kind. You were the same age when you lost both of your parents and had to shoulder the responsibilities of your family's vast holdings. I have no sympathy for '*Madame Deficit,*'" Jeremy said with feeling.

"Jeremy, for shame—using her brother-in-law Provence's cruel nickname."

"*Je suis désolé,* Madame, but she earned it even before the diamond necklace affair. And she's called much worse—'*l'Autri-Chienne,*' '*Co . . .*'"

"Jeremy," Eugénie said, interrupting him, "*ça suffit!* Her involvement in that scandal is old news, and totally false at that. That silly, pretentious man finally admitted that the queen had refused the necklace and had had nothing whatsoever to do with his feeble plan. Isn't it enough that, in the three years since then, the queen has withdrawn from the public eye and all the things she used to enjoy? She's become a virtual recluse at Versailles, venturing out only when coerced. *Alors,* if there's nothing more, I'd best go prepare for the Marquis de Lafayette's visit."

Realizing that he had upset the person who meant everything in the world to him, Jeremy said quickly, "Forgive me, I went too far."

"You're forgiven, dear Jeremy. The queen does seem to bring out the most extreme emotions. She's either loved or despised, nothing in between. But, really, I must go—unless there's something further?"

"There is. Now, more than ever, there are those who openly come out and criticize her." He reached up and picked an orange from a nearby tree. Peeling it, he continued, "They blame her for keeping the court at Versailles, instead of letting it move back and forth between the palace and Paris. Once again, she lacks any concern for the burdens she places on others."

"Ah, Jeremy, you see, that's a perfect example of how untruths become fact. The queen can't be held responsible for the court's residing at Versailles. It was Louis's ancestor, Louis XIV, who built Versailles for the very purpose of putting some distance between the court and the gossipmongers of Paris. She may prefer the countryside to Paris, but so does the king with his devotion to the hunt, which he enjoys every day, rain or shine."

"I stand corrected, milady," Jeremy said, though he looked anything but contrite. "Oh, I almost forgot. I also noticed glaring absences at Court. At least one or two members from each faction were missing. Why, the king's own brother d'Artois was not in attendance. I would've assumed that he was with the queen or otherwise occupied, were it not for that pup." He gestured towards the dog sleeping contentedly. "The poor little thing was running from person to person, as if asking where his master was. D'Artois is devoted to all his horses and dogs, but that one was his favorite. They were inseparable."

"Jeremy, I never fail to marvel at your knowledge of even the most trivial things, but what's the dog doing here? Le Duc will miss him when he returns to court."

"I couldn't just leave the little fella. For all practical purposes, he's been abandoned. From what I heard, the duke won't be back any time soon. Word is, he was very angry at the change in the king's standing since the Bastille's fall. He left France, taking a small fortune with him to raise a mercenary army to reinstate the king's absolute authority when he returns."

"Jeremy, what you say supports the rumors I've heard that members of the nobility are emigrating or planning to emigrate to the United States, or perhaps to some friendly European soil, to escape the growing hostilities. So far, I haven't heard that any have left from this region, but we're insulated down here." The countess looked off for a moment, deep in thought.

Mentally shaking herself, she looked back at Jeremy and smiled. "Of course, the pup is welcome here. We'll call him 'Émigré.'"

At her words, the pup raced over to nestle in her skirts and promptly fell back to sleep. "How quickly loyalties shift," Eugénie said, leaning over to pat the little dog's head. "Jamie returned from Paris last night with yet another alarming report. He said the talk in the taverns is that the queen plots to mine the National Assembly, poison the king, and replace him with d'Artois and that she's written her brother, Emperor Leopold, asking him to send a force to invade France!"

Jeremy rolled his eyes. "Certainly, I've no sympathy for the queen, but that's absurd. No one can take that seriously."

"I couldn't agree more, Jeremy, but her enemies grow bolder every day. Who knows what they'll concoct next? Only God knows where it will end. If I'm hearing these monstrous things, surely they're reaching the king's and queen's ears as well. Speaking of that poor man, how did you find the king?"

Jeremy finished an orange section, and then replied, "He seemed harried, lacking his customary patience. He was more preoccupied than ever. When it was my turn to come forward, his face visibly brightened. He immediately announced the end of the court's business for the day and, with me in tow, retired directly to the stables."

"That poor, beleaguered man," Eugénie murmured.

"The king has a most discerning eye for horseflesh. He took our entire lot and demanded more," Jeremy chuckled. "If he were as adept with people as he is with horses, his kingdom would be as fine as his stables."

Eugénie couldn't help smiling, even though she knew she should chastise him for his impudence. But how could she? What a remarkable person he'd grown up to be. She looked at him with pride. There was little of the young boy in the man who stood before her, except for the boundless energy and curiosity that still, at times, caused dissension in her household. "Ah, at least that transaction was a bright spot in his day," she sighed. "Now I *must* go and prepare to receive the Marquis de Lafayette." She rose and moved towards Jeremy to take his arm. Jeremy stepped back, holding up his hands.

"*Non,* Madame. The long ride from Versailles has left little difference between me and my horse."

"Jeremy, you must think me a prig that I would mind the perfume of the stable. I spend so many hours of the day as the chatelaine, I rarely have time to be with my precious beasts. Now, give me your arm and let me enjoy the pleasure of your ride vicariously."

With a smile, the young man bowed and offered her his arm. Together, they strolled down the graveled path, with the pup scampering along behind them.

"The king kept eyeing Roan IV," Jeremy said, chuckling. "Had his Highness not been called away, no doubt he would have taken the horse right out from under me!"

Eugénie threw back her head and laughed, imagining the king's bulging eyes feasting on the beautiful stallion.

II

Members of the household dallied in the hallway, hoping to catch a glimpse of the famous Marquis de Lafayette. Oblivious of his audience, the people's hero strolled arm in arm with his hostess down the wide corridor.

"Gilbert, you're so kind to come all this way. You can imagine how impatient I am to hear from you firsthand what's been taking place in Paris," Eugénie said, smiling up at him. "Buried down here, I'm simply starved for information."

"Madame," the Marquis replied skeptically, "I sincerely doubt that, knowing the extensive network you have in place."

"I do have my sources, that's true, but there's nothing like receiving it straight from the horse's mouth."

Lafayette laughed. "Knowing your love for those beasts, I'll take that comparison as a compliment."

Eugénie chuckled as she led him into the *petit salon* and gestured for him to join her on the settee facing the fireplace. "Understanding how little time you have to yourself as commander of the newly formed Garde Nationale, I'm doubly grateful for your making the trip down here," she said as she picked up the crystal

17

carafe from the table beside her and filled two goblets with Bordeaux from the château's vast cellar. Handing one to her guest, she saluted him with the other.

"*Ma chère* Eugénie," Lafayette replied, sipping the wine, "no matter the extent of my duties, I'll always make time to personally keep you informed, as long as it's in my power to do so. Our families share a long history together, not to mention the political views we've held in common. Your friendship means the world to me."

"Thank you, Gilbert, as yours does to me." The two friends savored their wine, for the moment lost in their own thoughts. Eugénie observed her guest without appearing to. Early on, they had both been drawn to the American patriots' cause and had spent many an evening speculating about a France built on liberty and equality.

The patter of raindrops on the windowpanes interrupted Eugénie's reverie.

"*Dieu merci,* you arrived before the storm. What a downpour we're having," she exclaimed.

Lafayette nodded with feeling. "*Oui!* I am certainly grateful for that. Will the rain harm the grapes?"

"No," his hostess answered, "the storm's almost passed, and tomorrow's sun should prevent any mold from forming."

"*Bon,*" Lafayette said, holding his glass up to the light, admiring the deep ruby color. "Yours is one of the finest Bordeaux in France. It would be her loss and mine if any harm came to this year's crop."

"Thank you for the compliment, sir. But, speaking of storms, I hope the rumors that have reached me exaggerate the situation in

Paris. I'm bursting with impatience to hear all about it. You must tell me everything, down to the smallest detail."

Lafayette's expression turned grave. "I don't know what you've heard, Eugénie, but I can attest to how volatile the conditions have become. What began as a reasonable act of a fearful citizenry seeking arms to protect itself has turned into mass hysteria and violence bearing little resemblance to the intellectual idealism that propelled the Americans' revolution.

"Forgive me if I become long-winded, but in order to understand the situation that exists today, it's imperative to lay out the events that led up to it. You and I were two of the nobility whose urging finally compelled the king to call the Assembly of Notables to address the country's financial woes and to undertake steps to set up a constitutional monarchy. That body of men came by its nickname 'the Not-Ables' honestly." He chuckled and then continued in a serious tone. "They wasted no time stepping out of the line of fire, advising the king to call the Estates-General. As you know, Jacques Necker, le Ministre de Finance, for all intents and purposes the head of the government, gave the Third Estate, the chamber of the people, a vote of two compared to one vote for the nobility and clergy chambers. In the resulting uproar and confusion, the Third Estate proposed a vote that was taken which united all three Estates into one chamber."

Eugénie nodded, "Creating the National Assembly."

Lafayette nodded. "In this unified body, the commoners outnumbered the nobles and clergy six hundred twenty-one to five hundred ninety-three."

"How the tables have turned," Eugénie breathed.

"Yes, indeed," Lafayette agreed. "All this occurred in May, but by well into June, the Assembly had done nothing but work on framing a constitution. The deplorable state of the royal finances hadn't been addressed, tax collection was seriously in arrears, and the people's desperate condition was escalating daily. For all the so-called political reform, nothing had changed. The jackals were circling and holding the king responsible."

Eugénie's expression was grim. "Granted, the royal treasury has been worsened by France's aid to the Americans' revolution, and it's true that the recent harsh winters and summer droughts have driven food supplies down and prices up. But the king inherited the grain and flour riots and the depleted treasury when he ascended the throne fifteen years ago. From the start he's been a champion of the people. They must know that he's made it his purpose to try to reduce privilege, eliminate the corruption of the court he inherited, and create a fairer tax structure."

"*C'est vrai,* dear Eugénie, but therein lies the king's dilemma. On the one hand, he's sought to take away from the influential and powerful, whose goodwill he needs, while on the other hand he's been unable to relieve the desperation of the poor, successfully isolating himself and alienating everyone."

Eugénie sighed. "Yes, and that isolation makes him an easy target for malicious rumors that would have been unspeakable only a short while ago. Did you hear the one that claimed that the king and his ministers set up the food shortages to justify the inflated prices, conveniently forgetting the recent extreme weather conditions? My overseer, Jamie MacKenzie, was in Paris in April when that rumor, later proved unfounded, set off the riot in Saint-Antoine that ransacked, burned, and looted the warehouse and even the home and gardens of Monsieur Réveillon. *Ce pauvre homme. Quel dommage!*"

Before Lafayette could comment, a liveried servant appeared in the doorway of the salon, announcing, "Madame, *le dîner est servi.*"

Once Eugénie and her guest were seated at the intimate banquette at one end of the impressive dining room, a servant presented the first course of crayfish in a light truffle sauce, served with a crisp Chablis.

Raising his goblet, Lafayette saluted his hostess. "*Superbe!* Eugénie, your table, as always, lives up to its reputation. What a shame to mar this feast with the grave matters we've been discussing, but we must press on.

"Exaggerated facts and false rumors have fueled much of the events lately," he continued. "The Réveillon warehouse riot, which you mentioned, was a perfect example. The rumor that Réveillon was cutting his workers' wages was completely false. It was not an occasion, as was put forward, of his workers rising up to redress a grievance. Not one of his workers took part in the riot. Instead, those malcontents came from across the Seine from the brewery and tannery district of Saint-Marcel."

Eugénie sighed and shook her head. "I'm told they call it 'the Paris Massacre.'"

Lafayette nodded. "When the smoke cleared, some three hundred lay dead and some three hundred more injured. Bad enough, but nothing like the rumor that nine hundred had been killed. We'll never know, but probably the mob would have disbanded without incident had not the Duchesse d'Orléans, returning from the races at Vincennes, insisted that the soldiers holding back the rioters break rank to let her carriage through."

"That foolish woman!" Eugénie said with disgust. "Even in the best of times that district's known to be dangerous."

"My thoughts exactly," her guest agreed. "As you know, that was not the first incident of its kind in Paris or in the countryside, but it was by far the worst. Since then, fear has stalked the streets of the city. No one feels safe. Even the meekest bear arms, as if they were a talisman against disaster. Weapons cannot defeat poverty, hunger, and despair.

"Meanwhile the National Assembly sits behind an armed guard and plans its constitutional monarchy. Such a government has been our dream for so long, both yours and mine, ever since we saw what rights and privileges could do for the American people." Lafayette was interrupted by the arrival of the next course, young partridge in a pinenut and orange sauce, surrounded by garden vegetables and *Gruyère macarony de Naples*. For a moment, Lafayette's brow cleared and he remarked with a chuckle, "Ah, *macarony de Naples,* Minister Calonne's favorite. If only his plans for the king's finances had been as sound as his palate."

For a few minutes they enjoyed the meal in silence. Then, noticing that her guest was becoming increasingly lost in thought, Eugénie asked, "I heard that the young student Camille Desmoulins gave a stirring speech just days before the attack on the Bastille. Was it triggered by Minister Necker's dismissal?"

"Ah, Eugénie," the Marquis said with a smile, returning his gaze to her face, "you've caught me woolgathering. I do apologize. Yes, you're well informed. That young man reminds me of Mr. Patrick Henry, though I fear his motives are not as pure. On July twelfth—and I mention that date because of subsequent events—it was reported to me that Desmoulins brought the crowd to a fevered pitch when he leapt on a table outside the Café de Foy, haranguing the king and condemning him for Necker's dismissal. The same afternoon I was organizing regiments of the militia to patrol the districts to keep order, he was inflaming the crowds."

"I'm sure you managed to have everything well in hand," Eugénie ventured.

"I thought so at the time, but clearly the cauldron was boiling just below the surface. I can't express to you the climate that had come to pervade that fair city. The cafés of Palais-Royal had always been gathering places for citizens and students, but increasingly they'd been getting out of hand, their habitués inciting each other to riot, with rumors flying and fear begetting fear. Add to that the continuing food shortages, and you have a people who are hungry, desperate, and fed up with empty promises. Fear stalked the streets. Paris had become a tinderbox."

His face tightened. "The very next day after Desmoulins's speech, bands of people swarmed the city streets, looking for arms for protection. The militia was out, as well, seeking additional weapons. The numbers had swelled by nightfall when they arrived at the Hôtel de Ville. There they learned that the arms and powder had been moved from there to the Bastille."

Eugénie's face turned ashen. "What you're saying is far worse than what my agents reported to me."

"It was a night and a day such as Paris had never seen. The people rising. The people on the march. It was a classless throng—men and women, both young and old, nobles, merchants, students, peasants. Meanwhile, word had reached the Governor of the Bastille, Bernard-René de Launay. He wasted no time in trying to fortify the fortress, though he had limited food, no source of water inside, and only a small Swiss regiment and some pensioners to guard the whole fortress.

"The crowd dispersed overnight, but the next morning nine hundred Parisians arrived at the gate of the Bastille, which ironically is in the same neighborhood as Réveillon's burnt-out warehouse. I've wondered since if that earlier riot was a portent of things to come."

"Who made up the crowd at the Bastille?" Eugénie asked.

"Artisans and cabaret owners from the Saint-Antoine district, delegates from the Hôtel de Ville, well-heeled merchants, soldiers who'd deserted their posts, and many desperate people who'd recently come to Paris from the countryside."

"Something about this doesn't make sense," Eugénie said. "Surely there's more to this than Desmoulins's speech, no matter how inflammatory it was."

"Yes, you're right. The heightened number of militia in the street, instead of quelling the people's fears, fed the rumor that troops were there for a more sinister purpose. After the Réveillon bloodbath, the people were desperate for arms and powder to protect themselves. From all reports, the people arriving at the Bastille that morning were frightened but not hostile."

"Then where did it all go wrong? What happened?"

"I can only tell you the sequence of events reported by eyewitnesses," Lafayette replied. "Governor de Launay agreed to meet with two Hôtel de Ville delegates to discuss the request for arms. The crowd grew increasingly restive as time went by and nothing happened. Then came the sound of distant gunfire, and the tinderbox exploded. The mob swarmed into the outer courtyard.

The drawbridge chains were cut, the bridge crashed down, and the mob rushed into the inner courtyard.

"In the mêlée, it's not clear who fired first. After that... bedlam. Over the next few hours, the ranks of the attackers grew. Around five o'clock they broke through the final barrier, disarmed the defenders, and freed the seven inmates." Lafayette paused. "Sadly, it didn't end there. The mob turned its pent-up fury on de Launay. They marched him through the streets, jeering and spitting on him. Finally, when he could stand it no longer, he turned on one of his persecutors. What little control existed up to that point, snapped. They fell on him and hacked him to death. Then they stuck his severed head on a pike and raised it above the cheering crowd."

Eugénie stared at Lafayette, a look of horror on her face. "What you describe is far worse than I was told — a world gone mad. You and I have always believed in and worked to further freedom and equality, but this, this... "

"I know, dear Madame." The Marquis covered her hand with his and said, "We can't condone the excesses of the mob, but I devoutly believe that the outcome of that day served an important purpose."

"With murder and mayhem?" Eugénie gasped.

"Eugénie, we must look at the larger picture. How long have the French people waited to see the king and the National Assembly make good their promises to address food shortages and unemployment?

"The people saw Necker's dismissal as an attempt to prevent these reforms. The Parisians were furious and took action. Because of that day, a municipal government for the city of Paris was set up and the Garde Nationale for all of France was established, for the first time in France's history. The mob's actions were extreme, but good came out of them. Important strides were made.

"Don't you see, the Bastille had become a symbol of oppression, representing all the wrongs of the old régime. The fall of the Bastille meant the end of the king's military power in Paris. That power now lies, as it should, in the hands of the people. Also, the Bastille's downfall lanced a festering boil. It gave the people an outlet for all their pent-up anger and frustration. The next day, as the Garde's commander, I ordered the fortress razed to the ground. That didn't keep scavengers from selling bits and pieces as souvenirs, but, as a symbol, the Bastille was no more."

Eugénie smiled wanly. "It is so very alarming to me, Gilbert," she said quietly. "The actions you describe are of the utmost bestial nature. Is this the behavior of a thinking body that can mindfully govern?"

"Eugénie, this was one of the most propitious moments in the history of France. The revolution has begun! What you and I have talked about, believed in."

Eugénie still looked concerned, but let him continue.

"The king had the forces to crush the uprising, but he showed his good faith by not doing so. He believed in the people and the need for reform. To prove this, it was mandatory for him to make an official visit to the new municipality of Paris. When he came before the National Assembly at the Hôtel de Ville and re-instated Monsieur Necker, that body roared its approval. Finally, we knew he was one of us when he accepted the tricolor cockade that I presented to him. *Vive le Roi!* It was a great moment—a fitting conclusion of the old and the beginning of the new." Lafayette's eyes glowed, reliving the moment. Eugénie considered raising her misgivings, but instead rang the small silver bell at her right hand.

Immediately, a servant came into the room bearing a silver platter with two domed lids. He set one at each place and then, with a flourish, lifted both domes simultaneously, revealing a pale-pink, shimmering substance in delicately cut glass goblets.

"Madame," Lafayette said, smiling, "unless I miss my guess, this is the newest craze of the French court, what they call ice-cream."

"*Oui, c'est vrai,*" Eugénie said, pleased at the effect of her surprise. "Every member of the household has been taking turns perfecting the recipe. So far, Marie's peach version has been the best. You must be the judge." She pretended to hold her breath as the Marquis tasted the first mouthful.

"*C'est magnifique! Délicieux!* I've never tasted anything so delectable."

"I'm delighted," Eugénie said, her eyes sparkling. "Won't Marie be proud."

"Tell me. How is Marie? What a brave young woman she was to accompany you to the American colonies . . . what would it be, fourteen years ago now?"

"Ah, yes," Eugénie murmured, remembering how, commissioned by her cohorts, a long-standing, influential group of like-minded nobility, which included Lafayette, she had crossed the Atlantic to determine the American patriots' intent, vis-à-vis the British crown, and report back her findings. "What wonderful people I met! How quickly I was won over to their cause! My dearest Marie, who had no choice but to fall in with my schemes, is now happily married to the giant Scot, Jamie MacKenzie, with a beautiful daughter, Jacqueline."

"Who is this Jamie? You mentioned him earlier." Sipping the coffee that had accompanied the dessert course, Lafayette raised an eyebrow at his hostess. "I daresay, Madame, you have a rare household."

Eugénie laughed. "You flatter me, my lord. It seems quite usual to me. Jamie was the first mate of Captain Bridger Goodrich, whom I met through the Whittingtons, the family I stayed with while I was in Virginia. The Goodriches were a very successful shipping family in Virginia before the American Revolution. But returning to Jamie... Besotted by Marie, Jamie happily gave up seafaring to oversee the château and represent my interests in Paris."

"You're fortunate in your network of 'representatives,' milady," Lafayette said, then lowered his voice. "Indirectly, I consider myself to be one of them. You're as informed as any Hôtel de Ville delegate or courtier at Versailles. I applaud you." A glance of understanding passed between them. "These days, that knowledge is invaluable for your protection. The mood in Paris, since July fourteenth and the destruction of the Bastille, has deteriorated and daily grows more dangerous. Political clubs and newspapers are springing up in increasing numbers. Even the countryside's not safe. *Faites attention.*"

"I will do that, Gilbert. Both Jamie and Jeremy have reported the same information to me. They also say there's a growing demand for the king to move to Paris, away from the influence of the courtiers of Versailles."

"It augurs well that the people wish to be near him," Lafayette said, nodding.

"That can be interpreted in more ways than one," Eugénie retorted. "Be that as it may, I'm quite safe here. I have the loyalty of the people in this valley. They will protect the château and its land as they would their own. Our bond, which goes back for centuries, is based on reciprocal trust and service. Also, you haven't heard of my most recent enterprise."

"I tremble to hear," Lafayette said with a laugh, "knowing of some of your past escapades."

Eugénie joined in his laughter. "I agree, some have been less successful than others, but this scheme is both Jamie's and mine. Over the past few months, we've replaced several vineyards with wheat. To begin with, wheat uses much less labor and can be harvested more than once a year, which are two good reasons for the change. In addition, I've become increasingly concerned about the shortage of grain. With this increased output, we can supply both those who have no access to any and those who can't afford the price of what is available. I've enlarged my granary and we process the grain and make our surplus flour available to the château's people and to those outside, as well. Even with the recent harsh winters, we've had plenty for all. Jamie's transports are seen delivering flour and spreading goodwill even outside of this valley, some as far as Paris. The Château de Beaumont is known for its open hand far and wide. Altruism and self-interest can make good bedfellows."

"What a brilliant enterprise, Eugénie! If only all of our nobility had your enterprise and sense of obligation. But tell me more of the shipper Bridger Goodrich and your stay in Bermuda. I never did hear the full story."

"Now that's a whole evening's discussion in itself," Eugénie protested, "and it's already quite late if you're to rest well before your early departure in the morning."

"How right you are," Lafayette said, looking at his timepiece. "Speaking of my early departure, I'll be quite annoyed if I see your bright face at that early hour." When Eugénie started to speak, he raised his hand. "No, my dear, I'm adamant about this. You'll be doing me a favor. It's quite an effort for me to be charming first thing in the morning."

"I can't imagine you anything but thoroughly gallant under any circumstance, but if that's what you wish..."

"Indeed it is," he said patting her hand. "Ah, Eugénie, this has been a most pleasant interlude. It reminds me of gentler times." As his hostess started to rise, Lafayette stepped quickly to pull out her chair.

"*Merci beaucoup,* Gilbert," Eugénie said, "both for your kindness and for the generous gift of your time. We're witnessing history, you and I. The next few months should be most interesting."

"Yes, indeed," the Marquis agreed.

III

Eugénie awoke the next morning to a tap on the door.

"*Entrez,*" she said, reaching for the cream-colored peignoir draped on the chair by her bed. "Ah, *bonjour,* Marie!" Flipping her chestnut hair over the collar of the robe, Eugénie smiled at her longtime retainer, who was more a friend and confidante than a servant.

"How bright you look this morning," Eugénie said, as Marie walked through the door bearing a large silver tray. It was always apparent to Eugénie when Jamie returned from one of his trips. Marie simply glowed. Theirs had been a happy union from the start.

Eugénie's own marriage ten years before was of short duration, ending tragically when Comte d'Armagnac died of a broken neck during a hunt when his mount balked at a hedgerow.

"Pan-cakes, my favorite *petit déjeuner.* I can smell them from here. Oh, Marie, you spoil me. We did finally perfect that Virginian recipe, didn't we? But what are you doing here? Surely, in this huge household, there was someone else who could serve me so that you and Jamie could enjoy a bit more of the morning together."

"Mistress, after all these years, I wouldn't miss sharing these quiet moments with you before your day begins," Marie said, setting the breakfast tray on Eugénie's lap and plumping up the pillows behind her back.

" 'All these years'? We've just reached our prime. I don't consider that at thirty-two I'm in my dotage."

"It's fine for you to say," Marie said under her breath, "unlike some of us..."

"Oh, hush your muttering. Mmmmm! *Bon, très bon!*" Eugénie interrupted herself as she exclaimed over her first bite of the honeyed pan-cake. "These pan-cakes bring to mind our great adventure in Virginia. What a time that was, but I wouldn't be eighteen again for anything in this world. Gracious me," Eugénie said, sounding almost like a Virginian, "that was a time, wasn't it?" Her fork stopped midway to her mouth and Eugénie looked off, her eyes soft.

"You're thinking of Captain Goodrich," Marie said gently, recognizing the telltale signs. Eugénie's eyes cleared and she looked back at Marie.

"Yes, dear friend, I'm thinking of Bridger. He was a part of that time, and he and it will always be a part of me. Sometimes I wish, I wish... But never mind. You know, I received a letter from him recently. He and his Elizabeth had their fifth child—now five daughters!—and every single one of them with the middle name Bridger. Never let it be said that the man has no vanity. He said that either he's meant to make up for the five sons his mother and father had, or that, given his history of adventures, one Bridger Goodrich on this Earth is enough." Eugénie laughed.

"He plans to come to France in the autumn and will be gracing us with his company, no doubt to try to persuade your Jamie to return to his seafaring ways." Then Eugénie's mood changed abruptly. "As treacherous as those times were, at the beginning of the American Revolution, they pale in comparison to the events that are happening now in France. Marquis de Lafayette's news from Paris was alarming." She quickly recounted to Marie the gist of their dinner conversation.

"Earlier this morning," Marie said gravely, "one of the château's agents arrived and said that he was attending the queen's morning reception when a messenger came and reported to her that the Comte d'Artois and others from the inner circle, even the queen's personal advisor, Abbé Vermond, had fled to the border."

"Like rats from a sinking ship. Oh, *pauvre* Marie Antoinette," Eugénie murmured. "Did the agent say how the queen reacted to this news?"

"Only that at first she paled, then she lifted her eyes to the messenger and thanked him, appearing to give his message 'no more attention than if he'd been reporting the arrival of an orange tree.' These were the very words of our agent. Then he said the queen dismissed the messenger and gestured to the next petitioner."

"Her strength and courage have always been underestimated," Eugénie said. "She'll need both now as never before." Suddenly, she could sit still no longer. She put her tray on the counterpane and, pushing the damask bed-hangings aside, she slipped out of the huge, ornately carved four-poster and walked over to the window. She looked out, oblivious to the view of her gardens that usually gave her such pleasure. After a moment, she turned back. "Marie, did the agent happen to mention seeing Madame de la Tour du Pin with the queen?"

"Yes, in fact he did. Apparently, the queen was standing amongst her ladies, wearing nothing that distinguished her from them. The messenger, mistaking Madame de la Tour for the queen, began making his report to the wrong person. You've always said they bore a striking resemblance to each other. The queen, with her love for practical jokes, let the farce play out until she heard the nature of the message and then she stepped forward."

"Oh, the queen and her practical jokes," Eugénie said. "Did you know that, dressed as a nun, she once fooled the king? What a jokester she is. I doubt she's indulged herself in such light moments lately, poor thing. We must make a trip to Versailles to show our support for Their Majesties. The king's command performance at the Hôtel de Ville after the fall of the Bastille must have been the ultimate humiliation. I pray there are cool heads who can design a constitution of reform and still preserve the monarchy."

"Isn't that the purpose of the Assembly?" Marie asked.

"We shall see. Intent and outcome are worlds apart, dear Marie." Just then, chimes struck the hour. Eugénie looked over at the gilt and marble clock that sat on the painted commode by her bed. The clock had always been a favorite of hers. She especially liked the reclining cupids on either side of its face.

"Good heavens, look at the time! I need a distraction from these dark thoughts. A good ride will clear my head."

Marie helped her mistress slip into her deep-blue riding costume with its signature split skirt, while thinking, You're even more beautiful than you were when Captain Goodrich fell in love with you fourteen years ago. Your skin is as bright, your figure as lithe. You'd hardly know that you'd birthed two stillborn babes. What is the source of your strength and courage?

It was a refreshed and invigorated mistress of the château who galloped across the pasture later that afternoon. With a whoop of delight, Eugénie sailed over the stone wall on the back of Roan II and trotted to the paddock, outstripping Jeremy on Roan II's son. When Jeremy joined her a split second later, Eugénie took a long look at the young man and his mount and said, her eyes twinkling, "It's a shame the soft life has robbed you of your competitive edge."

Jeremy rolled his eyes, thinking, The soft life? Lost my competitive edge? But he said, gallantly, "No, rather, it's a mystery, Mistress, how you defy every minute, hour, week, month, and year that measure the rest of us mere mortals. It's as though the gods have bequeathed you eternal youth. I must say, you inspired Roan II today." The words were barely out of his mouth before the great stallion arched his neck and danced sideways, pinning his son, Roan IV, and his offending rider against the paddock fence.

"See there, Jeremy," Eugénie said, chuckling, "The Roan is insulted by your critique of his performance. It was he that inspired me!" At her words, The Roan shook his head up and down. Laughing, the two riders dismounted and led the horses into the stable. At once, Jeremy's quick eyes noticed an unfamiliar horse whose coat, dark with sweat, was being rubbed down just inside the building.

"'Pears we have a visitor," he said, taking the reins from his mistress's hands. "I'll take care of the mounts."

"*Merci,* Jeremy. I'd best see who's arrived." As Eugénie walked away, she called over her shoulder, "Maybe a few extra carrots will reinstate you in The Roan's good graces." With a laugh she was gone.

Entering the château, Eugénie recognized one of the queen's messengers pacing back and forth beneath the four-tiered crystal chandelier that dominated the entrance hall.

"Jean," she exclaimed with concern, "has something happened to the queen?"

"*Non,* Comtesse de Beaumont," the young man answered, bowing. "Her Highness sent me with a letter that she commanded me to bring to you with all speed and to await your answer."

"Thank God," Eugénie said with relief. "Why are neither you nor your horse displaying the royal livery?"

Jean ducked his head and then raised troubled eyes to meet her gaze. "Recently, Madame, it's been unsafe to travel the countryside bearing the royal coat of arms, especially when traveling alone."

"I see," Eugénie murmured and then said briskly, "Go and have some refreshment while I read this. I'll have my reply ready when you return."

"*Merci,* Madame," the servant said, bowing, and disappeared down the hall.

Eugénie broke the seal as she went into the *petit salon.* She walked back and forth on the blue-and-gold-patterned rug several times before she sat down at her writing desk. She ran her hand over its smooth tortoiseshell surface and began to read.

My dear Eugénie,

I hope this letter finds you well. You've been too long from court. We're enjoying a pleasant season here, but something seems amiss with my animals at the Hamlet. My treasured cow, dear Blanchette, and my favorite sheep, Noir, are as usual, but the others are causing me some concern. You're so wise about animals. It would be a great help to me if you'd give me your counsel about these sheep, goats, and cows. I'm planning a little diversion on the first of October next, at the *Petit Trianon*, which I think you'll find amusing, just a small gathering to celebrate the autumnal season. We'll speak then. I remain your friend, M. A.

How very odd, Eugénie thought—the queen's seeking my counsel about animals. It's so chatty and informal, even for her. Clearly, it's a summons to court, but why two months in advance? When your queen commands, you obey. Is it to put me on notice, for some reason or another? But the animals, the allusion to her favorites? Ah, *je comprends!* The animals must be the courtiers and her inner circle. She must mean that two of her close favorites are loyal, but she questions the rest. Yes, that's it! She's disguised her true meaning, fearing this letter might fall into the wrong hands. If she's using the animals as a subterfuge, then the "gathering" must be something more than a "little diversion."

At that moment, Marie appeared in the doorway.

"Mistress, which apartment should I make ready for Madame de Staël?" Noticing Eugénie's expression, she went quickly to her and said, "You look alarmed. What's happened?"

"Marie, being so far removed from Paris and Versailles, I'd hoped to avoid becoming entangled in court intrigue, but it's not to be. The queen has summoned me to Versailles."

"That's surprising," Marie said. "The queen has never had

more than a cordial regard for you, because of your friendship with the Marquis de Lafayette."

"Yes, the queen heartily dislikes him for his strong voice in favor of reform. She's always kept me at a distance for the same reason. I find her change of heart quite odd. What do you make of this?" she asked, handing Marie the letter.

After reading it, Marie frowned. "How curious. All this talk about animals." Eugénie told her her theory and Marie burst out laughing. "Forgive me," she said, "but perhaps she's drawn an apt comparison."

Eugénie chuckled. "You do have a way of lightening the moment, Marie. Yes, it would seem there are several meanings to this piece. Isn't it interesting that, just this morning, I was saying we should make a trip to Versailles, and then this letter arrives?" She rubbed her forehead and let out a sigh. "With so much on my mind, I'd completely forgotten that Madame de Staël was coming today. Please have Sophie and Renée prepare the green apartment for her. I'll be fascinated to hear her thoughts about the recent events and the return of her father, Monsieur Necker, as the Minister of Finance."

IV

The sun was setting over the hills when a coach and six came rumbling down the long avenue of plane trees. It broke out of the shadow of the trees into the golden light of the courtyard. Circling the huge fountain where Neptune sat on his throne, surrounded by frolicking mermaids and dolphins, it pulled up in front of the château.

The summer sky glowed with streaks of crimson, apricot, and golden-peach, making the perfect backdrop for the young, full-figured woman who descended from the coach clothed from head to toe in flaming russet. Her hair, bathed in the rosy evening light, was dressed simply and hung to her shoulders with a blue, white, and red cockade prominently displayed at her temple. Jamie MacKenzie stepped forward, bowed, and offered his arm.

"Baroness de Staël, welcome to Château de Beaumont. The Comtesse will be pleased that you've arrived."

Taking the proffered arm, the Baroness tapped Jamie playfully on the wrist. "Jamie, have we returned to the formalities since my last visit? Dear, dear, 'Germaine,' *s'il vous plaît!*" Looking around her, she said, "What a magical kingdom Eugénie has created. Were I so fortunate to have such a pleasant haven, perhaps I'd cease my wanderlust and settle down."

"I doubt even Mistress Eugénie's magic could accomplish that," Jamie retorted.

"How right you are!" Germaine laughed. "But I see she was successful with you. Although I imagine the charming Marie may have had something to do with it, too." As they started towards the stairs, the large oaken doors opened and Eugénie flew down the steps, her arms outstretched.

"Germaine!" The two women embraced and then stepped back. Still holding on to each other's arms, they appraised each other closely.

"*Ma chère amie,* you look magnificent!" they said in unison. Eugénie put her arm around the younger woman's shoulder and led her up the stairs and through the doorway.

"Isn't it always the way?" she said. "We simply pick up right where we left off. You do look superb. What a glorious color you're wearing, 'though far from the queen's choice for this season."

"It's not only about color that the queen and I disagree," Germaine said tartly. Just then, the footmen came down the hallway laden down with trunks and other traveling paraphernalia. "Dear Eugénie, don't be alarmed," her guest said, laughing at the expression on her friend's face. "With my father's reinstatement, I'm just now returning to my beloved Paris from London. I don't intend to outstay my welcome at your splendid château, tempting though it may be."

"I hope you'll stay a fortnight, at least, and celebrate my birthday on the twelfth of August," Eugénie said, guiding her friend up the wide staircase.

"I wouldn't miss that occasion for the world," Germaine replied. "Will we have time to enjoy your delicious invention before we dine this evening?"

"*Mais oui.* I've been waiting for you."

"That's right," Germaine said, nodding. "You've long since discarded the formal practice of late-afternoon dining. *Dieu merci!* I firmly believe that only after a full day of observation and contemplation can the mind turn to the lofty pursuit of intelligent conversation. The process must not be interrupted prematurely by attending to the needs of the stomach. I don't think truly intelligent discourse is possible before the sun goes down."

A short time later, as dusk began to creep across the sky, Eugénie and her guest, engulfed in Turkish robes, approached a wall of boxwood at the far corner of the château's extensive gardens. They passed through the opening in the hedge into a secluded nook, which was dominated by a rectangular pond. At one end, a natural spring bubbled through the stones that formed the pond. In the center, a waterfall cascaded from a statue of a dancing Pan playing his pipes.

"It's lovelier than I remember," Germaine said, testing the water with her toe. "Mmmmm, the spring has warmed it to perfection." Dropping her robe on the grass, she plunged in. Eugénie joined her and soon the two women were paddling about, by turns submerging themselves and floating on their backs beneath Pan's watchful eye.

Later that evening, in the informal dining room, the chinoiserie mirror that dominated the space captured the two women deep in conversation.

"After my long days of travel, that quick dip in your heated pool was so refreshing. It returned me to myself. The trips are exhausting by carriage. I simply don't understand how armies can survive those long marches. Which reminds me, what's this I hear about the approach of Austrian armies?" Germaine asked, sipping Eugénie's deep-ruby-colored Bordeaux.

"I've heard that rumor," Eugénie replied, nibbling a bit of roasted capon. "I've also heard that it's categorically untrue. Nonetheless, it's caused universal alarm, which has served to unite the citizenry and has made them even more suspicious of the queen, if that's possible. It must be something in the air. Every time I turn around there's another rumor announcing the imminent arrival of the queen's relative and his Austrian armies. But what of you, Germaine? I've not seen you since before the birth of your daughter. And the Baron. Is he still in Switzerland?"

"*Sacrebleu!* Has it really been over three years?" Germaine exclaimed. "My daughter, precious child, flourishes, due in no small part to the quiet, settled life she lives with her father in Switzerland. It's perfect for my dear precious, but for me, *mon Dieu,* I would expire of boredom."

"But surely the Baron must miss you."

Germaine gave her friend a look that said it all. "Shall we say that my brains and his beauty are the perfect combination for a child, and leave it at that? For two people who are as different as the Baron and I, it's very convenient that he's obtuse in the extreme. How else would I have the life that I love, coming and going as I please, enjoying my dalliances where I find them, without the encumbrance of a jealous, besotted husband panting after me? Imagine if the Baron had called out Louis XV's illegitimate son? *Oh, là!* What a scandal that would have been! Instead, I leave him to tend to his sheep, his clock collection, and anything else he chooses in that godforsaken part of the world, and I'm free to travel and to entertain my intellectuals and politicians. *Quel arrangement!*"

Eugénie, a few years Germaine's senior, was always amazed at her friend's blunt delivery and liberal way of life. It was, she thought, their flouting of convention, each in her own way, that formed the cornerstone of their close friendship.

"Ah, what's this?" the Baroness asked as a servant placed the next course before her.

"It's the newest thing from court since that delicious concoction, ice-cream, was introduced," Eugénie replied. "It's a potato, a very satisfactory root plant. We've discovered that it's quite versatile." The food under discussion formed a dome-like shape above the edge of its dish. Germaine dipped in her spoon, capturing the browned crust and the fluffy substance beneath. With eyes closed, she relished her first bite.

"Mmmmm, potato cheese soufflé! What will your François think of next?"

Germaine, known for her rapacious appetites, made short work of it. "Eugénie," she said as she sat back with a look of supreme pleasure on her face, "that was a triumph! I must have the recipe. My salons will be the toast of Paris, the great minds of our day conversing over potato cheese soufflé de Beaumont! *Voilà!*"

Pleased with the success of François's creation, Eugénie promised, "You won't leave without a store of the potatoes and the recipe. We'll make your cuisine as well as your salons the talk of Europe. Tell me of your plans. Your friends must be languishing in Paris awaiting your return."

"Ah, bien sûr!" Modesty had never been Germaine's long suit. "I've put the Messieurs Talleyrand, Condorcet, David, and Lafayette on notice to assemble themselves and others of equal note at my *hôtel* on the evening of my arrival in Paris. It will be a grand redux."

"That it will," Eugénie agreed. "You've plucked the cream from each faction — the revolutionary bishop, the brilliant modernist, *le peintre de la révolution,* and the noble revolutionary. What a galaxy!"

At that moment, Émigré dashed into the room and leapt onto his mistress's lap. "Whom have we here?" Germaine asked, reaching over to scratch behind the puppy's ear.

"He's the newest addition to our household. Jeremy rescued him from court. The poor bewildered little thing was a casualty of the Duc d'Artois's abrupt departure. We call him Émigré."

The Baroness threw back her head and laughed. *"Drôle,* Eugénie, *très drôle!* Well, he looks none the worse for it. The queen must deeply miss Le Duc. He was a delightful diversion for her. Who'll act with her in her plays now? In spite of the gossip, I know for a fact that there was never anything between them. The queen, for all her defiance of court etiquette, is an innocent."

"I quite agree with you," Eugénie said. "I believe she truly is an innocent, but truth has little to do with her growing legend. Someone recently misquoted Jean-Jacques Rousseau's work, saying that the queen said, 'Let them eat cake,' when she was told of the people's bread shortages. My sources report that it's been repeated and repeated until now it's become fact."

"*Sacrebleu!*" Germaine exclaimed. "Anyone with the brain of a mouse knows it was Louis XIV's wife, the Spaniard Marie Thérèse, who made that unfortunate remark long before Marie Antoinette was born! Oh, if there's one thing I abhor more than ignorance, it's malicious ignorance!"

"I can see," Eugénie said drily, "that your presence is sorely needed in Paris. Malicious mischief and ignorance are reaching new heights, in both word and deed, particularly where the queen's concerned." Suddenly, Émigré was on his hind legs covering his mistress's face with kisses. "*Oui, oui, je comprends.*" She turned to her friend. "He's announcing that it's time to retire. Who am I to deny the little tyrant?"

V

The days slipped by, filled with visits to neighboring châteaux and preparations for Eugénie's birthday soirée. During one such visit to the Baron and Baroness Conti's nearby estate, the talk of the day was the National Assembly's newly adopted Declaration of the Rights of Man and Citizen. Over a lavish midday meal the guests and their hosts hashed over the radical changes it embodied and grappled with its three main tenets: that the nation, not the king, was the locus of sovereignty; that all men were born free and equal; and that the primary purpose of the government was to protect the liberties of the citizens.

When the meal drew to a close, Germaine de Staël stood and raised her glass. "This is a happy day! This document institution-alizes the revolution. To France and her patriot-king!"

Everyone at the table rose to their feet and cheered. After the clamor died down, Lisbeth Conti's dinner partner offered her his arm and led her to the salon for the customary demitasse and dessert.

Henri Conti bowed to Eugénie. "Shall we?" She smiled up at her host and they followed the others from the room, each lost in thought, the silence between them broken only by the rustling of Eugénie's taffeta gown.

Handing his guest a delicate blue-and-white-patterned cup, the Baron joined Eugénie on the settee that flanked the French doors in the spacious salon. "A penny for your thoughts, Madame," he said softly.

"Ah, Henri," she answered, letting out a long sigh, "my thoughts are all over the place. I'm not sure they're worth a penny."

He nodded. "As are mine. I've known you since childhood, *chère* Eugénie, and have treasured our friendship, no small part of which is based on our common political views. On the one hand, I agree with your outrageous friend that this is a happy day for France. On the other, I have some concerns that I hesitate to voice for fear that they'll be misconstrued in our present company's euphoria for the revolution."

"It sounds as though we're wrestling with similar concerns," Eugénie agreed. "I'll try to put them in words that make sense." She paused to take a bite of her biscuit and a sip of coffee. Then, placing them on the mother-of-pearl table in front of her, she turned to her host, her silver eyes vivid in her earnest face.

"I'm in total accord with the Declaration's principles and applaud their Jeffersonian ring."

"As do I," Henri murmured, munching on pastry.

"But will these lofty principles birth working institutions? And where does the king stand? He's one of my chief concerns in all this."

The Baron nodded. "With good reason. You heard our neighbor who'd just returned from court say that, true to form, the king vacillates back and forth. According to him, the king accepts the Declaration but poses questions and asks for changes that suggest he 'doesn't grasp' the full meaning and significance of it. Does he understand that it alters for all time the world he and we were born into?"

"Which all of us here have sought for so long," Eugénie added. "But, unlike you and me, the others may not have thought through the implications. With privilege abolished, so too are class distinctions, titles, and dress codes—the very underpinnings of this society. As much as I'm in favor of their elimination, it will be no easy matter to put the changes into practice."

"Equally daunting," replied the Baron, "is how to carry out the new separation of power that makes the king the executive, but with limited authority; that makes the Assembly the legislative arm; and that completely overhauls the judicial system, putting into place a jury system, elected judges, and Departments to replace the local and provincial governments.

"Eugénie, it is a bright new day for France, and let's hope we French are up to its challenges. *Ça suffit*," he said, brushing crumbs off his fawn-colored breeches. "I've monopolized you for far too long. Now that we've exhausted every weighty political wrinkle facing our heroic delegates, let's join the others and enjoy some lighter fare."

Later that afternoon, in the comfort of the de Beaumont coach, Eugénie and Germaine sat back against its gold brocaded cushions and watched the lush fields of vineyards that passed by the open windows.

"This valley harbors some rather extraordinary intellects,"

Germaine remarked, as she tucked a stray lock of hair back under her turban. "I certainly hadn't realized the extent of the revolutionary fervor here. In my attachment to Paris, I may have overlooked some important participants for my salons."

Eugénie smiled indulgently at her friend. "Yes, we do have one or two very fine minds to our credit down here," she said drily. "When I chose to remove myself from court, I didn't exile myself completely from intelligent discourse."

The Baroness, for once, lost her aplomb. "Oh, dear, I didn't mean that the way it sounded. You know how I value your intelligence, but you've thwarted my efforts at every turn to draw you into my salons. Particularly now, I lament the lack of your attendance. Your experience with the American patriots would be such an asset to my gatherings." The younger woman sputtered to a halt.

Eugénie reached across the carriage to pat her hand. "Germaine," she said, her eyes twinkling, "I consider it a feather in my cap that for a moment I threw you off guard. As to the other, I have my own ways of being a part of the movement. Speaking of which, I'd like to have the benefit of your objectivity, which you have both by virtue of being Swiss and by having returned so recently to France. Am I the only one who sees a dangerous crossroad ahead?"

Germaine's usual lighthearted expression turned solemn. "I love your country and salute the direction it's taking, but I don't see the same unity of purpose and ideals amongst your countrymen that united the American patriots. To begin with, theirs was a political action without the countervailing forces that exist here, forces that—correct me if I'm wrong—are already having an impact on the effort."

Eugénie was quick to answer. "What you say is true. There's a subculture of peasants, laborers, and others who make up a large portion of France's population. They have huge grievances, yet no political say. There are some amongst them who riot in the cities and roam the countryside wreaking havoc. They're not a voice for liberty. They're a voice for violence and anarchy. They could be pawns in the hands of the unscrupulous and easily manipulated. I fear that long before this is over they'll be the ones dictating the terms."

Germaine's face was pale in the bright sunlight. In a voice just above a whisper she said, "Surely, you're letting your imagination run away with you. I've never known you to be a pessimist. What you describe is not the grand vision we spoke of today, but a disaster."

"Perhaps you have been away from France too long," Eugénie said gravely, "and, if I may be so blunt, perhaps you traffic too much with those of like minds to be in touch with what is really going on in France today. I'm not a pessimist. I am only being pragmatic." She shivered in spite of the warmth of the day and pulled the scarlet cape closer around her shoulders.

"But perhaps I'm wrong. Who am I to predict the future? I only pray that there are cool, informed heads to advise the king, and that he heeds their counsel. He hasn't the political interest or the intellect of a Jefferson, Adams, Madison, or Franklin. Thank God, your father is once again at his elbow. I hope he wastes no time turning his attention to the unemployment and the food shortages. The people cannot subsist on 'liberty, equality, and fraternity.'"

"What of this Mirabeau?" Germaine asked, changing the subject. "His name was on everyone's lips today. Where does he fit in? It appears that he's held in very high regard."

"You speak of Honoré Gabriel Riqueti, Comte de Mirabeau." Eugénie smiled at her friend, appreciating the change of subject. "He has his detractors, but not in this quarter. He'll be attending my soirée. You'll meet him then. He was a Deputy from Aix and Marseilles to the Estates-General. He's a brilliant orator and a powerful presence. Mr. Jefferson respects him as a representative of the people and as a reformer." She laughed. "You'll recognize him on sight, for, as Mr. Jefferson has said, he is 'mountainously ugly.' You'll hear much of him in Paris. Be prepared, for he and your father seldom see eye to eye."

"Oh, ma chère," Germaine said with a chuckle, "what an extraordinary description! How is he received by the king and queen?"

"Well," Eugénie replied, "as you know, the queen is offended by anything that's even the slightest bit crude or coarse. She can't abide the king's coarse sense of humor and his crude language. In spite of Mirabeau's noble heritage, his appearance and attitudes are much more of the people. When he appears, she either ignores him or leaves the room. To say that she isn't one to mask her feelings is an understatement. Now, the king, on the other hand, appears to be very impressed with the man."

"It sounds to me," Germaine interrupted, "as though this person, Mirabeau, and my father seek the same thing. Why would they be at odds?"

"Oh, Germaine, you've put your finger on the crux of the matter. It's the difference in political personalities. Do you really want me to go into it?" At her friend's flutter of the hand, Eugénie continued, "Mirabeau, Talleyrand, and Sieyès are the leaders of what is now called the Club of 1789. They stand squarely on the side of establishing a new governing state based on a constitutional monarchy. Opposing them is the rival group led by Barnave, which is adamantly antimonarchical."

"You don't mean it!" Germaine said with alarm. "There are those who would abolish the monarchy entirely?"

"Yes, there are. So far their influence is negligible, but their numbers are growing, aided by a membership that allows non-deputies to join for a very low membership fee. The nature of this group, as you can imagine, is quite different from the other. The core of both groups comes from like backgrounds and old shared friendships, but they mean nothing in the face of their present different political positions.

"But you were asking about the differences between your father and Mirabeau. Necker is seen by many to be a savior, but there's a growing wariness about anyone who's foreign. Mirabeau shares that attitude. He's also highly skeptical about your father's financial plan. At every opportunity, he speaks out against it, saying it won't work. Another example of two leaders with opposing views in the ranks of this revolution."

"My father wishes to levy taxes to avoid bankruptcy. How can Mirabeau argue with that?" Germaine asked.

"Mirabeau's not convinced that bankruptcy is inevitable."

"Then the man's a fool. The state of the treasury is deplorable. Anyone can see that!"

"I'm not debating that point. I'm explaining Mirabeau's position and how it differs from your father's. Mirabeau says that even if bankruptcy should occur, it's not such a bad thing, because the burden of it will fall where it should—on those who can afford it, not on the masses. It's an interesting logic. Oh, here we are," Eugénie exclaimed, as the carriage pulled up in front of the château. The two women alighted and swept through the doorway into the hall.

"Eugénie, our conversation has left me breathless. I'll need some time to digest all that you've said. If you don't mind, I'll repair to my rooms and do just that." With a nod and a smile Germaine disappeared up the stairway.

Eugénie had just settled at her desk in the *chambre de soleil,* which she had designed to match the one she had seen at the Whittington plantation in Virginia, when Jamie appeared in the doorway.

"I trust your visit to the Contis' château went without incident," he said, sitting down across from Eugénie.

"Jamie, I know you fret about my traveling unattended with so much unrest in the countryside, but I never go without two footmen and a very robust coachman."

"They'd hardly be a match for the brigands who are roaming abroad," Jamie grumbled.

"Yes, our trip both going and coming was uneventful," Eugénie said, ignoring his remark, "but the conversations were lively and very informative. What have you there?" she asked, gesturing at the sheaf of papers in Jamie's hands.

"These are the midmonth reports from the granary and the vineyards. We harvested the wheat crop ahead of schedule, as you know. It appears that we'll have a bigger grain supply than usual."

"That's wonderful!" Eugénie exclaimed.

"And the same is true of the vineyards." Jamie couldn't help beaming. "We expect to go to harvest the first of September, little more than two weeks from now. This summer's warm, sunny days and the infrequent rainfall over the last two months have raised the sugar levels ahead of schedule."

"Jamie, I'm so pleased."

Jamie held up an official-looking document, barely containing his excitement. "This afternoon one of our agents delivered a copy of the Declaration of the Rights of Man and Citizen."

"Bon, bon," Eugénie said, wondering how her agent had managed to accomplish that feat. "It dominated our dinner conversation today. I can't wait to read it word for word. I'm particularly interested in the description of the separation of power."

"Why that part especially?" Jamie asked.

"Because it might be seen by some as creating a gap between the king's camp and the people's representatives in the Assembly."

"I see," Jamie said. "It would certainly contradict the principle of a unified state that the majority has been clamoring for."

Eugénie nodded, pausing to worry the pearls at her neck. Clearing her throat, she said with feeling, "We've certainly come a long way, but the Declaration glosses over the fissures that exist in this society. These fissures run deep and are deepening daily. They can be ignored only at our peril." A look of concern passed between them.

"Well, Jamie, it certainly should be a lively soirée."

VI

AUGUST 12, 1789

The clouds that threatened on the morning of Eugénie's birthday disappeared during the day, and by evening the sky was ablaze with the colors of the setting sun as carriages arrived in front of the château and discharged their passengers.

Eugénie stood at the top of the stairs, resplendent in a diaphanous silk gown whose transparency exposed the layers of color underneath. Shades of lavender, turquoise, apple-green, golden-yellow, peach, and apricot shimmered to the surface as she moved. Her naturally high color took on a rosy glow and her chestnut hair turned deep auburn in the amber light. Her hair was dressed simply, allowing the deep waves to tumble freely to her shoulders. Her silver eyes sparkled as she welcomed her guests one by one.

The celebrants followed Eugénie into the inner courtyard where refreshments were being served. Eugénie moved from one group to another, joining discussions about the fall of the Bastille, Monsieur Necker, and the newly adopted Declaration. She noticed the tricolor cockade, the emblem of the revolution, on shoulders, sashes, and shoes, even as fobs on watches. As she looked around her, her hand toyed with the one she wore at her throat.

After the furor in Paris and the increasing incidents of violence in the countryside, here, at least, there's tranquility, she thought. Eugénie glimpsed Lafayette and Germaine, strolling arm in arm, deep in conversation. As she watched, they met up with Mirabeau and Lucien Isnard, one of Mirabeau's many young protégés. The four exchanged greetings, and Lafayette and Mirabeau continued on in one direction while Germaine and the young Parisian drifted off in another. She watched as others, in the same manner, drifted together and then apart as though performing an intricate minuet.

"Eugénie," Lafayette said at her elbow a short time later, "how beautiful you look tonight. And what a glittering array you have brought together for this special occasion."

"Gilbert," Eugénie said with a smile, looking up at him, "I must return the compliment. How dashing you look in the new uniform, bearing the colors of *La Patrie*."

Lafayette looked down at the uniform of the revolution. The coat was blue with white lapels. The facings and vest were white, as were the red-trimmed leggings. "*Merci,* Madame," he said, clearly pleased. "Yes, the new uniform announces the colors of the monarchy, the people, and *La Patrie* quite well and brings a much-needed *esprit de corps* to our ranks."

At that moment, Eugénie saw her majordomo gesture to her. "Ah, it's time to go inside for the feast my chef has spent the whole week preparing. It's a shame to leave this beautiful evening, but I can't have my guests subsisting only on hors d'oeuvres and wine, now can I?"

Lafayette laughed and replied, "No, I should say not." Then he bowed low before her and offered his arm, saying, "Comtesse, may I have the honor?"

Eugénie gave him a radiant smile and placed her hand lightly on his arm. *"Avec plaisir,* Monsieur, but we must dispense with our titles in this new world of ours," she chided him as she led her guests into the château.

"Ah, bien sûr, but old habits die hard, *n'est-ce pas?"*

At Eugénie and Lafayette's approach, the arched gilded doors swung open. Before them, running the length of the vast dining salon, was a banquet table set for the one hundred guests. Down the center of the table was an artfully designed trellis, around, through, and over which wound grapevines from which hung fat clusters of deep purple-red grapes. The same theme of the leafy-vined trellis was repeated throughout the room, covering the walls and arching across the ceiling. The gold candles, platters, and table settings on the gold tissue overlay cloth complemented the richness of the purple-red and green colors of the trellis. The overlay appeared to float above the cream brocade skirt that cascaded to the floor. Gilded grape clusters dripped from the large golden bows that swagged the cloth at intervals along the table's length. The same gold clusters were repeated in the massive chandeliers, whose bright candlelight added to the golden glow, kissing the crystal goblets at each place and setting them sparkling. It was as though the sun had been captured within this indoor arbor.

Eugénie noticed that the natural setting was the perfect backdrop for her guests' informal attire, which had become *de rigueur* since the fall of the Bastille. Not one woman in attendance bore the extraordinary head dressings so popular until just a few weeks ago. She smiled, remembering a gathering where the Duchesse de Chartres had inserted hair pads for height and added false hair for length to support a model of her son's nursery. Another had constructed a live bird in a birdcage to ride atop her mountain of hair. The lengths they went to! Eugénie smiled at her unintentional pun. Oh, the countless stories of how those vertical structures caused hair loss, toothaches, headaches, and eyestrain, not to mention harboring fleas and lice, and how, to accommodate these fashion statements, ladies were forced to sit on the floor of their carriage or hang their heads out of the window! My queen, Eugénie mused, you were ahead of your time, dressing your hair in an unpowdered, natural style long before the revolution made it mandatory.

Her thoughts were interrupted as the first course of *coquilles Saint-Jacques* arrived. When she saw that everyone was served, Eugénie rose, holding aloft a goblet of her '72 vintage Bordeaux, and said, "*Bienvenue, mes amis!* Please rise and join with me to toast *la belle France, notre patrie, et le Déclaration des Droites d'Homme.*" A cheer burst forth as the guests rose and toasted the new régime. Seated once again, her guests turned to their food, and conversation soon rippled up and down the long table.

"But what faith," said one, "can we put in a monarch whose only entry in his journal on the day the Bastille fell was 'Rien'?"

"But surely you realize he was referring to his lack of success in the hunt that day," came the reply.

"Even more damning," the other retorted with a look of disgust, "after the fall of the Bastille had been reported to him, the king still made no other entries in his journal for that day. My point stands."

"As Mr. Jefferson said of the queen," another guest was saying, " 'She is inflexible of will and stupidly obstinate.' He said of Louis that 'His queen has absolute sway over his weak mind and timid virtue. She is disdainful of restraint, indignant at all obstacles to her will, eager in pursuit of pleasure, and firm enough to hold her desires, or perish in their wreck.'"

At the mention of Jefferson's name, those in the vicinity of the speaker fell silent and listened. When the one who had been speaking paused, another spoke up. "With all due respect to the great Mr. Jefferson, you must agree that there are some glaring inconsistencies between his brilliant political writings and his private dealings. He conveniently overlooks his population of slaves when he speaks of life, liberty, and the pursuit of happiness. But, putting that aside, speaking of the queen, those who are close to her, who don't depend on hearsay, hold her to be impulsive, but also intelligent, as well as a devoted, loyal, caring, and generous mother and friend."

"Are you suggesting..." the earlier speaker began.

Lucy de la Tour du Pin interceded at that moment, saying, "In this time of revolution, perhaps we should credit the queen for liberating us, by her example, from corsets and stays." Appreciative laughter met her words. "Furthermore, as we sit here tonight, we reflect her movement towards simpler styles of dress and accessories. I don't see a powdered head amongst us."

"To Lucy, ever the diplomat!" applauded her dinner partner.

Encouraged by that response, Lucy continued, "It's often been said that I closely resemble the queen in appearance. Perhaps that was my entrée into her inner circle. But, for whatever the reason may be, I have witnessed her wit, intelligence, and courage. She's the spirit of an age that embraces art, innovative architecture, music, and the laws of nature espoused by Jean-Jacques Rousseau."

"It's unfortunate, then," a nearby person grumbled, "that she hasn't limited herself to those endeavors and saved France from her meddling in affairs of state." The explosive moment had passed and the conversation moved on to other topics.

On the heels of a musical fanfare, servants arrived and paraded whole suckling pigs and sides of venison around the long table. Then the guests watched as they carved them on the sideboards that ran the length of the room and served the succulent meats with a flourish. Next came a course of assorted fowl *en croûte,* followed by local cheeses. A murmur of admiration met the finale, a mound of *glace de vin* served in a spun-sugar swan that floated on a custard lake.

As the guests were enjoying this delicacy, Mirabeau, feeling at his oratorical best after several glasses of wine, pronounced in loud tones, "What is bankruptcy, if not the most cruel, the most iniquitous, the most unequal, and the most disastrous of all taxes?"

Eugénie looked up sharply, thinking that he'd made a complete about-face from just a few weeks ago.

"At all costs, we must avoid . . . " Mirabeau's neighbor began, but was interrupted by his dinner partner on the other side.

"Avoid! We're in the throes of it, even as we speak!"

Suddenly, a shot rang out, silencing the room. Alarmed, Eugénie rose from her chair and turned towards the sound. Others began to rise.

"Non, non," Eugénie said, *"Asseyez-vous, s'il vous plaît."* She turned and spoke quickly to the footman who stood behind her chair and then resumed her seat as the man walked swiftly from the room.

The guests sat frozen in their chairs. Almost immediately, Ja-

mie appeared in the doorway and walked quickly over to Eugénie. Her face betrayed nothing as he whispered urgently in her
ear. She listened intently, nodding several times. When Jamie had
finished and stepped back, Eugénie rose and stood quietly for a
moment. When she spoke, her voice, clear and strong, carried easily in the large room.

"*Mes amis,* just now a band of ruffians, led by an Englishman
with whom I had the misfortune of crossing paths in Virginia,
was discovered on this property attempting to set fire to the east
wing of the château. In the ensuing fight, one of my people was
critically wounded." Her guests turned to each other, their faces
stricken with shock and fear. "The criminals have been apprehended and placed under guard. The leader, one Mr. Darby, is a
dangerous scoundrel of the first order. He uses his professed loyalty to monarchies, wherever they exist, as an excuse to create
mayhem. This isn't the first instance of his wickedness. But, this
time, we have the evidence to make sure it will be his last. Several
witnesses saw him shoot my guard.

"I'm sorry that this unfortunate event has marred an extraordinary evening of dear friends and good will, but perhaps it's a
timely message to us all that these are dangerous times. It would
behoove us to listen closely to voices raised in passion, be they for
our side or for another, and to plumb the true nature of the person behind the voice."

Servants arrived on the heels of her words to replenish the wineglasses, but the hour was late and the festive spirit had gone out of
the evening. The guests rose and began to make their *adieux*. After Eugénie had accompanied them to their carriages and bid each
a safe journey home, she went with Lafayette in search of Jamie.

Once Eugénie had determined that little damage had been done to the château, she left Lafayette to attend to Darby and his brigands and went quickly to the bedside of the wounded guard where he lay surrounded by his family. She knelt down beside him and took his hand in both of hers.

"You're so young, Claude," she whispered, "so pale." As she leaned over him to brush his hair back from his forehead, Claude opened his eyes, which were bright with pain.

"Mistress," he said softly. As Eugénie watched, his eyes grew dim and then vacant. Eugénie lowered her forehead to the lifeless hand still clasped in hers.

"Claude," she said, "you have not given your life in vain. Darby will pay in full for your sacrifice. He'll not live to see another sunset." Eugénie rose from her knees and embraced each member of the family. She then slipped quietly away, leaving them to mourn their loss.

VII

THE FOLLOWING DAY

The next morning, Eugénie met with Jamie and Jeremy in the *chambre de soleil*. Eugénie was very disturbed by John Darby's reappearance in her life. He was a villain of the first order. His attempt on her life in Virginia still gave her nightmares.

She plunged in without preamble. "You spoke with Darby. What did you learn from him? Was it a random attack or was it specifically aimed at me, at the château—what? Or was it part of a larger plan? And how in God's name did he breach our defenses?" Unable to sit still, Eugénie jumped to her feet and began pacing back and forth.

"As you might expect," Jamie replied, "Darby wasn't forthcoming, but one of his henchmen was all too eager to speak up, hoping for clemency. It seems that Darby has been busy at work both in England and France. He uses whatever is at hand to incite rioters, just as he did in Virginia during the American Revolution. The informant said that Darby hadn't mentioned you by name, but that he'd bragged that, as he said, 'with only a woman in the way,' this château would be an easy target to attack and plunder."

Eugénie stopped her pacing and looked at him, narrowing her eyes.

"I know, I know. He underestimated you, to his sorrow," Jamie said.

"He breached our defenses," he went on, "by slipping his carriages in amongst the guests' coaches and hiding his men under tarpaulins. He'd prepared well. Disguised as a peasant, he came to the château several weeks ago to beg for bread. He struck up a conversation with our baker, Gerald, and learned of your birthday soirée. Increasingly, we're hearing of châteaux being attacked, ransacked, and burned. I've every conviction that they're the work of Darby and his accomplices or others of his ilk."

Eugénie shivered, imagining Darby so near. "This time," she said with feeling, "we were fortunate that, except for Claude, nothing worse happened. There will be other 'Darbys' who will use these unsettled times to spread their mayhem. We must be more diligent."

"I suggest we close the granary and the kitchen to those outside of the château. They make us too exposed," Jeremy said.

"No, Jeremy," said Eugénie firmly. "I will not eliminate the only source of grain and bread for many of the families in this area. They count on us. To do what you suggest would mean that Darby and his like will succeed in their schemes to control through fear. Instead, we must increase our patrols and add armed guards at both the granary and the kitchen. We also must heighten the vigilance of our network."

"It's a different world we live in now," Jamie said quietly. "It was changing even before the fall of the Bastille. The incidents of violence were increasing then, but now they've become commonplace. We must be even more alert. I'm in agreement with Jeremy. Most of our people are like Gerald and aren't apt to make the judgments necessary to keep you and the château safe. Even when we're here, Jeremy and I can't be everywhere. As often as not, one or both of us is absent from the château."

"No, Jamie, absolutely not. I will not limit access to the kitchen and granary in any way," Eugénie said unequivocally, "but I'm willing to make some concessions, one being that from now on only one of you at a time will be away from the château." She paused and then spoke with feeling. "I will not allow the rabble to dictate to us. They'll learn that their terrorizing only makes us stronger. Furthermore, we have an obligation to the hungry, and we will fulfill it as long as we possibly can. You and Jeremy must select others to aid you in safeguarding the château."

Both men started to protest, but Eugénie held up her hand to silence them. "No, you will not change my mind on this."

A fortnight later, Eugénie was in the rose garden deadheading the spent blossoms, a task she enjoyed. It kept her hands busy and left her mind free to roam at will. She noticed one of her men standing in the shadows nearby. Good, she thought, Jamie's increased the vigilance without drawing undue attention to it. Thankfully, we've enjoyed some peace and quiet since the Darby incident and Germaine's departure.

She chuckled to herself, remembering Jamie's description of what had occurred on the morning after the attack, when he and Lafayette had taken the prisoners to the newly formed Department of Bordeaux. She recalled Jamie's telling her that the recently appointed official in charge was so dazzled by the great

Lafayette's appearance that he mistook the prisoners for new recruits for the local militia. The official had rushed off to procure uniforms for Darby and his men, before Lafayette was able to break through the man's excitement to correctly identify the prisoners. Then, chagrined at his mistake, the man had hustled Darby and his men through the judicial process at an almost unseemly rate.

Jamie had told her that Darby, having been sentenced to die, along with the other prisoners, had met his death exhibiting more dignity than he had displayed during his life. Thinking of what might have happened, a chill seeped through her, in spite of the warmth of the September sun. There will be others like him, she thought. Men of his kind flourish in the midst of social upheaval. Whether they're counterfeit monarchists or false revolutionaries, their numbers are on the rise.

Eugénie shook herself mentally, shrugging off the dismal thoughts. I must turn my mind to something more pleasant. In less than a month I leave for Versailles. The trip will do me good. I've been too long buried down here in the countryside. I'm jumping at shadows and seeing sinister meanings where none exist. The court gossip and backstabbing will be the perfect distraction. Although, she laughed to herself, after one day in that company, I know I'll be desperate to escape.

With a lighter spirit, she set about clipping a bouquet of pink, golden, white, and apricot blooms, making sure to add several of her namesake "Eugénie" blossoms to the mix. When her rose basket threatened to overflow, she started up the path towards the château.

She looked up at the cloudless sky and realized that it had been a long time since she'd allowed herself the leisure to stroll in her gardens and enjoy the sound of birdsong and the warmth of the sun. As she approached the wide stairs of the veranda that ran the full length along the back of the château, she saw Jamie in close conversation with a man who looked vaguely familiar.

"Mistress Eugénie," Jamie called to her, "Mr. Randolph Whittington and I were just coming to find you." Eugénie rushed up the steps. Handing the basket of roses to Jamie, she reached out to clasp Randolph's hand in the American fashion.

"Randolph Whittington," she exclaimed, "I'd know you anywhere. You're the image of your father! How wonderful to meet you after all these years. You've arrived just in time for tea, one of the many customs that I've adopted from your parents. Though, truth be known, I usually substitute coffee for tea. Will you join us, Jamie?"

"Thank you, Madame, but I must attend to my paperwork, which I've put off for too long," he answered. "I'll give these flowers to Marie and inform her that you're ready for the tea cart."

"*Merci beaucoup,* Jamie," Eugénie said, as she linked her arm through Randolph's and led him through the French doors into the château. Once in the salon, she gestured for him to sit beside her on an oversized jacquard-fabricked sofa.

Randolph looked around him, admiring the cream-on-white damask cloth that draped the floor-to-ceiling windows that alternated with pairs of double doors along the veranda wall, the gilt-wood console tables topped with deep-green marble flanked by veneered occasional chairs, and the four gracefully arranged seating areas. He noticed that the accents of turquoise, pale green, and rose, dappling the chair and sofa brocades, were repeated in the unusually large paintings that hung at intervals along the walls. To his eye, the use of color and scale gave the large formal room a feeling of friendly welcome. Eugénie watched her guest's appreciative gaze travel around the room and light on a painting that hung in the alcove to the right of the ornate fireplace.

"My goodness, is that a painting of Oak Grove?" Randolph asked, turning to Eugénie.

"Yes, it is," Eugénie answered, clearly pleased. "I'm delighted you noticed it. It's one of my most prized possessions. I commissioned Thomas Jefferson's daughter, Martha, who's such a talented artist, to paint it for me. I found, once I returned to France, that your home and family held so many fond memories for me that I simply had to have a painting to remind me of those happy days. I've only to look at it and I'm immediately back in Virginia, riding on The Roan in that beautiful countryside, catching up on the local gossip with your sisters or sharing one of Opa's delicious dinners surrounded by your wonderful family. As hair-raising as those days were, they were some of the happiest of my life." Eugénie smiled, remembering.

"Oh, Randolph, forgive my rudeness," she said with dismay. "Your mother would be appalled. You must be exhausted and in need of refreshing yourself after your long journey, and here I am reminiscing about old times." Eugénie jumped to her feet. "Come, we must see to your baggage and show you to..."

Her words were interrupted as Marie came through the door carrying a cut crystal bowl filled with roses. As she walked into the room, the sunlight streaming through the windows glanced off the bowl's facets, creating pools of rainbows on the walls and the Aubusson rug.

"Oh, Marie, how beautiful! Randolph, I'd like you to meet..."

Again, she was interrupted, but this time by her guest.

"Miss Eugénie, I've already made Marie's acquaintance, but I would have known her on sight from my family's description. We met when I first arrived. She kindly saw to my belongings and showed me to the most charming bedchamber that overlooks the river. I'm overwhelmed by the gracious hospitality of your household."

"Randolph, I'm pleased that you've been so well looked after," Eugénie said. "Now that your immediate needs have been attended to, at long last, may I formally welcome you to Château de Beaumont. I was so sorry to miss entertaining you during your Grand Tour."

"It's my pleasure to finally meet you," Randolph said. "You surpass all my expectations. I couldn't imagine that anyone could equal the picture my parents drew of your beauty and grace. How wrong I was!"

"Ah," Eugénie said, coloring prettily, "I see that your Grand Tour didn't dim your Southern charm."

Randolph laughed. "As the fourth and last of the Whittington children, I was more indulged than my brother and sisters. I'm not known for my silver tongue—in fact, most usually quite the opposite. Jack, Bess, and Kate can attest to that. My bluntness dismayed my mother and father once too often. They dispatched me off for the Grand Tour to England and the continent in the hope that the experience would smooth my rough edges.

"It must have had some effect, since I'll be attending the October fête at Versailles. When I received that royal invitation, you could have knocked every member of my family over with a feather." He threw back his head and laughed. "I guess I must have comported myself well enough when Mr. Jefferson presented me at Court during my tour. It certainly didn't hurt to have that great man's patronage." Nor did your handsome face and manly carriage, Eugénie thought.

Marie, who had been standing quietly by, turned as a footman came through the door pushing the silver tea wagon. He lifted the large tray from the cart on which a lavish tea had been spread. After placing it on the table in front of Eugénie, he turned and took a position by the door.

"Marie, you've thought of everything. *C'est magnifique!*"

Marie smiled and said, "Mistress, if there's nothing further, I'll take my leave, to help Jacqueline with her studies."

"Certainly, Marie. Nothing is more important than my god-daughter's schoolwork. We must do everything we can to prepare her for her place in this new world of ours."

Marie spoke briefly to the footman and left the room. Turning to her guest, Eugénie asked, "Randolph, may I serve you coffee or tea?"

"I, like you, prefer coffee, thank you," he answered, "with just a little sugar. I hope, Miss Eugénie, that my letter reached you and that my arrival didn't come as a surprise."

Eugénie sprinkled sugar from the muffineer on his coffee, then handed him the delicate Sèvres demitasse. "The post has become more and more unreliable, but I did receive your letter. I'm happy that you went out of your way to travel to the Bordeaux to visit me. What a shame you missed my dear friend the Baroness de Staël, and by only a few days. She's always hungry for news of your United States, not to mention the company of *un bel homme.*"

Randolph chuckled. "I'm sorry to have missed her. Her reputation has even reached across the Atlantic. Will she be attending the October fête?"

"The queen bears no kind feelings towards the Baroness," Eugénie answered as she sipped her *café au lait,* "resenting, as she does, Monsieur Necker's policies. And as for Germaine, having been away so long from her beloved Paris, I doubt that she would have attended even if she had been asked. She much prefers the gossip of the Palais-Royal cafés to the intrigue of court." Eugénie shook her head. "That city's gossip has reached monstrous proportions, and the scandal-mongering press has become even more hyperbolic and sensational since the fall of the Bastille. Monsieur Marat's *L'Ami du Peuple* has many avid readers. At this distance, I must depend on the reports of my agents to separate the wheat from the chaff."

Randolph nodded. "I was cautioned to land at Marseilles to avoid the confusion in Paris and the surrounding area."

Eugénie smiled at her guest, thinking, We're chatting just like old friends. It's as though we've known each other for years instead of a few brief moments.

"'Confusion' is an understatement," she said. "The Parisians are bent on firing up the revolution, but with very little direction. A short time ago, *les poissardes*' conduct at La Fête de Saint-Louis indicated just how much times have changed. They demonstrated none of the traditional obeisance to the king and queen at the annual reception for the market people of Paris. *Les poissardes* led the procession of twelve hundred to Versailles. It was an unruly lot.

Had it not been for the presence of the Garde Nationale, things might well have gotten out of hand. The food shortages are the reason for their anger. It's hard not to sympathize with them, but on the other hand, the king and the queen, isolated by their own choice, aren't in touch with or prepared for the harsh wind that's blowing across this land."

"Why this isolation?" Randolph asked, sampling the *petits fours*. "I understood that the king was popular with the people."

"Ah, bien sûr," Eugénie replied. "In most quarters, the king is still the beloved father figure, but the queen's behavior has offended many, both inside and outside of the court. Except for attending the biennial Art Exhibitions at the Salon Carré, she's withdrawn completely from the public.

"She was deeply offended when she was unjustly held responsible for a public scandal a few years ago. Ever since then, she's been the target of even more lewd rhymes and rumors. I'm afraid her reputation has gone from bad to worse, and the king's bond with the people has suffered because of it.

"Ça suffit. You've been more than patient with my prattling along about the affairs of France. We shall be in the midst of it at Court soon enough." Seeing that Randolph had finished his refreshments, Eugénie stood up, saying, "While there's still light, let's go to the stables and give Jeremy a chance to show off the new generations of the Virginian bloodstock. I believe the most recent coupling of Roan II is producing a foal, even as we speak."

VIII

As the last week of September approached, the household began to prepare in earnest for the journey to Versailles. Eugénie spent the mornings with dressmakers, haberdashers, and other suppliers, leaving only the afternoon hours to manage the demands of the château.

It was on one such day that her patience finally ran out.

"They'll simply have to make do without me for an hour or two," she said to Émigré. She whistled to the little dog and together they slipped away from the hubbub of the household. After stopping by the kitchen to pick up a cup of steaming apple cider and a treat for the pup, they set off for the garden gazebo, which had always been Eugénie's refuge. She walked down the graveled path as quickly as the hot cider allowed, followed closely by Émigré, who rarely left her side. The fall of the Bastille seems a lifetime ago, she thought, as she approached the white circular structure, and, at the same time, as if it happened yesterday. She stooped to pick up the pup and carried him up the stairs into the gazebo.

"Escape! Peace at last," she said out loud. She put Émigré down, placed her cup on one of the tables, and quickly lost herself in the enjoyable task of pulling brightly colored cushions and pillows out of the bench cabinets that lined the circular wall. After she'd massed them along the bench tops, she stepped back to view her handiwork.

"What do you think, Émigré?" As if in answer, the little dog wagged his tail even faster than usual. "A bit more turquoise here, you think, and two more crimsons over here? Yes, perfect. Now, where shall we sit?" With her hand at her chin, her eyes traveled over the tones of green, orange, red, yellow, blue, and purple that surrounded her. She turned her head this way and that as though the choice of cushion were tantamount to a decision of state. Finally, the puppy preempted her and trotted over to a cushion and plopped down. Eugénie laughed and settled down beside him.

"How clever you are! Yes, it's definitely an apple-green day." Leaning forward, she picked up the cup of cider that happened to be sitting on the table right in front of her and took a sip. "Mmmm, cinnamon-clove with just a hint of lemon. Delicious!" She pulled the puppy onto her lap and fed him his treat. Giving his mistress a grateful lick, he burrowed his head under her arm and was soon fast asleep.

Eugénie leaned back against the cushions, thinking how contented she felt. The simple act of playing with the pillows and cushions never failed to restore her. She remembered the many happy hours she and her mother had spent together doing the same thing.

Sipping the cider and smoothing the puppy's fur, she let her mind roam back over the busy schedule of the last few weeks — the comings and goings of her neighbors to the château to discuss the current events, the harvesting and crushing of the grapes, attending salons at nearby châteaux, taking part in the local races where The Roan's line had distinguished itself, once again. She smiled, thinking of Randolph's enthusiastic participation in it all.

Slowly, her smile faded as she thought about the continuing food riots and the rumors she'd heard about desperate women waylaying grain carts and carrying away the sacks on their backs. Thank God, Jamie's grain deliveries have gone without incident. Her eyes grew heavy. She was just slipping off to sleep when she heard the sound of footsteps coming quickly down the garden path.

She put the sleeping Émigré down on the floor and reluctantly rose to her feet. Who could it be? she wondered. Eugénie crossed to the gazebo steps and looked up the path. She had barely smoothed the expression of shock off her face and started down the steps when the unexpected arrival looked up, saw Eugénie, and called out in a strident voice, "Eugénie Devereux, why, there you are! Finally! I've been lookin' all over for you. Your nice Marie offered to come with me, but I said, 'Now, no need to bother yourself. Just point me in the right direction and I'll find your mistress myself.' I never thought it would be so far! What a big garden you have here. Why, I just know it must be even bigger than the one at the Governor's Palace in Williamsburg! I've never in all my born days seen so many statues. Why, you must have picked clean every single last quarry in France. Not that we don't have our share of quarries in Virginia, but I swear on the Bible, I have never seen the likes of this! And all these bushes and things—you put our piddly Virginia plantations to shame. Wait 'til I tell those Whittington girls. They'll be pea-green with envy." With these last words, a breathless Amelia Stanton came to a halt in front of Eugénie.

"Amelia, what an unexpected surprise," Eugénie said, amazed that she managed to recall the woman's name.

"As my daddy always says, I am just full of surprises," Amelia said as she smoothed her skirts and fluffed her blonde curls. The gesture immediately reminded Eugénie of the ball in Virginia fourteen years ago at the Governor's Palace when Amelia, completely oblivious to his discomfort and lack of interest, had attached herself to Bridger Goodrich.

She also remembered a later occasion when, with great glee, Amelia Stanton had brought the news to the Whittingtons of the Goodrich family's fall from grace and expulsion from Virginia. It was all Eugénie could do to keep a cordial expression on her face. What a thoroughly unpleasant individual. *Mon Dieu,* what am I to do with her?

Eugénie's silence went unnoticed by Amelia as she chattered on. "I declare, I am so good at surprises. Why, I didn't even tell that handsome Randolph Whittington about my little surprise for you. You see, he and I made the crossin' together. Oh, that odious boat! But that's behind me. I will not say another word about that rude captain and those disgustin' passengers. I was downright overjoyed that I didn't have to come up with excuses to avoid their little gatherin's and card parties. I declare, were it not for me savin' poor Randolph from a fate worse than death, he would have had to endure more of them than he did already. But, thank the good Lord, that's all behind us."

Finally, she took a breath. Tossing her blonde curls, she smiled brightly. "Now, wasn't it clever of me to resist writin' to let you know about my surprise visit? I had so many friends to see in London, I didn't know exactly when I'd be comin'. And I couldn't just keep you hangin' from one day to the next, now could I? Certainly not! My upbringin' just wouldn't allow it. Momma would be so appalled, she'd fall right down and die of mortification." Her mind flitted on. "All those beautiful parties, just for little ole me! But finally, I plainly had to put my foot down, no, not another luncheon, not another tea, not another anything. I know it broke their hearts, but they understood once I told them I couldn't wait another minute to see my dear, dear friend Eugénie Devereux. And now here I am! Isn't it just wonderful? If I say so myself, I did it just perfectly."

Amelia finally paused for another breath. Schooling the dismay from her features, Eugénie said, "Welcome to Château de Beaumont, Amelia. You have most certainly taken me by surprise." Looking over Amelia's shoulder, Eugénie saw Marie coming down the path leading a procession of servants bearing trays.

Following Eugénie's gaze, Amelia exclaimed, "Oh, thank the dear Lord!" She turned to Eugénie and patted her arm. "I do hope you don't mind, Sugar. I just mentioned to your Marie that I was simply famished and look, here she comes with a feast fit for a king. I guess it's all right to use that expression over here. Back home, we'd never think of sayin' such a thing."

As the servants approached, Amelia went into action. Grabbing her skirts in both hands, she dashed up the gazebo steps. "Here, girls, bring your trays right up here. There's plenty of room for everything on these cunnin' little tables." She managed to whisk a parsnip sandwich off a passing tray as she plopped herself down on a cushion and wasted no time diving into the laden platter in front of her. She patted the cushion beside her and said between bites, "Come on over here and sit down, Eugénie. You make me nervous standin' there. You've just got to try one of these precious little tarts. They're the best thing I've had to eat in a month of Sundays. I'm just dyin' to hear every little thing about your fascinatin' life over here in France. My, my, isn't this delicious!" Amelia demolished one platter after another, barely finishing one delicacy before grabbing the next.

Eugénie and Marie exchanged a look. Under her breath Marie said, "I've had an apartment prepared for Mademoiselle Stanton in the east wing. Her servant is there, now, unpacking for her."

"Marie, we're leaving for Versailles in two days' time," Eugénie whispered in dismay. "I can't leave the château at her mercy. I guess there's nothing for it but to include her in our plans. She's only just arrived and already she's driven me to distraction. How can one person so set my teeth on edge? Thank God for Randolph. I'll press him into service. They're both Virginians, after all. Mary Whittington, forgive me!"

Marie managed not to laugh at her mistress's outburst and instead smiled sympathetically. Eugénie gave Marie's hand a quick squeeze and said, "*Merci,* Marie, for attending to all this. Now, I'd best act the gracious hostess." As Marie and the other servants filed out of the gazebo, Eugénie went over to join Amelia.

"I do declare, Eugénie," Amelia said peevishly, "how you do go on with your Marie. Back home, my girls wouldn't dare interfere when I'm entertainin' a special guest. For all the world, I wouldn't think of leavin' my newly arrived guest all alone to eat by herself. If I didn't know better, I'd think you weren't happy to see me. Why, I'd lose my appetite if I thought my special surprise was puttin' you out for even the teeny-tiniest moment." Eugénie glanced at the ravaged platters and thought that somehow Amelia had managed to carry on regardless.

Suddenly, Amelia spied Émigré curled up asleep at Eugénie's feet.

"Oooo, what a cute little fluffball! Why, it's a little doggie. You know, dogs just love me." She reached around Eugénie to grab the pup. Émigré's eyes flew open. He jumped up and backed away, making low, menacing noises in his throat.

"Well, I never!" Amelia exclaimed. "What is the matter with him? I declare, I've never seen such a nasty, ill-tempered creature. Eugénie, how can you have such a dangerous animal around? Why, he might just attack someone for no good reason." Amelia glared at the puppy. Émigré looked her square in the eyes, snarled, and glared right back. Amelia jumped and scooted down two cushions. Recovering her bravado, she said, "Really! In all my born days, I have never seen the like!"

Eugénie picked up the pup and settled him in the crook of her arm. "Shhhh, it's all right. It's all right." Émigré gave the offensive intruder one last look, turned his back on her, and promptly went back to sleep.

"Amelia, I don't know what came over him. He's always so friendly. He must have mistaken you for someone else."

Somewhat mollified, Amelia muttered, "Oh, whatever," and picked up another tart.

"Amelia," Eugénie said briskly, "your visit is indeed a surprise and one that I wish we could extend." She prayed that God would not strike her dead for the falsehood. "But, in two days' time I must leave for Versailles."

Amelia's face lit up and she cut Eugénie off, saying, "Sugar, I know all about the October fête. The Whittingtons were just pleased as punch when their Randolph received his very own personal invitation. Oh, my, my, it was the talk of the county. I, of course, would certainly have received one if I'd been on a Grand Tour and been presented at Court. It was clear to me that I was obliged to fix this oversight. I wrote my friends in London to let them know that I'd just love to stop by and visit with them on my way to this occasion in France. Of course, they were just dyin' for me to come immediately and stay for several weeks, but, with all my obligations at home, I simply couldn't tear myself away a second sooner.

"Everyone, but everyone, at home was so alarmed about all the dangers of travelin' alone all that way across the ocean and all the rumors about the uprisin's in Paris and the riots all over France. But I wouldn't hear any of it. They all might be afraid and shakin' in their boots, but not me." She lowered her voice conspiratorially. "Eugénie, honey, I'm goin' to tell you a secret. But you mustn't breathe a word to another livin' soul."

She paused for effect, drew in a deep breath, and took a large bite of pigeon galantine. After she had swallowed it, she daintily wiped a bit of aspic from her mouth and took a sip of tea. Leaning towards Eugénie, she looked her straight in the eye and said, "I've learned something very important about myself. Something I've never realized before. I haven't told another livin' soul, but I'm sharin' it with you because you're such a dear, dear friend." Momentarily overcome, she paused, then drew herself up and announced, "I am a truly brave and courageous person!" Eugénie, expecting something of real importance, was caught completely off guard. Misreading the look on Eugénie's face, Amelia struck her knee with her fist and said emphatically, "Yes, indeed, I am the most truly brave and courageous person I have ever known. I'm sure it's hard for you to grasp all this at once. I must confess, when it first came to me, when I first understood the magnitude of this realization, I honestly thought I was goin' to faint. You just never know what you're made of until you're confronted with a life test."

Amelia went on, "Here I was in the midst of all these people talkin' about fearsome this and frightenin' that, dangerous this and dangerous that. Then, out of the blue, as clear as the nose on your face, it came to me that, bein' the brave, courageous person that I am, it was my bounden duty to meet this challenge. I put my foot down and said, 'I am goin'!' And do you know what happened?"

Eugénie tried to think of a reply, but not a thing came to mind.

Caught in the throes of her emotion, Amelia flung her arms up in the air and announced, "All of a sudden, every little thing fell into place. There was Randolph Whittington, the perfect escort to accompany me on my dangerous voyage. I'm still not clear what happened to him when we docked in London. I'm sure I told him to meet me... Oh, never mind. I knew I'd see him here, sooner or later. He must have been distraught not to find me, but what was I to do? My friends were there and I couldn't keep them waitin', now could I?"

It took every ounce of Eugénie's self-control to sit there and endure the silly woman's nonsense.

Oblivious, Amelia prattled on. "Next, I hatched up this wonderful surprise for you, which, I don't mind sayin', to this day I don't know how I managed to overcome so many obstacles. But, knowin' how much my visit would mean to you after all I did for you durin' your stay in Virginia, I was not goin' to let anything, not anything stand in my way. Finally, miracle of miracles! My dressmaker had some orders for ball gowns that were canceled." Amelia giggled. "I just happened to be in her shop at the time. And do you know, with just a few itty-bitty alterations here and there, she made them just right for me. As I said, every little thing just fell into place. Now isn't that grand?" Amelia looked at Eugénie expectantly.

Eugénie was speechless. Happily, she was saved from having to respond because at that moment Randolph, still in his riding clothes, bounded into the gazebo. Émigré jumped off Eugénie's lap and dashed over to him. For different reasons, his arrival was met by two bright, welcoming smiles. The transformation of Randolph's face from eager anticipation to complete consternation was almost comical. Too late, he covered his dismay by picking up the pup and burying his face in Émigré's fur.

"Amelia!" he managed to say in a strangled voice.

With blonde curls bouncing, Amelia leapt to her feet, rushed over to him, and flung her arms around the startled man. With a yelp, Émigré jumped out of Randolph's arms and scurried back to Eugénie.

"Randolph Whittington," Amelia exclaimed, "if you aren't a sight for sore eyes!" She stepped back and looked up at him through pale lashes. "I was just sayin' to myself, where is that handsome boy? I've been keepin' Eugénie company. After all, I couldn't have her eatin' this beautiful tea all by herself. We've been havin' the most wonderful time reminiscin' about old times, whilin' away the hours, just waitin' for you. Now, aren't you ashamed, keepin' two beautiful women waitin' all this time?"

Randolph looked hopefully at Eugénie, but her raised brow told him, in no uncertain terms, that there would be no help coming from that quarter. Resigned, he turned back to Amelia.

"Ah, Miss Amelia, when did you arrive? I didn't know Miss Eugénie was expecting you," he said, making a valiant effort not to draw back as Amelia locked her arm through his. Carefully extricating himself, he fairly shouted, "Keep your distance!" At Amelia's shocked face, he continued in a more restrained tone, "Ah, pardon me, that is to say, I'm quite ripe after my ride. I'm not fit for close company." Amelia, looking somewhat appeased, stepped back.

"I hadn't heard that you were planning a visit here," he said lamely.

Seeing that Randolph was on the brink of committing another faux pas, Eugénie took pity on him.

"Randolph, you must be in need of some refreshment after the rigors of your afternoon. Marie prepared a feast for an army. Please stay and join us." Randolph threw a look of gratitude at Eugénie and stepped aside to let Amelia resume her seat.

Placing himself as far away from her as possible, he turned to his hostess and said, "Thank you, Miss Eugénie. I certainly could use a little sustenance just now."

IX

"*Zut!* Where is Amelia?" Eugénie said under her breath, as she paced back and forth in front of the assembled coaches and mounted footmen. "Drat her. I've a mind to leave without her." It had taken no small effort on Eugénie's part to secure Amelia's inclusion in the de Beaumont party for the royal fête.

Eugénie walked over to Jeremy and Randolph, who were talking quietly astride their horses. Only The Roan, whose reins Jeremy held, seemed to share his mistress's impatience to leave. Eugénie caught Jeremy's eye and, looking at him pointedly, said, "Not one word, Jeremy, not one single word, or so help me..." She left the rest unsaid as she swung up onto The Roan's back. Eugénie had chosen to wear her green, split-skirt riding costume instead of the breeches and jacket she often favored when riding at the château. Considering the occasion, she had been willing to make this partial compromise with convention, but some inner voice had led her to tuck the other clothing, along with a knitted cap, into one of her smaller valises.

"Yes, Ma'am, Miss Eugénie," Jeremy replied, reverting to the broad Bahamian drawl of his childhood. "I wouldn't consider sayin' one single word. No, Ma'am, not a single one."

In the few days since Amelia Stanton had arrived at the château, she had managed to disrupt everything and everybody. In retaliation, Jeremy had marshaled the troops. At Amelia's approach, every able-bodied member of the household, from the highest to the lowest, would scatter, leaving only the older, less nimble servants to contend with her commands and demands. Those unfortunates affected deafness, which caused Amelia to raise her naturally shrill tones to a near ear-splitting pitch.

Jeremy, unable to resist additional mischief at Amelia's expense, had encouraged the servants to reverse Amelia's orders whenever possible. If she demanded a cool compress for a nagging headache, she received hot bricks for her bed. Her gowns invariably were returned to her more wrinkled than when they went out to be pressed. The decrepit mount they gave her was never quite able to keep up with the other horses on the morning rides.

Just when Amelia, feeling at her wits' end, was about to berate the first unlucky servant to cross her path, Jeremy, the instigator, would magically appear and smooth her ruffled feathers. The result was that the entire château population seldom went a day without a good laugh at the poor woman's expense.

Eugénie was torn between upbraiding Jeremy for his mischief and laughing at his pranks. The irony of Amelia, the consummate snob, turning for sympathy and company to a black, Bahamian horse trainer was lost on no one.

The Roan, who had been pawing at the ground and tossing his majestic head, settled quickly under Eugénie's familiar hand. Stroking the horse, Eugénie mused over Amelia's tardiness. She found it particularly puzzling, considering her guest's outspoken eagerness to quit the château as soon as possible and be on her way to Versailles.

The night before, Amelia's parting words to Eugénie had been, "For the life of me, Eugénie, I can't understand how this château is still standin'. I've never in all my days seen such triflin' servants. Not a one of them has a brain in their head. Why, even your Marie can't perform the simplest task I give her—that is, when I can find her. My people at home would be soundly thrashed if they carried out my orders anywhere near as poorly as the service I've suffered here. Really, Eugénie, how ever do you put up with this?"

Eugénie turned to gaze suspiciously at Jeremy, who was whistling under his breath, with a look of supreme innocence on his face.

"Jeremy," she said, her voice deceptively low, "if you've contrived one last bit of mischief for Mademoiselle Stanton to cause this delay, I will..." Before she could finish, Amelia came hurrying into the courtyard, followed by her maidservant, Betsy.

"Lawd above, how did it get to be so late? I'm fairly breathless, I've been rushin' so! I do not know what on Earth came over me last night. I swear, I was asleep before my head hit the pillow." Eugénie's gaze was riveted on Jeremy. "The next thing I know, Betsy, here, is shakin' my shoulder tellin' me that everyone's in the courtyard ready to leave. I've never in my life slept so late and I have this awful headache. It must be all the stress and strain I've been under lately. But, here I am. Betsy, what in heaven's name are you waitin' for? Get in the carriage this instant!"

Amelia hoisted up her skirts, preparing to climb into the coach, when she looked around and exclaimed, "Why, where is Countess de Beaumont?" Just then, her eyes alighted on Eugénie seated on The Roan. Amelia's eyes widened in shock. "My dear Eugénie, surely you don't intend to ride horseback—astride, no less—all the way to Versailles. What will people think?"

"Amelia," Eugénie replied, trying to keep the exasperation out of her voice, "that is exactly what I intend to do. I find the opportunity for a ride quite irresistible." When she saw Amelia open her mouth to speak, Eugénie cut her off, saying, "This arrangement is by far the most enjoyable for everyone. If you please, Amelia, settle yourself in the coach and we'll be off. We're entirely too late getting started as it is." Not waiting to see if Amelia followed her thinly veiled command, Eugénie turned The Roan towards the gates and galloped off down the avenue of sycamores.

The next two days of travel passed without incident, in spite of Amelia's constant complaining that the coach was rattling her teeth and breaking every bone in her body. Amelia realized, after the first day, that her exhortations to stop every few miles to relax and refresh were of no use. The coachman was the only person, except Betsy, within earshot and he, like the rest of the party, had no wish to prolong the journey. Eugénie, Randolph, and Jeremy rode ahead, enjoying the beautiful countryside and relishing their distance from the querulous Amelia. Eugénie was glad that, at the last minute, she had thought to have Marie ride in the second coach with the baggage, relieving her of Amelia's company.

It was a subdued Amelia and a thoroughly cowed Betsy who stumbled from the coach on the evening of the second day. Amelia's fighting spirit returned in part when she looked about her and saw that they had arrived in a small courtyard in front of an unprepossessing inn. Eugénie, Randolph, and Jeremy were nowhere in sight.

"Betsy!" Amelia's voice rose to its usual strident pitch. "Go into that place this minute and find Mistress Eugénie. I will not stay here. This is not to be tolerated!"

The young black woman looked at her mistress, horrified, and said, "Miss Amelia, I cain't go into no public place unaccompanied. You knows that. My mammy would whup me within an inch of my life if'n I was to do such a thing."

Amelia grasped Betsy's arm and gave her a shove towards the inn. "And I'm goin' to whip you within an inch of your life if you don't!" Betsy, seeing Amelia's immediate threat to her person as being far more dangerous to her than her mother's distant one, chose to follow her mistress's command and hurried into the inn.

With her face wreathed in smiles, Amelia glided over to the coachman, who was giving orders to one of the inn's stable boys. She pushed her way in between them, interrupting their conversation, and said in broken French, "My dear man, *je suis bien sûr* that *il y a un terrible* mistake. I distinctly recall the Countess de Beaumont *dit nous* that we'd be staying *au château* of the Duke and Duchess of Sully, *ce soir.*" With a bright smile, she looked up expectantly at the coachman. The man stared blankly at her and then stepped around her to continue his conversation with the stable boy.

Her nerves frayed to the breaking point, Amelia again stepped in between the two men. She shook her finger in the coachman's face.

"Listen, whatever your name is, I'm talkin' to you and I expect you to listen! Now..." At that moment, a burly man, well into his cups, swaggered up and threw a thick arm around Amelia's waist.

"What have we here?" he said in guttural French. "A damsel in distress?" Amelia looked first at the arm around her waist, then up into the leering face above her, and let out a bloodcurdling shriek. Pushed past all endurance, she slumped forward in a dead faint. Had it not been for the ruffian's arm, she would have collapsed in a heap on the cobblestones.

Amelia's scream reverberated through the inn. Eugénie, who had been trying to calm the hysterical Betsy, ran to the open doorway, followed by Randolph.

"Zut alors," she cried, seeing a brawl in full tilt taking place in the courtyard, with Amelia lying on the ground in the middle of it. The coachman and footmen were exchanging blows with what appeared to be a motley group of local rascals.

Eugénie sprang into action. Seeing the coachman's discarded whip, she grabbed it and, snapping it in the air, waded into the fray. Her expert handling of the whip sounded like gunshots, which accomplished the desired effect. The men froze in place, but when the locals saw that it was a mere woman, they resumed their attack on Eugénie's men. They halted abruptly when the whip found several marks. Nursing their rising welts, the attackers ran towards the entrance of the courtyard. At a gesture from Eugénie, the coachman took the whip and hastened their departure by following behind them and snapping the whip above their heads.

Eugénie hurried over to Amelia, who was just beginning to

revive. She reached down and helped the dazed woman to her feet.

"Oh, Amelia," she said under her breath, "what am I going to do with you?"

Amelia moaned and rubbed her forehead. Turning bewildered eyes to Eugénie, she said, "Eugénie, an evil, evil man attacked me!" She looked wildly around the courtyard. "Where is he? Where is he?" Bursting into tears, she crumpled in Eugénie's arms and wailed, "I'm so afraid! I'm so afraid!"

A short time later, Marie was serving a modest supper to the weary travelers in the small sitting room adjoining Eugénie's bedchamber. As Eugénie ladled vegetable soup into her bowl, Marie bent close to her ear and whispered, "Betsy is still prostrate in her mistress's bedchamber. I left some bread and cheese at her bedside. I daresay she'll sleep through 'til morning."

"*Merci,* Marie," Eugénie replied in low tones. "God willing, by this time tomorrow, we'll be rid of them. The French court doesn't know what it's in for."

Amelia, who had declined Marie's offer to serve her in bed, spoke up for the first time since they had sat down at the table. "Eugénie, why ever did you bring us to this horrible place? If we were at the Duke and Duchess's château, as we were supposed to be, I wouldn't have come within a hair's breadth of losin' my life, or worse, at the hands of that disgustin' creature and I wouldn't be forced to eat this, this... food that's not even fit for barnyard animals!"

"Amelia," Eugénie replied quietly as though calming a fretful child, "we were well past the de Sully château by midday. By stopping here overnight, we'll only have a short trip to Versailles tomorrow. I expect to arrive there well before midday. You've had a very difficult time. Perhaps it's best for you to retire and get your rest. Marie, would you please assist Amelia, since Betsy is indisposed?"

"Yes, Mistress," Marie replied.

"In the morning, Amelia, it'll all be behind you," Eugénie said soothingly.

"Oh, yes, tomorrow, it'll all be behind me," Amelia parroted. With no more ado, she rose from her chair and swept from the room.

X

The sky was a brilliant blue and the crisp air was laden with the rich scents of autumn as Eugénie's entourage approached the outer gates of the Palace of Versailles. They quickly passed through, after the gateman gave their documents a cursory inspection. In short order, Eugénie's party, as well as Amelia and her servant, were directed to apartments in the west wing of the palace, but several blocks apart, much to Eugénie's relief.

Eugénie and Marie were still unpacking their trunks and baggage when they heard a rap on the outer door. Marie opened it to see Jeremy, dressed in his finest, followed by a young man whose livery announced his position in the queen's personal guard. The footman followed Marie into the room and presented himself to Eugénie, holding a small silver plate on which lay a note with the royal seal. Eugénie took the note and, breaking the seal, quickly scanned the contents. Frowning, she read it again more slowly.

"Zut," she said under her breath, "how silly of me to hope for an afternoon all to myself." Looking up at the messenger, she smiled and said, graciously, "Please tell Her Majesty that I'm delighted to attend her this afternoon." When she heard the door

close behind the servant's departing back, Eugénie collapsed into the nearest chair.

"Will I never be done with Amelia Stanton? How did she manage to worm her way into an audience with the queen this very afternoon?"

Jeremy turned from picking through the basket of fruit on the carved vitrine next to the marble fireplace. "That's a mystery I can solve," he said.

"Well?" Eugénie watched the young man choose a particularly large red apple and take a bite. Marie unsuccessfully tried to squelch a giggle.

Finally, Jeremy said, "As I heard it, Miss Amelia was no sooner shown to her room than out she popped in a frock that must've set her pappy back a pretty penny." He took another bite from the apple before continuing. "She made such a racket ordering everyone around, I thought for sure you could hear it all the way over here. It wasn't long before she'd had some soul run poor Mr. Randolph to earth. Just like a fox after a hare, she was.

"Next thing, Mr. Randolph's man was dispatched to the royal apartments with a note written in Mr. Randolph's hand, but under the close eye of Miss Amelia, beseeching an audience for Miss Amelia Stanton, his very dear friend from Virginia. Last I heard, Miss Amelia was flouncing around in the gardens with Mr. Randolph in tow, looking for her next prey." Jeremy munched on his apple, his eyes twinkling. Eugénie burst out laughing.

"Oh, Jeremy," she said catching her breath, "how on Earth do you find out all this? Is it your boyish charm, or have you stooped to listening at keyholes?"

"I have my ways. I have to admit, sometimes it does take a bit of wit and charm. But that one's no challenge at all. All I have to do is follow the havoc she leaves in her wake and lend a sympathetic ear to the bodies strewn in her path," he replied, looking quite pleased with himself. Then his face turned serious. "There's been a change of plans for tomorrow evening."

"Oh?" Eugénie looked up, hearing his somber tone. "What is it?"

"The ministers have stationed the Flanders regiment at the palace. They feel recent events dictate strengthening the guard for the royal family."

Eugénie, rising from her chair, began to pace. She picked up a small figurine of a shepherdess and turned it slowly in her hands.

"Oh, la Pauvre Bergère," she murmured, using one of the queen's nicknames. Holding the figurine, she walked over to the window and stared out. Taking a deep breath, she turned back to Jeremy. "Have you heard anything else?"

"Only that the royal guard's traditional banquet of welcome for the new regiment will take place, instead of the royal fête. I hear that it'll be more elaborate than is the custom, that members of the court will attend, and that the royal family is expected to make an appearance. It'll take place in the Château Opera."

A chill skittered down Eugénie's spine. "But that's an enormous place. They must indeed be planning an elaborate event and expecting great numbers. Can such extravagance be wise, given the extensive poverty in the country and the state of the treasury? No doubt, it'll be yet another example of excess laid at the queen's feet."

Jeremy nodded in agreement. "Madame, if there's nothing further, I'd best be off to oversee The Roan and the other horses.

With the Flanders regiment's arrival, the stables are filled to bursting. I wouldn't trust my brother, if I had one, to look out for their welfare."

"Yes, yes, Jeremy," Eugénie said, "be off, then, and keep your eyes and ears peeled." She turned to Marie. "I have a sense of foreboding about this. Unpack only the bare necessities. Should the need arise, we must be prepared to leave at a moment's notice."

The ladies of the court had turned out in force for the queen's audience. Marie Antoinette appeared to be in high spirits, chatting, in her informal fashion, with everyone who approached her. But Eugénie, who had not seen the queen since the fall of the Bastille, noticed that there were signs of strain around her eyes and a nervous tremor in the motion of the fan she held in her hand. Only when talking to her close friend Princesse de Lamballe did the queen seem her usual lighthearted self.

Eugénie visited with Jeanne Louise Henrietta Genet Campan, knowing that, as one of the queen's favorites, her assessment of the queen's health and state of mind could be trusted. Out of the corner of her eye, Eugénie followed Amelia's progress around the room. It amused Eugénie that she seemed to have an unerring nose for the loftiest titles and the most renowned gossips.

"Ah, the Virginian," Jeanne Louise said, seeing the direction of Eugénie's gaze. "Already she's cut a wide swath. I understand she arrived with your party. A friend of yours?"

"Yes, she does make her presence felt," Eugénie said drily. "No, not a friend, more of an acquaintance." Just then, Jeanne Louise rose from her chair.

"There's the queen's signal. She very much wants to have a quiet moment with you." Surprised, Eugénie followed her onto the balcony where the queen stood looking out at the Orangerie.

"Isn't it comforting," said the queen pensively, aware of the two women's approach, "that the bees, year in and year out, move from blossom to blossom, tree to tree, without a care in the world." Eugénie and Jeanne Louise said nothing, leaving the queen to her thoughts. After a few minutes, she turned towards them and they dipped into deep curtsies. Marie Antoinette reached out and took both of Eugénie's hands, as Jeanne Louise withdrew.

"It's been far too long since you've visited," the queen said brightly. "What can the Bordeaux offer that the powdered heads of this illustrious court can't provide?" Then the gaiety vanished from her face. "No, let me start again. I'm so in the habit of idle chitchat that I do it without thinking and, by doing so, I do you a great disservice. I rarely have the luxury of enjoying discourse with someone I truly admire. I don't intend to waste it.

"You and I are the same age," she went on. "You were fifteen when you lost both your parents when the British frigate sank your family's merchant ship. I was that age when I lost my home and everything I held dear when I left them to come to this strange country to marry a boy as young and as naïve as I. We, you and I, have been given great opportunities and great burdens. You're a credit to your family's name and to your country. I'm called frivolous, extravagant, headstrong—and worse. I know these things, though I pretend to the contrary."

Suddenly, her eyes shimmered with tears. "People think it very easy to play the queen," she said softly. "They're wrong. The constraints are endless. It seems that to be natural is a crime." She looked away and then turned back, her gaze clear and hard.

"Eugénie, all the hateful slander hurled at my name touches me not at all. Let them do their worst. I must be strong for the king, my children, and my loyal friends. I cannot allow myself to waver in front of them, or all will be lost. But there are a few, a precious few, whom I hold in the highest regard and with whom I trust I can bare my soul. You're one of them."

Eugénie was stunned. "Your Majesty, I'm honored..."

The queen raised her hand dismissively. "*Ma chère* Eugénie, it's not necessarily a compliment. I'm known to be an abysmal judge of character." She laughed self-deprecatingly. "But in your case, I know I'm right. You've suffered such loss in your lifetime — your mother, your father, your husband, your babies."

At Eugénie's startled look, the queen said, "Oh, yes, I know all about the loss of the babies." She paused for a moment and looked down, murmuring, "My babies, my precious babies, are my salvation. What would I do without them?"

The queen grasped Eugénie's arm in a surprisingly strong grip. "In spite of everything, Eugénie, or perhaps because of everything, you're a person of strength and character. One day, I may need to call on you. You'll know my messenger by this token." She pointed at the plain, slim band on her wrist. "I hope to God such a day will never come, that it's just one of my foolish fancies."

"Your Majesty, you do me the highest honor. I and all that I have are yours to command," Eugénie said, sinking into a deep curtsy.

In a lightning change of mood, the queen drew Eugénie up and said, "Eugénie, have you noticed how closely some of my courtiers resemble sheep, goats, swine, and cattle? Forgive me,

Blanchette. I fear I insult you by such a comparison." Linking her arm through Eugénie's, Marie Antoinette turned and re-entered the salon.

Scanning the room, the queen said under her breath, "Nothing's changed." Turning a bright countenance to Eugénie, she winked. "And, if I'm not mistaken, your very dear friend, Mademoiselle Stanton, bears a very close resemblance to me, poor thing, even to her excessively high forehead and protruding eyes." Marie Antoinette threw back her head and laughed merrily. The transformation of the queen was so complete that, had it not been broad daylight, Eugénie would have sworn that she had dreamt the whole thing.

XI

The vast space of the Château Opera was ablaze with candlelight. The regimental uniforms were in sharp contrast with the host of bedecked courtiers, striking a martial note amidst an ocean of elaborate costumes and jewels, wine and food. The evening had begun quietly enough. The shift occurred gradually. By the time the queen and king made their appearance, the atmosphere in the room fairly crackled.

To resounding cheers, the queen moved through the room, holding the four-year-old Dauphin in her arms. When she circled back and stood by the king, the assembled rose to their feet as one, enthusiastically toasting the royal family. In the midst of this uproar, the royal family withdrew, but the toasting continued.

Caught up in the spirit of the moment, Madame de Maille, who was seated at Eugénie's table, impetuously ripped the revolutionary cockade from her bodice, brandished it aloft, and flung it to the floor, exclaiming, *"Vive le Roi!"* Several other ladies followed suit and the volatile atmosphere exploded, amidst deafening cheers and shouted toasts. Ladies plunged into the crowd, handing out white cockades for the king and black ones for the queen.

Eugénie watched the courtiers eagerly grasping these offerings and pinning them on their clothing. Don't they understand, she thought, that these are acts against the revolution? What, dear God, will be the consequences of this night? I'd better find Amelia before she's swept up in this madness.

Just then, Amelia appeared in front of her, clutching the arm of a young soldier. Before Eugénie could speak, Amelia, swaying slightly, announced, "Eugénie, isn't this the most excitin' evenin'? I'm havin' the most wonderful time! I am green-eyed over all the beautiful gowns and jewels. Have you ever seen the like? Won't I just have a thing or two to tell my friends back home? I simply can't get over the beautiful gowns. I've a mind to speak to the queen about having her dressmaker—now, what's her name? Rose, Rose something—Rose Bertin, that's right, I'm goin' to speak to the queen about havin' Rose Bertin make some new gowns for me."

Looking down at her own exquisite dress, she plucked at it distastefully. "Just look at this thing! It's downright pathetic! How am I supposed to hold up my head wearin' such a rag? Did you see the queen? Wasn't she just grand? And that cute little baby. Which reminds me, all evenin' long, everyone's been tellin' me that I'm the spittin' image of Queen Marie Antoinette. Isn't that somethin'? Now, of course, those nice people were just tryin' to make me feel at home." She paused, waiting to be contradicted. When no contradiction was forthcoming, she continued, "I have to admit, I was tickled pink."

She preened and batted her lashes up at the soldier, who seemed to be hanging on her every word. "You know," she said, including Eugénie in her glance, "it's enough to turn a person's head, but not mine—oh, no, certainly not mine."

Amelia paused and wrinkled her forehead in thought. "Now, why was it I came over here? Oh, yes, I remember. Hans! Hans, this is Eugénie. Eugénie, this is Hans." She pointed proudly at the young man as though he were a prize exhibit. "He's in the regiment that just arrived at the palace." Hans bowed deeply to Eugénie and then resumed his rigid, upright posture. Patting Hans's shoulder, Amelia gushed, "Isn't he just the most handsome thing?" Before Eugénie could respond to either the introduction or the question, Amelia sped on. "I always say there's nothin', nothin' in this world more absolutely irresistible than a handsome man in a handsome uniform. Well, here's the livin' proof!" Amelia emphasized her point by whacking Hans on the shoulder. To his credit, he did not lose his self-possession and continued to beam at her.

"Hans, here, doesn't speak much English. But who needs it? All I have to do is look into his big, beautiful brown eyes and everything I want to know is right there. I declare, Eugénie, I am dizzy, just plain dizzy with the queen, with Hans, with... with just everything!" She flung her arms wide, encompassing the room. The gesture threw her off balance and she would have fallen had Eugénie not caught her around the waist and Hans braced her from the rear.

"Amelia," Eugénie said, trying to break through Amelia's drunken euphoria, "it's getting late. Let me help you back to your apartment."

"Late? Late! The evenin's just begun!" Amelia pronounced, pushing Eugénie's hands away. "Anyway, whatever do I need your help for, Eugénie Devereux, when I've got this wonderful, handsome Hans here?" Amelia purred up at the young man and stroked his chest.

She turned back to Eugénie, her voice hard. "And to think I felt sorry for you over here all by yourself. I left all the fun I was havin' to come over here and take you to meet all my new friends. I can see, now, that you're jealous, just plain jealous. Well, you can just sit here, for all I care. Come on, Hans." She whirled around and flounced off, dragging Hans behind her.

Shaking her head, Eugénie looked after Amelia's retreating figure. Then she made her *adieux* and called it a night.

XII

The following afternoon, Eugénie and Randolph strolled in the gardens, enjoying the brisk autumn weather.

"Isn't it an interesting irony," Eugénie said to her companion as they paused to admire a larger-than-life-sized grouping of gods and goddesses frolicking in a massive stone fountain, "that I should have been in Virginia on the brink of your revolution and now you're here in my country at the beginning of ours?"

"Aye, it is," Randolph agreed, smiling at her. "The threads of our lives intertwine in some grand scheme beyond our understanding." He turned away from her and dabbled his fingers in the spray of water that cascaded into the base of the fountain. "Eugénie, you've avoided the subject that lies between us. I'm most embarrassed about it. I'm speaking of Amelia Stanton."

Eugénie reached out and placed a comforting hand on his arm. "Randolph, I won't have your conscience burdened for one moment by her behavior of last evening."

"You're too kind, Madame!" he cried, swinging back to face her. "She is willful, selfish, and rude! I'm ashamed that she's a fellow countryman of mine, a Virginian, from my own county, no less. And I'm ashamed that through me she foisted herself off on you, and now has thrust herself on the queen and the French court. At home, I thought her little campaigns harmless enough, but she's taken her manipulations to new heights over here. I fear the harm she could cause in these unstable times.

"After you left last night, she made a complete and utter fool of herself, prancing about, dragging that poor officer behind her. She kept yelling, 'Long live the king!' at the top of her lungs, and snatching the black and white cockades from the ladies and gentlemen of the court and sticking them all over herself. She failed to see that she was the laughingstock of the evening, not 'the belle of the ball,' as she kept saying to me in that braying voice of hers."

"Randolph, I agree that Amelia is far from harmless. More than that, there are those who could easily play on her vanity and use her for their own ends to foil the best interests of the revolution and the king and queen. Intrigue is rife at Court in the best of times. Traveling through France, as you have on this trip, and witnessing last night's debacle, you can see the state of affairs that could find Amelia as a pawn in someone's unscrupulous scheme.

"Sadly, the unifying spirit that prevailed from the beginning of your American Revolution is not the case here, at least at this point. The students, the bourgeoisie, the nobles, and the church all vie for control, each pursuing their own narrow interests. Power is seductive. Were it not for the tenuous hold of the people's loyalty to the Crown, I fear what would happen. But there's nothing to be gained by following that train of thought. What of Amelia? Have you seen her today?"

Randolph shook his head. "No, I've not had the dubious pleasure, but I did speak to Betsy, who assured me that Amelia's still in the land of the living, 'though just barely.'" In spite of his low spirits, he managed to laugh. "It appears that God is having his just retribution on that lady for her excesses of last evening." The amusement left Randolph's face as he took Eugénie's hand and looked down into her eyes. "I'm glad we've had these moments together before I depart."

"Oh, must you leave so soon? I was hoping to enjoy your company during my time here at Court. I feel it's my duty to remain long enough to be sure that last evening's events don't have unfortunate repercussions for Their Majesties." Eugénie's voice took on an urgent note. "Randolph, I think it would be very unwise for Amelia to remain, once you're gone. Also, who'll escort her safely out of France?"

Randolph looked alarmed. "Surely, you don't believe she's in danger?"

"It's more that Amelia is a danger to herself and to others than the other way around. She's headstrong and unpredictable—a dangerous combination. There's no telling what she might do. Furthermore, as you know, travel is precarious at best in these times. It was a miracle that she arrived at Beaumont unscathed. And in the short time she's been here, conditions have worsened."

Randolph nodded. "I spoke with her last night at the banquet about my plans to depart tomorrow. I felt honor bound to invite her to join me. But she turned up her nose at my offer. So, I say, she's made her bed. Let her sleep in it. I'm done with her!"

"Randolph, you've gone above and beyond the call of duty," Eugénie said. "Like a cat, Amelia seems to have at least nine lives. I just pray that she has one or two left. Considering the company she's keeping, she'll need them."

As they were talking, they continued down the path, which led to another fountain display that featured a life-sized Neptune, his wife, Amphitrite, and their son Triton.

"The sculptures in these gardens are magnificent. Many appear to be by the same hand," Randolph said, admiring the piece before them.

"You're correct. The brothers Lambert-Sigisbert Adam and Nicolas-Sébastien Adam created many of the sculptures here. Their *atelier* had the greatest reputation in all of France. They worked in many mediums, using terra-cotta as well as lead casts. Their pieces are some of the finest legacies of France. I'm so pleased you've had the opportunity to visit Versailles and see"—she paused and smiled—"for better or worse, the world of the Bourbons. Once the new order is established, I don't know how much of the old ways and how many of these riches will survive. Already, monuments and symbols of privilege have been defiled and destroyed in Paris and throughout the country. I only hope that Versailles will weather the storm."

In the predawn light, Eugénie saw Randolph Whittington off the next morning. There was no sign of Amelia, who Marie reported had been seen cavorting late into the night with her new friends. Promising to plan a get-together of Eugénie and the Whittington family as soon as possible, the friends embraced one last time. Then, Randolph swung up on his mount, his saddlebags laden to overflowing with Eugénie's letters and gifts for the Whittingtons. He wheeled his horse around and cantered off down the avenue of trees. Eugénie stood waving at his departing figure until Randolph turned, gave one last jaunty salute, and disappeared from view.

XIII

OCTOBER 5, 1789

Eugénie shot straight up from the trunk she was packing. "Marie, what in heaven's name was that?" It was late afternoon, five days since the infamous regimental banquet. Life at the palace, to all appearances, had settled back to normal.

"Mistress," Marie began, but was interrupted by a loud knocking at the apartment door. Marie hurried to open it and Jeremy strode into the room.

"Jeremy," Eugénie exclaimed, "what's that noise? It sounds like drums!"

"Mistress, it is drums! I was already coming to relay an urgent message for you from the Marquis de Lafayette when that racket started."

"From Gilbert? A message?" Eugénie asked, her hand at her throat.

"A messenger from the Marquis arrived here a short while ago from Paris and sought me out. He had much of import to tell me."

Jeremy plunged on. "This morning early, the tocsin was rung in Paris calling forth the women of the marketplace to gather and march on Versailles to demand bread. The messenger reported that Paris has been in an uproar since word arrived there of the regimental banquet and the dishonor done that evening to the cockade of the revolution."

"*Mon Dieu,*" Eugénie whispered.

Jeremy's words came in a rush. "To make matters worse, following that evening, black and white cockades have been showing up in substantial numbers in the streets of Paris. That night has come to represent the height of, not only debauchery and excess, but high treason, as well. I just came from the village of Versailles. The women of Paris are arriving by the thousands, armed with cannon, cudgels, and other weapons. It's their drums you hear."

Eugénie's face went stark white. "I must find the queen. She'll be terrified!"

Marie and Jeremy looked at each other with alarm. "*Non, non!*" Marie spoke first. "You must look to your own safety."

"Marie's right, Madame. We must leave Versailles with all haste," Jeremy said, his usual composure shattered. "The messenger also said—I forgot, in all the excitement—that Lafayette, with at least fifteen thousand of the Garde Nationale, is even now on his way here to intercept the mob and maintain order. But you know as well as I do that he's not the adored leader he once was. I fear what'll happen when those two forces come together."

Eugénie looked at her devoted servants standing before her. She read the concern for her in their eyes. "Your loyalty has never been more precious to me than it is at this moment, but I can't leave before I know that I've done everything in my power to ensure the queen's welfare."

"*S'il vous plaît,* Mistress," Marie beseeched her, close to tears, "I fear for your life, should these people find you in the queen's company."

"*Chère* Marie," Eugénie said, putting her arm around her servant, "these people aren't monsters. They only come to make their demands for food known to the king and queen. In any case, they can't breach the royal guard. I'm confident that they'll be granted an audience with Their Majesties and a reasonable conclusion will be reached."

"I beg to differ with you, Mistress," Jeremy argued. "I've been in their midst and seen the rage and hopelessness in their eyes!"

Eugénie held up her hand to silence him. "*Ça suffit!* We've no time to waste. Marie, finish the packing and see that the baggage is loaded into the coaches. Jeremy, go at once and alert our guard. Ready the horses and coaches and assemble everyone in the grove by the west gate. It's little known, even to those at the palace. We'll make our departure from there. I'll meet you as soon as possible."

The words were barely out of her mouth before Jeremy bowed briefly, turned on his heel, and left the room. As Marie returned to the packing with new urgency, Eugénie went to one of her valises and yanked out the pair of breeches, jacket, and cap that she had stuffed in it before leaving the château.

"*Vite,* Marie, help me with these hooks and buttons," Eugénie said, wrestling with her gown.

Marie turned and saw what was in Eugénie's hands. "Mistress!" she exclaimed, horrified. "Surely you aren't attending the queen in that garb!" Then Marie's eyes narrowed. "What are you planning that you need to pass as a man?"

"Marie, indeed I am wearing this garb, as you call it. The queen is oblivious to the etiquette of dress. As to schemes, I've none at present, but this disguise that's served me well in the past could prove useful if the need arises. No more talk. *Vite! Vite!*" Marie's lips thinned in disapproval, but soon her nimble fingers dispensed with the gown and undergarments. In no time, Eugénie, dressed in breeches and jacket with the cap stuffed in her waistband, hastened out the door.

Eugénie was breathless by the time she arrived at the Belvedere pavilion where she hoped to find the queen. To her relief, the guard posted at the entrance indicated the queen's presence. He recognized Eugénie and ushered her to the queen. Oblivious to the stares of the ladies-in-waiting, Eugénie rushed forward to Marie Antoinette.

"Your Royal Highness, a mob from Paris has arrived at the village of Versailles! For your welfare, I urge you to retire to your apartments!"

"*Chère Eugénie, quel joli garçon vous êtes,*" the queen said, her blue eyes twinkling. "You've given me the first bit of pleasure I've had this whole day long." As Eugénie began to speak, the queen interrupted her. "*Oui, oui.* I know of the Parisian women's arrival. Not more than a few moments past, a page brought me the news. I suppose I must return to the palace." Wearily, she rose from her seat and gestured to Eugénie to walk beside her. She linked her arm through Eugénie's and the two made their way out of the pavilion with the attendants trailing behind.

As they started up the graveled path, the queen lowered her

voice. "The world is too much with us, and we do so tire of its intrusions. What will it be this time?"

Once they arrived at the Salon Doré, the queen dismissed all but a few of her ladies. She indicated that Amelia Stanton should remain.

Marie Antoinette whispered to Eugénie, "That one's resemblance to me may prove to be of some use." The calculating look on the queen's face was not lost on Eugénie.

When the others had withdrawn, the queen looked about her. Clapping her hands, she exclaimed, "Come, come! I'll have no long faces in my presence! Quick, bring the dice. Bring the cards. Let us while away these dreary hours of waiting for who knows what, with a bit of gaming." Hastily, chairs were drawn up to tables and soon the sound of the rolling of dice and the shuffling of cards filled the silence. The queen's spirit was infectious. Amelia Stanton's high-pitched giggle punctuated her frequent winning hands. Even the queen paused in her dicing to watch Amelia's unbroken streak of luck.

"Let's hope it's contagious," she murmured.

As the long hours crept by, the queen sustained the group's level of gaiety through sheer force of will. Dressed in her favorite shade of pale lavender, which set off her large, vivid blue eyes, she stood out amongst her more elaborately gowned attendants. Her strawberry-blonde hair was swept up away from her face, held in place by simple tortoise combs, allowing several strands to escape, which masked her exceptionally high forehead.

Eugénie never left her side and witnessed the queen's only lapse during the endless afternoon when she murmured, in an aside to Eugénie, "I know that they're coming for my head, but I've

learned from my mother not to fear death. I await it with resolution." Shocked by the queen's words, Eugénie began to protest,
but Marie Antoinette had already recovered and was laughing at a
clever rejoinder by her dear friend Princesse de Lamballe. Eugénie
looked with admiration at her queen, who appeared to have nothing more important on her mind than the next roll of the dice.

The minutes dragged on. Eugénie, whose nerves were stretched
to the breaking point, looked over at Amelia. *If I hear her cackle
one more time, I'm going to grab her by the throat and strangle her!*
A courtier burst through the door, startling her from her thoughts.

Bowing to the queen, the man announced, "I come from His
Majesty to report that the immediate crisis has passed! Still in his
hunting clothes, he met with the Parisian women's representatives. He assured them that he supports the Declaration of the
Rights of Man and confirmed that he had already given the order
that any grain wagons held outside of Paris be delivered to that
city posthaste."

An audible sigh passed through the room. Eugénie, who had
been watching the queen's face closely, saw no visible change in
her expression, which had remained brightly attentive throughout the report. The only telltale sign of her true feelings was the
agitated fluttering of her fan, which was hidden from all but Eugénie, who sat slightly to the left and to the rear of the queen.

"Ah, bien," Marie Antoinette said, rising, as she bestowed a brilliant smile on the young man. "We appreciate your bringing us this
news. We must go now and gather the children and join His Majesty.
Comtesse de Beaumont, you'll attend us, *s'il vous plaît.*" The courtier bowed and withdrew, as the ladies stepped aside to make way for
the queen, who swept from the room, followed by Eugénie.

XIV

The royal family and Eugénie ate a quiet supper in the king's apartments in the Salon de l'Oeuil de Boeuf. The children, sensing the tension, huddled in their parents' arms. Over their small heads the king looked fondly at his wife and patted her hand.

"*Ma chérie,* it promises to be a long night. You and the children retire and seek what rest you can."

"But what of you, Louis? You also need to conserve your strength."

The king sighed deeply. "I fear this afternoon's *entente* will not last. I must stay and be ready to meet with my people, should the need arise. There'll be rest enough for me later. In the meantime, I'll summon my ministers and seek their counsel."

Suddenly the queen's composure broke. "I don't trust their counsel. We're not safe here! We must flee! Leave this place to those odious commoners, and the Devil take them."

The king looked alarmed but his voice was gentle. "There, there. Don't upset yourself. Remember the children," he admonished her.

"But the gunshots, the cannon!" Her voice began to rise.

"*Oui, oui, je connais.* Put your mind at rest. The coaches have been assembled in the Grand Écurie. Should we have need of them, they'll be ready for us. Our personal guard is loyal. This afternoon, when I rode up the Grande Avenue, they stood united and firm. They'll defend us to the last. It's nearly midnight. You must take the children and get what rest you can."

Witnessing these intimate moments between her two sovereigns, Eugénie felt increasingly uncomfortable. She rose and said in a low voice, "Your Majesties, I have outstayed your generous hospitality. I..."

"Eugénie," the king said, addressing her informally, an unusual breach of decorum for him, "your character and grace shine through even that lowly costume you affect. You've always been a premier subject of our realm. This day most especially, you've been a singular comfort to the queen. You have our deepest gratitude."

"*Merci beaucoup,* Your Majesty," Eugénie replied, her voice barely above a whisper. At that moment, a page appeared in the doorway. Alarmed, the king and queen turned as one to look at him.

"Sire, the Marquis de Lafayette with the Garde Nationale is at the very gate of the Cour Royale! He and a contingent of eight officers request an audience."

The king looked at the queen, a hunted expression in his eyes. "Oh, dear, dear," he murmured to her, "I'm afraid events have run beyond our control. Ever since the Duc de Maille reported to me yesterday that 'Paris is marching here with guns,' I've feared this moment would come." He turned back to the messenger and said, in a resigned voice, waving his hand in an almost dismissive fashion, "Bring the Marquis and his officers to us." The page bowed, turned, and withdrew.

"Madame," the king said firmly, "take yourself and the children to your apartments and get some rest. Wait for me there. I'll join you as soon as I'm able."

The queen laid her hand against his cheek, her eyes meeting his. Rising gracefully, she said, "We'll await you with loving hearts." She moved quickly to Eugénie, saying, *"Ma chère amie,* we shall always remember how the pleasure of your company sustained us through this long day. It's come time for you to depart." Then she took Eugénie's hands in hers, speaking urgently. "Those who have shown us loyalty must look to their own safety. Mademoiselle Stanton, with her close resemblance to me, would be well advised not to tarry. If she's wise, she'll depart with you."

"I'll endeavor to persuade her, Your Majesty. Know that I'm ever at your service . . . "

"Oui, oui, je connais, je connais," the queen said. Surprising them both, she embraced Eugénie and said with feeling, *"Allez! Allez! Vite!"* Then she gathered the children and led them through the door at the far end of the long room. Eugénie turned and bowed to the king, who sat slumped in his chair, staring at his hands. She was just moving towards the near door when she heard the staccato sound of booted feet. Before she could make her escape, the Marquis de Lafayette and his officers strode into the room. He looked neither left nor right, but marched across the room, knelt in front of the king, and kissed the royal ring that was extended to him.

Speaking in clear tones, he said, "Sire, I thought it better to come here and die at the feet of Your Majesty than to die uselessly on the Place de Grève."

An unreadable expression flitted across the king's face, then he said, "Arise, sir! What do you seek of me?"

The Marquis arose and stood at attention. "The Garde wants to resume its former duties at Your Majesty's side."

His words were met with silence as the king gave the soldier standing before him a long, measuring look. Then, holding Lafayette's gaze, he said simply, "Well then, let it do so."

Eugénie slipped unnoticed from the room and hurried down corridors filled with soldiers standing at stiff attention and courtiers whispering in clusters. She finally came to one of the queen's antechambers where her ladies had gathered. As she walked into the room, she was stunned to see that they had resumed the afternoon's activities of gaming and gossiping. Eugénie hurried over to Amelia.

"Amelia, come, we must leave at once. We haven't a moment to spare!"

"Leave? Whatever are you talkin' about? I'm right where I'm supposed to be. I am here playin' cards with my friends. And look at all these lovely winnin's. It must be my lucky day. Sit down if you must, but stop botherin' me. I'm busy."

As Amelia reached for the dice, Eugénie grabbed her arm. "What are you doin'?" Amelia shrieked. "I said..."

"Amelia, the Parisians are at Versailles with weapons and cannon."

"I know that, you ninny," Amelia interrupted, wrenching her arm away. "That's why I'm doin' my best to follow the queen's example..."

Before she could finish, Eugénie grasped the arms of Amelia's chair and jerked it around to face her. "The Garde Nationale is at the palace gates. Lafayette is closeted with the king. There have already been skirmishes between the Parisians and the Palace guard. The situation is escalating! The queen, herself, commanded me to leave and to take you with me!"

Momentarily, Amelia lost some of her bravado, but then she squared her shoulders and jutted out her chin. "Well," she said to Eugénie, "some of us may turn tail and run at the first sign of danger, but not I. I'm stayin' right here with the king and queen and all my friends. You're just creatin' a tempest in a teapot. The king will straighten out those troublemakers. And the royal guards won't let anything bad happen, anyway. Now, shoo, shoo. You're goin' to ruin my luck!" With a toss of her head, Amelia pulled her chair back around and said to her companions, "Don't pay her any mind, she's just bein' a rain crow. Now, where were we?"

During the heated exchange, the ladies seated near them looked at each other with alarm and several slipped from the room. Eugénie looked at Amelia with disgust, shook her head, and left the Virginian to her games.

Taking a circuitous route, Eugénie finally made her way to the grove where Jeremy and the coaches were waiting. At her approach, Marie leapt down from the coach.

"Oh, thank God you've come!" she said. "We've heard scattered gunshots, and a contingent of soldiers only just left after telling us that there's been an outbreak of shooting between the Garde Nationale and the royal guard! I'm so glad you're safe."

"Marie, I'm so sorry to have worried you. I would've been here sooner, but I wasted precious time trying to persuade Amelia to join us. Oh, that foolish woman! Without her, we won't need the second coach. Jeremy! Oh, there you are," Eugénie said as the young man materialized at her side. "I'll ride with the footmen and the coach to de Beaumont. You remain here until the events of this night have played out. Then report back to us at de Beaumont."

"What of the other coach and four?" Jeremy asked.

"Return them to the stables for now and bring them with you when you return to the château," Eugénie replied. Taking his hands in her own, she said, "Take every care, Jeremy. You're precious to me."

"And you, also, Mistress. Godspeed and *bonne chance,*" the young man said solemnly. Then he melted into the shadows and was gone.

"Let's be off," Eugénie said, swinging up onto The Roan. Marie climbed back into the coach as Eugénie moved amongst the footmen, setting their formation. With a gesture from her, the coachman pulled out and the mounted men fell in alongside and to the rear. Eugénie cast one last look back towards the palace as she stuffed her hair up into her knit cap and pulled it down over her head. Turning The Roan, she set off down the lane after the coach.

The night was dark and silent except for the occasional hooting of an owl. Eugénie shivered, hoping it was not a portent. As they made their way by the fork of the road that led to the village of Versailles, a group of Parisian revelers, sated with food and drink, stumbled across their path.

"Who goes there?" yelled out a drunken woman, shaking her fist at the coach. The coachman brought the carriage to a halt and the footmen closed in around it, their hands on their firearms.

Eugénie, counting on Marie's quick wit, remained silent and fell back amongst her men. Before anyone could approach the carriage, Marie stuck her head out of the window.

"I'm a midwife on my way to deliver a child in the next village," Marie spoke clearly, using a voice of authority. "If you wish to escort us, be quick about it. There's no time to lose."

" 'Tis an awful fancy carriage for a midwife," another woman snarled, spitting on the ground. Before Marie could reply, a magnificent woman astride a huge stallion pulled up to the coach's window. She struck a flint and leaned forward, peering at Marie. In the circle of light, had not her beauty, height, and extraordinary horse set her apart from the others, her plumed hat and bright-red riding coat most certainly would have. Apparently reassured by what she saw, the horsewoman sat back in her saddle, resting her hand on the pistol at her side.

"I am Theroigne de Mericourt," she announced. "Who might you be, who travels in such a conspicuous carriage?"

"*Je suis Marie de Ville,* a simple midwife," Marie replied quietly. "I've been called to my cousin's house in the next village, for she's gone into labor. I beseeched these kind soldiers to escort me to her." Marie's voice caught. "The babe's two months early! I had nowhere else to turn. It was they who found the coach, truly a miracle on a night like this." Gesturing at the coach, Marie said slyly, "Some of the fancies, no doubt planning to flee this night, will soon discover their means of flight has gone missing." Leaning further out of the coach, Marie reached out to the rider, imploring her, "Please, I beg of you, let me pass for the sake of my cousin and her babe. Also, if they catch me in this carriage..." Marie stopped, covered her face in her hands, and wept.

Theroigne de Mericourt looked long at Marie's bowed head, then backed her horse away from the coach and called out, "Let the carriage pass! This midwife does our cause a service, by absconding with the possessions of one of the enemies of the revolution. Let her pass. We've better fish to fry." Brandishing her saber aloft, the Amazon whirled her mount around and, followed by the mob of women, set off back towards Versailles.

Relieved beyond words, Eugénie moved The Roan to the head of the procession and, without looking back, raised her arm in the air and gestured to her party to set off. Fearing the mob might change their mind and come after them, she spurred The Roan to greater speed and soon left Versailles well behind. They traveled through the night without stopping. Just before dawn Eugénie and her company took advantage of a secluded grove of trees to refresh themselves and to see to the needs of the horses. Taking only a few minutes, they were soon on their way again.

They avoided the highways and took the less-traveled roads. Eugénie set a breakneck pace throughout the rest of that day, stopping only briefly as night fell. She was determined to reach the safety of the château's walls by the middle of the next day.

Eugénie finally allowed herself to relax as the small party crested the hill that marked the beginning of the Garonne valley. In just a few hours we'll be home, she thought, her spirits rising. She pulled back on her reins, letting some of the footmen take the lead as she waited for the coach to come up alongside her.

"Henri," she called up to the coachman, "I say, we've all earned an extra tot this day." She affected a broad English accent, causing all within earshot to laugh heartily. "And, Marie, my simple midwife..." Her words were cut off by gunshots coming from a dense thicket. Stunned, she saw a footman fall from his horse. One of his comrades quickly dismounted, scooped him up, and slung him across his saddle, then turned to face the attack. Henri cried out and slumped sideways on the coach bench as a group of ragtag highwaymen burst from the underbrush and rushed towards the carriage. The footmen, who had already assembled, turned as one and, with pistols blazing, plunged into their midst.

Panicked, the coach's horses lurched forward. Eugénie leapt from The Roan's back onto a shaft of the moving coach and scrambled up beside Henri. With one hand she pulled her coachman back against the seat and grabbed the reins from his limp hand with the other.

"Hold on!" she yelled above the gunfire. With his good arm, the coachman obeyed his mistress's command as Eugénie urged the horses forward. Already terrified, they needed little encouragement. The Roan trumpeted and galloped out ahead.

Out of the corner of her eye, Eugénie saw a horseman racing up alongside the coach.

"No!" she screamed, reaching down to grasp the pistol lashed to her ankle. She turned and took aim. Her eyes widened in shock.

"Bridger!"

His blue eyes laughed up at her as he doffed his tricorn and laid it against his heart. "At your service, Madame," he shouted above the noise of the coach wheels and the pounding horses' hooves. "It seems I'm forever rescuing you from marauders and scoundrels. If memory serves, you were wearing that same fetching costume at our first meeting."

For the first time in days, Eugénie threw back her head and laughed. Bridger's reference to her adventures in the colony of Virginia and her near-death experience on the island of Bermuda so many years ago made the intervening time melt away. She saw him again as the young, reckless captain of the *White Heather,* who had captured her heart and saved her life. Suddenly, her expression changed to alarm as she looked back over her shoulder.

"Bridger, the highwaymen! My footmen!"

"Fear not, your men have the rascals well in hand," Bridger reassured her. "I came upon the fracas, recognized your livery, and knew you couldn't be far away. So I set off to rescue you, my forever damsel in distress."

Eugénie tossed her head. "I was doing quite well without your assistance, thank you." She smiled, realizing Bridger had successfully distracted her from her concern about her men. "A damsel in distress," she muttered.

Bridger laughed up at her. "Unless I'm mistaken, I believe I hear them approaching." Amazed, as always, by the acuteness of Bridger's senses, Eugénie looked back down the road and saw a cloud of dust in the distance.

"Whoa," she called out to the horses. Pulling back on the reins, she brought the coach and four to a halt. Bridger dismounted and reached up to Eugénie. His strong fingers circled her waist and he lifted her down as though she were no more than a feather in his hands. As her feet touched the ground, the shock of the last few days overwhelmed her and she began to tremble. Bridger gathered her into his arms, cradling her head under his chin.

"There, there, little one. It's over. You're safe," he crooned. "I'm here." The strength of him seeped into her.

Oh, how I've missed you, she thought. How I've missed you!

Lifting her chin, Bridger looked down into her silver eyes wet with unshed tears.

"Yes, I know," he murmured, as always reading her thoughts as clearly as if she had spoken them out loud, "and I you." He drew her even closer into his embrace and kissed her gently. Resting his head against hers, he whispered, "Every moment without you is a lifetime." Hearing the clatter of the footmen's horses, they pulled apart and turned to look back up the road.

Moments later, Eugénie's men drew up alongside the coach and the footman in the lead dismounted and hailed Bridger.

"Captain Goodrich, it's been too long since ye've paid us a visit."

"Aye, it has, lad," Bridger replied, clapping him on the back. "But it appears, Charles, you've managed to keep yourself busy." Bridger looked back down the road. Charles laughed and the others joined in.

Scanning her men for injuries and losses, Eugénie interrupted the camaraderie. "Charles, please give me an accounting of the attack."

"Mistress, it was a rout," Charles said with pride. "All but two are dead. Those two lit out and ran for their lives. Were it not for Jean's being so sorely wounded, we would've pursued them. Except for Jean, we came through unscathed."

"God be praised!" Eugénie breathed. "Come, help Jean and Henri into the coach so that Marie can tend their wounds. Charles, if you'll take Henri's place on the coach bench, we'll be under way."

With Eugénie and Bridger in the lead, it was an exhausted and travel-worn company that straggled into the château's courtyard early that afternoon. Just as Eugénie slid from The Roan's back, Jamie burst through the door of the château.

"Mistress Eugénie, thank God you've returned! Ever since a messenger came this morning with news of the march on Versailles, I've been beside myself with worry." Seeing Marie stepping down from the coach, the tall Scot ran to his wife and enfolded her in his arms, pressing his lips to her hair. "*Ma chère, ma chère!* Oh, how I feared for you."

"It's been a harrowing experience beyond imagination, Jamie," Eugénie said, her voice heavy with fatigue. Looking tenderly at her servants' reunion, she continued, "Marie and the footmen were the true heroes of the story."

Jamie, who had been lost to everything but his wife, lifted his head to see Bridger standing nearby, smiling at him.

"Captain Goodrich!" Jamie gasped. They quickly closed the distance between them and the captain and his former first mate held each other in an embrace that spoke to the deep and abiding friendship they shared. Stepping back, Bridger looked closely at Jamie.

"Domestic life suits you, my friend."

Eugénie gave the two men a chance to enjoy the moment and then said, "We all have much to tell each other, but first we must see to the wounded and tend to the horses."

XV

Early the next morning, as Eugénie was tightening the girth of The Roan's saddle, she looked up to see Bridger coming into the stable. She paused, a smile lighting her face. At times his absence in her life was almost unbearable. Thank God, she thought, that as a shipper with extensive trade routes he's built a clientele that brings him to England and France—and to me—as often as it does. As he strode towards her, Bridger let out a low whistle.

"Eugénie, your beauty takes my breath away. A night's sleep has magically erased all the ravages of the last few days." He stroked The Roan's neck, but his eyes were on Eugénie. "I knew I'd find you here with the stallion."

"Ah, Bridger, far more than a night's rest, just having you here is my restorative. Isn't this the most glorious day? Jeremy will bring the world to us, soon enough. For now, let's rejoice in this beautiful place and in being together again."

Infected by her mood, Bridger clasped her around the waist, swung her up, and twirled her around. Setting her back on the ground, he gave her a kiss that left both of them breathless. In the circle of each other's arms they gazed at one another, relishing their nearness. Eugénie's hand caressed his cheek. His fingers captured a lock of her hair, stroking it between his thumb and forefinger.

"When I'm with you again, I realize that I've not taken a full breath since I left you," he whispered, "that the ache in my heart has lifted."

"Oh, Bridger, with you my soul returns. I'm whole again. Without you, my life does go on, but when you come back to me so does my soul. I can feel again. The light is brighter, the birds' song clearer. The fragrance of a rose is so heady my senses reel. I live." Her eyes shimmered as she looked up into his face. Embracing her head with his hands, he tenderly kissed her eyelids and her trembling lips.

"Come, come, sweetheart, our minutes together are slipping away and we've yet to retest the speed of our horses against these beautiful hills of yours, as we promised on my last visit. Now, unless you're reneging..."

"I certainly am not, sir!" Eugénie leapt onto The Roan's saddle. "I'm off, catch me if you can!" she called over her shoulder and flew out of the stables.

"You haven't the advantage you think," Bridger called after her. He whistled and his black stallion, Montross, with saddle in place, trotted out of his stall. Bridger ran alongside him and vaulted into his saddle just as the horse broke into a run. Bridger saw Eugénie out ahead, galloping up the path between the hillside vineyards. In seconds, he closed the gap. Side by side, they hurtled up the ridge and down the other side, neither giving ground.

They tested each other's horsemanship and their mounts' hearts as they broke out into the meadow of the Garonne valley. Eugénie laughed, exhilarated by the wind in her face, the man at her side, and the feel of the horse beneath her. Up ahead, the Garonne River flowed lazily by, sparkling in the October sun. The Roan inched ahead, his competitive juices responding to the black challenger beside him. But it was not to be. With the finish line in his sights, the black surged forward, first meeting The Roan's speed and then surpassing it. Barely ahead, Montross reached the bank of the river. Swerving to avoid plunging down the slope, the stallion reared high and trumpeted his victory. The Roan, a split second behind, stopped at the river's edge. He shot the victor a disdainful look and lowered his head to nibble the grasses at his feet.

Eugénie and Bridger laughed at the interplay between the two horses. Bridger pulled his water flask from his pocket and took a long drink. He turned to Eugénie, his eyes filled with mischief.

"Rematch? Montross and I will settle for nothing short of a clear victory. Considering the adverse conditions you were laboring under, such as The Roan's exertions over the past few days, not to mention..." At Bridger's words, The Roan pawed the ground, whinnied, and then turned and nipped Bridger's hand.

"Well," Eugénie said, her silver eyes glinting dangerously, "I'd say my horse has spoken for both of us. We don't stoop to using excuses. Keep them for yourself, sir. You'll need them, I promise you. This time the victory is yours, but be warned: The Roan and I have your measure now and are only provoked and inspired by your patronizing attitude." So saying, Eugénie slid from her horse and, assuming an air of total indifference, rummaged in her saddlebag. She pulled out her flask and a bundle tied with string. After taking a sip, she untied the bundle and offered bread and cheese to Bridger.

"Ah, no wonder!" Bridger exclaimed. "Handicapped by such a burden..."

"I warn you," Eugénie cut in, snatching back her offerings. Chuckling, Bridger dismounted and took both of her hands in his. He kissed her fingers and took a large bite out of the cheese.

"Mmmmm, delicious! Forgive me, sweeting, for teasing you. It's irresistible. Every facet of you delights me," he said, his eyes darkening. "In the time we have together, I'm going to devote myself to enjoying as many of them as I can, so that later I'll have those memories to keep me company."

Eugénie pursed her lips and looked up at him impishly. "I forgive you, sir, but The Roan is not so easily won over." Raising his brow at her, Bridger pulled two carrots out of his pocket and held one out to The Roan, who hesitated not one second before lipping the reward. Smiling, Bridger gave the other one to Montross. Munching happily, The Roan nuzzled Bridger's arm, making him laugh.

"Oh, you Judas!" Eugénie yelled at the horse. "Couldn't you have held out for at least a little while? Won over by a carrot!" The Roan neighed, rolled his eyes, and nuzzled Bridger again. "Clearly," Eugénie said laughing, "you have the key to both of our hearts."

Bridger pulled her, the cheese, the bread, and all, into his embrace and said softly, "And for that I count myself truly blessed. May it always be so."

Suddenly, both horses lifted their heads and looked back across the meadow.

"Lady, you've dulled my senses. There's a rider approaching. Ah, I believe it's Jamie." Bridger whistled shrilly and waved to his friend. Jamie turned his mount and headed in their direction. In no time, he pulled up in front of them.

"Jeremy's returned," he said without preamble. "He's eager to give you his report." Before the words were out of his mouth, Eugénie and Bridger were back in their saddles. The three turned their horses around and streaked across the meadow.

"They broke into the royal apartments?" Aghast, Eugénie looked up at Jeremy. Her spoon rattled against her coffee cup. Bridger, who was sitting beside her on the settee, reached over and took her hand. Jamie, leaning against the mantel, looked at Jeremy in horror.

Jeremy, still in his travel-stained clothes, nodded. "After the king's audience with the Marquis, the situation appeared to be in hand. The royal guard was in place. Most of the mob had withdrawn to the village. Some of the women, though, followed Monsieur Stanislas Mailliard to the Assembly room. You remember him, the one who tried to take all the credit and glory for the fall of the Bastille? What an imposter," Jeremy said derisively under his breath. "Those women and the ones in the kitchen stuffed themselves with food and drink and fell asleep. With everything apparently quiet, the king dismissed his bodyguards and his other attendants."

"What was he thinking," Eugénie whispered, "after everything that had happened?"

"At some point during the night," Jeremy continued, "some of the mob discovered that the royal carriages were assembled and ready. They attacked the servants who were stationed there and led the horses away. At around five o'clock in the morning, a group of about three hundred women managed to find an unlocked door that led directly to the Cour Royale. Meanwhile, others broke into the Cour de Marbre and headed up the stairs to the royal apartments."

"*Oh, mon Dieu!*" Eugénie breathed.

Jeremy looked at her sympathetically, then went on, "One of the guards fired into the crowd and there was pandemonium. Seeing the mob surging up the stairs, the guard just outside the queen's apartments called a warning to her through the door and was summarily shot. The queen fled with the children through the passageway that connects her apartments to the king's. A company of the Garde Nationale found the royal family there in the Salon de l'Oeuil de Boeuf and rescued them from the attackers.

"Where, in God's name, was Lafayette all this time?" Eugénie asked.

"He'd retired for the night, thinking all was well, since the king had agreed to the women's requests and had guaranteed food for Paris. Most importantly, the king had agreed to consider their demand—'request,' if you will—to return the seat of government to the Louvre Palace in Paris." Eugénie chewed on her lip, thinking. Such a move might be politically expedient for the moment, but can he afford to remove the buffer between him and the capricious Parisians that Versailles's distance from Paris gives him? Only time will tell.

She turned her attention back to Jeremy, who was saying, "I was told that, the minute Lafayette heard about the assault, he rushed to the palace and persuaded the king to go out and speak to the Garde Nationale who had accompanied Lafayette to restore order. The king met with the Garde and somehow elicited their loyalty. Encouraged by this, he went out on the balcony overlooking the Cour de Marbre and told the crowd gathered there that he would keep faith with 'the love of my good and faithful subjects' and that he would return to Paris. A great cheer went up and the king repeated what he'd said to the Garde, that his royal guards weren't guilty of the accusations aimed at them. At that moment, the Marquis, in a brilliant move, pinned a tricolor cockade on the hat of one of the king's bodyguards, thus bringing the royal guard into the fold."

"Ah, yes — Gilbert. What a brilliant move," Eugénie whispered.

"But his finest moment was yet to come. His masterstroke was persuading the queen to go out alone on the balcony to face the people."

Eugénie's hand flew to her mouth. "She must have been so afraid — afraid beyond words."

Never a fan of the queen, Jeremy nodded, saying with admiration in his voice, "There she stood alone before them. Lafayette stepped out beside her, bowed, and kissed her hand. I was standing in the crowd. It was a heroic moment and the crowd went mad, cheering them both and shouting, *'Vive la Reine!'* "

A stunned silence filled the room. "It's nothing short of a miracle," Eugénie finally said.

"That it was," Jeremy agreed. "A few hours later, a huge cavalcade, I'd say nearly sixty thousand strong, set off for Paris. The magnificent procession included the king's ministers, the Deputies of the National Assembly, and the whole French court. Lafayette rode beside the royal coach and the Garde Nationale rode in formation in front and behind it. Oh, I almost forgot: Included in the entourage, pulling up the rear, was every conceivable transport, loaded with flour, surrounded by a motley group of the Parisian mob."

"Truly, a singular moment in the history of France," Bridger observed. "They accomplished a fairly bloodless *coup d'état,* all things considered."

"Aye," Jamie agreed, "the royal lion has been declawed. With the king bending to the will of the people and retreating to Paris, the people have won the day. I wonder if that's occurred to the king? Be that as it may, there's reason to celebrate. The revolution progresses."

Jeremy took a deep breath. "The euphoria of the moment was marred by one thing, though. Amongst the crowd, there were Parisians parading the slain bodies of the royal guard on pikes. It was a grisly sight and it couldn't have been lost on the royal family."

"How they must have suffered," Eugénie said. "My heart goes out to them. The kings of France have never trusted the Parisian mob and now King Louis has handed himself over to it. I've a strange premonition that the royal family will never see Versailles again. How will the queen bear it? I fear her Hamlet, her precious Blanchette, and her other pet animals are lost to her forever. I pray she's unaware of how drastically her life has changed." Eugénie let out a long sigh. "Jeremy, did you see or hear anything of Amelia Stanton?"

Jeremy nodded. "Yes, but only in passing. It would seem the lady has attached herself quite securely to the court. Just as the procession set off, I caught a glimpse of her in one of the carriages immediately behind the Garde Nationale that followed the royal coach. At first I thought the queen had been separated from her family, so closely does Mistress Stanton resemble her. I realized my mistake when she called out to a mounted soldier in the

Garde. The minute she opens her mouth, no one would mistake her for the queen."

"I imagine we've not heard the last of her escapades," Eugénie said, shaking her head. "Perhaps she'll provide some much-needed amusement for them. The Tuileries is not Versailles, but Paris does offer many diversions to distract the queen. Overall, this may have turned out for the best."

The others nodded in agreement.

"Captain Goodrich," Jeremy said, breaking into the silence, "there's much to show you at the stables. There are new additions as well as some training techniques I've introduced. Also, that's a fine stallion, your Montross. If Mistress Eugénie and you are in agreement, I know a filly he just might take a shine to."

"My stallion and your filly, you say?" Bridger winked at Eugénie. "Montross is a rambunctious fellow. I wonder if your filly has the spirit to match him."

"Indeed, sir, I wager . . . " Jeremy began hotly, then grunted, realizing the joke was on him. He added, good-naturedly, "Well, sir, I guess I'll just let you be the judge of that."

Bridger rose and walked over to the young man. "No time like the present. Shall we?"

Jeremy stepped aside. "After you, Captain." Bowing briefly to Eugénie and Jamie, the two turned and could be heard discussing training methods as they walked down the hall.

Two weeks later, Marie knocked on the door of the small salon where Eugénie was enjoying a rare solitary moment playing with

Émigré and the new pup, Crème Douce, that had been sired by Marie's Puff.

"*Entrez,*" she said, cuddling the white fluffy little fellows under her chin.

Marie smiled at the pups and handed three missives to Eugénie. "They just arrived by separate messengers. None awaits a reply."

"*Merci,* Marie. Please see that the messengers have refreshments before they depart. Oh, and take Émigré and Crèmie with you. They indulge me, but I know they're happier frolicking outside." Marie whistled and the pups, after a quick lick for their mistress, scampered over to her and followed her out of the room. Eugénie looked at the three letters and opened the one addressed to her in the familiar hand of her friend Thomas Jefferson. She read it quickly. He wishes me to make welcome his personal friend, Mr. Robert Morris, she mused. Mr. Morris is traveling in France and would like to bring to my attention an intriguing proposition that could possibly be of interest to me. He's expected to be in the Bordeaux within the month. Anyone referred to me by my dear friend is certainly welcome at de Beaumont. An intriguing proposition, hmmm. She put the letter aside and opened the next. Recognizing the royal seal, she read it eagerly.

Chère amie,

I'm sending you a copy of a letter I wrote to Mercy d'Argenteau, my Austrian Ambassador, the day after we arrived at the Tuileries. Here's the letter. "Rest assured I am well. Forgetting where we are and how we got here we should be content with the mood of the people, especially this morning, if bread does not lack... I talk to the people; to militiamen; and to the market women, all of whom hold out their hands to me and I give them mine. Within the city I have been very well received. This morning the people asked us to stay. I told them that as far as the King and I were concerned, it depended on them whether we stayed, for we asked nothing better than that all hatred should stop, and that the slightest bloodshed would make us flee in horror."

Eugénie looked up from the letter. *If I'm reading correctly between the lines, it seems the queen is putting a good face on it and making the best of the situation.* She glanced back down and read the postscript.

I wished you to know that the family and I are well and settling into this new life. You are in my prayers; please keep me in yours. I remain...

Ah, perhaps this chapter has had a happy ending after all and the revolution can now proceed smoothly. Dear God, let it be so. Putting the queen's letter down, Eugénie picked up the last one, which she saw at once was from one of her agents in Paris.

Madame, the royal family is now secure at the Tuileries. The National Assembly, today, has proclaimed that Louis XVI's official title will no longer be *roi de France et de Navarre,* but will be *roi des Français.* I report to you additionally that Monsieur de la Tour du Pin has overseen the locking and boarding up of the Palais de Versailles. I'll keep you informed of events as they occur.

Eugénie's earlier elation vanished. *In one day, his grand palace and his kingdom have been taken from him. He's now the head of the French people, only. But at their whim... and for how long?*

XVI

FEBRUARY 1790
Château de Beaumont

"Bloody Hell!" Bridger exclaimed, walking into the salon with Eugénie. "What is that racket?"

Eugénie clapped her hands over her ears. "They never said it would take this long or make this much noise."

"What?" Bridger shouted.

Eugénie grabbed his arm and hurried them both out onto the terrace, down the stairs, and into the gardens away from the din. When they were finally some distance from the clatter, she sat down with a sigh on the bench that overlooked a fishpond.

"What, in God's name, is going on in there?" Bridger asked, settling beside her.

"It's a new composition for moldings and cornices that the English brothers, the Adamses, patented recently. If I'd had any idea that it would take this long and create such havoc, I never would have started. I thought for sure that our stay these past two weeks with the Dumas at their lovely château would have been ample time for them to install the new moldings. What are we going to do now?"

"I'd suggest an extended voyage on *White Heather*," Bridger grinned at her wickedly, "but the February winds off the coast are hardly conducive to a pleasure sail."

Eugénie smiled, remembering the voyages they had shared on Bridger's ship, first sailing from Virginia to Bermuda and later making the Atlantic crossing. She remembered how they, both so young, from such different backgrounds, had met in that young land on the brink of revolution. How they had found something in each other there that was so powerful and consuming that time, distance, and long absences could not lessen its intensity.

She stood and drew him up beside her. "Well, at least it's late afternoon. Soon, they'll be finished for the day," she said, leaning over to snap a twig off the hedge that fronted the pond. She held it to her nose, sniffing deeply, and handed it to Bridger.

"What gift is this, sweetheart?" Bridger asked. "Mmmmm, delicious. It's familiar, but I can't place its name."

"It's rosemary, for remembrance and friendship. It's also an herb that enhances lamb and chicken dishes, and makes a refreshing potpourri. I've noticed, if I'm drowsy, a quick inhale of its fragrance and I'm rejuvenated in an instant."

"Remembrance, you say," Bridger murmured. "I'll carry a sprig with me when I leave and it'll be a constant reminder of you, not that I need rosemary for that."

Eugénie leaned into him and rested her head on his shoulder. "I hate to talk of your leaving, even though I know you must go all too soon," she said softly.

He lifted her chin and gently kissed her parted lips. "Then we shall talk of it no more. Come, show me these shrubs and things and tell me their special properties. I'm ignorant of the subject. Such things have never held much fascination for me, but you, my enchantress, have me waiting with bated breath to learn every-thing there is to know about them."

Taking up his lighthearted tone, Eugénie replied, "Beware what you wish for. This subject happens to be a favorite of mine. I'll have you either asleep in no time or running for relief back into the cacophony!" She grabbed his hand and set off down the garden path. "Many of these plants are in my kitchen garden, but I intersperse them in my formal ones, as well, for texture and scent. Many are not indigenous. My sea captain friends bring them back from their journeys."

"Beware, yourself, milady, that you don't cause my jealous na-ture to rear its ugly head. I trust the generosity of these friendly sea captains is limited to a plant now and then," Bridger growled.

"Fear not, Captain Goodrich, for only you are the captain of my heart." Bridger grumbled under his breath and tucked her arm closer through his.

"Now, here we have a bay hedge, which the ancients said gives power. It also intensifies the flavor of soups and sauces." She laughed as Bridger plucked a leaf and proceeded to chew and swallow it.

"I feel the power coming over me," he announced, lifting Eu-génie and twirling her around until she cried out.

"Your power's dizzying. Put me down this instant!"

Chuckling, Bridger obeyed, but held her shoulders until she stopped swaying.

"Really, Bridger, if you eat everything I show you, I won't be responsible for the outcome. Now, behave yourself! Here, hold on to these sprigs. That should keep your hands busy. Tomorrow, I'll work them into a potpourri as a talisman for you."

"As you command, Madame, so shall it be," Bridger said, but his eyes gleamed dangerously.

Ignoring his look, Eugénie continued, "Here we have a yew hedge. Ouch! Have a care, it's prickly," she said sucking her thumb. "The yew is a defense against witches and their spells."

"Clearly, it's ineffectual against your charms, sweeting, for I'm thoroughly bewitched by you." He gathered her to him with his free hand, and kissed her deeply. "I am and shall forever be under your spell, sweet witch."

"Bridger, is it any wonder that I love you so? On the contrary, it's I who is charmed by your lips and your pretty words. Now, where was I? Oh, yes, holly with its red berries is both a Christian and a pagan symbol. The red berries are the symbol of Christ's blood. The combination of holly and ivy, sacred to the god Bacchus, is a protection against drunkenness and is a familiar sight at Christmastime, especially in England. In the old days, holly and ivy were a common sight at the pagan winter solstice celebration."

They walked along further until they came to a high hedge of deep-green, glossy leaves. "I certainly know holly and ivy, though not their special properties," Bridger said, running his finger over the leathery leaves of the hedge. "I recognize this plant from the plantations we used to own in Virginia. What's its name?"

"It's laurel. It's no surprise that you recognize it. The hardiest of the laurels is from England. It was transported early on to America. It's said that it protects the land and symbolizes honor."

"An important ingredient for our potpourri." Bridger broke off a cluster of leaves and added it to his bouquet.

Looking across at an ancient oak that stood sentinel at the edge of the gardens, Eugénie exclaimed, "Mistletoe! We must have mistletoe."

Following her gaze, Bridger said, "Ah, mistletoe. Now, that's a familiar sight. Many are the times at Christmas I've captured a fair maid in a doorway beneath a cluster of it."

"You did, did you?" Eugénie looked at him archly. "Well, there are other purposes for mistletoe. It's said to be a protection against evil spirits and it's also supposed to promote peace. You might say it's the European answer to the olive branch. If we had a firearm, we could shoot it out of the tree, as we do at Christmas."

"Fair lady, yardarms, masts, and trees hold no challenge for us. Remember when you climbed *White Heather*'s mast? Compared to that, this tree will be child's play. You wish a spray of mistletoe, a spray you shall have."

In seconds, skirts and all, Eugénie found herself standing on a low, sturdy branch of the oak tree, gripping the trunk for dear life. She made the mistake of glancing down. "Oh, Bridger."

"Just follow me as you did on *White Heather*," Bridger said over his shoulder. "Your hand follows my hand; your foot, my foot. Here we go." In no time, they were halfway up the tree and standing together beneath a huge cluster of mistletoe. "It may not be Christmas, but...," Bridger said, looking up at it. Supporting her against the tree trunk, Bridger kissed her.

For a moment, lost in each other, they forgot where they were. Eugénie's foot slipped. She grabbed Bridger's shoulder, passion forgotten, replaced by fear. Steadying her, Bridger whispered, "To be continued. We'd best complete our purpose here before your nearness overwhelms me again." So saying, he reached up, broke off a healthy portion of the mistletoe, and let it drop through the branches to the ground. "Mission accomplished. Follow me."

Once more on terra firma, Eugénie cocked her head. "Ah, blessed silence. They've finished for the day." Bridger reached for her, but Eugénie pushed his hands away. "No, sir. I've lost my head twice already with you this day. The idea, at my age! Climbing a tree, of all things, and then being swept away by you and the spell of the mistletoe like some foolish young maid! We could have toppled to our death!"

"But we didn't, did we?" Bridger said with a grin. "And when did you, of all people, start counting your days and fearing little escapades? You and I are not cut from that cloth. That's for the faint of heart."

"How right you are," Eugénie said. "Oh, how I've missed you. Sometimes the role of chatelaine weighs too heavily on me. I need you to remind me that life is not to be hoarded, but to be spent with gay abandon. Thank you for that." She reached up, pulled his face down to hers, and kissed him with all the passion of youth and the richness of experience.

"And I thought I was the one giving the lessons!" she flung over her shoulder as she grasped her skirts in both hands and sprinted up the path towards the château.

He caught up with Eugénie as she dashed up the terrace steps. Laughing, she ducked under his arm and ran across the terrace and burst through the doors into the grand salon. Bridger grabbed her from behind and was about to swing her around when they saw Jacqueline standing in the doorway across the room. Bridger's hands fell to his sides and Eugénie straightened her skirts and assumed a dignified air.

"Oui, chère Jacqueline. Qu'est-ce qu'il y a?"

Jacqueline stood awkwardly plucking at her skirt, her face turning in rapid succession from pink to white, embarrassed to witness her beloved mistress and godmother frolicking in such a girlish fashion.

Eugénie smiled as she walked towards her godchild. "Captain Goodrich is such a scamp. I don't blame you for being shocked at our display, but," with a Gallic shrug, "we all seem to revert to childish antics around him, *n'est-ce pas?*"

Jacqueline giggled, but answered primly, *"Oui, Madame."*

"Alors, now that we've returned to our senses, was there something you came to tell me, Jacqueline?"

"Oh, oui, Madame!" The young girl's eyes were alight with excitement. *"Maman lui prépare une chambre et Papa est avec lui dans le salon."*

"Lui? Qui est 'lui'?" Eugénie asked, trying to be patient.

"Oh, je suis désolé! L'américain!" Jacqueline announced, proudly.

"Ah, that explains everything," Eugénie said under her breath. Out loud she said, *"Merci,* Jacqueline. If you will, please take us to him. Come, Bridger, we mustn't keep the mysterious American waiting."

Jacqueline curtsied to the two men sitting in the book-lined room and stepped aside for Eugénie and Bridger to enter. Jamie looked up and smiled at his stepdaughter. Both men stood as Eugénie came through the door, followed by Bridger. Eugénie was pleased to see that refreshments had been served.

Jamie stepped forward. "Comtesse de Beaumont, may I present Mr. Robert Morris from America." Ah, so this is Tom's friend, Mr. Morris, Eugénie thought as she moved forward, extending her hand in the conventional American manner.

"I'm honored to meet you, Comtesse," the American said, grasping her hand in both of his.

"Oh, please, sir, call me Eugénie. We French are dispensing with formalities left and right, as you may have heard, following in the footsteps of our American brothers. May I introduce you to Captain Bridger Goodrich." Eugénie stepped back gracefully and drew Bridger forward. The two men sized each other up. An expression flickered in Morris's eyes as he held out his hand.

"The captain's reputation is well known to us in America. His exploits stalled our navy on many occasions during our war for independence, but, since then, it's reported that he's come to the aid of some of our ships beleaguered by the Barbary pirates."

To Eugénie's relief, the awkward moment passed when Bridger took the outstretched hand. "I expect we all share a common goal where those rascals are concerned. Only together can we protect the seas, our ships, and our cargo."

"New circumstances forge new friendships," Morris agreed blandly. Just then, Marie appeared at the doorway, indicating to Eugénie that her guest's apartment was prepared.

"Robert, if you'll come with me. I'm sure you'd like some time before supper to rest and refresh yourself from the rigors of your journey."

XVII

A fire blazed on the enormous hearth and the candles glowed in the three massive Venetian chandeliers that hung above the long dining table, lending warmth and coziness to the winter evening. Large chinoiserie urns filled with branches bursting with pink blossoms were banked along the wall of French doors, complementing the pale green silk-covered walls and heralding the promise of spring.

"What a magnificent display!" Robert Morris said, admiring the unseasonable show of color. "Is your climate so far ahead of ours?"

"They are magnificent, aren't they?" Eugénie answered, delighted at her guest's frank appreciation. "Their beauty is all the more striking because they're so out of season. I learned the trick of forcing buds from Mary Whittington during my stay in Virginia."

"Well, I must export the practice back across the Atlantic to my home in Pennsylvania," her guest replied. "Our winters are harsh. A spray of blossoms would be a feast for the eyes. Speaking of feasts, what is this delicious dish?"

"It's a tuber called the potato. It was introduced to our King Louis by the horticulturalist Auguste Parmentier. Alone, I find it rather dull, but with a little imagination, it's quite versatile. For instance, this evening, using the skin as the *ramequin,* the chef mashed the white center and mixed it with butter, Gruyère, and scallions. When it's accompanied with fruit and nuts, I find it very satisfying as a light supper. I've been serving it quite often, lately." Eugénie gestured to the footman to repass the platter of potatoes.

"Indeed, quite delicious," Robert agreed. "Yes, I think I'll have another."

The evening continued with Eugénie and Robert Morris sharing various husbandry methods. Even Bridger contributed one or two over the course of the conversation. As the dessert dishes were cleared and Eugénie and her guests were enjoying the last of the château's Bordeaux, Morris's face turned grave.

"It's a shame to introduce a somber note into this pleasant evening, but I'd best get to the point of my visit."

I wondered when he would broach the subject that brought him here, Eugénie thought. The cultivation of crops and the breeding and raising of livestock would hardly be sufficient for him to brave the Atlantic winter seas and France's political climate.

"Miss Eugénie, I believe you received my letter of introduction from Mr. Jefferson, preparing you for my arrival?"

Eugénie nodded. "Yes, I did. I was delighted to hear from him. Tom and I met when I was in the colonies before your revolution. We became fast friends when we discovered we had much in common, sharing our love for horses and our political philosophies. He often made the trek down here when he was the

Ambassador to France. Forgive me, I digress. In his letter, Tom praised you highly, saying that you were a financier and in the shipping business and that you arranged the financing for the purchase of supplies for General Washington's army. He mentioned an 'intriguing proposition.' It must be very intriguing indeed, to bring you to France during these unsettled times."

Giving her guest a moment to collect his thoughts, Eugénie suggested, "There's coffee, tea, and a delicious Portuguese wine awaiting us in the library. Shall we?"

Morris rose from his chair, saying, "A fine idea, Miss Eugénie. May I help you with your chair?"

Bridger, who had been observing Robert Morris closely, was relieved that whatever he had sensed lurking beneath the man's urbane manner was finally going to come out in the open. His jaw tightened as he wondered what had brought the American this long way. Whatever it was, he knew that the American expected Eugénie to play an important role—one that would be dangerous for her.

Too restless to sit, Bridger shook his head when Eugénie gestured for him to join her on the sofa. He moved over to the fireplace and leaned against the mantel, his arms folded across his chest. The casual pose belied the expression in his eyes, which watched Robert Morris intently. Morris, deep in thought, settled into one of the sofa's companion chairs.

Once the refreshments had been served and the servant had departed, Morris took a deep breath, drew a letter from the pocket of his black broadcloth waistcoat, and handed it to Eugénie.

"I had a devil of a time smuggling that past the government agents."

"Yes, an unfortunate inconvenience of the revolution. Since the Comité des Recherches was established this past summer, without warrants or cause, the agents search everyone, even imprisoning without warrants. The wrongs that existed in the old régime persist, but in a new guise. Fear of brigands and invasion is valid, but..." She started to say something and then stopped. "I apologize for our overzealous citizens."

"It's the natural course of a new social order. We in America, to some extent, still suffer the same growing pains. But back to the purpose of my visit. This letter I've brought from Mr. Jefferson will cast some light on my mission."

Eugénie began to read out loud what appeared to be a part of a longer letter.

... with powers so large as to enable him...

"Him?" Eugénie looked up questioningly.

"He refers to your King Louis XVI," Robert answered.

Eugénie nodded and continued to read.

... as to enable him to do all the good of his station, and so limited as to restrain him from its abuse. But he [has] a queen of absolute sway over his weak mind and timid virtue; and of a character the reverse of his in all points, with some smartness of fancy, but no sound sense... proud, disdainful of restraint, indignant at all obstacles to her will, eager in the pursuit of pleasure and firm enough to hold to her desires, or perish in their wreck. Her inordinate gambling and dissipations, with those of the Comte d'Artois and others of her clique, has been an item in the exhaustion of the treasury, add to that her inflexible perverseness and opposition to reform. I have ever believed that had there been no queen there would have been no revolution.

Eugénie raised her eyes from the letter and gazed out of the window into the darkness. A log popping on the grate sent out a spray of sparks and brought her attention back into the room.

There are three epochs in history signalized by the total extinction of national morality. The first was of the successors of Alexander, not omitting himself. The next, the successors of the first Caesar, the third our own age.

Eugénie folded the letter and handed it back to Morris. "He expressed many of these thoughts to me on his last visit," Eugénie said. "I didn't know he'd formalized them in writing. The 'extinction of national morality' he speaks of... I wonder if a national morality is extinguished by the initiation of a new social order, or if, prior to the change, the loss of a national morality is one of the causes that sets into motion the change in the social order?" She looked up and met Bridger's eyes, then turned to see Robert Morris gazing intently at her.

"Robert, I don't think you came this long way to discuss political philosophy. Where do Thomas's words lead us?"

"To be blunt, milady, reading between the lines, our Mr. Jefferson, even at such a distance, sees the king as being too weak and the queen too perverse to carry out the will of the people. Why, they already have taken actions to obstruct it. It's a short step for this society, devoid of a national morality, to find cause to... well, remove the obstructions."

Eugénie gasped. "Surely you don't think...?"

"Indeed I do, Eugénie," he said gently. "I'm not alone in this.

Recently, a contingent of the constituency of which you're a member that sent you as agent to our shores at the brink of our revolution came across the Atlantic to meet with me and other Americans of influence and substance to express their fears and to present us with an ambitious proposition."

"As patriots and revolutionaries yourselves, surely you wouldn't countenance counterrevolutionary actions," Eugénie said sharply.

"Nay, Madame, we would not. We listened to your countrymen because they were not counterrevolutionaries. They, like you, believe in the necessity of the change underway here. They're divided over whether to institute a constitution of the people and by the people, as we have, or a constitutional monarchy."

Eugénie nodded. "Yes, I see this division and it's tearing this country apart. I myself stand for a constitutional monarchy." She sighed. "Even though at times it's hard when the king and queen work against their own best interests."

"Aye, that they do," Robert agreed. "The Frenchmen we met with are very concerned for the safety of the king and queen, but they're also concerned about the political ramifications should the king and queen be executed, which they know is being considered in some quarters.

"Regicide is a dangerous step to take. The disastrous results are well documented. In every case, down through history, it has precipitated a backlash that not only buries the perpetrators of the deed, but also reverses the direction of the needed political and social changes.

"As if that weren't enough, your queen is the scion of the most powerful royal family in Europe, who'll waste no time marshaling forces to avenge her death. An invasion, which is now no more than the figment of paranoid minds, will become an immediate reality. Austria will quickly be joined by every other monarchy of the Western World. For they can ill afford to allow their people to witness such an act's occurring with impunity. Only a swift and harsh response would suffice, throwing all of Europe into war."

Eugénie closed her eyes and raked her hand across her forehead. She asked in a whisper, "What is this proposal you speak of?"

"The proposal is that concerned Frenchmen, in conjunction with us Americans, rescue King Louis XVI, Queen Marie Antoinette, and their children from themselves and the clutches of misguided patriots and spirit them out of France to the United States to a safe haven, a town designed and built expressly for the purpose of relocating and protecting the French royal family. Are you with us?"

XVIII

"Dear God, how did it come to this?" Eugénie exclaimed, later that evening, as Marie helped her prepare for bed. "Perhaps I'm naïve, but I still believe that wise heads will prevail and we'll bring France through this transition without sacrificing the monarchy." In the mirror, she watched Marie's deft fingers slip the pins from her thick chestnut hair. Soon the dark mass flowed down her back and Marie's rhythmic brush strokes smoothed out the tangles as they soothed her taut nerves. "Where did it start to go wrong? When did the king lose the devotion of his people?" She pictured his waddling gait, his slumped posture, and his permanent squint caused by his poor eyesight. "He certainly isn't as kingly in appearance as his predecessors, but is that enough for his people to turn from him?"

"Mistress, an accident of birth thrust our king into a role for which he was unsuited."

"Ah, *c'est vrai, chère* Marie. Were it not for the climate of our times, Louis XVI would have been left alone to enjoy his hunting, his maritime pursuits, and his journal, while his ministers carried out the affairs of state. Instead, the Crown demands more of him than he's equipped to give.

"Still, the people must see that he's harmless enough and is a true friend to them. After all, as far back as '83, it was he who invited the throng into Versailles to view Monsieur Montgolfier's balloon launch. It certainly was an unprecedented moment, bringing all the classes together like that. Some say 'foolhardy' and the first step in the disintegration of the social fabric."

Bridger and Eugénie were continuing the discussion the next morning, as they rode away from the château. "Mingling the classes can be a dangerous thing," the captain remarked. "You can't, one minute, put everyone in a crucible and, the next, expect the less fortunate to return to their hovels content with their lot. The reverse is also true. Your queen plays at being a shepherdess, but indulges herself with lavish feasts that are made possible only by the labor of the peasants. She dallies with the ordinary citizens at the boulevard theaters, which the king in his wisdom has avoided and has asked her not to attend, but to no avail."

"What you say is true," Eugénie said, "but you have to start somewhere. I applaud the reduction of privilege, such as the abolishing of coats of arms and titles. I particularly appreciate the introduction of the more informal dress, even at Court. There's no harm in these changes. In fact, I think they're all for the good. They help break down class distinctions and bring more equality to the classes. They support the purpose of the revolution — one citizenry, one *patrie* governed by elected officials, not appointed ones."

"But, Eugénie," Bridger broke in, "years of the ingrained habits of servitude and privilege don't vanish with the stroke of a pen. Abolishing the constraints you mention and promising 'liberty, equality, and fraternity' opens a Pandora's box. Acts of violence are no longer isolated events—the defacement of the coats of arms on carriages and church pews, the game riots in the countryside, the strangling of prize white doves in their dovecotes, the burning of symbolic mannequins on Pont Neuf in Paris, just to name a few of the more petty ones. I'm not even mentioning the great riots in Paris or the recent march on Versailles. Liberty and equality are heady stuff. How can you expect people with no experience with power, property, and privilege ... ?"

"*Ça suffit!*" Eugénie snapped, glaring at him.

Bridger started to say something but thought better of it, and they rode down the country lane in silence.

The early signs of spring and the sight of the winter harvest stacked in the fields were lost on Eugénie as she wrestled with Bridger's words. After seeing Robert Morris off to finish his journey, she had been glad when Bridger suggested a morning ride. It seemed the perfect opportunity to clear her head and come to a decision about the American's proposal. As she grappled with the cross-purposes that existed in her country's revolution, her mind went back to the rousing words of Patrick Henry that spring day, so long ago, in Virginia, and the eloquence of the Americans' Declaration of Independence.

Voicing her thoughts, she said, "The American patriots found a way to unite for a common goal and built a new nation. Now, they've penned their Constitution, but it was fourteen long years in the making. We have just begun."

Bridger looked over at the woman who had absorbed every waking and sleeping moment of his life since he met her fourteen years ago at the Whittington plantation. He had loved her then and he continued to love her, even though their lives had gone in separate directions—hers back to France, his to the island of Bermuda, where he'd married, made a family, and continued his livelihood at sea. Their time together was precious and made possible only because his shipping business demanded that he periodically spend time across the Atlantic.

"Yes, sweetheart, you have just begun," he said quietly, "but there are certain truths that'll make it difficult for your infant revolution to grow into manhood. The Americans weren't burdened with a peasantry. They had the luxury of self-government in every town and county, which they practiced and honed for years before they undertook their war for independence. They weren't strapped with a monarchy. They were divesting themselves of one. The monarchy was the very symbol they fought against. They were also an educated people. Daughters, as well as sons, received at least a basic education.

"These conditions are a far cry from the composition of your countrymen. Education and self-governing are hardly universal here. Only the few understand and wield power. The vast majority has no experience with it whatsoever. The smallest taste of power is too rich for them to stomach without its going to their heads and turning them into brutes, as you've seen. Now that they've had a taste of it, they'll want more. They're dancing in the streets today, because they bent the king and queen to their will. The euphoria won't last. What'll be the next demand, and the next?"

"Ah, Bridger, my head spins with it all. I can't fathom what the future will hold, but, at least, I've reached a decision about one course of action. I will join Robert Morris's group and help set up his bold plan. I pray God we won't have to implement it, but we must prepare for the possibility."

"Eugénie, isn't it enough that you've joined the activists in Bordeaux and put into place a network of agents that range up and down and across France? Must you undertake this scheme to preserve and protect a king and queen with whom a growing faction is thoroughly disenchanted, if not actively interested in discarding? This growing radical faction, let me add, would consider your undertaking to be in direct opposition to its goals for France. Should these people get wind of such a plan, you'd be their enemy!"

"Bridger, we've had this conversation, or one like it, so many times. We are not so different, you and I. I may take risks for my political beliefs, but are the risks you take at sea any less grave? We made a pledge to each other, long ago, to celebrate the gift of our love without restraint. We haven't the luxury of time, but neither do we have the burden of convention. Only yesterday, you reminded me that we laugh in the face of danger, even though the danger may take different forms. Rejoice with me in my passion for what I believe in, as I rejoice with you in yours, that our hearts may be light and our minds unfettered by the hobgoblins of fear and doubt."

"Dear heart, I'm chastened by your words. Yes, we must be forever grateful for the rare gift that we bring to each other. Forgive me for wanting to keep you safe and beyond harm. I offer you all that I have and all that I am, to assist you with this endeavor should the need arise. I was momentarily taken over by mundane worries. I'll see that it doesn't happen again," Bridger said to her with a mixture of love and mischief in his eyes.

Eugénie closed the distance between their horses and reached across to bring Bridger's lips to hers. Their kiss was interrupted as the two horses began to paw the ground and toss their heads.

"I see they're impatient for their apples," Bridger laughed, reluctantly ending the embrace. Joining in his laughter, Eugénie slipped from her saddle.

"This seems as good a spot as any for our picnic," she said, spreading a tricolored cloth on the ground under the canopy of a majestic oak. "Oh, I almost forgot. Jamie told me this morning that the moldings and cornices will be completed by the end of the day."

"Heaven be praised," Bridger said.

It was late afternoon before Eugénie and Bridger started up the avenue of trees that led to the château.

"What a wonderful day. A few hours in nature's arms renews my spirit like nothing else," Eugénie said.

Bridger shot her a cocky grin. "Like nothing else?" he murmured, "Hmmm, perhaps I've been delinquent in my..." His words were cut short by an angry shout.

"Unhand me, you lout! Do you know who you're dealing with?"

Eugénie and Bridger looked at each other with alarm. Spurring their horses to a run, they galloped through the courtyard gate to see an exceptionally short, rotund man in Jamie's grasp. When Eugénie and Bridger clattered up to within inches of the stranger, his eyes widened with fear and he shrank back. Eugénie sprang from her saddle.

"Jamie, *qu'est-ce qui se passe?*"

Keeping a firm grip on the man, Jamie replied, "This man, who calls himself Monsieur Renaud, arrived unannounced and proclaimed his intention of taking up residence at de Beaumont. I was simply dissuading him of that and sending him on his way."

"Thank you, Jamie. I'll take it from here." Jamie released the unwelcome visitor, but stood nearby.

"I'll have your identification card for this!" Renaud blustered, shaking his fist in Jamie's face. "No one manhandles Marcel Renaud with impunity. I'll..."

"Monsieur, I'm sure we can straighten out this misunderstanding," Eugénie said, interrupting the little man. "I'm Madame Eugénie Devereux..."

"I know who you are," Renaud lashed out, turning on her. "You're the high and mighty owner of the Château de Beaumont. I know who you are," he snarled, the layers of his chin quivering with indignation. "And," he said, drawing himself up to his full but meager height, "I am Monsieur Marcel Renaud, member of the regional council. Throughout the district, we're quartering our members in suspicious domiciles."

With an effort, Eugénie kept her voice calm and her expression bland. What a pompous fool, she thought. "Monsieur Renaud, I'm sorry that you've come this long way for nothing. Like you, I am a patriot. I support the revolution. My efforts on its behalf are well documented. I've heard nothing of the new protocol you speak of, which I would have been informed about as a member of the Gironde council. I recognize the importance of your position and that you're only doing your duty as you see it." Renaud preened at her flattering words.

"But," Eugénie continued, "in my capacity as a member of that council, I'll vouch for this château and its people and assume the responsibility for seeing that all is as it should be in accordance with the revolution. You may report this to the regional council. I'm sure it's quite burdensome to cover such a wide territory. I'm happy that I can relieve you of the need to oversee Château de Beaumont. Jamie, if you would, please see that Monsieur Renaud has ample refreshments to sustain him for his trip home."

Nodding to Renaud, Eugénie said, "Citizen, I applaud your efforts for the revolution. *Vive la France!*" With that, she turned on her heel and left the regional councilman staring after her, his mouth gaping open.

Recovering himself, he shouted after her, "You've not heard the last of this or seen the last of me, I promise you, Mistress Eugénie Devereux!"

"Jamie," Eugénie said, a short time later, "send a rider immediately to the regional office and learn what you can of this new protocol. Also, find out if Monsieur Renaud is who he claims to be. What an odious man! It's clear he's been elevated beyond his capabilities. Combine his limited intellect with a rage that emanates from his every pore and we have a man not to be taken lightly. Unfortunately, I doubt we've seen the last of him."

"You'll have the information on the morrow," Jamie promised and, bowing, left the room where Eugénie and Marie were hard at work adapting clothes to the requirements of the revolution.

Eugénie's hands paused momentarily as she looked out the window. "All seems so tranquil, but, in the blink of an eye, everything can change." With a lightning mood shift, she picked up the striped fabric on her lap and shook it out. "I rather like these new styles—no stays, no corsets, no fuss. The revolution has been the making of the queen's dressmaker. Long before it was *de rigueur,* Rose Bertin was fashioning loose, simple muslins and using cotton and white lawn for the queen. On the other hand, I imagine that the queen's jewelers, Messieurs Bohmen and Bassenger, and her hairdresser, Monsieur Leonard, have fallen on hard times. Remember the eighteen-inch-high hair styles complete with windmills, country scenes, plumes, and combs that he fashioned for her?" With a shrug, Eugénie quipped, "Oh, well, one man's gain is another man's loss."

"*C'est ça,* finished, at last!" Marie said, snipping the hemming thread of the gown she had been altering. "Mistress, this'll be quite fetching on you, *je pense.*"

"Let's see, Marie," Eugénie said, standing up. She took the gown from Marie, held it against herself, and looked down at it. "Hmmmm, white linen and muslin. Rather plain, wouldn't you say?" Running her hand over the fabric, she wrinkled her nose. "It certainly doesn't feel as good as silk and satin. *D'accord!* No sacrifice is too great for our revolution."

"Mistress!" Marie muffled a giggle, looking around for hidden ears and eyes.

"At least, Bridger will like the deep scooped neckline," Eugénie said, exchanging a smile with her servant. "Maybe we can brighten it up with a red and blue sash. Were it left to me, I'd simply wear peasant trousers like the *sans-culottes,* a muslin shirt and jacket, and be done with it."

"And give Monsieur Renaud and his like more grounds for criticism?" Marie asked drily.

Eugénie's eyes flashed. "I doubt that his small mind would be satisfied even if I paraded about in a madras kerchief, red waistcoat, short skirt, and *sabots*!"

"Mistress, you jest, but such conformity to the new fashion might serve you well."

"At least such a costume would have more snap than this," Eugénie said, and tossed aside the offending gown. Picking up a rough jacket from the pile at her feet, she set to work again. "This *carmagnole* will be much improved with a blue and red cockade on the shoulder." She looked at the clothing on the floor around her and said with a sigh, "This has been an endless task, but once we've finished what's here, the household should look suitably revolutionary."

"Why did Captain Goodrich and Jeremy go down to the stables at this hour?" Marie asked, as she put the finishing stitches on a skirt before setting it aside and picking up another *carmagnole* from Eugénie's stack.

"They went to help with a mare that's foaling early." Eugénie's hands stilled. Marie looked over at her and was concerned to see a shadow pass over her mistress's face. "Now, with the coming of March, Bridger will soon be returning to the *White Heather*." Her bleak expression tore at Marie's soft heart.

"Oh Marie, it's become so natural to look up and see him standing there, to look forward to his company at the end of the day. To have him here at Christmas. To watch the old year out and the new year in, with him beside me. It's been such a wonderful time, the longest we've ever had together, and we've used it to the fullest. In a lifetime, many small lifetimes. For us, the ordinary things of daily life are extraordinary." Suddenly, her face brightened, "The new foal, colt or filly, shall be named Bridger of White Heather."

"Are you considering making free with me, woman?" Bridger asked, striding into the room and startling them both. His face was ruddy from the chill of the night air. Seeing his look, Eugénie felt the color of her cheeks heightening to match his.

"Oh, sir, if you only knew."

XIX

That night, their passion reached an intensity that left them breathless. At one point, as Bridger drove Eugénie to staggering heights, brilliant colors exploded behind her eyelids and she felt the pounding of her heart stop just before he nudged her over the edge. Together, they soared into the firmament.

Later, he lay beside her, propped up on an elbow, his head cupped in his hand. He looked down at her, sleeping peacefully. Her face, as always, fascinated him. Her silver eyes were hidden behind lids fringed with thick, dark lashes that lay gently on cheeks more chiseled now than in her youth. Her skin, still flushed with passion, was as smooth as when he first saw her. The lips that he had first tasted in his dreams so long ago were slightly parted, inviting. Their etched fullness, always quick to smile, could, he knew, just as easily taunt, chastise, soothe, or seduce. One hand was tucked beneath her chin, a chin too square for conventional beauty. On its surface was the shadow of a cleft. He resisted kissing it and, instead, lifted a stray burnished curl and wound its silkiness around his finger. The feel of it brought back the many intimate moments they had shared over the years. His lips curved in a smile, remembering.

"How will I protect you when I'm gone?" he murmured. Lost in his thoughts, he was startled by her whisper.

"*Mon amour,* what's causing the furrow between your beautiful eyes?" Eugénie reached up to smooth his brow.

His face cleared as he took her hand and kissed each fingertip before turning it over and kissing the palm, sending a flutter through her.

"Scheming, dear one. Scheming how best to keep you here at my beck and call every day and every night for the rest of our lives."

Laughing, she framed his face with her hands and pulled him down to her.

Eugénie groaned and burrowed deeper into her pillow, willing herself back to sleep, but the early morning sun streaming through the windows and the thoughts whirling in her mind proved too much for her. She rolled over and sat up, shoving her hair out of her eyes. Bridger, fully dressed, stood at the window looking out. The rustle of the sheets drew his eyes to the bed.

"Good morning, sleepyhead." He smiled as he walked over to the bed and sat down beside her. He leaned over and gave her a kiss. Pulling back, he looked at her closely.

His expression turned serious. "You've never looked lovelier —your eyes soft with sleep, your hair framing your face. My love, how I shall miss you." During their months together, the haunted look had disappeared from her eyes and the strain from her face. "You're ready for whatever may come, my strong, brave Eugénie."

"You're leaving," she said.

"Yes, my love, but only for a few days. I'm off to Marseilles to oversee the preparations for *White Heather*'s voyage. I should be back in a few days, a week at the most. If the winds are fair, we shall set sail by the spring equinox, or by the end of March at the latest."

She took his hand, raised it to her lips, and then held it against her cheek. She looked up at his face. Their eyes met and spoke volumes. Playfully pushing him off the bed, she said, "Give me a moment to attend to my toilette, and I'll give you a proper send-off."

A short time later, Eugénie and Bridger walked into the stable-yard. Eugénie was surprised to see it deserted even at that early hour. She smiled, thankful that they would have these last moments alone together. Bridger's stallion stood saddled and ready at the hitching post. Hand in hand, they walked over to Montross, who tossed his head and whinnied a greeting. Bridger turned Eugénie to him and drew her into his arms. Leaning back, he looked down into her face and traced the line of her cheek with his finger. He captured an errant curl and slipped it behind her ear. Her eyes shone up at him, reading his thoughts.

Roughly, he pulled her to him and kissed her deeply. She reached up around his broad shoulders and interlocked her fingers behind his neck. Finally, breaking the kiss, she rested her head against his chest, savoring the smell of him and the texture of his jacket. She felt the steady beat of his heart beneath her cheek. The moment stretched out as they rocked gently in each other's arms. As one, they leaned back, their arms slipping down to encircle each other's waist.

"See to young Bridger while I'm gone. Since he's my namesake, I've a vested interest in that fine colt. Between Jeremy and me, he's become somewhat spoiled." He smiled into her eyes.

"Used to a diet of carrots and apples, is he?" Eugénie said, trying to look stern.

"Aye, he is," Bridger answered, looking not the least bit remorseful. With that, he gave her a light slap on the rump and vaulted into the saddle. "I'll be back before you know it."

"See that you don't let those dockyard wenches delay your return," Eugénie said, tossing her head.

Bridger laughed. "There's only one wench in that port with sails trimmed to my liking." He saluted her and, with a flick of the reins, turned Montross and cantered out of the yard.

Later that afternoon, Eugénie was poring over the household accounts when a light knock on the door broke through her concentration. She looked up to see Jamie in the doorway.

"*Qu'est-ce qu'il y a,* Jamie?" she asked, putting down her quill.

"I just received the information from the regional council about Renaud and the quartering protocol," he answered.

"From your face, it doesn't appear to be good news. Come, sit down and tell me."

Jamie lowered his tall frame into the chair across from her and said gravely, "The protocol was passed by the Assembly and each locality may implement it 'according to need,' which gives wide discretionary powers to the regional authorities. When our agent reported Renaud's actions to the regional officials, they confirmed that he was the representative for this area. From what the agent could glean, representatives such as Renaud have tremendous latitude because their specific duties aren't clearly defined."

"As I feared," Eugénie murmured.

"Mistress, we have ways to keep him from sniffing around here. I'll personally see that he doesn't bother you."

"*Merci,* Jamie," Eugénie said, smiling at him, "but perhaps it would better serve our purposes to keep him where we can see him."

"Surely, you don't mean to have him stay here at the château!" Jamie exclaimed.

"That's exactly what I mean. Isn't it better to appear to be compliant and feed his overblown pride than to resist and invite his retaliation? He's fully capable of making our lives miserable, and after yesterday I think he fully intends to. Jamie, our revolution is riddled with those of little integrity and petty minds whose positions of perceived power go to their heads. We've heard too many stories of people questioned and imprisoned on the trumped-up charges of a disgruntled neighbor or official, or detained without any charges at all. None of us is immune. Should Renaud choose to take such action against us, no doubt we'd ultimately be released, but not without a great expenditure of resources and time. Isn't it far better to avoid it altogether by practicing a little cunning instead? Who knows, our Monsieur Renaud may unwittingly be a source of useful information."

"Perhaps so," Jamie replied, rising, but he looked none too convinced as he left the room.

Again, a rap on the door interrupted Eugénie. She turned to see the footman Nicolas standing just inside the door. She closed the heavy ledger with a thump. It was clear that the remainder of the accounting would have to wait for another day.

"*Oui, Nicolas, entrez,*" Eugénie said with a tired smile, beckoning him forward.

"Madame Devereux, a messenger just delivered this. I hesitated to interrupt you, but it bears the royal seal." Bowing, he held out the letter to her.

"*Bien, Nicolas, merci beaucoup.*" The footman turned on his heel and left the room. Eugénie quickly broke the seal and began to read.

Ma chère amie, thank you for your kind letter. As you may know, more and more of the court are leaving and taking refuge beyond our borders. Those who do remain act as though Louis and I have the plague and make themselves scarce more often than not. Just as well, for I find their endless prattling and the accompanying undercurrents difficult to bear. My inner circle stands firm in their loyalty. Your Amelia Stanton continues to be an amusing diversion.

My time is consumed with the children. How precious they are to me. They're the center of my universe. Were it not for them... Their bright little faces quicken my heart. The Dauphin is such a brave little man. Not for a second does he show how he must feel about the limits placed upon him and the curtailment of so many of his activities. We're all suffering from the constraints we've been living under since October. Is it only five months since we left Versailles? I sometimes think I'll never see it and my dear animals again. But I mustn't think about that or I know I shall go mad.

These walls sometimes feel like a prison. I seldom go out

anymore. The streets are dirtier than ever and the ragged bands roaming the streets are even more uncivilized than I remember. If only the Assembly would make up its collective mind about what it intends to do with the new régime. From the little news that manages to get to me, it seems that the Assembly has broken into warring factions, each one more concerned with outmaneuvering the others than governing the country. Did you ever expect to hear me discussing politics?

The children and I did go on an outing to the Bois de Boulogne yesterday. Louis's burdens are so heavy, I sometimes like to give him a few hours of peace and quiet, so we left him to his ship models and had a lovely picnic by the lake. The ducks and ducklings enchanted us all and we returned refreshed and replenished. The children's rosy cheeks were my reward for braving the dirt and stench of the streets.

Today, poor Louis has been deluged with new demands from the Assembly. He looks so weary these days, I fear for his health. I trust you are well and springtime is blessing that beautiful valley of yours. Please know what a comfort your letters have been to me. I remain...

Eugénie sighed as she placed the letter with the others in the drawer of her desk. *La pauvre reine,* she thought. I imagine the situation is far worse than she's willing to put into words. Eugénie locked the drawer and reattached the key to the chatelaine that hung at her waist.

A few days later, Eugénie rode into the stable on Roan II to see Jeremy mucking out one of the stalls, muttering under his breath.

"Jeremy, whatever are you doing? Surely, we have enough hands to attend to that chore."

"Miss Eugénie, I'm a good leader only as long as I perform the same tasks that I ask my men to do. Today, if I hadn't found useful work for these hands, they might have found their way around a certain person's neck and strangled that person."

"Stop talking in riddles. What 'certain person' are you talking about?"

"I'm talking about Renaud's messenger," Jeremy said, his voice rising in anger, "who, as we speak, is strutting about in the kitchen making a nuisance of himself."

"Why didn't he depart after he delivered his message?"

"My very question!" Jeremy answered, becoming even more incensed. "That's when he climbed higher on his high horse and announced that he would give his message to Madame Devereux and to Madame Devereux only! And that's when I decided, rather than grabbing him by the throat and throwing him to the ground, that I'd come here and do something useful."

"I see," Eugénie said, trying not to laugh. The outraged expression on his face made him look just like the little boy she'd brought back to France with her from Bermuda so many years ago. "A worthy decision, indeed. I'd best go and find out what this messenger has to say. I was hoping to hear something from Bridger by now."

"Oh, Ma'am," Jeremy quickly reassured her, "Captain Goodrich's messenger came just after you left on your ride, to say you should expect the captain by the end of the week. That dithering idiot knocked it clean out of my mind." Her bright smile almost made Jeremy forget his anger with the messenger.

Eugénie hurried into the château, pulling off her gloves as she went. She stopped short when she saw several valises piled just inside the door. At that moment, Marie and an unfamiliar man came rapidly down the hall. As they drew near, she observed the man's rough peasant garb. Could this nervous, uncertain little man be Jeremy's messenger?

"Madame Devereux?" the man said deferentially.

Eugénie nodded and said, *"Oui, Monsieur. Je suis Madame Devereux."*

He snatched off his cap and stood twisting the red and blue cockade on its brim, clearly overwhelmed in her presence.

"Oui?" Eugénie said encouragingly.

As though coming out of a trance, the fellow began haltingly. "Uh, I come to bring you a message from Monsieur Renaud. He'll be arriving here soon." He stopped, gulped, and finally stammered out, "I brung his baggage." He gestured at the pile.

Ah, Eugénie thought, Monsieur Renaud is already on his way here. Her silence heightened the messenger's discomfort. He began to babble.

"Nice place ye got here. I never seen such, so grand and all." His voice trailed off and he shifted from one foot to the other as he looked around for some avenue of escape. Seeing his distress, Eugénie fixed a look of polite interest on her face.

"Citoyen, comment vous appelez-vous?"

"Je m'appelle Pierre. Pierre. My name's Pierre, Mistress."

"Ah, Pierre." Eugénie gave him a brilliant smile. He was so overcome that, had he been a pup, he would have been wildly wagging his tail. "On your way here, you must have passed the messenger I sent to the regional office to convey my wish that the château work as closely as possible with that office to ensure the implementation of the protocols of the revolution." The simple man's eyes glazed over and his mouth gaped open. Eugénie altered her tack. "Citizen Pierre, you've accomplished your duty admirably." Pierre dipped his head, blushing. "When should I expect Monsieur Renaud?"

Relieved to have a question he could answer, Pierre said quickly, "One day, Mistress, two at the most."

"*D'accord*. Pierre, Marie will find lodging for you."

"*Non! Non!*" Pierre's nervousness returned tenfold. "I can't stay here! Wouldn't be fittin'! My orders was to deliver my message to Citizen Devereux and to her only about Monsieur Renaud's arrival, deliver his bags, and report back *tout de suite. Tout de suite!*"

"I'll be sure to tell Monsieur Renaud of your diligence," Eugénie said. "Marie, we mustn't delay Citizen Pierre's departure a moment longer." Relief flooded the poor man's face.

At that moment, Jeremy came through the door. He did a double take, seeing the messenger's transformation.

"*Merci,* Madame Devereux, *merci!*" Pierre said, pulling on his forelock in the traditional gesture of respect before clapping his cap back on his head. He turned and scurried through the door, almost knocking Jeremy down in his haste.

"Jeremy, how could that poor little fellow have so undone someone like you? For shame!"

"Madame, he may have been putty in your hands, but ask Marie." He looked beseechingly at Marie, but when no aid was forthcoming, he continued. "Before you came, he was strutting about like the cock of the walk, making demands. He had no manners. He..."

"I see, I see," Eugénie chuckled. "He didn't pay you your due, is that it?"

"The likes of him shouldn't set foot..." Jeremy began.

"Jeremy, Jeremy," Eugénie chided him, "you and I, all of us, had best come to terms with the new régime. He and others like him are more and more in positions that will affect our lives. It behooves us to help them, in spite of themselves. We can ill afford to be arrogant or treat them lightly. Now, Jeremy, if you will, please take this baggage to the old overseer's cottage. Marie, will you please see that it's aired and made ready for Monsieur Renaud's arrival. Jeremy, if you found poor Pierre difficult, you'd best prepare yourself for Marcel Renaud. I'm not asking that you like the man, but you will be civilized. He'll serve our purposes splendidly."

XX

Two days later, the household was bustling with the arrival of Monsieur Marcel Renaud.

"How such a forlorn little man could turn this well-run household upside down in a matter of a few hours is beyond me," Marie muttered as she carried a tea tray into her mistress's sitting room.

Eugénie looked up from the letter she was writing. "Pardon, Marie. What did you say?"

"Nothing, Mistress." Her quick glance over her shoulder answered Eugénie's question.

"Our Monsieur Renaud has even managed to upset my unflappable Marie," Eugénie murmured. "It's no wonder the revolution moves in fits and starts with such efficient bourgeoisie oiling the machine. Fear not, *ma chère* Marie, Monsieur Renaud may stir about all he wants, but the ongoing workings of the château will prevail, in spite of his officiousness."

"Mistress, I hesitate to question your orders, but, when you agreed to his calling out the entire château population for his inspection, I was hard pressed to hold my tongue. And Jamie or Jeremy..."

"Marie, Marie, don't you see? He played right into our hands. His eyes fairly popped out of their sockets when he saw the number of our people and the extent of their health and well-being. It put to rest his view that the evil chatelaine stood daily brandishing her whip over the heads of her downtrodden, impoverished retainers.

"I particularly enjoyed the moment when he asked young Lucille how she minded working dawn to dusk as a scullery maid, and she retorted, How else was she to repay her beloved godmother, Mistress Eugénie, who'd not only given her the food on her table, the clothes on her back, and the roof over her head, but had also rescued her from the clutches of her cruel and heartless father, who'd never done an honest day's work in his life, but only sat around swilling spirits, working her like a slave and complaining about the unfairness of his lot."

Eugénie laughed. "After three or four more similar testimonials, our Monsieur Renaud threw his hands up in defeat. The crowning moment was when Virginie drew herself up to her full impressive height, placed her fists on her ample hips, and said right into his face, 'Monsieur Renaud, if'n you don't stop wastin' our time with this stuff and nonsense you're goin' to find yourself with nothin' but an empty dish come suppertime. You may have time to spare lookin' for what you call "revolootionary breaches," but the rest of us have work to do.' When Virginie marched off with her girls in tow, you could've knocked the poor man over with a feather."

Marie giggled, remembering the scene Eugénie described. "I hadn't looked at it quite that way, but we did rather put him in his place, didn't we?" With her composure once more intact, Marie settled down by the fireplace and took up the darning.

The château survived the first day of Renaud and was just settling down for the night when the sound of hooves clattering into the courtyard brought Eugénie to her feet. She put down the pamphlet she had been reading in the library and hastened into the main hall. Before she could reach the front door, it flew open and Bridger strode in, followed by the chilly night breezes that set the candle flames dancing in the wall sconces. Bridger's eyes lit up at the sight of her. He swept her into his arms and gave her a hearty kiss.

"Has it only been a week?" Eugénie breathed. A movement in the shadows caught Bridger's eye. He slowly released Eugénie and moved in front of her, his hand gripping the pistol at his hip.

"Who goes there? Come forward!" Bridger commanded. An apparition in a nightshirt and cap, which sat askew upon a grizzled head, separated itself from the gloom and inched into the candlelight. Bridger, not recognizing Renaud in his disheveled state, looked questioningly at Eugénie, who was equally startled by the man's appearance. Seeing Renaud's slack features and bloodshot eyes, it was clear to Eugénie that the official had continued to enjoy a quantity of liquid refreshment after his evening meal. She smothered a smile and tucked away the information.

"Monsieur Renaud, I trust that you find your quarters satisfactory?" Eugénie asked, subtly questioning his presence in the main house and making a mental note to secure the locks in the future.

Unaware of the comical picture he presented, Renaud drew himself up, clearing his throat several times.

"My rooms are fine, just fine. I was making my nightly rounds when I heard a commotion in the courtyard and came to investigate." Going on the offensive, he turned on Bridger. "Sir," he asked sharply, squinting myopically up at Bridger, "who are you and what is the meaning of your breaking curfew?"

"Monsieur Renaud," Eugénie said smoothly, "I believe you met Captain Goodrich on your first visit. He's a renowned shipper. He's been away this week attending his affairs in Marseilles, preparing for his voyage home across the Atlantic."

"Ahem, ahem, I see, I see. Well, just this once, sir, I'll overlook this breach of protocol. In the future, see that your comings and goings coincide with the prescribed curfew."

"Monsieur Renaud, in the future, I'll endeavor to the best of my ability to uphold the rules and regulations of the revolution, but the tides are a demanding mistress that conform to no man." Bridger spoke smoothly, but his eyes gleamed dangerously.

"Good, good. See that you do. Now, I must retire and get the rest I require to perform my rigorous duties. 'Til the morrow, then." Renaud attempted a dignified retreat, but he turned too suddenly, causing him to stagger. He regained his equilibrium and tottered down the hall. Bridger chuckled, his eyes following the official's unsteady passage. Eugénie put a restraining finger to his lips until they heard the distant sound of a door slamming.

"Dear heart, I never thought I'd leave you with any degree of eager anticipation," Bridger said a few days later, as Eugénie and he were enjoying a rare, solitary walk in the gardens, "but that ubiquitous man's interference in this household has me constantly stepping in to quell tempers, restore order, and keep Jamie and Jeremy from coming to blows with the little twit. At the end of the day, if I've caught a glimpse of you, much less spent even a few quiet moments with you, I count myself lucky. The demands of the sea will be child's play after this!" He paused and caught her around the waist.

Her hand reached up and absentmindedly stroked the hair that curled over his collar. She looked up at him, her eyes glistening with unshed tears.

"I almost welcome the horrible man's presence. He'll distract me from the long days that stretch out ahead of me, empty of you. Oh," she moaned, throwing her arms around him and holding him close, "each parting weighs on my heart more heavily than the last. One day the accumulated weight will crush it and it will simply stop."

He tightened his arms around her and tucked her head under his chin. "Eugénie, as long as there's breath in my body, my heart will call out to yours across whatever distance separates us. Distance is nothing to us." He took her hands in his and gazed down into her face. "Now, my gallant Eugénie, again the world taps us on our shoulders. Word came to me this morning that my first mate is alarmed about the unusual activity in Marseilles. His informants think that an ordinance closing the port to all departing foreign vessels is imminent. There's even talk of cargoes being seized, and other reprehensible acts are being committed that violate maritime law. I depart the château at dusk and we sail with the morning tide."

"Bridger," Eugénie cried in alarm, "are *White Heather* and your crew safe until then?"

"The messenger assured me that no action can be taken until additional gendarmes and other officials are in place. That'll take time, but I'll not tempt the fates."

"No, you mustn't," she said firmly, her pain at his leaving forgotten in her concern for his safety. "Shouldn't you leave immediately? I fear for you, traveling in the dark."

"Fear not, my love. In daylight, traffic clogs the highways. The darkness suits me better. More importantly, how could I, in all conscience, leave you alone to face Renaud's legions of local officials at this noon's reception?"

A shadow flitted briefly across Eugénie's face. "*Zut!* I'd almost forgotten his most recent ploy to feed his insatiable self-importance!"

She drew a weary hand across her brow. "*Merci, mon coeur,* for reminding me of my duties. I'd best go help Marie with the preparations. That man has burdened her beyond belief. Drat him!"

"And I'll endeavor to keep him out of Jeremy's and Jamie's path." Bridger grinned and swung Eugénie up into his arms. "But only after I've had one last sustaining kiss for my efforts." It was a tender kiss, sweetened with the knowledge that their remaining hours together were all too brief.

Reluctantly, Eugénie and Bridger pulled apart and turned their steps towards the château. He laced his fingers through hers and said urgently, "Promise me that you'll keep yourself safe in all things, but most especially in regard to Robert Morris's scheme." At her nod, his voice softened. "My love, I'll be with you again before you know it. This year will pass and I'll return to you by next year's spring equinox. 'Til then, you're with me always."

"And you with me," Eugénie whispered as they reached the terrace steps and went their separate ways.

XXI

Eugénie leaned against the paddock fencing, watching the colt, Bridger, gamboling in the pasture. Had it truly been a year and a month since he had foaled? Whether he was alone or with the other yearlings, his antics endeared him to everyone at the château. She whistled softly. Bridger froze in midleap, turned in her direction, and, with a speed that defined him as a future champion, galloped over to her. Eugénie opened the gate and the colt pranced through. He nuzzled her pockets, looking for hidden treasure.

"You scamp," she scolded. "Have you no manners?" The colt shifted and nibbled at her neck with his soft lips. "That's more like it," Eugénie laughed, giving him a sugar lump. Stroking his withers, she admired the glossiness of his deep chestnut coat as he crunched on his treat. Thinking of the man for whom the colt was named, she lifted her gaze to stare off across the field, a distant expression clouding her eyes. Over a year had passed since he had left, but she remembered the last words he said to her as though it were yesterday.

"I didn't know my heart before I beheld your face. With you and only with you does my heart beat in my chest. Only at the sight of you does it leap with joy. I've no use for it when I'm away from you. You gave me my heart. Now I give it back to you for safekeeping. Guard it well while I'm gone. Know that wherever you are, there will I be also." Bridger, she thought, I've guarded it well this long, long year, tucked away with my own. She flung her arms around the colt's neck. Burying her face against his cheek, she drew comfort from his stillness.

What a year it had been. Inspired by the anniversary celebration for the fall of the Bastille, the nobility and the royal family made substantial donations to the treasury, which included melting down much of the royal silver plate.

The Assembly targeted the Church, wresting away its power, abolishing tithes and privilege, demanding from the clergy oaths of loyalty to the State. Poor Louis was caught once again between Church and State. How could he condone making outlaws of the clergy who refused the oath . . . and yet how could he not?

The plight of the people had not changed since the Bastille fell almost two years before. They still clamored for food, while the fortunes of the Assembly leadership rose and fell. What had become of the principles that inspired the revolution? Had they been set aside only to be brought out when it was convenient for the leader of the moment to secure his position or justify his actions? Did demeaning the king and the clergy serve the universal principles of liberty, equality, and brotherhood or did they simply feed a free-floating lust for power?

Hearing footsteps on the gravel behind her, Eugénie turned to see Marie coming down the path. "Marie, don't tell me you've managed to slip away from Monsieur Renaud's clutches?" The two women laughed companionably. "Only you have found the key to that man. You have him fairly eating out of your hand. He follows you around like a puppy."

Marie smoothed Bridger's mane. "Actually, I feel sorry for him. He's had a hard life. Orphaned so young, he never had the luxury of a mother's love."

Eugénie rolled her eyes. "You make him sound almost human. If he weren't so officious and obnoxious, the rest of us might be more sympathetic. I don't want to waste another breath on him. I happily leave him and his travails to you. Is everything in readiness for Monsieur Danton's arrival? I look forward to meeting this revolutionary. Comparing the real man to the reputation should make for an interesting evening."

Marie looked more closely at her mistress. She saw the strain on her face. Without the softening effect of Bridger's company, her mistress's concern for her neighbors as well as for the Château de Beaumont, caused by the ever-increasing number of attacks on châteaux and travelers by the brigands roaming the countryside, had taken its toll on her.

"Yes, Virginie and the girls have prepared a veritable feast, though she grumbles that it's better fare for livestock than people."

"Well, we were told Monsieur Danton's choices. If it suits the man's palate, somehow we'll survive. It's Renaud who may not live through the visit."

Marie laughed. "I know. His chest is so puffed out, I'm afraid he's going to burst his buttons. He takes full credit for Monsieur Danton's coming to the château. He can barely sit still. No sooner does he sit down than he's up again, checking this or that. To use his words, 'To be in the presence of such a prominently noteworthy citizen is the greatest honor ever bestowed upon this château.'"

Eugénie couldn't help but laugh. She put a halter over Bridger's neck and the two women began walking the colt towards the stableyard.

"Captain Goodrich should be arriving any day now, shouldn't he?" Marie asked.

"Yes," Eugénie said, her face lighting up, "any day now." As if on cue, they heard the sound of hoofbeats. "Could it be?" Eugénie gasped. She handed Bridger's lead to Marie and started to run, but before she had taken more than a few steps two riders wheeled into sight and drew up in front of her in a cloud of dust. Jeremy was the first out of the saddle.

"Look who overtook me on the road. No telling what rascals you'll find riding abroad these days!" A travel-worn Bridger leaped down from Montross. With a small cry, Eugénie threw herself into his arms, causing him to stagger back.

"Had I known I'd receive such a reception, I'd have ridden all the harder to get here," Bridger laughed, pulling her close. His dusty appearance and Montross's sweat-darkened coat were clear proof that neither had spared any effort to reach the château.

"All's well with the world, once more," Eugénie breathed, hugging him to her.

When Bridger came up for air, he looked over Eugénie's shoulder to see a beaming Marie and his namesake. "Is this young Bridger?" The colt's head had shot up when Bridger first spoke.

Now that Eugénie and Bridger were standing apart, the young horse looked at the man with the familiar voice. Pulling Marie with him, he pushed between Eugénie and Bridger and nipped at Bridger's sleeve.

"Ah, you remember me," Bridger chuckled, stroking the colt's neck. "I'm afraid you'll have to wait for a treat. Montross ate every one." Seeing a groom approaching to tend to the colt and Montross, Eugénie linked her arm through Bridger's and started towards the château.

As he walked down the courtyard steps, Jamie stopped short at the sight of Bridger. A broad grin replaced the look of concern on his face. He rushed forward and the two men embraced.

"Captain, welcome back!"

Bridger cuffed him on the shoulder. "It's good to be back, Jamie."

"Better than you know," Jamie murmured, causing Bridger to look more closely at his friend.

"I see you're still flourishing under Marie's loving care," Bridger said lightly. Marie and Jamie exchanged a warm look. Bridger knew that, with Jamie's forthright nature, whatever was causing the signs of strain around his eyes would soon come to light. He did not have long to wait.

"Mistress Eugénie, we just received a message from Monsieur Danton."

"Oh?" Eugénie asked, her pleasure at Bridger's arrival dimming as she saw the shadowed expression in Jamie's eyes.

"His trip has been postponed for the foreseeable future."

"What possibly could have happened to prevent him from coming? He was so adamant about his schedule." Jamie started to speak, but Eugénie interrupted him. "*Venez, venez,* let's go inside. We've kept the captain lingering long enough. Bridger, I'm sure you'd like a few minutes to get settled." Bridger nodded, hoisted his saddlebags up on his shoulder, and followed her through the doorway.

"I'll see to some refreshment," Marie said, turning down the hall, as Jamie followed Eugénie into the small salon.

Eugénie patted the cushion beside her. "Here, sit down, Jamie, and tell me what the messenger had to say." Jamie sighed and sat down, dragging a tired hand across his brow.

"Madame, Monsieur Danton wanted to assure you that only the most dire circumstances would cause him to postpone his trip. These are the events the messenger reported. On Monday past..."

"That would be April eighteenth? Ah, Bridger, good, you're here. Continue, Jamie."

"Yes, Madame, on April eighteenth, the start of Holy Week, the royal family was confronted by a mob as they were departing for their property in Saint-Cloud. As we know, the king has been very ill and wished, no doubt, to have a short respite from the tensions surrounding him. Apparently, Lafayette arrived and commanded the National Guardsmen with him to disperse the mob. The soldiers refused."

Eugénie exclaimed, "It sounds just like the *contretemps* that occurred between the General and the Garde on that horrific night at Versailles. I thought that had been an isolated event. This report seems to confirm the rumors that Lafayette's influence is waning."

Bridger's expression mirrored the alarm on Eugénie's face.

"Why would the Parisians take such an aggressive action? Clearly, much has changed in the year since I've been gone."

"That it has," Eugénie answered. "The Hapsburgs have gathered troops at our border. Invasion is more and more a reality. Since you left, the widespread fear and the ever-increasing lawlessness in the streets have emboldened the Parisian mob. The king's wish to leave for Saint-Cloud is too close in time to the conflict that arose over the desire of his aunts, Adelaide and Victoire, to go to Rome for the beginning of the Lenten season."

"Conflict? What conflict?"

"In February," Eugénie said wearily, "the aunts' proposed trip brought to a head the battle that's been raging over the Assembly's decrees, which place the State above the Church and call for all the clergy to swear an oath of loyalty to the State, outlawing those who refuse. Finally, the king reluctantly signed the decrees into law. The aunts' trip was seen as a clear statement of their stand against the authority of the State, and the responsibility for their behavior was laid at the king's feet.

"Mirabeau, who was the foremost champion of the decrees, was at the same time outspoken against any infringement of the aunts' freedom of movement, saying that that freedom was central to the spirit of the revolution. He argued effectively in the Assembly to let them go. At the same time, the broader issue dealing with restricting the movement of émigrés was before the Assembly. Mirabeau unflinchingly condemned any restrictions that would contradict the basic freedoms set out in the Declaration of Rights. It's a mess."

"It sounds to me as though the Assembly is on its way to legislating a tyrannical state," Bridger said quietly.

Eugénie nodded, her eyes grave. "There's no question about that. To protect *La Patrie,* they're eroding the liberties of the people. There, I've finally put into words the fears I've had these past months." She took a deep breath. "And now the great Mirabeau is dead."

"Dead?" Bridger asked, shocked.

"At the beginning of April, that clear, strong voice for liberty fell silent forever. I can only imagine how much we'll miss him in the days to come. There's no one to take his place—no one. Without him to stem the tide, I fear for the course of this revolution."

Eugénie stood up and moved restlessly around the room. "*Alors,* you can see that the king not only has little influence over the affairs of state, but also has less and less say over his own circumstances. Jamie, did the messenger say anything else?"

"Yes, Mistress. According to the messenger, Monsieur Danton praised the crowd for showing its good will in allowing the king and queen to return to their apartments without further incident."

"The crowd's good will... allowed the king... That's utterly mad! What can the man be thinking?" Eugénie exclaimed, but waved to Jamie to continue.

"The next day, April nineteenth, now a week ago, the king demanded that the Assembly honor his right to travel the given radius from Paris."

"My God!" Bridger said. "It's come to that? The king must beseech the Assembly to travel to one of his own palaces?"

Silence enveloped the room. Then Jamie finished. "Because the debate continues, Monsieur Danton is remaining in Paris."

"Oh, my heart goes out to Their Majesties. Daily, they're subjected to humiliation heaped on humiliation. The palace is nothing short of a prison. I can't imagine how they bear it, especially the queen. I, for one, wouldn't blame them if . . . " Eugénie stopped in midsentence when Marie entered the room, carrying the tea tray, followed closely by Renaud.

"What is this I hear? Monsieur Danton will not be arriving as planned?" the official barked, bustling past Marie and planting himself in front of Eugénie.

"He's been detained by urgent business of the Assembly," she replied vaguely, wondering how much he had heard.

Crestfallen, Renaud dropped his rotund, short body into the nearest chair. "All my special planning, for nought." He looked close to tears.

"May I pour you some tea? Marie, the *petits fours* look particularly appetizing." Eugénie gave Renaud a sidelong glance. She knew that an appeal to his stomach would ease him over even the most severe disappointment. The effect was remarkable. His head bobbed up. He nodded, as his plump hands gathered up several of the pastries and piled them on a plate. With his spirits visibly on the mend, he rounded on Bridger.

"Captain Goodrich, here you are again!" he snapped. "It may not be healthy for you to remain in France. Foreigners are not welcome." He paused midbite, looking from Eugénie to Bridger, and said craftily, "Sir, were it any household but Madame Devereux's, I'd find your comings and goings highly suspicious. I'm aware of the depth of your, er, friendship. Nothing gets by me, I assure you. I trust your papers are in order, but you will present them to me forthwith."

"I wouldn't have you derelict in your duty, Monsieur Renaud. Miss Eugénie, if you'll excuse me?" Bridger said smoothly, but the look he gave Renaud made the little man's blood run cold and he quickly pushed another sweet into his mouth.

Renaud waited until Bridger was well out of earshot and said, "That man bears watching. Madame, it would be a shame if your, um, friendship should bring suspicion down on this household. Even my influence would not be sufficient to protect your good name," he added.

Eugénie burst out laughing. "Monsieur Renaud, my horse, The Roan, is more of a political animal than Captain Goodrich. It's been an argument of long standing between us, his complete and utter lack of interest in anything remotely political. Were it up to him, he'd relegate all of it to the ash heap." As Bridger strode back into the room, Renaud, who had a retort teetering on his lips, thought better of it and instead clamped his mouth down on a *petit four* and gulped some tea.

Holding out a sheaf of papers, Bridger said, parroting Renaud, "My papers, sir. I trust you'll find them in order."

Renaud cleared his throat, snatched the papers, and said petulantly, "Humph, I'll peruse them at my leisure, after I've had my tea."

When Eugénie was sure the château had settled down for the night, she made her way to the stables. Glancing about her, she shivered as she pulled her cape closer. She tapped lightly on Jeremy's door. When it opened a crack, she pushed it open further and slipped inside.

"Mistress! Is something wrong?" Jeremy said with alarm, stepping back.

"Shhh!" Eugénie whispered, walking over to the fireplace where the flames danced cheerfully upon the grate. Leaning towards them, she rubbed her hands together before turning back to face her trainer.

"Jeremy, you must leave for Paris, tonight."

"Tonight? Paris? What's happened?"

"It's nothing I can put my finger on. It's not just one thing. Over the last month, Renaud's been receiving more and more visitors. Also, he's been going away more frequently, for what he calls his 'duties.' For a loquacious, transparent fellow, he's become increasingly silent and mysterious. Something is brewing. I feel it. I'm certain that Danton's planned visit, the matter of the aunts, the confrontation described by today's messenger, and now the king and queen's virtual imprisonment are all building to something.

"This is too sensitive for our usual system of agents. I trust only you to be my eyes and ears in Paris. I count on you to find out what's afoot in the streets, in the Assembly, and beneath the surface of the king and queen's narrowing world. Pay particular attention to Danton and the pious Robespierre. They're the ones to watch.

"I'll be meeting with my constituency soon and I must be kept apprised daily of the actions in Paris to safeguard our mission to rescue the royal family. You're the only one at the château who has the documents as well as a legitimate reason to be in Paris. It'll be hard to spare you here, but anyone else's absence would be suspicious and would alert Renaud."

Eugénie stepped forward and held out a letter and a pouch.

"Deliver this letter to Danton. In it, I express my regret that he had to postpone his visit and my hope that it will be rescheduled at his earliest convenience. I also offer you into his service, with a horse from our stable as a token of my regard." She smiled for the first time. "Even we revolutionaries appreciate good horseflesh and the service of a trainer of your reputation.

"This is an extreme course of action, but it's the only way I could think of to work you in close to him." Jeremy's eyes lit up with anticipation. "His pride will make him an easy target, but beware. Don't underestimate him. From everything I've heard, he's ruthless and cunning. Pack and be off as quickly as you can. There should be sufficient funds in the pouch to sustain you."

While Eugénie was speaking, Jeremy had begun stuffing his belongings in his saddlebags. Eugénie started to leave, but turned back and gripped his arm.

"Jeremy, don't take any unnecessary chances. Promise me you'll take every care." Jeremy looked at her intently. In his dark eyes, she saw the depth of his feelings.

She hugged him to her and whispered, "Go with God."

XXII

THE FOLLOWING DAY

The next morning, a petulant Renaud stopped Eugénie and Bridger as they were leaving the stableyard on horseback.

"English," he said imperiously, "I've read your papers. They're sufficient, but as you are not a citizen of *La Patrie* you will report to me when you leave the château and apprise me of your destination. Any breach of such and the largesse of *La Patrie* will be withdrawn. Do I make myself clear?"

Bridger cocked his eyebrow at the man's rude manner and delivery, but he kept his voice level. "Monsieur Renaud, you make yourself eminently clear. Madame Devereux and I..."

Eugénie raised her hand, effectively cutting off Bridger's next words. Sitting up straighter in her saddle, she matched her tone to Renaud's. "Monsieur Renaud, Captain Goodrich is a guest in my home, as are you. As long as you enjoy this hospitality, you will abide by the rules of common courtesy, which are extended to you and to all who reside under my roof. Moreover, I will remind you that we of the revolution espouse universal equality and brotherhood. As one of our fellow men, Captain Goodrich shall receive the benefit of these principles. This once, and only this once, shall

I overlook your egregious lapse in adhering to the principles of our revolution. I trust it will not happen again. Do I make myself clear?"

At her words, Renaud's complexion took on an unhealthy flush, but he managed to choke back his anger. "Yes, Madame, you do." He straightened his jacket and attempted to put some authority back into his voice. "May I ask where Jeremy is this morning? I specifically asked him..." When Eugénie's silver gaze flashed dangerously, he stumbled to a halt.

"Jeremy has gone to Paris to work in the service of Monsieur Danton."

The little man's mouth fell open and he squeaked, "Paris! In Monsieur Danton's service!" Eugénie couldn't suppress a smile of satisfaction, but didn't grace his reaction with a response. Instead, she clucked to The Roan. The horses broke into a trot and clattered out of the stableyard, leaving a stupefied Renaud staring after them.

"You certainly gave him his comeuppance," Bridger chuckled. "Don't you think you were a little hard on the poor fellow?"

"Hard on him!" Eugénie exclaimed. "He's fortunate that I didn't toss him out on his ear. He's been more and more impossible these last months. The only way to deal with a bully is to bully him right back. I've had to bite my tongue and remember he's been of great use to us. How else would I be able to warn our neighbors of the night raids his officious bureaucrats have planned, or to avoid certain days and times for our meetings? Even so, every so often it's necessary to put him in his place. Enough of him. I won't have him ruin this beautiful day and the pleasure of our ride."

Bridger nodded. "I wholeheartedly agree. Tell me, why are we leaving the château for the meeting with your compatriots? I thought you'd found a way to have them here without raising Renaud's suspicions."

"Without Jeremy, our clever subterfuge no longer works." She laughed. "When I think of those skilled horsemen and crack shots pretending to train under Jeremy to be members of the local militia, it's all I can do to keep a straight face."

"Surely, no one, not even Renaud, would've been taken in by that ruse."

"*Au contraire,* as veterans of the masquerade, they were quite convincing in their roles. Had I not known the scheme, they would've fooled me."

"Extraordinary," Bridger said.

"Bridger, I've a bone to pick with you on an entirely different subject."

At her tone, Bridger looked at her sharply. "And what might that be?"

"I don't see why you felt it necessary to accompany me to this meeting. I'd never forgive myself, should something happen to compromise you. Renaud's statement about foreigners is true. You can ill afford to be associated with this operation. Also, on the first day of Jeremy's absence, your presence at the château would have been a great help to Jamie."

"Jamie is fully capable of managing on his own," Bridger said with some heat. In a gentler tone, he continued. "Forgive me, dear heart. The last thing you need with all that's on your mind is my short temper, but I'm hard pressed to curb it when you treat your safety so lightly, traveling alone, knowing how dangerous it is. So long as I'm here, I'll escort you whenever and wherever you choose to go. I can live with the risk for myself. What I cannot live with is the thought of something happening to you. No!" He raised his hand to ward off her objections. "There will be no further discussion or I'll return to the château, pack my bags, and be gone."

Eugénie looked over at his stern profile and surprised them both by bursting out laughing. "You rascal! You know I'd agree to anything to keep you with me. But let this be fair warning to you: Don't play that card too often, or, in spite of 'our, um, friendship' the threat will lose its power."

Bridger laughed at her perfect imitation of Renaud. "Milady, consider your warning taken. As you well know, for me to carry through with such an act would be the worst hardship I can imagine, short of losing you altogether." They exchanged a meaningful look and rode on, thinking their own thoughts.

After a short while, Bridger broke the silence. "Who'll be at the meeting?" he asked as their two mounts forded a wayward stream and scrambled up the bank on the other side.

Eugénie smiled. "I wondered when your curiosity would overcome your indifference to our politics. Let's see. General Louis de Noailles will be there. He's by far the most prestigious of our group. He's a brother-in-law of Lafayette's. He distinguished himself in the Americans' war, particularly in the battle of Yorktown. I don't know how much longer he'll be able to stay in France. His voice is repugnant to the radicals, especially Robespierre, even though he has an illustrious record in the National Assembly and has been responsible for many of the liberal measures that have reduced the privileges of the nobility. Antoine Omer Talon is another one to take note of. His list of credentials includes Chief Justice of the criminal court of France, the head of the royal secret service, and the prosecutor of the conspirators who led the mob to the Bastille. He's long been an advisor and confidant of the king."

"I can't imagine he's very popular with the radicals, either," Bridger said under his breath.

"Another is Captain Aristide Aubert du Petit Thouars, whose hand was permanently crippled from a wound he suffered fighting in the Americans' war. His friends call him 'Admiral.' Then, there's Charles Bue Boulogne. My father admired his expertise at buying and selling property, both here and abroad. The others who will probably be present are Messieurs Homet, LaPorte, Le Fevre, Brevost, and d'Autremont.

"The consortium my father was a member of has disbanded. It's too politically dangerous. It exists today as a loose association. It's no longer the political and economic force it once was, or the sub rosa advisory council to the French monarchy. Should, however, a person who has belonged to this group need aid of any sort, there's still a commitment to help that person, regardless of the cost. The membership, which goes back countless generations, covered the whole political gamut. This is still true today. There are staunch royalists, moderates, and radical revolutionaries.

"I know a list was compiled at the time of the fall of the Bastille that includes many of us. Those on the list are persona non grata, and many have fled France. Those of us who remain believe we can still serve the revolution and our country. But who's to say what tomorrow will bring?"

"Hmmm," Bridger said, mulling over her words, and then asked, "Will the Americans be at the meeting as well?"

"*Je ne sais pas.* I do know that Robert Morris, their leader, has returned to Philadelphia. His partner, John Nicholson, Pennsylvania's comptroller general, may attend. I don't know if Étienne Girard will be there. He goes by 'Stephen' now that he's an American citizen. He's a Philadelphian banker. Another one I don't know about is Pierre, now Peter, Donceau. I've not met the other Americans. Their involvement to date has only been communicated at the meetings through the ones I've mentioned."

"Aren't you afraid someone will infiltrate the group and do you harm?"

"Certainly anything's possible, but considering the extent of our safeguards and our familiarity with each other—there's no one who hasn't been vouched for by several others—I find such a possibility very remote. Let me see if I can explain it to you. Although the French and the Americans in this group are committed revolutionaries, we French have been, are, and, to our last breath, will always be fiercely loyal to our monarchy."

Bridger nodded. "I can understand that. I feel the same loyalty to my clan. I see why you and your cohorts are willing to risk so much to rescue your king and queen, but why the Americans?"

"As Morris told me so eloquently, 'We Americans owe you French, and most especially your king, a huge debt of gratitude for the financial and military aid you contributed to our Revolutionary War. Just as important'—I remember him smiling when he said this—'my partners and I see this as an opportunity to repay that debt and to benefit financially as well, which we also happily offer to our French brothers.' "

"Ah, speculators." Bridger smiled. "Now, that's something I can appreciate, though it's right dangerous, I suspect."

"More dangerous than trading on the high seas, buying and selling in capricious foreign markets, at the whim of the weather and as the target of pirates?"

"All right, all right," Bridger said, throwing his hands up and startling Montross, "you've got me there. I daresay I've dealt in my world for so long, I carry those risks as lightly as I carry the coat on my back and think nothing of it."

Having made her point, Eugénie smiled at him and flicked her reins, calling over her shoulder, "We're far enough from the château, now. We can drop the pretense that we're out for a leisurely ride. We have a good hour of hard riding ahead of us. Let's go!" The two riders took off down the roadway, setting a fast pace.

Eventually they crested a hill and pulled up to give the horses a well-deserved rest. Below them a river meandered through pastureland that stretched as far as the eye could see.

"There, see the old grist mill? That's our meeting place."

Bridger looked skeptical. "It looks abandoned."

"That's why it's perfect for our purposes. It belongs to a relative of Arnaud LaPorte's. It hasn't been used since the active commerce moved downstream to the more heavily populated areas."

They wasted no time galloping across the meadow. Dismounting, they guided the horses into the shed next to the mill. From the number of horses inside munching at the hay bins, it was clear others had already arrived.

"Good," said Antoine Omer Talon, the ex officio leader of the group, "it's settled, then. John and Charles, you'll return to Pennsylvania and meet with Robert, as soon as possible, to locate land for the settlement. Eugénie, your name for the town, Azilum, is well chosen. Unless I miss my guess, before this revolution plays out, there will be many who'll seek sanctuary there. Admiral, you said you had some preliminary plans for the town?"

"Yes, I've sketched out most of it and I've made a list of the materials and the style for the buildings that I think would be the most suitable, given the need for speed and durability."

"*Bien!* Share them with us, if you will."

Captain Aristide Aubert du Petit-Thouars shuffled the sheaf of papers adroitly, despite his crippled hand. "I envision a tract of land that, for our needs, must encompass about sixteen hundred acres, preferably on a river to facilitate the movement of materials and people."

Excitedly, John Nicholson interrupted him. "I may know of such a site. Damned if Robert and I haven't seen just what you've described. I'm not sure of the exact acreage, but I know there's land available of about that size along a horseshoe curve on the Susquehanna River in Pennsylvania."

"Can you tell us more about it?" asked André Brevost.

"It's lush riverbed land. It's called 'missicum' by the Indians, which means 'meadows,' and 'standing stone' by others because of the stone shaft that stands high in the water near the western bank of the bend. Its stark wilderness is beautiful beyond words, and the width and depth of the river are perfect for our needs. I think the land will be available for a very good price. Robert, Charles, and I can get all the particulars, if you all agree." The group nodded enthusiastically.

Aristede continued. "According to my plan, we would need about three hundred acres for the town itself. It would have a market square of about two acres right in the middle of town. To reach the square from the river, I envision a wide avenue, more like a road, perhaps even one hundred feet wide to allow for carriages coming and going concurrently with wagons and other conveyances, as well as foot traffic. A gridiron of roads would feed out from the square. They, too, would be wide, though not as wide as the road from the river. Along these streets, I've laid out four hundred and thirteen building lots of about half an acre each. Around the market square would be all the shops and other needs of a town—a chapel, a schoolhouse, a theater, and so on.

"In the areas beyond the town, I've allowed for larger, uncleared lots for farms and future growth. We also would have to make room for dairying, sheep-raising, orchards, gardens, a mill, a blacksmith shop, and distilleries, as well as places to manufacture everyday needs, such as soap, gunpowder, glass, and fertilizer, to name a few." Mumbles of approval met his words.

"We have to get these buildings up quickly, so I see them as rough-hewn log cabins, but with the conveniences of chimneys, windows with glass, shutters, and deep front porches."

"Admiral, you've given this much thought. I commend you," de Noailles said. The others nodded in agreement. "But we mustn't lose sight of the main purpose of this town. Why not take the prototype you've described and simply enlarge it?"

"That would work," the Admiral said. "It would be feasible to expand the design to three stories. We could widen the hallways and add additional fireplaces and chimneys. We could put in small-paned windows and enlarge the main salon to make it more grand." An affirmative murmur passed through the room as long hours of conjecturing began to take shape and become concrete.

"With the river so near, there must be springs that we can

divert to bring running water to the house for the . . . persons who'll go unnamed," spoke up another in the group.

"It might be a little extravagant, but worth the effort," agreed another.

"Fine, it appears we're well on our way, thanks to you, Admiral. Considering your fine plan for Azilum, I suggest you be the one to get it started and oversee its progress, once Robert, John, and Charles have procured the land," Omer said. "All in favor say 'Aye.'"

A unanimous "aye" swept the room.

"Fine, that's settled. Shall we have some refreshment before we adjourn?"

XXIII

On the way back to the château, Eugénie and Bridger stopped at a small wayside inn. Once they had attended to the horses, they wandered hand in hand through the elaborate parterre that circled the sides and back of the inn. The gardens were bathed in the light and shadow of the late-afternoon sun.

"Oh, how beautiful," Eugénie sighed, crouching down to cradle a deep-pink cabbage-sized peony in her hands. Its radiant color seemed to pulse in a shaft of sunlight. "Mmmm, the fragrance!" She looked up at Bridger to see him smiling down at her, a tender look in his eyes.

"If only I were an artist," he said, gazing at her, "I'd capture you forever just as you are right now, your eyes shining, your face flushed with delight, surrounded by these beautiful flowers."

Eugénie laughed and rose to her feet. "Ah, my poet. Fortunately, the lovely portrait you paint doesn't include The Roan's strong perfume that clings to me."

"Since the artist reeks of a similar perfume, he's completely oblivious to yours," Bridger chuckled. "Come, let's go freshen ourselves and see if the cuisine measures up to the gardens."

The inn's fare was plain, but carefully prepared. A serving maid hovered nearby, whisking away each course almost before they had put down their forks. Their wineglasses were replenished so often that Eugénie began to feel giddy.

"What they lack in artistry, they more than make up for in efficiency. What's more, I don't remember ever enjoying a roasted pigeon as much. Perhaps the wine has dulled my memory." Eugénie giggled and raised her goblet to toast Bridger. "Or perhaps it's the company that adds the special spice." A shadow crossed her face. "Or maybe it's the sum of the day."

"How is that, dear heart?" Bridger asked, interlocking his fingers with hers.

She looked off through a lace-curtained window, then drew her gaze back to him. "As much as I dearly love the château and my people," she said softly, "to spend a day away from all of it gives me such a lift; to be with you, riding in the countryside; to be a part of the mission, a mission that I believe will save my beloved France from political suicide. Oh, forgive me. I meant not to bring up any of that to spoil the day. As I was saying, the sum of this day and now the unexpected pleasure of this charming inn have given me such a feeling of lightness, a... *zut,* I haven't the words to express how I feel!"

"I see it in your face and in your eyes, which are far more eloquent than any words," Bridger said. "There's a light about you. It was what I saw in the garden that inspired what you called my poetry."

"*Mon chéri,* I'll hold your words and this day close in my heart in the days to come." She reached across the table and put her hand over their linked fingers. Smiling into her eyes, Bridger raised their hands and kissed her fingers, one by one, as though learning their taste and texture for the first time. Gently putting her hand down, he beckoned to the serving maid, who came forward and curtsied.

"*Oui, Monsieur. Voulez-vous quelque chose?*"

"*L'addition seulement, s'il vous plaît, Mademoiselle. Nos soupers étaient délicieux! Merci beaucoup.*"

She colored prettily at his compliment and said in perfect English, "Madame and Sir, it was my pleasure to serve you."

Eugénie and Bridger crested the ridge that bordered the de Beaumont lands and paused to look across the pastures to the château. Aided by the moonlight, they could see the courtyard swarming with activity. Alarmed, they streaked across the field, down the long avenue of plane trees, and through the gates into a scene of pandemonium. The château was ablaze with light. Soldiers on foot were dashing back and forth while others on horseback were milling about dangerously close to the members of the household, who clustered together, trembling with fear.

Eugénie and Bridger sprang from their horses. Even in the chaos, Jamie's head and shoulders stood above the crowd. They rushed over to him where he was arguing vehemently with a soldier who was brandishing a pistol in the tall Scot's face.

Eugénie forced her way between the two men and confronted the soldier. "What's the meaning of this? Put down that pistol at once!"

Responding to her tone of command, the soldier stepped back, but quickly recovered himself. "Step aside, Madame! You're interfering with my investigation."

"Investigation! What investigation? By whose authority do you and these soldiers trespass on my property and disturb my household?" Turning her back on the soldier, Eugénie addressed her servant. "Jamie, *qu'est-ce qui se passe, ici? Qui sont ces hommes?*"

"Mistress, it's Monsieur Renaud. Captain Brion..."

Jamie's words were cut short as the captain seized Eugénie's arm and yanked her around to face him. "I'll ask the questions, Madame," he said sharply. Bridger and Jamie stepped forward, but before they could take action, Eugénie looked pointedly at the hand on her arm and slowly lifted her cold, silver gaze to the soldier's face. He had the grace to drop her arm and look chagrined.

"Captain Brion," she said quietly, "I'm Eugénie Devereux, the chatelaine of Château de Beaumont. I'll have a suitable explanation for your presence or I'll go this minute to the proper authorities and have you brought up on charges of trespassing."

Brion started to speak, thought better of it, took a deep breath, and said, "Madame Devereux, I apologize. I wasn't aware to whom I was speaking. I and my company were sent here to investigate the sudden disappearance of Monsieur Marcel Renaud."

"Disappearance?" Eugénie asked, startled. "He was here this morning."

She looked questioningly at Jamie, who shrugged and replied, "Mistress, I'm completely in the dark. He left after noon, saying that he was going to an important meeting. *C'est tout.* He's in the habit of coming and going, sometimes for days at a time. I thought nothing of his absence this evening."

"Captain?" Eugénie asked, turning to Brion.

"I was called in to investigate when he failed to arrive at his meeting. This was a very crucial one, according to his associates, who agreed that he was conscientious to a fault and overzealous in his attention to his obligations. After exhausting what information there was in Bordeaux, we were dispatched here to the château, where I was told that he's been residing."

"In the middle of the night?" Eugénie said incredulously. "Surely, Captain, the morning would have sufficed, which would have saved my household from being thrown into such an uproar."

"We were told to move with all speed because there's reason to believe that some misfortune may have befallen Monsieur Renaud. When we arrived, only a short time before your return"—he paused, his gaze flicking over to Jamie—"your man here was obstructing my investigation by refusing entry to the residence."

"And rightfully so," Eugénie retorted. "Monsieur Renaud has been staying in the overseer's cottage, which stands quite a distance from the château. There's no reason for you to investigate this building."

"I fear we must search the whole property. According to one of your grooms, Monsieur Renaud's mount returned to the stableyard early this evening, but, as yet, there's no sign of Renaud himself."

"Captain Brion, if Monsieur Renaud has met with foul play, which, to this point, hasn't been established, I'll do everything in my power to assist you. In the meantime, my household is my first concern. You and your men may set up camp on my land tonight, or you may depart and return on the morrow. There'll be no investigation of this property this night. My people have been disturbed enough as it is. I leave you in Jamie's capable hands to make your arrangements." Without waiting for Captain Brion to agree or disagree, Eugénie and Bridger made their way through the congested courtyard and disappeared into the château.

"*Sacrebleu!* Where can that wretched man be? His presence is aggravating enough, and now his absence has thrown us all into a turmoil." Eugénie let out a long breath, as she breakfasted with Bridger, Jamie, and Marie the following morning. "No doubt he fell off his horse and is lying under some hedgerow as we speak. He's an abominable horseman. It's a miracle something hasn't happened to him before this. As if there weren't enough to contend with already, now we have the captain and his men to deal with. We must get to the bottom of this as quickly as possible so we can return to more serious matters."

"They made camp in one of the southwest pastures," Jamie informed them. "I expect we'll be graced with the captain's presence before long." At that moment a servant appeared in the doorway.

"Yes, Maisie?"

"Oh, Mistress," Maisie answered, wringing her hands, "someone's been in Monsieur Renaud's apartment!"

"Oh, dear God, what next! Marie, kindly go with Maisie and let me know what you find. I simply must finish the accounts before the captain arrives, which, I've no doubt, will be all too soon."

Eugénie had hardly settled at her desk when Marie, without her usual composure, hurried into the room.

"Monsieur Renaud's rooms have been ransacked, his papers and belongings strewn every which way. Even the furniture has been turned upside down."

"When was the last time anyone was in his apartment?" Eugénie asked, trying not to sound alarmed.

"Yesterday, after he departed. He barked at one of the girls earlier for disturbing him. He was particularly cantankerous all day, taking every opportunity to jump down anyone's throat who happened to cross his path. Jamie was thoroughly fed up with him by the time he left. Also, he was acting even more secretive than usual. I came across him more than once muttering to himself and looking furtively around."

"Maybe there's more to this than I thought. This is bound to bring suspicion down on the château."

"Should I send the girls to straighten his rooms?"

"No, we'd best leave them as they are. The captain will think the worst if we put them in order."

A short time later Eugénie heard booted footsteps coming down the hall. She rose and met the captain at the doorway. *"Entrez, s'il vous plaît,"* she said pleasantly.

Looking fresh in spite of the short night, the soldier bowed to her and walked into the room. *"Bonjour,* Madame Devereux. I've come to discuss my plan for the investigation. But, before I can speak about that, something has come to my attention that we must discuss first."

Anticipating him, Eugénie said, "If you're referring to the ransacking of Monsieur Renaud's rooms, it was reported to me early this morning. I posted a guard and, since then, they have not been disturbed."

"Eh bien. At the conclusion of our conversation, I'll personally

go to investigate. As to the broader investigation, over the course of the next few days, my men will scour the pastures, vineyards, and forests for any sign of Monsieur Renaud. Concurrently, two of my men and I will search each building on this property. I apologize in advance for any inconvenience this may cause you and your household, but I expect to have the full cooperation of you and your people."

Eugénie matched his cool tone. "You'll have our full cooperation. I'd add but one requirement to the plan you've outlined. An equal number of my people will join your men in searching the property and the buildings. You're an intelligent man, Captain. I'm sure that you understand the need for this."

He nodded. "That I do. It will be as you suggest."

"Bon," Eugénie said with a smile. "Let's assemble our people in the courtyard and carry out this distasteful task as quickly as possible." Eugénie rose, pulling her shawl more closely about her, and motioned to the soldier. "After you, Captain."

In short order, the château's people and the soldiers were gathered in the courtyard awaiting instructions. Eugénie and Captain Brion stood at the top of the steps looking out over the two groups that were jostling each other and exchanging glares and sharp words.

"Captain, it might be best if you announce the plan and I'll follow with instructions for my people."

"Merci, Madame. I appreciate your diplomacy."

The captain's voice rang out and his words were clear as he outlined how they would proceed. When he said that the château people would be part of the search parties, grumbling swept through the soldiers' ranks.

"We'll carry this out to completion in a cooperative spirit," he announced. "If I hear of one of my men so much as looking askance at the people of the château, that man will be confined to barracks in the blink of an eye."

Eugénie stepped forward and looked slowly around at the assembled faces. "Captain Brion, my people will cooperate with you and your men in every regard." The message was clear to her people.

The large group broke into smaller search parties with no further incident. While the units spread out to their assigned locations, Eugénie sent Marie to speak to each woman servant to ask if any had seen a stranger at the château the day before. She sent Jamie to ask the men the same question. No information was forthcoming. The long morning turned into a longer afternoon and evening. A section of breached fencing was discovered, but it led to nothing.

XXIV

The following afternoon, Captain Brion arrived with dogs. They created a stir, first sniffing one of Renaud's nightshirts, then running in circles in his cottage and wreaking even more havoc. Brion herded them outside and, with Eugénie and Bridger, followed the hounds on horseback. Baying and keening, the dogs tore down the road for a short distance, then dashed into the woods.

It was there that they found him, his body crumpled at the base of a tree, his eyes staring sightlessly up at the canopy of branches above him, strangled by a kerchief tied so tightly that the purpled skin bulged on either side of it.

"Dear God," Eugénie gasped. "The poor man. Why would anyone want to kill such a harmless person?"

"Ah, Madame, harmless he was not," Captain Brion replied as he struggled to restrain and leash the dogs. "I've learned since we last talked that he was an information collector *par excellence.* There were many who feared him and will celebrate his death, but only one, the one who silenced him, who took the ultimate step. I will find that one. With Renaud's death, we may conclude that it was his killer who went to Renaud's apartment to find incriminating evidence. I'll post one of my men there. I believe whoever killed him was unsuccessful in his first pass and will return."

"Surely he won't take that risk. It's no secret that you and your men are at the château."

The captain smiled mirthlessly. "He's a desperate man and I intend to encourage him to take that risk by appearing to withdraw with my men and making a big show of it. Fear not, the château will be well guarded, unseen, but well guarded nonetheless."

Bridger, who had crouched down to look more closely at the unfortunate Renaud, stood up and said, "Monsieur Renaud was quite the dandy. He wouldn't have owned such a kerchief, much less worn it to an important meeting."

"Bridger, you're quite right!" Eugénie exclaimed. "His personal vanity was monumental. He'd never have worn such a coarse fabric. He was forever saying that his skin was so sensitive he could only wear the finest silks, linens, and woolens. He was constantly complaining about his bedding. Now that I look at it more closely, I would swear the pattern isn't even French."

"A foreigner!" the captain exclaimed. "This becomes more and more interesting. But, foreigner or not, I will apprehend him—that I promise you. Madame Devereux, please accept my apologies for all the distress we're causing you. It would appear that we've solved the mystery of Monsieur Renaud's disappearance. If you'll bear with me but a brief time longer, I trust we'll soon have his murderer in custody and can leave you in peace."

Eugénie nodded and said, "Captain, that is my fondest hope. I'll return to the château and report our sad findings to my people and call off the search parties."

"If you would, please send some of my men back with a wagon so I can attend to Monsieur Renaud." Leaving the captain gingerly untying the telltale kerchief, Eugénie and Bridger rode swiftly back to the château.

Late that evening, true to his word, Captain Brion and his soldiers departed, with the wagon bearing Monsieur Renaud's body in tow.

"I feel terrible when I think of my last moments with Monsieur Renaud. I treated him so harshly," Eugénie said a few days later as she and Bridger sat having their breakfast on the terrace in the warm sunshine.

"If what the captain said is true," Bridger replied, "he was a reprehensible character, in over his head, a thoroughgoing rude scoundrel, who used his secrets to bully and threaten. Well, he finally pushed one of his victims too far. Didn't you wonder how such a lowlife had the means to dress in such a fashion or how someone of so little intelligence had progressed so far?"

"Bridger! Really! You think Renaud stooped to bribery?"

"Dear one, for someone of your wisdom and intelligence, you can be such an innocent." At Eugénie's outraged expression, he was quick to add, "Sweetheart, I don't insult you. That such motives never occur to you speaks to your innate integrity and honest nature."

"There are more and more Renauds since the revolution began. He seemed much like many others—no more, no less," she said, somewhat appeased.

"Well, happily now there's one less."

"Bridger, how callous!" She toyed with the plate in front of her. "I never even made the effort to find out if he had a family, anyone he loved or who loved him."

Bridger took her hand, turning it over to kiss the palm. "Sweeting, there are so many reasons that I love you, your tender heart not being the least of them."

Eugénie laughed. "One minute you insult me, the next you court me with pretty words." She cupped his face with her hands and kissed him softly on the lips. "Whatever am I to do with you?"

His lips curved. "Madame, I have a ready answer for you."

"You rascal! I certainly stepped into that one, didn't I?" She returned his smile, but then her expression turned serious. "I feel so on edge, the shadowy figures gliding through the darkness, watching us as much as they watch for Renaud's killer." She shivered. "A goose just walked over my grave. I pray the murderer's caught, and caught soon, before my nerves are completely shattered. The charade of normalcy we all play is taking its toll on everyone."

With a lightning change of subject, she continued, "By now, Jeremy must be in Paris. I haven't had a moment to think about him. I don't dare send a messenger for fear he'll be intercepted and interrogated by our 'phantom soldiers.' Perhaps I'm blowing things out of proportion."

Bridger shook his head. "If anything, you're taking all this remarkably in stride. Your world is upside down. Nothing is as it used to be. Danger is your constant companion. You're a revolutionary at odds with most of your peers, viewed suspiciously by those for whom you risk so much. Marauders travel freely in the countryside.

The château, your haven, is invaded from the outside by forces beyond your control. And you feel on edge? Dear lady, your fortitude in the face of it all is nothing short of a miracle."

Once again, the château people were called into the courtyard. They milled about, nervously questioning each other. Had another crisis occurred? Had Renaud's murderer been apprehended? Why had the chatelaine called them together?

Eugénie raised her hands to quiet them. "It's been several days since the soldiers withdrew, leaving a guard at the overseer's cottage. Renaud's murderer is still at large. The presence of the guard must not give any of us a false sense of safety. Avoid being abroad after dark. Even inside the walls, travel in pairs, and under no circumstances venture beyond the walls until this is over. I would never forgive myself if something happened to one of you."

Far back in the crowd, the young servant girl Nicole looked furtively at her lover, who stood with his friends a short distance away. Feeling her gaze, he turned slightly towards her, their eyes met, and he dipped his head. *Bon,* we meet as planned. She smiled, the danger mentioned by her mistress heightening her excitement.

Eugénie paused, looking out over her people. "I'm tardy in thanking each and every one of you for your steadfastness during these trying days. God willing, they'll be over soon."

A high, piercing scream ripped through the night. Eugénie shot up in bed. *"Jésus! Qu'est-ce que c'est que ça!"* She scrambled into the clothes that were laid out on the chair by her bed, grabbed her pistol, and dashed out of the room, colliding with Bridger. They hurried down the stairs and out into the moonless night. Others with torches had already congregated in the courtyard, fear etched on their faces. Eugénie seized the nearest torch.

"Go back! Return to your homes and stay there until I send word!" she shouted. Seeing Jamie, she rushed over to him. "See that my orders are obeyed." Bridger grabbed her arm.

"Eugénie, stay here and look after your people. Jamie and I..."

Interrupting him, she yelled, "No, you will not! Get out of my way! I don't have time to argue with you!" Yanking her arm free, she ran across the courtyard and through the gate. In a few strides, Bridger caught up with her.

"I should have known better than to try to stop you. If you're hell-bent on being foolhardy, you'll not do it alone."

They slowed their pace as they approached the forest, cocking their heads to listen.

"There," Bridger whispered, "I hear something over there. Follow me." They crept into the woods, veering to the left. After a few steps, Eugénie heard the thrashing sound that had caught Bridger's attention. It was coming from the direction of the overseer's cottage.

Suddenly, a voice boomed out, "Stand back or I kill her!"

Bridger and Eugénie froze and looked around, but saw nothing. Bridger pointed to himself and motioned to the left. Eugénie nodded and continued forward towards the cottage. As she broke through a curtain of branches, her torch illuminated a clearing where four soldiers had their pistols trained on a stranger, who was squatting down and holding a knife to the servant Nicole's throat. He squinted at the light, but didn't loosen his grip.

"Back! Back!" he bellowed.

Eugénie's mind registered the foreign accent as she quickly took in the scene around her. Both Nicole and the servant Pétion were bound hand and foot. The boy appeared unconscious, blood seeping from a gash on his forehead. The soldiers started to move in, circling the desperate man. He suddenly lurched to his feet, dragging Nicole up with him, using her as a shield.

"I kill before, I kill again, if..." His words caught in his throat as a shot rang out. A look of shock crossed the man's face just before his eyes rolled back. The knife fell from his hand and he slumped forward, collapsing on top of Nicole.

Eugénie ran over and pulled the dead man off her servant. Nicole crumpled into her mistress's arms, weeping piteously, as Bridger strode through the trees, a pistol dangling from his hand. Eugénie sent him a grateful look before turning to the soldiers.

"You may dispose of the body in any way the captain sees fit." She pointed to the scarf tied around the dead man's neck. "Please bring to his attention the similarity of this kerchief to the one that was used to kill Monsieur Renaud." Eugénie turned, unbound the weeping Nicole, and led her gently back towards the château. Bridger hoisted Pétion up on his shoulder and followed them.

Early the next morning, Eugénie, Bridger, and Jamie were in the morning room discussing the events of the night before. Marie came through the doorway, followed closely by Captain Brion. He bowed to Eugénie.

"Madame, I'm truly sorry that my men weren't able to inter-cept the Austrian before he attacked your people."

"No permanent harm was done, Captain. It seems you've learned the identity of Renaud's murderer. He was the killer, was he not?"

"Yes, he was. He was an Austrian spy. I've learned the whole sordid sequence of events. Renaud had learned his identity and purpose. Instead of turning the man over to the authorities, as he should have, he approached him and threatened to expose him unless he agreed to pay Renaud an exorbitant bribe."

Eugénie and Bridger exchanged a glance. "Don't look so smug," she said to him under her breath.

"Pardon, Madame?"

"It's nothing, Captain, please go on," Eugénie said sweetly, smiling up at him.

Startled by her sudden warmth, the captain stammered, "Um, uh, I'm here to report these findings to you and to assure Captain Goodrich that no charges will be brought against him for ridding the district of that miscreant. Also, I'm happy to report that this is the last you'll be seeing of my men and me. I commend you for the shining example you set during this whole affair. Your strength of character exemplifies the best of our revolution. Should there ever be any occasion when my men or I can be of any assistance to you in the future, you have only to ask. If there's nothing more, I'll take my leave."

"Thank you for your kind words, Captain Brion." Listening to his stilted delivery, it was all Eugénie could do to keep a straight face. "I sincerely hope there'll be no need to call on your services in the future."

Captain Brion bowed, turned on his heel, and left the room.

XXV

Taking in the sounds and smells around him, Jeremy sauntered along the congested street clogged with pedestrians and conveyances of every size and shape—the ripe smell of offal and garbage almost unbearable in the stifling summer heat; the din of vendors hawking their wares vying with the clatter of wagon wheels and wooden clogs; the familiar sight of mangy dogs scratching in the gutters for scraps. Ah, the joys of Paris in the summer! he thought, dodging a wagon. Beneath his nonchalant manner, his eyes missed nothing.

As he approached the arcades of the Palais-Royal, a filthy urchin tugged on his sleeve, imploring him with huge, red-rimmed eyes. Jeremy dropped a few coins into the grimy outstretched hand. The little beggar blinked twice as if surprised at the unexpected windfall and melted quickly into the crowd. Jeremy understood the signal. The king's man has arrived at the café. Without appearing to, Jeremy increased his pace and was soon entering Café de Foy, the popular gathering place for students and hotheads.

The midday regulars were well ensconced. We certainly won't

have to worry about being overheard in this racket, he thought, as he sighted the king's man sitting at one of the less-crowded tables. He worked his way through the room, making a show of looking for an open seat. A serving maid sidled up to him, smiling provocatively. He returned her smile and lightened her tray of an overflowing tankard of ale.

He threw down a few coins and said, *"À tout à l'heure, peut-être, mademoiselle."* She tossed her head and moved off in the direction of her next quarry. Quaffing the brew, Jeremy arrived at the table and tapped the courier on the shoulder.

"Pardonnez, Monsieur. Is this seat taken?"

"Non, non. Asseyez-vous, s'il vous plaît."

Jeremy sat down and the two men struck up a conversation befitting new acquaintances. When Jeremy was sure that no one was showing any interest in them, he lowered his voice and asked, "Pierre, what's come of the matter we discussed when we met last?"

"It's going forward with all speed," the man replied. "It's planned for two months and three days before the friar's birthday. *Entre nous,* I didn't think the old man had it in him." Pierre chuckled as Jeremy calculated back from August 23, the birthday of Louis XVI. His eyes widened.

"Mon Dieu, that's but a week away! Have you made the arrangements I spoke of?"

Pierre nodded. "Yes—and in spite of him, I might add. He wanted to forgo an escort, but, when I pointed out how dangerous travel has become and what could happen to his sister and her children, who're accompanying him, he relented. He was very relieved that you'd be one of the escorts. I've chosen the others extremely carefully. But what of you? Won't you be missed?"

"I laid the groundwork for the possibility of absences when I first arrived. Monsieur Georges understands. I must announce my departure to him immediately, so he won't see any connection between mine and that of the friar, next week."

"You'll share my lodgings in the meantime."

"Ah, Citizen, it's been a pleasure," Jeremy said, raising his voice, "but I must be off. I've a harsh taskmaster, who, I've no doubt, is tapping his foot at this very minute."

"Speaking of feet," Pierre said jocularly, "as a cobbler, I couldn't help but notice that the Parisian streets have taken their toll of your shoes. If your master can wait but a little longer, you can accompany me to my shop and I'll outfit you with some new ones."

Jeremy resisted smiling at Pierre's clever ruse and clapped him on the back. "Lead away! What are a few harsh words, when my vanity is at stake?"

Jeremy looked around the small, drab room that would be his quarters for the week. Dropping his sack on the floor, he flopped down on the plain trestle bed to test it. Lying back, he rested his head on his crossed arms and reviewed the plan that Pierre had mapped out. *So, the royal family is planning to escape. I pray I won't rue the day, but Mistress Eugénie's message was clear: that I'm to protect and assist them in any way I can. Monsieur Fersen's plan seems simple enough. Odd that he, an officer in the Swedish regiment of the French army and a favorite of the queen, if not her lover, should play such a central role in the matter. Already* the queen's making changes, demanding one large, cumbersome *berline* for the whole family instead of Fersen's recommendation of two coaches, which would be immeasurably faster and safer with the king and queen separated.

Will the king be able to carry off his disguise as a valet simply by wearing a round hat and a plain coat? Will his poor eyesight give him away? *Et le pauvre petit Dauphin* dressed like a girl? *Mon Dieu!* The idea of the queen's reversing roles with the children's governess is just as preposterous. Will the long-suffering Madame de Tourzel be convincing as the fictitious Baronne Korff, supposedly on her way to Frankfurt with her retinue? Will their papers pass muster? At least "nurse" Madame Elisabeth will be there with her quick wits in case her brother bungles. All of this, to travel to a misbegotten garrison in the Austrian Netherlands. How has it come to this?

Jeremy frowned, remembering the touching scene he had inadvertently witnessed when, as Danton's messenger, he had delivered to the king yet another humiliating demand from the Assembly and had seen the queen prostrate herself before her husband.

Weeping pitifully, she had cried, "No, no! No more! How long will you suffer these indignities? How long will you offer up yourself to these monsters, who pick you apart, piece by piece? When will you stand your ground and say, 'Enough!' I beg of you, I beg of you, if you won't look to your own safety, think of the children—think of your family!"

The king had gently raised his wife to her feet, Jeremy recalled, and, lifting her chin, had looked down into her streaming eyes and nodded. That was the moment the die was cast. And we're but the pawns in their play. Will our sacrifice save them, should it come to that? On that note, he turned over and fell into a deep sleep.

Shortly after the midnight chime, Axel Fersen and Jeremy spirited the king out of the palace and past the guards. The night was moonless. Jeremy could barely see his hand in front of his face. Silently, they navigated the gardens of the Tuileries without mishap and slipped into the grove of trees where Jeremy could faintly make out the silhouette of the large coach. He heard the rattling of the six posthorses' traces. "At least," he said under his breath, "we'll get off to a good start, since I chose each beast myself, for speed and stamina."

The king stumbled climbing into the coach and would have fallen, had Jeremy not rushed over and caught him. Jeremy braced himself to hoist the king's bulk up into the carriage, where he was met by the gleeful whispers of his children.

"Where's their mother?" the king whispered to his sister, Elisabeth.

"*Je ne sais pas,*" she answered worriedly.

The minutes stretched on with no sign of the queen.

"*Zut,*" Jeremy muttered. "Where can she be? Did she lose track of time? Did she lose her way in the dark? Was she found out and detained?" His nerves were strained to the breaking point. He couldn't stand still any longer. He made his way over to Fersen, whose anxiety was palpable, and whispered, "Shall I go back and look for her?"

"I don't know. I don't . . . " They heard footsteps approaching. Gripped with fear, they turned in the direction of the sound.

The queen staggered towards them.

"I thought I'd never make it!" she gasped, her breath rasping in her throat. "First, I saw Lafayette's carriage, but I managed to keep him from seeing me. Then, I got completely confused and lost my way, going down one path after another. But, thank God, I'm here now! Are the babies safe? The king?"

"Yes, Your Royal Highness," Fersen answered, his voice light with relief. "Come, we must leave at once," he said, gently handing her up into the coach. She turned and touched his sleeve. "Fear not, I'm accompanying you," he said as he closed the carriage door. The escort mounted their horses and the entourage set off for Porte Saint-Martin and all points northeast towards Montmédy.

Instead of making a headlong dash, the unwieldy coach lumbered along at a snail's pace, which set Jeremy's teeth on edge. They traveled through the night without incident. At dawn, woefully behind schedule, they reached Meaux, only 26 miles into a journey of more than 200 miles.

"At this rate," Jeremy muttered, "we'll be fortunate to reach the border by Bastille Day."

The soldier riding beside him chuckled. "I see you've not enjoyed the experience of traveling with the family before. This is record-breaking speed, compared to their usual pace." He winked at Jeremy. "'Monsieur Durand' seems quite jovial. I overheard him teasing 'the governess' about the state of her buttocks, jostled about as she's been. I heard only a choked response. No doubt, her complexion turned well nigh the shade of a beet. Between you and me, his humor has always been a source of friction between them."

The dark covered Jeremy's embarrassment. He managed to say, "They may concern themselves with such trifles as their bums, but there's another part of my anatomy that's wedged in my throat and will be there until we safely deliver them to their destination."

They continued on their way through the countryside as morning turned into afternoon. Much to Jeremy's relief, they only made a short stop in Châlons at five o'clock, in an effort to make up some time. His spirits lifted as he looked out over the peaceful landscape of ripening vines, which reminded him of the Bordeaux. They had seen little traffic along the way, and none that took any notice of them.

The road leveled out and the coachman urged the horses faster. Too late, he saw up ahead a narrow bridge veering off to the right. To no avail, he pulled back on the reins. The carriage careened across the bridge. With a sickening crunch, one of the wheels caught a stanchion. The coach came to an abrupt halt, the harness straps snapped, and the horses collapsed to their knees.

The king staggered down from the carriage to survey the damage. After conferring with the coachman, he clambered back into the coach and emerged a moment later with a map. "By the time we make the repairs, we'll be even further behind schedule," the king groaned. "At this rate, how will we reach Pont de Somme-Vesle in time to meet Marquis de Bovillé's military escort? I despair that more than this wheel has come off our journey."

"Sir," Jeremy said, stepping forward, "if I may suggest, I'll go ahead and inform them of this accident and prepare them for your delayed arrival."

"Excellent! Excellent!" the king said, clapping Jeremy on the shoulder. "I'm more and more in your mistress's debt. *Ça va!*" He tore a button from the vest that was concealed by his plain coat. "Here, this'll identify you as my messenger. Go, go with all speed!" Jeremy bowed, dashed back to his horse, swung into the saddle, and galloped off.

XXVI

Jeremy arrived at his destination in record time. He entered the village and looked around. The promised escort was nowhere to be seen.

"Zut alors," Jeremy cursed under his breath. He dismounted in front of the local tavern, tied his horse up to the hitching post, and entered the drinking establishment. Sauntering up to the bar, he let his gaze travel around the room and saw the patrons clustered together talking excitedly. The proprietor, his ham-sized hands braced on the wooden surface, looked Jeremy up and down.

"What'll it be?" he asked in an unfriendly tone.

"An ale, if you please, sir," Jeremy answered blandly, noting the man's reaction to seeing a black man in gentleman's clothes, the revolution notwithstanding.

When the mug was thumped down in front of him, Jeremy said, adopting the colloquial speech pattern, "'Tis a fine establishment ye have here. No wonderin' you draw such a crowd." He raised the tankard, gesturing with it to the still-glowering man. "To you and yours, sir. May your days stretch out before you just as fair as this one." He took a long swallow. "What do I owe you for this fine refreshment?" In answer to the man's reply, Jeremy placed several coins on the bar, substantially more than was called for, but not enough to cause suspicion. The bartender's eyes gleamed and his manner warmed up considerably.

"*Merci beaucoup,* Citizen. Truth spoken, this crowd be here 'cuz of the excitement earlier this day."

"Oh? And what excitement might that be?" Jeremy asked mildly, showing no more interest than if his host were discussing the local crop.

The man leaned towards him. "We're a law-abidin' town. No need for those soldiers intrudin' in here disturbin' us. We pays our taxes and we lives our lives. No call and no cause." Jeremy nodded sympathetically, sipping his ale. "No call, I say. We came out in force and met 'em head on. Their leader said something I couldn't hear, but those 'at could said it didn't make no sense. They dallied around a while and then rode off. We showed 'em, we did. It was a thirst-makin' business, times bein' what they are. So, I reaps the benefit and pulls a few extras for the parched throats. It don't take too much," he confided behind his hand. "It's the most excitement we've had since old man Barnoit got drunk and fell into the livestock water trough."

Jeremy mentally rolled his eyes. "Seems clear to me why the good townsfolk might be stirred up over such a thing."

"They'll be settlin' down soon. Weren't so long since those troublemakers left. Truth be, you might've seen their dust as you came into town."

"Well, sir," Jeremy drawled, taking his last swallow and wiping his mouth with the back of his hand, "I'd best be gettin' on. 'Tis a long way I have to go before I can lay down my head. Workin' man can't be lingerin', no matter how good the company."

"Welcome, any time," the bartender said heartily.

As Jeremy made his way to the door, he looked back over his shoulder and was pleased to see that the man's attention was taken up by a group of townspeople leaning on the bar and chattering amongst themselves.

Now what do I do? Jeremy wondered, mounting his horse. Do I try to catch up with them or do I rejoin the royal family? The soldiers could have gone in any number of directions. Whatever I decide, I had best do it quickly before I become another source of interest for the good townsfolk. I think I'll press on. At best, I'll come on them, and at worst I'll reach the next stopping point and wait for the coach.

Jeremy halted his horse on the bank of the Aisne river, just outside of Sainte-Menehoulde. He had seen no sign of the soldiers. He slid down from his saddle. He pulled some bread and cheese out of his saddlebag, sat down on a large boulder, and prepared to wait.

The shadows lengthened as time wore on. Finally, his patience at an end, Jeremy stood up and began to pace. "It's going on eight o'clock," he said out loud to break the long hours of silence. "Where can they be? Were they waylaid in Pont de Somme-Vesle? Perhaps I should have waited for them there." At that moment, he heard the unmistakable sounds of rattling harnesses and hoofbeats and the coach broke through the trees, followed by the loyal escort.

The king's face lit up when he saw Jeremy, but sagged when he heard what the young man had to say.

"Then we'll have to proceed without them." Tapping the ceiling of the coach, the king yelled out of the window to the coachman, "Move on, sir, and make haste!" Falling back against the seat of the coach, he said under his breath, "Will this interminable day and interminable journey never end?"

As "Baronne Korff" presented her papers to officials in Sainte-Menehoulde, Jeremy went off in search of the elusive military escort. Again, the tavern proved to be a source of information, but this time it was far more disturbing. Jeremy hastened back to the entourage and was further alarmed to see one of the postmasters peering into the coach. Before he could be seen, Jeremy turned his mount, proceeded out of town, and took shelter behind a high wall. It was not long before the coach came into view. Jeremy gestured to the coachman to stop and quickly approached the carriage. The king leaned out of the window. *"Oui? Qu'est-ce qu'il y a?"*

"Sir, the news of your escape has preceded you!"

"Oh, dear God!" the king groaned. "I thought the procedures were excessive and that one postmaster seemed to take an undue interest in us. Well, we've no choice but to go on. Was there any word of the escort?" he asked hopefully.

"No," Jeremy admitted. *"Je suis très, très désolé."* The king, a stricken expression on his face, rapped sharply and the coach set off again.

Darkness fell as the desperate party flew through Clermont heading towards Varennes. A stunned silence had enveloped the weary travelers. Even the whimpering of the children had stilled, and the king and queen clutched each other's hand, staring straight ahead as if to will themselves to Montmédy.

When they arrived in Varennes, they were commanded to halt by an official, who walked up to the carriage and leaned in the window. "In the absence of the mayor, I, Procureur Monsieur Sauce, am acting in his stead. Worrisome rumors have reached me that force me to thoroughly scrutinize each and every traveler. Your papers, please." Once again, the papers were handed over. "*Merci beaucoup.* If you will follow me." Slowly the party descended from the coach.

Travel-stained and fearful, they followed Monsieur Sauce to an official-looking building. Leaving the escort in the vestibule, Sauce ushered the others into the mayor's office. He sat down behind an impressive desk and motioned for them to be seated while he examined the papers. After a few minutes, he looked up at them.

"Your papers appear to be in order." He stood up and extended them to "the Baronne." "You may continue on with your journey." His words were barely out of his mouth when a man rushed into the room. The king turned and his eyes widened with apprehension. He quickly schooled his expression, but his hand tightened on the arm of his chair.

"Monsieur Drouet, what is the meaning of this intrusion?" Sauce asked sharply.

"Detain these people!" Drouet commanded. "This man and this woman are the king and queen. They're attempting to flee to the border! I recognized them when they stopped in Sainte-Menehoulde. The royal family escaped Paris this very night. These people are they, disguised though they may be!"

"Sir, you are outside your jurisdiction. Their papers are in order. I cannot detain innocent people!"

"When the authorities learn that you had them and let them go, they'll show you little mercy! Why do you suppose they fled in this direction?" Drouet asked slyly. "Because, you dolt, it's the shortest distance to the border from Paris." He raised his voice and whirled, pointing a finger at the queen. "Where, no doubt, they'll be met by an army of her family, who've been looking for any excuse to invade France."

At his words, the queen shrank back and pressed a hand to her trembling lips. Taking a deep breath, she pulled her dignity around her and met her accuser's eyes with a cool stare.

Monsieur Sauce was clearly shaken, but still he spoke firmly. "I repeat, Monsieur Drouet, that you're outside of your jurisdiction. I'm taking these people to my house, where they'll stay until I can resolve this."

When Sauce led the group through the vestibule, the king pulled Jeremy aside, told him what had happened, and said quietly, "Keep your eyes peeled. You won't serve us if you're swept up in this. Inform your mistress of the outcome, which, I fear, will be most dire. God be with us all."

As the bedraggled party made their way to Sauce's house, they passed through streets lined with people holding torches and the local militia shouldering firearms. Some looked at them curiously, others with open hostility. They were shown upstairs. After settling the children down, the queen sat beside her husband and took his hand.

"Those sweet innocents, they're already fast asleep. May God bless and protect them," she whispered.

They had just nodded off when a knock sounded at the door. Monsieur Sauce strode in, followed by an old man, who instantly recognized his king and fell to his knees.

"Ah, Monsieur Destez, *un juge de paix,* from Versailles," the king said softly. He gazed kindly at his subject. "*Eh bien,* I am indeed your king." Pulling the distraught man behind him, Sauce left the room.

"*D'accord,*" the king said, turning to his wife. "*C'est ça.* We'd best get what rest we can. The morrow will tax us to our limits."

After spending a fitful night alternating between hope and despair, the king and queen were almost relieved when Monsieur Sauce arrived at their door as dawn's first light crept through the window. He bowed slightly and in an expressionless voice said, "Make yourselves ready and present yourselves downstairs."

Trailed by the little ones and the other members of their party, the king and queen moved with dignity into Sauce's small sitting room where Sauce, head bowed, a triumphant Drouet, and two other men stood waiting for them.

"Monsieur and Madame, we've come as messengers from the Assembly." The queen's eyes turned cold at the effrontery of the salutation. "It's the ruling of that body that you return to Paris under armed guard."

"The insolence of that 'august' body!" the queen hissed. The king shook his head without looking at her. The two men brushed past him and led the small party out to their coach. The king quickly looked around, scanning the crowd for Jeremy. Relieved not to see him, he turned and assisted the queen and the children into the coach. Settling himself beside his wife, the king fixed his gaze on his children sitting across from him and ignored both the throng of armed citizens who lined the streets and the Garde Nationale troops who fell in alongside the carriage as it started the long journey back to Paris.

XXVII

LATE JUNE 1791

Paris

"I'll have his resignation if not his head!" Georges Danton shouted to Robespierre, his audience of one. He stormed around the room, slamming his fist down on his desk for emphasis. "He, *le grand Marquis*," he snarled sarcastically, "only he, according to him, could bring Louis Capet to reason. Reason! When, in his coddled, decadent life, has he ever been exposed to reason?" He paused for breath, his huge head bristling with outrage.

"Citizen," Robespierre purred in his uniquely high-pitched voice, "we couldn't have designed the drama better. They've played right into our hands, with the Marquis, a convenient scapegoat, to boot." He smiled, as he used the end of a quill to scratch his scalp beneath his elaborately dressed hair. His eyes grew dark and cold. "Let's not forget that Citizen Capet is simply the goat of the hussy. It's she who's brought about his downfall. It's she who, like a worm in *La Patrie's* gut, wriggles this way and that, drawing unseemly attention to herself while feeding on the organs of *La Patrie,* laying *La Patrie* open to invasion by foreign hosts."

Watching his fellow member of the Jacobin Club, Danton saw a hot light flare in the eyes of the Deputy from Arras. He looked at him more closely, this man known for his consistency in a changeable world, for his "unimpeachable integrity," always being the champion of virtue and freedom in a world riddled with vice and tyranny, who, with his vaunted calm, seared his audiences with his righteous indignation. Was this man showing the first crack in his moral earnestness and exhibiting the emotions of lesser men? Danton tucked the thought away to chew on later.

Robespierre plucked an orange from one of the many bowls of oranges that were always at his fingertips. With a glance, he offered one to Danton, who shook his head. After examining the fruit, Robespierre tore into its skin, peeling off strips with intense concentration. Observing this, Danton felt strangely uncomfortable and looked away.

"Yes, yes," Robespierre murmured almost to himself, "the harlot is central to the plot that led to their ill-conceived flight, and we shall keep her there. Citizen, don't fret yourself unduly with the likes of Lafayette and Louis Capet. They are but small players in this drama. In the interests of *La Patrie,* it's our obligation to make this clear universally. *La Patrie,* first, foremost—*La Patrie,* above all else."

Jeremy, who was in the anteroom waiting to announce his return, heard the exchange between Danton and Robespierre. Not wanting to make his presence known, he slipped quietly from the room.

"Your network of informers, Danton, must be ever zealous," Robespierre said, delicately wiping his fingers on the linen square at his elbow. "Your reports of foreign troops assembling at our northern and eastern borders have been invaluable. A situation is building that we cannot deny much longer, except to our own detriment. The voice of Paris speaks when her citizens destroy symbols of the king and the monarchy.

"This flight, this egregious deed, has once and for all undermined our more moderate political brethren's faith in a constitutional monarchy. Even Condorcet has abandoned that myth. He is now actively working to end the institution of the monarchy. Yes, Citizen Danton, we—you and I—chosen instruments of *La Patrie,* need only bide our time and wait for the opportune moment to help her enemies, both from within and from without, to defeat themselves. If I read the signs correctly, we've not long to wait. *La Patrie,* the new France, will rise victorious!"

Jeremy walked down the street watching the rockets, squibs, and serpents, which were set off to celebrate the capture of the king and queen, lighting up the night sky. He slipped into a raucous, smoke-filled café, bought a tankard of ale, and sat back to listen to the gossip.

"And, then, at Epernay," someone was saying, "their coach was stopped to pick up Barnave and Pétion, who, representing the Assembly, were sent to escort them back to Paris. Now, listen to this. Those officials didn't ride alongside. They didn't sit on the seat facing the king and queen. *Non! Sans permission,* they sat themselves down right there between them!"

Shocked at the cavalier disregard for the long-held convention of the *ancien régime* that dictated the specific distance to be maintained from royalty, a nearby companion exclaimed, "*Non! Mon Dieu!* How the mighty have fallen!"

"Attendez! Ce n'est pas tout! When the Capets ate, Pétion and Barnave ate!"

"No!" the other breathed.

"Yes! And when nature called, when Pétion or Barnave needed to..., yes, yes, the coach stopped!"

How can this information have reached the man on the street even before the royal coach has arrived back in Paris? Jeremy wondered. And when were the monarchs' titles signifying respect and privilege dropped and replaced with "Monsieur and Madame Capet"? Jeremy's attention was suddenly drawn to another conversation.

"Look to yourselves, Citizens. Don't venture abroad without some way to protect yourself. Invading troops are massing at our borders, if they haven't actually breached them by now. I hear tell that Varennes has already felt the foreigners' wrath for capturing the Capets and sending them back to Paris. Look alive! You could pass one of them on the street, this very day! They disguise themselves cleverly and are infiltrating us on all fronts, in the Assembly, in the clubs... why, in this very café!" The speaker of these dire warnings and his companions whipped around wide-eyed, scanning the room.

Just then, a man crashed through the door, shouting, *"Allons! Allons! Ils viennent!"* The patrons scrambled to their feet and ran out of the café.

Jeremy was swept along with the crowd. When they arrived at the city gate, a huge throng had already gathered. Jeremy saw a sign that read, "Anyone who applauds the king will be beaten, anyone who insults him will be hanged." As the royal coach progressed slowly through the multitude, he noticed that most failed to remove their hats and that the Garde Nationale interspersed amongst the throng gestured their defiance with their rifles.

Jeremy waited a few days before going once again to Danton's office. He need not have worried that Danton would make a connection between his departure and the flight of the king and queen, so distracted was the man by the repercussions stemming from that flight and the subsequent return of the royal family.

Danton looked up as Jeremy entered the room. "Ah, you're back. I trust your errand was successfully concluded?" The question appeared to be rhetorical, since he continued on before Jeremy had a chance to reply. "Wait in the anteroom, if you will. This meeting shouldn't take much longer." Danton waved a sheaf of papers at the man sitting across from him. In the split second that Danton's guest had turned towards him, Jeremy recognized Antoine Barnave. Jeremy bowed, backed out of the room, and closed the door behind him.

Interesting, he thought—Danton's meeting with one of the leaders of the Feuillants. Considering that it's a very large, influential faction and one that's usually opposed to the stands taken by Danton, Robespierre, and Pétion, I can't think of anything that would bring these two men together, unless it has to do with the furor over the declaration the king left behind when he fled. I still don't understand why he did that. It has confounded his supporters as well as his enemies. Foolish man.

"In summary, then," Danton said to his guest, "the king's declaration seems to fall into two categories—the first being his litany of complaints: childish whining about feeling intimidated by some combination of things that, he says, caused him physical fear for his family and himself; complaints about the size of his allowance; and something about their accommodations at the Tuileries not being suitable for the royal family. Bosh!

"The second category is, by far, the more troublesome. He discusses the restraints placed on the monarchy by the Assembly's decrees and the paradox embodied in a constitution that sets forth a role for a monarch but gives him no power to carry out the role, including the power to make treaties, the power to appoint domestic and foreign representatives for France, and the power to lessen the extent of punishment. Have I summarized adequately?" Danton sent Barnave a penetrating gaze from beneath his heavy brows.

"More than adequately," Barnave said, nodding. "Do you suppose the declaration was meant to justify the flight?"

"Who can understand the twistings and turnings of that mind?" Danton went on. "How can we consider this declaration seriously when he apparently didn't, since he fled into the night for the nearest border, leaving the document behind to be accidentally discovered and read? The man is either a traitor or an imbecile, which is also my assessment of Lafayette, who allowed the family to slip right through his fingers! And now we have the Cordeliers, those extremists, screaming for 'tyrannicide,' as they call it."

Danton tore at his hair, adding to its already disheveled appearance. "As if we didn't have enough cooks stirring the broth already, now we have Cordorcet printing a translation of the revolutionary Tom Paine's pamphlet. He calls the king 'Louis Capet' and states that, by removing himself from the seat of government and fleeing, Louis collapsed the monarchy, thereby ipso facto establishing France as a republic, a nonmonarchical system. And now," Danton said, rolling his eyes, " 'Monsieur' d'Orléans is seeking membership in the Jacobins?"

"That one, the self-proclaimed Monsieur Philippe-Égalité," Barnave replied contemptuously, "is a weathervane that swings whichever way the wind blows. As for Paine, he always advocates the most extreme position. We might come to his thinking eventually, but not yet." Danton nodded in agreement.

"To return to the matter at hand, Citizen Danton, we must combine our resources in the Assembly before this wagon rattles off the track completely. I hear that your associate, Robespierre, embracing ambiguity, has expressed his view that the constitution that's under consideration offers France the best solution — a republic with a monarch." He shook his head. "Self-canceling, as I see it."

Danton, not wanting to be drawn into either defending or opposing Robespierre, said, "Since the role of the king is the center of the controversy, perhaps the most politic step is to replace him, at least for the moment, with some form of 'executive council.' "

Barnave looked skeptical and shook his head. "I fear, as do most in the Assembly, that deposing him, even temporarily, will lead to war with Austria."

"Perhaps it is too precipitous," Danton agreed, "but we must put forward something that will temper the emotional heat that's threatening to burst out into a full-fledged conflagration. What if we propose 'suspending' the king's role until we can finalize the constitution?"

A slow smile crept over Barnave's face. "That might be subtle enough to bring the members of the Assembly together and lower the temperature to the point that the constitution can successfully be completed. You realize that we are in actuality casting him aside, but using a pretty phrase to make it palatable?"

"Why don't we incorporate some words of another revolutionary, the master of pretty phrases, Mr. Jefferson?" Danton suggested, with an answering smile.

"Well put," Barnave said, saluting him. "I'll discuss this proposal with Duport and the Lambeths and together we'll work our people around."

"I'll take it to Robespierre and Pétion, and we'll do the same." The two men rose from their chairs and a rare look of accord passed between them. Danton moved around his desk, put an arm around Barnave's shoulders, and walked him to the door.

XXVIII

"Jeremy, we must celebrate this day, the thirteenth of September 1791!" Danton shouted above the din in the street. "Finally, finally, we have a constitution. Louis has accepted it. It is done! We'll float a hot-air balloon, complete with tricolor ribbons, to officially announce it. I predict there'll be dancing in the streets! The constitutional monarchy has arrived! And with it, those who sought a republican democracy are neutralized. We've created a nation in which all citizens are equal. Gone are the nobility, heredity, titles, and privilege. No longer will we fear popular insurrection or the martial law and bloodbath of July, for the people have emerged victorious! And we've saved the monarchy in the process, so we need not fear an invasion by the foreign forces at our borders. We've accomplished the impossible!"

"What of the clubs and the press?" Jeremy asked. "Have they sheathed their claws in this present state of euphoria?"

Danton looked sharply at Jeremy, but decided that his turn of phrase was more a matter of the young man's poor grasp of the language than an intended slight. "With the constitution in place, their purpose has been served. There's something to be said, though, for curtailing some of the more radical press. As for the clubs, their voices will always provide an important function for the state. Any attempt to curb them will be rejected summarily, although I've heard rumors of such from certain quarters. They'll come to nothing."

Danton was quiet for a moment, lost in thought. "The regulations of May and June that banned multisignature petitions and labor collectives are worrisome, but so far they've not been acted on, and I doubt they will. They're the weapons of those who'd seek to quell the politics of the street. We won't allow that to happen, even though those who champion the bans say that without them there'll be anarchy, pointing to the strikes and labor riots of last spring."

He made a derogatory sound in this throat. "Strikes and labor riots are elements of a free society and will be dealt with accordingly. Robespierre and I are in complete agreement on this. The constitution ensures freedom—of assembly, of speech, of the press. It's the job, then, of the leaders to protect these freedoms and to keep them within bounds. Also, he and I don't feel that the revolution is over, as some others do, merely because we have a living, breathing constitution. There's still much to be done to establish the government system in practice that now only exists as a blueprint on paper."

The two men strode on in silence. Jeremy mulled over Danton's words. Danton, his earlier elation somewhat diminished, pondered the schism that still existed between the disparate political factions that harbored differing political goals.

"There are those," Danton spoke so quietly that Jeremy had to step closer to hear, "who would have some 'ideal virtue,' as they call it, at any price, even at the price of the state's stability. Virtue cannot put food on the table or keep our enemies at bay. Virtue, I spit on it!"

One late afternoon, Marie hurried into the kitchen garden, where Eugénie was weeding a patch of herbs. "Mistress, a letter just arrived from Jeremy."

Eugénie stood up and took the letter from Marie's outstretched hand and began to read it out loud.

Jeremy wrote to Eugénie:

... Mistress, on September 29th, the Constituent Assembly was no more. Its last act was to vote on Le Chapelier's legislation, legislation that only the other day Danton was turning his nose up about, because, as he told me, it would narrow the freedoms of the clubs and place controls on popular political action, especially in Paris. It was a lively scene in the Assembly with Robespierre going after Le Chapelier. He used every tool at his disposal to drive home his point that such restrictions contradicted the constitution they had just passed, carrying on about France as a "republic of virtue" as though this "republic of virtue" was the panacea of all ills.

This "virtue" business doesn't sit well with Danton, I can tell you. It may eventually drive a wedge down the middle of the Jacobins. As far as I can see, this "virtue" does nothing but support mob violence. Danton and Robespierre are definitely at odds over the issue of "stability" versus "virtue." On this subject, Danton is closer to the moderate Barnave than Robespierre.

Now, France has a new governing body. It's called the Legislative Assembly. It has the prodigious responsibility of enacting the fledgling constitution. The Feuillants, led by Barnave, number 264; the Jacobins 136; but more than 400 Deputies aren't aligned with any particular faction. In spite of what Danton said the other day, there's a strong republican sentiment both inside and outside the Assembly. Barnave, Alexandre Lambeth, and Duport are doing everything in their power to quash it and strengthen the central core of the state to combat insurrection and counterrevolution. Although he doesn't publicly say so, I believe Danton is in total agreement with this. It seems to me that Robespierre, by contrast, is overjoyed with the mobs, the outrageous press, and the lack of discipline in the army and navy that keep Paris at a constant boiling point and that infect even the farthest corners of France.

Robespierre has started his own paper, *Le Défenseur de la Constitution,* as a convenient forum for his political voice. The man is gaining political force and influence. I wouldn't be surprised to see him heading up the whole thing before too long. I'm not sure that such a turn of events augurs well for those of a more moderate persuasion, but that remains to be seen.

Even with the constitution and the Legislative Assembly in place, Danton, Robespierre, and others hold the view that the revolution isn't over. As you can see, there's no unity of thought here. Will a spark set off this volatile powder keg? Or will some universal goal emerge? If so, in what direction?

I'll continue to keep a vigilant eye, but I pine for the Bordeaux. This Paris is stifling and it stinks of all manner of odors. I remain, your devoted servant . . .

"Dear Jeremy. Whatever would I do without his ears and eyes and his invaluable letters, more important now than ever? But," Eugénie sighed, "how I wish he were here in his beloved Bordeaux. What a price I exact from him."

"No more than you exact from yourself," Marie said, joining her mistress as Eugénie returned to weeding the garden. "If you had no obligations here, you would be in Paris. It's not your way to be on the sidelines."

"Ah, *c'est vrai,* Marie." Eugénie stood up again, stretching to relieve her protesting muscles. "This Robespierre appears to be more and more a force to be reckoned with. Speaking of men and their papers, have you read Monsieur Jacques-Pierre Brissot's *Patriote Français?*"

"No, I leave political rhetoric and such to Jamie."

"*Ma chère* Marie — ever the reluctant revolutionary," Eugénie said with a laugh, bending over again. "Unless I miss my guess," she said more seriously, "Brissot and his followers are emerging from our own region as a political force to be reckoned with, vying with the Jacobins as the most radical members of the Assembly. We know now that the Austrian spy's presence wasn't such an odd thing after all. Concerned as the Austrians are for the queen and the royal family, I'd be surprised if there isn't an active Austrian network throughout France, for that matter. The spy was here specifically to report on the activities of Brissot and his followers. Brissot is an outspoken republican, as are Armand Gensonné, Henri-Maximin Isnard, and Pierre Vergniaud. They were at the dinner I attended two weeks past. They're effective orators, especially Vergniaud. Using our regional name, they call themselves Girondists and are in the vanguard of the growing movement for a republic. Oh, Marie, it doesn't bode well for the future of the monarchy. Considering the implications of that movement, the continuing insults to the king by the Deputies, as bad as they are, pale in comparison.

"I've heard that the Deputies sit in his presence with their hats on in the Assembly and relegate him to an ordinary chair on the same level as the president. As if all that weren't enough for the poor king to bear, he's battling with the Assembly over proposed legislation to enact severe measures against the émigrés who have fled France and set up camps just beyond our borders, and to criminalize the priests, who refuse to swear an oath of loyalty to the state."

"Is it true," Marie inquired, "that, since the royal family's return from Varennes, there's been a flood of the nobility, the priests, and the military officers emigrating?"

"Indeed so. As many as a third of the officers have left France."

"*Mon Dieu!* I'd no idea it had reached such proportions." Marie looked at her mistress with alarm. "Jamie mentioned something about a declaration by Emperor Leopold. That it could mean war," she whispered.

Eugénie shook her head. "I don't know what the Emperor's intent was, but the effect is clear. It's fueled the growing fear of foreign invasion, and it's given the Deputies the excuse they needed to demand that the king's brothers return and that the émigrés' camps be broken up or else their lives will be forfeited and both their property as well as that of their family members still in France will be confiscated."

"Mistress, this government is proving to be as brutish as the one we overthrew."

"That it is, Marie, that it is. Each action both within our borders and without seems to be moving us closer and closer to the point of no return. Unless something happens to reverse the course, I believe war is inevitable. The foreign coalition now stands firmly behind the émigrés and the king's brothers, and our government runs headlong to meet them."

The weeding of the kitchen garden forgotten, the two women grasped hands and stared into each other's eyes. "Our revolution from the start has posed a threat to all the monarchies of Europe. Couple that with those monarchs' outrage at the treatment of Louis and his family..." Eugénie whispered, "I dearly hope our king and queen do nothing further to tip the balance."

Eugénie had no sooner sat down for dinner with some neighbors when a messenger, accompanied by Jamie, appeared at the doorway.

"Madame Devereux, pardon the interruption, but I think you'll want to hear the news this messenger brings."

Eugénie's fork paused in midair. "What news have you, sir?" she asked of the messenger, quietly putting down her fork.

The young man doffed his *bonnet rouge* and spoke quickly. "Madame Devereux, two days past on December 14th, the king appeared before the Legislative Assembly. He vehemently condemned any invasion of France by the European monarchs. His words were met with wild applause. Monsieur Brissot, head of the Diplomatic Committee, also made a speech, after which Monsieur Narbonne was empowered by the Assembly to prepare for war. The king was made Commander-in-Chief. Lastly, the Assembly issued an ultimatum to Austria, giving that nation until

March first to abide by the French-Austrian Treaty of 1753." His message delivered, the young man and Jamie withdrew, leaving Eugénie and her guests in a stunned silence.

Eugénie was the first to speak. "A tactful move by the king. He has nothing to lose. He's aligned himself with the French people against his brother-in-law, Emperor Leopold, which should spike rumors to the contrary. War can only play into his hands."

"I see your direction," said the man on her right. "If the war goes well, his authority increases as the Commander-in-Chief. Should it not fare well, however, he must believe that the Austrian coalition will invade France and restore him to the throne." Eugénie and the other guests around the table nodded in agreement.

After that night, messengers arrived daily at the château. Eugénie's head spun trying to keep track of the ministers in Paris who moved in and out of office as the nation prepared for the war that now seemed inevitable. Her worst fears were realized when a message came to report that the new ministry was composed almost entirely of Brissot and the Girondists, making the Assembly more warlike than ever. It was no surprise, then, when the next messenger informed her that the king's brothers had been declared traitors and their lands seized. What of the royal properties? she thought. Surely they wouldn't... Daily he's more and more isolated. What next?

She hadn't long to wait. On February 7, after France refused to comply with Austria's demands that full powers be restored to the king, that Alsace be released by France, and that Avignon be returned to the Pope, Austria formally declared her alliance with Prussia.

The date of France's ultimatum to Austria, March 1, came and went. When the Bordeaux region received the news that on April 20 the king had declared war on Austria, there was an orgy of celebration in the countryside. Eugénie held her breath, waiting for the moment when the celebrants realized the price they would be called on to pay.

The year 1792 witnessed a country spinning out of control, hurtling towards disaster. Early reports from the fronts were catastrophic. The French armies' lack of discipline made them impossible to command. With the armies in increasing disarray, many officers feared for their lives and either resigned or fled France. The combination of food shortages and the high prices for what was available brought the frequency of attacks on food sources to an all-time high.

One long day at the château succeeded another. Jamie oversaw the steady stream of wagonloads carrying foodstuffs leaving the château for the nearby villages. Eugénie and her people strove to satisfy the long line of beggars that grew longer by the day at the château's gate.

It was after one such day that Eugénie and Marie were in the library sewing. More and more over the last months, Eugénie had found herself seeking the quiet solace of that room. The strength of the dark wood paneling comforted her. Surrounded by her father's books and her mother's needlepoint cushions and pillows, she felt assured of the permanence of things. The portrait of her mother and father above the heavily carved mantelpiece brought them close to her and renewed her courage and her faith in her fellow man, a courage and faith that they had instilled in her. She looked up to see their eyes looking down at her and felt their presence.

The rapidity of the recent events had jarred Eugénie and shaken her to her core. Not even when she learned that her parents had died at sea had she been so thrown off kilter. She was alone in the world then, but still it was a world she knew and understood, a world her parents had prepared her for. She had easily assumed on her young shoulders the responsibilities incumbent in her role. Not even when she traveled across the Atlantic on a mission to learn the American patriots' purpose, and was caught up in the Bermudians' dangerous plot to aid the Americans, had she questioned her path or flinched from the certain risks she faced. She had met the challenges in her life. She had embraced them. They were the sum and substance of who she was and who she had become.

When had she learned fear? A primitive, pervasive fear that had crept in, catching her off guard, consuming her, a fear from which she had no protection.

"It's not for myself that I fear," she murmured so softly that Marie would not have heard the words had she not been watching her mistress closely, concerned by her stilled fingers and her bleak, expressionless eyes.

"What is it?" Marie asked, reaching over to clasp Eugénie's hand. Eugénie started at her friend's touch and turned towards her, her eyes refocusing.

"Marie, *ma chère,* I was just thinking back, thinking of all we've shared."

"Aye, 'tis easier than thinking of the days ahead."

"Are you ever afraid of what's happening or what may come of all this?"

Marie took a deep breath. She had never known her mistress to waver. She was deeply shaken by the fear in Eugénie's voice.

"No," she answered simply. "Jamie, Jacqueline, and you are my world. It's not my way to question what lies ahead. That's for others. So long as my days are filled with those I love and care for, whether in sunshine or in shadow, I'm content."

"Ah, Marie," Eugénie sighed, feeling the weight lift off her heart, "how like you to use the words of that beautiful ballad of war from Jamie's native land to express what I needed to hear. 'In sunshine and in shadow.' Let the shadows do their worst. *Chère amie,* you have restored me." Eugénie looked over at Marie and thought, not for the first time, You are truly a brave heart. Whatever would I do without you?

Marie's words sang in Eugénie's heart and buoyed her spirits as she rode out the following afternoon on The Roan. She was eager to test the speed and stamina of her old friend. The great horse pricked his ears and whinnied. Bridger, she breathed. Could it be? The long, endless days of his absence vanished as she reined in The Roan and looked out across the meadow. Faintly, she could make out a cloud of dust and two riders galloping towards her. Bridger! Jeremy! With a cry, she tapped the stallion with her heels and the eager horse took off at a gallop.

The three flung themselves from their saddles and threw themselves at each other, embracing tightly as though it had been a lifetime since they had last been together.

"Race you to the stables!" they cried in unison. Neck and neck, they tore into the stableyard and jumped from their saddles, laughing.

"You've both lost a step," Bridger observed loudly.

"My win!" Jeremy proclaimed.

"The Roan by a nose," Eugénie shot back at both men.

"We'll call it a draw," the three shouted simultaneously.

His honor restored, The Roan nuzzled Montross and his grandson, Thistledown, and led them with regal bearing towards the grooms who had rushed from the stables to see what all the commotion was about. They joined Eugénie in welcoming back the travelers, then affectionately clapped the horses on their rumps and led them away.

XXIX

By common accord, they decided to hold the world at bay for one evening and devote themselves to the pleasure of each other's company. Jeremy set the tone with his light banter. The supper that night had all the gaiety of bygone days. Eugénie looked around the table, relishing the moment and toasting each of them with her eyes — the ex-Virginian sea captain, the Bahamian horse trainer extraordinaire, the giant Scot, the steadfast servant and friend, their beloved daughter now coming of age, and I, she thought, looking inward, the French countess, now a revolutionary. We come from different heritages, but we are here now, together as we were meant to be.

She waited for the laughter at Jeremy's description of his latest outrageous exploit to die down.

"Please join hands," she said quietly, her eyes bright as she looked into each face, one by one. "Dear Lord, Our Heavenly Father, hear our prayer, we beseech Thee. We thank Thee for the laughter, family, friendship, and love we share this night. Bless this house and all the people within her walls, and all those who abide on this property that has fed, clothed, and sheltered so many for so long through Thy bountiful goodness. Give us strength and courage in the days to come. Help us to know Thy will and to see Thy will be done. Bless this country, this France. In the name of Thy Son, Our Lord Jesus Christ, we pray. Amen."

"Amen," echoed the others. Not another word needed to be said. She had said it all. They rose and embraced each other and retired for the night.

"In my recent travels from here to the coast and back again, two subjects seem to be on everyone's tongue," Bridger said at breakfast the next morning, buttering a crisp croissant. "The first is something called the 'Austrian Committee.' From what I could glean, it refers to anyone set on undermining France, whether they be Austrian or those they call false patriots."

Jeremy nodded. "I've heard the same. There's a hue and cry to root out these false patriots, these traitors, these 'Austrians,' and destroy them. The new symbol of the true patriot is the *bonnet rouge*. Even some officers in the armies are wearing it instead of the tricorn."

"Yes," Eugénie murmured, "we've seen it worn here, in the marketplace. And the other topic, Bridger?"

"The second, no less alarming, is the rumor that there are forces in the country hell-bent on starving the people."

"I, too, heard this in my travels north and east of Paris," Jeremy agreed. "The same was true at every stop I made coming home."

Eugénie nodded, pressing her lips together.

"I've also noticed more and more people affecting the peasant dress," he added. "To be called *sans-culottes* is a badge of honor.

Breeches and hose are cast aside for fear of being linked to the old ways. Robespierre's the exception. Even though he persists in dressing in the old manner and powdering his hair or wearing a wig, his star continues to rise."

"I've seen the change of dress in increasing numbers," Jamie interjected. "More and more merchants and professional men are flocking to the new costume. And the sentiment in the street grows daily more disrespectful of the king."

"Before, it was the queen whose name and character were the target, but since that poor family was dragged back from Varennes, now the king is ridiculed, as well," Marie said sadly.

"Yes," Jeremy agreed. "In Paris, they call him Louis le Faux or Le Faux-Pas, but that's by far the least of it." Jeremy let out a long breath and took a sip of coffee. "For the first time, I truly fear for the king," he said quietly.

Eugénie's face paled. "What, Jeremy, what's happened?"

"Much has happened since my last letter," Jeremy replied. "To begin with, the king, as a gesture of his good faith, agreed to the Assembly's demand that he give up his personal guard."

"*Mon Dieu!* What could he have been thinking?" Eugénie exclaimed, her hand at her throat.

"There's more. Even as he agreed to this, he adamantly refused to withdraw his vetoes concerning the clergy and the émigrés. He vetoed the Minister of War's proposal to assemble twenty thousand soldiers in Paris from the provinces. On top of that, he dismissed the Brissot ministry!"

Seeing the shocked faces in front of him, Jeremy shook his head.

"But as bad as all that is, it's not the reason I'm here." He looked down at his hands and gathered his thoughts. "The events that I'm about to report to you are of such a nature that I feared to entrust them to a letter. I've yet to fathom the magnitude of them. They occurred on the 20th of June. An organized demonstration made up of the most extreme elements of the Parisian districts, clubs, and societies congregated in large numbers at the Tuileries. Even though they came with petitions and arms, they were a mannerly crowd in the beginning.

"The leader, Santerre, requested that the Assembly read their petition, saying something about wanting nothing more than to plant a liberty tree at the Tuileries to protest the ministry's dismissal. While the Deputies debated this request the demonstrators went ahead and planted the liberty tree in the Capuchins garden."

"They may have called it a protest against the dismissal of the ministry, but it seems much more sinister to me," Eugénie said, gravely.

Jeremy nodded. "How right you are, Miss Eugénie, as you'll see. By the time the Deputies agreed to allow them to come in, the huge crowd had become worked up and, singing 'Ça Ira,' they marched into the Manège where the Assembly was in session and then proceeded on to the palace grounds."

"'Ça Ira,'" Eugénie murmured, "has become the popular song of the revolution and never fails to incite a crowd. I can only imagine what the royal family thought, looking down from their windows."

"One thing led to another. The cannon, part of the demonstration that had lagged behind, now caught up with the throng. It was impossible to control its mass in that mob, and it ran over and killed some of them. In a misguided effort to avoid further casualties, someone inside opened the gates to the palace."

Eugénie looked at Jeremy in disbelief. "What an act of colossal stupidity! What were they thinking?"

"Clearly, they weren't," Jeremy said drily and then continued. "The mob poured into the palace and confronted the king in the Salon de l'Oeuil de Boeuf. They waved weapons in his face and hurled insults at him, demanding that he withdraw his vetoes and bring back the ministry. One member of the crowd thrust a *bonnet rouge* at the king, who calmly put it on his head and with remarkable self-possession lifted a goblet and toasted France.

"I was in the clubs doing my usual reconnaissance when I learned about this carefully orchestrated demonstration. I followed along with the crowd and watched the nightmare unfold. Throughout that long afternoon, the king never lost his dignity. Only that saved him from even more abuse, or worse.

"Finally, Pétion, who, as you know, is the presiding head of the Assembly, arrived with some lame excuse for not coming sooner. He managed to convince the mob to leave. I heard later that the queen, who was in her own apartments, suffered the same treatment. It was a horrifying afternoon, and it showed just how defenseless the royal family is and how tenuous their safety."

"A mob overrunning the palace, in their very apartments! *C'est incroyable!*" Marie exclaimed. The stern expressions on the faces of Eugénie, Bridger, and Jamie mirrored her words.

"What's happened since?" Eugénie asked, not wanting to dwell on the effect of those horrendous events on the king and queen.

"I would've come here that night, but I waited to see what repercussions occurred so I could gauge the political state of mind. There was a backlash in the king's favor. Even for the most unfeeling, this rabble had gone too far. Pétion was suspended for his wretched performance. Rumor has it that he delayed to give the mob time to do what the Assembly hadn't the stomach to do."

"No!" the others cried in unison.

"Oh, yes, the mood in Paris is ugly. I've heard support in the street for even the most extreme actions. But to continue, there was talk of removing the Dauphin from his family for his own safety, and Lafayette spoke in front of the Assembly, calling for the clubs to be closed down, the press muzzled, and petitions banned. So far, nothing's come of that. For the moment, Paris is paralyzed with shock, which, no doubt, will spread through the country. What effect this all will have in the long term, I can't say. Still, inflammatory rumors abound—about a royal plot, for one—but that's hardly new."

"Jeremy, you make no mention of any punishment for the demonstrators. That says much," Eugénie remarked. "One thing's sure: There's no turning back the clock. From the start, relations have been strained between the king and the various Assemblies, but the day you describe," she shook her head, "the actions of that mob... It's clear the king has no real power. The monarchy serves only at the pleasure and whim of the capricious forces that now control France."

"Using fear as a whip, power and malice drive Parisian politics," Jeremy said grimly. "Troops are arriving daily from the provinces. They're called *Fédérés*. They're nothing more than an unruly bunch spoiling for a fight. The city's an armed camp. There are forces and counterforces."

Jamie nodded. "I can vouch for that. It's happening here as well. The antigovernment camp is growing. The people are on the march. I hear many feel that, not only haven't conditions improved with the new order, but, in some ways, they're worse. This movement wishes for the old ways and a return of the power to the monarchy. This polarity is tearing the country apart," he ended bleakly.

"Meanwhile," Eugénie added, "the foreign coalition is massed at our borders and advancing in the northern and eastern territories. France is indeed a powder keg ready to explode, with the king and queen caught in the middle! I thought we'd have more time before we needed to approach the royal family with Robert Morris's plan."

"Where do the preparations stand?" Jeremy asked.

"I heard from him only last week. The town Azilum in America is already laid out and several buildings including the school and church are well under way. Houses are beginning to spring up and La Grande Maison is almost complete. But there's so much, so much left to do. He spoke of mishaps that stalled the original timetable, but he didn't elaborate. Several families of émigrés have arrived and joined the workforce. He has a core of investors, but he's disappointed not to have more by now. He said that he's taking on more of the costs than he originally intended, but his tone was optimistic. We must get word to him quickly that we must move more swiftly than we'd planned."

"The *White Heather* can depart on the morning tide," Bridger said quietly.

"Oh, Bridger," Eugénie cried, "you've only just arrived!" She let out a long sigh. "But you're right. We have no choice. You must go with all speed and deliver the message to Robert Morris."

"I'll put on extra sail." His eyes looked at her tenderly. "The summer winds are fair and strong. I'll be there and back in a fortnight."

She smiled up at him, knowing that even with his skill such a feat was impossible. "Bridger, if anyone can, you will. Promise me you'll take no risks."

His lips curved. "That's a promise I'll never make, Madame, but I'll return before you know I'm gone." A long look passed between them, and then she turned to Jeremy.

"Dear Jeremy, you must ride for Paris tonight. Assemble those you can trust so we can move the family at a moment's notice. Dear God, I pray we're not already too late."

XXX

"I declare," Amelia Stanton said, peering closely at her face in the mirror, "I am beginnin' to look a little peakèd. This sittin' around all day and all night is not good for my complexion. There hasn't been a ball or anything since I can't remember when. It's downright borin' around here. And all those filthy people starin' at us when we manage to go out in the carriage. Ugh, nasty. I'd rather stay right here in this old drafty palace and be bored to tears. No, I wouldn't. Let me think. There must be something I can think of to liven this place up before I go stark starin' mad!

"Oh, silly me. I've been on the wrong track all this time! I know just the thing. Home! Perfect. If I just get a move on, I'll be back in time for all the harvest parties. And me with all my stories to tell! I'll be the belle of the ball. Of course, I always am, but now even more so. Oh, won't those Whittington girls just be pea-green with envy. Oh, I can't wait! Why didn't I think of this before?

"I must speak to the queen, today, yes today, about makin' arrangements for a ship home. I know my leavin' is just goin' to break her heart. Oh, well, it can't be helped.

"Ouch! What are you tryin' to do, rip my hair out?" She glared up at the young servant who was trying to brush the tangles out of Amelia's blonde curls. "Give me that brush!" As she wrenched the brush out of the girl's hand, her arm knocked an atomizer off the dressing table. "Oh!" she shrieked. "You ninny, now look what you've made me do! Get out of here! Out! Out!"

The poor girl ran sobbing from the room. Amelia scowled after the retreating figure. She turned back to the mirror, piled the tangled mass on top of her head, and began sticking combs in every which way to hold it in place. Patting it, she smiled at her reflection.

"Perfect! Just the new look I needed. I know the queen will just adore it. I'll go show her at once." She picked up the yellow gown that was hanging on the dressing screen and looked around.

"Now, where's that girl got to? How does she expect me to get into this thing by myself? Once I tell the queen how useless that girl is, why, she won't take 'no' for an answer 'til I agree to use her own dresser. After all, it's the perfect solution. I'm sure she would've demanded it long since if she'd known the pitiful situation I've been puttin' up with."

She walked over to the bell pull and gave it a yank. "In the meantime, I'll just have to make do with whoever shows up."

The queen looked up from her needlepoint as Amelia Stanton sailed into the room. "*Mon Dieu!* She looks just like a haystack!" she whispered to her dear friend Louise de Lamballe. "Doesn't she realize how unflattering yellow is on someone with blonde hair? And what in heaven's name has she done to her hair? She has become such a trial. Every day there are reports about her. No one in breeches is safe. Yes, it's long since past time to send her packing." Then she straightened and quickly schooled her features.

"Ah, Amelia, I was just thinking about you. Louise, dear, would you please make room beside you for Amelia?" The queen's closest friend shifted over on the settee, bringing her closer to Marie Antoinette's chair.

Amelia flounced over to them, dipped a shallow curtsy to the monarch, and then stared down at Louise, clearly indicating that she intended to have her seat.

With a shrug, the young woman rose gracefully and turned to the queen, effectively cutting off Amelia. "Your Majesty, by your leave, there are some matters I need to attend to."

The two women exchanged a smile. "Of course, dear." With an amused expression, the queen gazed after her friend before turning back to Amelia, who had settled in and was munching on a puff pastry she had taken from the tray in front of the queen.

"Mmmmm, delicious! I'm so goin' to miss..., uh, I mean, I'm so sorry, Your Highness, so sorry to have to tell you this, but a very unfortunate thing happened this mornin'."

"Oh, what might that be, Amelia?" the queen asked, well used to Amelia's unending stream of "unfortunate things."

"My dresser—I can never remember her name—just up and quit this mornin', leavin' me at my wits' end," Amelia answered, pouting prettily. "Actually, it may have been a fortunate thing, after all," she said, patting her hair and preening. "You may have noticed my new hair style? I did it all by myself. Isn't it fetchin'?" Amelia looked brightly at the queen, turning her head from side to side.

"I should say so. Very becoming. It suits you perfectly," Marie Antoinette murmured drily.

"Why, it'll become the rage!" Amelia exclaimed, gaining momentum. She turned and, looking closely at a woman sitting nearby, said, "Well, with your round face, maybe not." She swung back to the queen, missing the venomous expression directed at her by the young woman. "But, for you, perfect! You can see how good it looks on me, and us lookin' so much alike. Well, you just say the word and I'll do up your hair just like mine. It's very easy and quick. It won't take but a minute or two. You don't even have to let on that it was my inspiration. I don't mind if you take all the credit. In fact, I insist on it."

When the queen started to speak, Amelia raised her hand. "Yes, yes, I insist, every bit of credit. There, it's settled. You just say the word. As my partin' gift..."

"Your parting gift?" The queen interrupted, not believing her good luck.

Amelia hurried on. "I know how important, how indispensable, I've become to you since I've come to court, not to mention how close we are. I know it's goin' to break your heart to see me go." She crossed her hands over her breast. "But I truly must get back to my poor daddy. I don't know how he's managed to survive without me this long. I truly don't. I'm just torn, torn, bein' so needed in so many, many places. Just torn. But you know how it is, bein' a mother and all, just how much you'd miss one of your babies."

Struck by her own melodrama, Amelia pulled a linen handkerchief from her sleeve and blew heartily into it. She failed to see the look of relief that passed between the queen and one of her ladies.

"Somehow, we'll have to make do," the queen demurred. "Family must come first."

Amelia sprang to her feet and flung her arms around the startled queen.

"Oh, I knew you'd understand. I just knew it. You're the kindest person in the whole wide world! I'd better go and finish, I mean, start on my packin', this minute. Why, it's only the ninth of August. I can be home before September." Grasping her skirts in both hands, Amelia whirled and fairly danced out of the room, passing the king on his way in.

Seeing the expression on his face, the queen hurried over to him.

"Louis, Louis, what is it?"

"Marie, please dismiss your attendants. I would have a moment in private with you."

When they were alone, he guided her to a window seat that overlooked the gardens. He looked out and in his mind's eye he saw the throng of armed demonstrators. *Has it already been seven weeks? It seems like yesterday.* He rubbed his brow with a weary hand and turned to his wife.

"I fear, my dear, that Joseph's Manifesto has had just the opposite effect of what we'd hoped. Instead of deterring the forces that range against us, calling for the French to rise up against the lawlessness that rules the land has only added fuel to the fire. I fear the days ahead. More and more troops are pouring into Paris. There's brawling in the streets. The *Fédérés* that have converged on Paris seize every opportunity to engage the Garde Nationale. The radical Marseilles contingent outshouts the *'Ça Ira'* with their *'Marseillaise'* battle song. I'm told the din is unbearable." The queen took his hand. "I'm the focal point of it all, this tortured political web—I, the last remnant of the monarchy. Every step I take only creates more dissension, more..."

"*Non, mon chéri, non,*" his wife protested.

"*Mais oui, mon chou.*" His gaze, which had been wandering around the room, lighting on a chair here, a tapestry there, came back to rest on her upturned face.

"*Ma chère,* I never meant any of this for you. We were so young, so young." He gently touched her cheek. "We, you and I, as different as the families and the countries that spawned us and joined us together." He shook his head at the mystery of it and continued on. "My agents report that there are those ready to rise who are fed up with the Assembly that pontificates but does nothing to lessen the burden of our people. On the one hand, such news gives me hope, while on the other I fear the government's reprisals."

"What can the Assembly do?" his wife asked. "It's in complete disarray. You dismissed the ministry. Pétion is suspended. What better time for a counterrevolution?"

"Marie, Marie, don't you see? The ministers, even Pétion, were fronts for the true powers in the Assembly — Robespierre, Marat, Danton, extremists all. The presidents, the ministers come and go, but these men and their followers prevail and on the surface reinvent themselves, depending on how the wind blows, but their purposes underneath never change. This time does not bode well for us, my dear, but I hold to my faith, to my love for you and the children, and to my belief that the true spirit of the revolution will ultimately prevail."

She held his hand more tightly and tried to muster the right words of encouragement. "Louis, we have been through so much together."

"That we have." He smiled at her and murmured under his

breath, "If only I hadn't agreed to dismiss our personal guard, leaving a mere two thousand to protect the whole Tuileries."

"Is there something you're not telling me?" the queen asked anxiously.

"No, no, my dear. Should the need arise, I've no doubt there will be those who'll stand by us." He patted her hand and kissed her cheek, a rare show of affection that caused alarm to leap into the queen's eyes.

In the middle of the night the clarion sound of the tocsin rang out. The queen summoned her attendants to her apartments. Amelia clutched her chamber coat about her and stared around her with wide eyes.

"What is that clangin'? Will it never stop?" she wailed.

With her arms wrapped around her son and daughter, the queen spoke quietly. "The ringing of the tocsin signifies an emergency. Until we know its nature, there's nothing for us to do but remain calm. I'm going to leave now and attend to my toilette. I suggest that all of you do likewise. Come, children." The words were barely out of her mouth when a servant burst into the room.

"Insurrectionists! The streets are teeming with them. They've taken over the Hôtel de Ville!"

"Go quickly, ladies," the queen said, maintaining her composure, "and prepare yourself for the day."

"Lord in heaven!" Amelia shrieked, "They're comin' for us! We'll all be murdered!" Princesse de Lamballe walked over to the hysterical woman, grabbed her by the arms, and shook her until her teeth rattled.

"Be quiet, you fool. The queen has enough to contend with!"

"How dare you!" Amelia screamed, her eyes blazing. The queen moved quickly to intercede between the two women.

"It's all right, Louise. Please take the children. I'll be with you shortly. Go, go." She pushed her reluctant friend in the direction of the two children, who stood clutching each other, their eyes wide in their pale faces.

"Dear Amelia, if you would, return to your rooms and . . . , oh, Sophie," the queen motioned a servant girl over. "Go with Mademoiselle Stanton to her apartment and exchange clothes with her." Amelia looked ready to faint. "Amelia," the queen said firmly, "there's not a minute to lose. By the time you return, Hans will be here to escort you to the coast."

"Hans? Here?" Amelia stammered.

"Yes, I sent for him. He's standing by. He'll accompany you and see you safely aboard a ship. Bring only a small valise. Now, hurry! Go!"

Amelia stood tapping her foot and clutching her small satchel in the king's anteroom. The king and queen sat talking quietly together, each holding one of the royal children. The queen's attendants and a few of the Royal Guard helped themselves to the hastily prepared food on the sideboards.

"What are we waitin' for? Why are we still here?" Amelia hissed at a thoroughly provoked Hans.

"I've told you. We're waiting for the appropriate conveyance, Mademoiselle."

"What are you talkin' about? There are plenty of carriages and coaches."

"We won't be traveling in that fashion. The wagon we seek had to be procured outside of the Tuileries."

"A wagon! I am not travelin' in a wagon!"

At that moment, Procureur-Général Pierre Louis Roederer, one of the members of the Assembly more loyal to the king, entered the room and strode over to the king. Making a small bow, he said, "Your Highness, all of Paris is on the march. Madness has swept the streets. I fear for the safety of you and your family, should you remain here in the palace. I'll escort you across the courtyard to the Assembly chambers, where you'll be safe."

"It's come to this," the king said with finality. "Come, my dear." He held out his arm to the queen and together they swept through the room, followed by the king's sister, Elisabeth, and the Princesse de Lamballe, who held tightly to the children's hands. The Swiss Guard stood at attention and the women curtsied as they passed. As they neared the door, Hans stepped forward.

"Sire, I request permission to remain here in your service."

"No, Hans," the queen interrupted. "You've been true and loyal to us." Her eyes twinkled briefly as her gaze took in his unusual attire, from his scuffed sabots to his red bonnet. "As such, I've entrusted Mademoiselle Stanton into your care. I know that you won't disappoint me." Standing ramrod straight, the soldier saluted. His eyes never wavered as the royal family walked through the doorway and down the hall.

XXXI

LATE SUMMER 1792
Château de Beaumont

"Marie, I don't expect Monsieur Brissot and the others to stay for dinner, but we had best be prepared," Eugénie said as she pulled a massive damask cloth from the linen closet and buried her nose in it. "Mmmm, there's just a faint hint of lavender. It's past time to replace the sachets. We've had such an abundant crop this summer, we should have more than enough for all the closets."

One by one, they removed the linens from the top shelf, sorting carefully through them to remove the stale sachets.

"Remember doing this with our mothers, how they taught us to fold each piece just so?"

Marie smiled at the memory. "Oh, yes. It seems such a long time ago."

"It does, doesn't it? I still miss my parents' counsel, but I'm glad they're not here now. They would have approved of the revolution as it began, but they would've deplored how it's deteriorated into little more than a power grab. I fear we haven't seen the worst of it."

"Your family has always lived by the very things the revolution set out to do," Marie said, "working side by side with their people, giving them a share in the abundance of the château and a fair reward for their labor. They even offered schooling for the château's people. But it was you who instituted a wage scale and a system of managers, whom you trusted to advance those under them with the ability to move ahead, even to the point of furnishing the means to pursue a profession."

Eugénie smiled at Marie's lengthy speech, because it was so unlike her. "The progress I made was possible only because of what Mother and Father and those before them set in place. I have the Whittingtons to thank for the innovative farming practices I brought back from their Virginian plantation. Jamie says we should expect good harvests across the board. The summer wheat we've put by should be ample to supply grain well beyond our needs."

The women worked steadily in a companionable silence, finishing the first closet and moving on to the next. By the end of the morning, all the linens had been turned, layered with fresh, fragrant lavender sachets, and returned to the closets that lined the long hall on the second-floor landing.

Eugénie arched her back and turned her head from side to side to stretch out her tired muscles. She leaned out of the window, breathing in the delicious smells of late summer. "Oh, Marie, it's turned into such a beautiful day!... What on Earth is that?" As she watched, a dilapidated wagon with a single bench seat, drawn by two mules, rolled to a stop in front of the château's steps. The driver pulled off his red cap and mopped his face. What had first appeared to be a pile of rags in the bed of the wagon began to move and shift. An arm reached out and grasped the side of the wagon. Next emerged a kerchiefed head, followed by shoulders wrapped in a faded shawl. The apparition snatched off the kerchief and shook out a mass of blonde hair.

"Hans!" The unmistakable voice carried easily to Eugénie standing at the open window. "You get back here this instant and get me out of this thing!"

Marie hurried to the window to see what had caused Eugénie's alarm. "Oh, dear God!" she exclaimed.

Horrified, the two women looked at each other. "It can't be!" Eugénie cried. "It just can't be! Not with everything that's going on. Amelia Stanton, of all people! Marie, what in heaven's name am I going to do with her? We have to get her out of here before Brissot and the Girondists arrive."

"The proverbial bad penny," Marie murmured, causing Eugénie to laugh in spite of herself.

"I'll go down and meet her," Eugénie said, regaining her composure. "You go and get Jamie and meet us in the morning room. Hurry! Oh, and bring some refreshments. Amelia can't resist food, especially sweets."

Marie sped along the hallway and Eugénie hurried down the stairs, muttering, "A plan, I must come up with a plan."

"I know! I know! I know!" Amelia ranted at the people around the table. Hans, his head bowed, looked near collapse. Eugénie, Jamie, and Marie simply stared at her. "You do not need to tell me that it's dangerous out there! Where do you think I've been all this time while you've been sittin' here in this nice cozy safe château? Only by the skin of our teeth did we manage to slip by one group of no 'count rascals after another. The countryside is just crawlin'

with them, but Paris, Paris is Hell on Earth! Never, never, never will I ever set foot in that hellhole again! Never again! Why, we barely escaped with our lives. Tell them, Hans, tell them what I've been through." Hans's head jerked up, but before he could utter a word Amelia continued to rave. "Has it only been a week? It's more like a lifetime! What a nightmare!"

Abruptly, she stopped and tears streamed down her face. "I've got to get out of this godforsaken place! I want to go home!" she wailed. She looked down at her filthy clothes and wailed louder, wringing her hands. "I can't go home like this! I am a sight. Look at me! Just look at me!" she stormed, as though anyone had been looking anywhere else for the last half an hour.

"Come, come," Eugénie said soothingly and handed the distraught woman a linen handkerchief. "Wipe your eyes and have one of these delicious pastries." Amelia was a sight, her eyes swollen, her dirty face streaked with tear tracks, her soiled blouse and skirt hanging in rags. She took the handkerchief and after wiping her eyes blew her nose so loudly that Émigré, who was snuggled at Eugénie's feet, jumped up, startled out of his late-morning nap. Eugénie patted his head and he flopped back down and was soon sound asleep once more.

"I couldn't eat a thing, not a thing," Amelia said pitifully. Her voice rose and she shouted, "How can you expect me to eat? I AM TOO UPSET!"

Seeing that the woman was on the verge of a complete collapse, Eugénie said quickly, "Amelia, you're absolutely right. How thoughtless of me. Marie, please take Mademoiselle Stanton up to my room." Eugénie stood up and fairly pushed Amelia into Marie's arms, mouthing words and pantomiming behind Amelia's back to hurry Marie along. "Amelia, after you've washed off the travel stains and changed into one of my gowns, you'll feel more like your old self."

Amelia sniffled and, leaning on Marie, left the room, mumbling, "Yes, change into one of your gowns."

As soon as Amelia was out of earshot, Eugénie turned to Hans.

"Hans, I'm sure the last week has been a harrowing experience for you."

The soldier's laugh was hollow. "That it was, milady, that it was. Mistress Stanton didn't overstate the extent of what we went through." He tactfully avoided Eugénie's other meaning. "As we headed south, we were overtaken by countless people fleeing Paris with only the clothes on their back. Word was that there was a massive uprising in the city against the government, against the royal family—against everything. We were told the bloodshed throughout the city was horrendous. At the royal palace, every member of the guard was slaughtered."

"*Oh, mon Dieu!*" Eugénie said, shocked.

Overwhelmed by exhaustion and despair, the young soldier dropped his head in his hands. "What am I to do? I have no regiment to return to. There is no regiment. All my comrades gone, all gone."

Jamie, who like many Scots had suffered the loss of all his people at the hands of the English at Culloden, knew the depth of the young man's pain. He put his arm around Hans's shoulders.

"Don't think about that now." He pressed the soldier's untouched snifter of cognac into his hands. "Here, now, drink this. Brace up, man." Jamie's firm voice had the desired effect. Hans sat up, took the glass, and downed it.

"Thank you, sir." His face was still pale, but his eyes had lost their haunted look.

A short time later, Amelia walked into the room. "Amelia, how well you look!" Eugénie said, genuinely amazed at the woman's transformation.

Amelia smiled coquettishly, showing some of her old spirit. Fluffing the skirts of one of Eugénie's favorite gowns, she settled on the chair next to Hans. "I simply couldn't resist this gown. Lavender is so becomin' on me, don't you think? It reminds me of the queen. You see, she and I share a particular fondness for this color." Looking up through her pale lashes, she held one of Eugénie's lace handkerchiefs to her nose and sniffed delicately. Sighing, she paused for a moment before stuffing it into her sleeve. She plucked a sandwich from the platter.

"Oh, I feel so much better, almost like my old self—that is, except for my poor, achin' bones. Eugénie, you can't imagine, you simply cannot imagine." Her words were barely understandable as she washed the mouthful down with a gulp of wine.

Clearly, Eugénie thought, you're on your way to recovery. "I'm delighted that you're feeling so much better," she said aloud. "Now, we'd best talk about your trip home."

"Yes, yes," Amelia agreed. Having ravaged the sandwich platter, she turned her attention to the tray of sweets. "A good night's sleep and I'll be ever so much better, I'm sure," she mumbled, her mouth full of bonbons. "Mmmm, I didn't realize how hungry I was. After all I've been through, the hardships I've suffered, it's truly amazin', it's a bloomin' miracle that I can get a thing down my throat." She picked up a cream puff and performed another miracle, swallowing it in one bite.

"Yes, Amelia, a good night's sleep," Eugénie said, trying to hold on to her patience. "Now, let's stay on track, here. Jamie, with an early start in the morning, a very early start, how long do you expect it would take to reach the coast?"

"I'd say we should be able to arrive there shortly after noon," Jamie replied, transfixed by the show of pure gluttony taking place before his eyes.

Looking like a startled rabbit, Amelia stared at them. "Early start in the mornin'!" she shrieked, aghast. "Oh, no, I couldn't possibly. No, no, no. I'll need a week, at least a week."

"Amelia, dear, much has changed since you were last here. The château is watched."

"Watched?"

"There are spies everywhere, reporting anything unfamiliar or unusual. They have lists of the people in every household. Unexpected arrivals are immediately suspect."

"Spies?" Amelia, her eyes wide with fright, swung her head around, expecting to see one lurking behind the draperies or hiding behind a chair.

"Whatever was I thinkin'? My poor poppa, how has he managed without me all this time? I cannot have him wait another week, certainly not, no, not another day, not another hour, not another minute. No, I must leave this very second!"

Somehow, Eugénie managed to resist grabbing the young woman and clapping a hand over her mouth. "Amelia, the morning will be soon enough." And, before she could be interrupted,

Eugénie continued, "Believe me, we'll do everything humanly possible to speed you on your way."

Jamie made a strangling sound and coughed behind his hand. Eugénie frowned at him, but said smoothly, "It wouldn't do for you and Hans to stay here any longer than absolutely necessary. As a member of the Royal Guard, it's very dangerous for Hans to be in this part of the country."

Amelia, who, at the mention of Hans's name, had cut her eyes at him and given him a melting gaze, suddenly looked at him as though he had the plague. "And with your close resemblance to the queen..." Eugénie let the words hang in the air.

It was all too much for Amelia. She sprang to her feet. "Tonight. I leave tonight. No, right now, right this minute! I won't stay a second longer!"

"Well," Eugénie said, trying to look unconvinced, "a good night's sleep..."

"No!" Amelia almost shouted. "I feel as fresh as a daisy. I leave this minute!"

"Jamie," Eugénie said, still trying to sound reluctant, "what do you think?"

"I can be ready at once, but Hans must have a chance to refresh himself and have a change of clothes."

"Fine," Amelia cut in. "Hans, you take all the time you need. I'm leaving immediately, right this minute. Yes, much better that we travel separately." She moved, putting space between them.

"Amelia, Hans's training and experience will be invaluable to you. You don't want to travel alone, these days. And," Eugénie added mildly, "there's no telling what the conditions aboard ship will be."

Amelia turned and looked at the young man with new eyes. "Hmmm, perhaps you're right. Yes, yes, you're right. It wouldn't do. It wouldn't do at all for a lady such as myself to travel out there alone at the mercy of who knows what. Hans, you may come with me."

"The question is," Eugénie continued as if Amelia had not spoken, "Hans, how do you feel about going to America?"

"Eugénie, whatever do you mean? Of course he wants..."

Hans gave Amelia a sharp glance, stopping her in midsentence. "Madame Eugénie, there's nothing for me here. I'll be able to start a new life over there." He turned to Amelia, his eyes soft. "And Mademoiselle Stanton will need protection on her journey. I'd be honored to accompany her on the voyage."

"*Bon, c'est ça,*" said Eugénie, satisfied. "Jamie, please see to Hans's needs and prepare a carriage. Amelia and I will go and put some things together for the trip."

When Eugénie ushered Amelia down the wide château steps, Jamie and Hans were already standing by the carriage. Marie hastened out of the door, carrying a large picnic hamper.

"Ah, Marie," Eugénie smiled at her, "how thoughtful of you."

With the moment of departure at hand, Amelia flung her arms around Eugénie. "I am so sorry to be leavin' so soon," she gushed, "but I know you understand. Now, if you ever come to Virginia, you be sure and visit us, you hear? Don't forget to write!" With unseemly haste, she scrambled up into the carriage.

When Marie handed the basket through the window, Amelia said sharply, "Marie, I do hope you put in some of my favorite petits fours." Marie nodded. "Oh, good, good! I am simply starvin'!"

Eugénie turned to Hans. "Hans, you're a very fine young man, I'd even say a saint."

Hans laughed, understanding her meaning. "She grows on you, after a while. In fact," he dipped his head, blushing, "I've become quite fond of her."

"Bless your heart," Eugénie said with feeling. *"Bon voyage."*

"Thank you, Madame. I hope one day I'll have the privilege of returning your kindness." He saluted and climbed into the carriage as Jamie swung up onto the bench. He flicked the reins and they were off.

Eugénie and Marie stood waving until the carriage was out of sight.

XXXII

During the month since Amelia Stanton's departure, the news from Paris was sporadic and alarming. Everyone at the château was on edge. The one bright note came when Jamie sent word that he had managed to procure passage for Amelia and Hans. He reported that, in Amelia's eagerness to leave France, she had been uncharacteristically cooperative and touchingly appreciative of the patient Hans, who seemed to grow daily in her esteem. Jamie returned to the château after he had seen the unlikely pair aboard ship and watched with his own eyes as the vessel set sail on the morning tide for America.

Eugénie's dinner for Brissot and the Girondists, which had been postponed when they were recalled to Paris to be reinstated in the Assembly, was under way in the château's candlelit dining room. The French doors were opened wide to the soft September evening.

Brissot, seated at Eugénie's right, was regaling her and his fellow ministers with a lively discussion about the central role that Dr. Guillotin's machine was playing in the restoration of order in

Paris. He had been enumerating the machine's feats in doling out death since they had sat down at the table. Oblivious to the elaborate feast before him, he had been drinking steadily all evening. Once again he raised his goblet.

"To La Guillotine, our blind and deaf lady, who services the high and the low alike! La Guillotine, our enforcer of *égalité!*" He threw back his head and drained the glass. Eugénie had long since lost her appetite. She shuddered as the others around the table joined in the toast. No one noticed when she failed to follow suit. Before Brissot could launch into another bloodthirsty discussion, Eugénie turned to him.

"Monsieur Brissot..."

"*Non, non,* Madame Eugénie, Jacques-Pierre, please call me Jacques-Pierre. This is a new day. We're all brothers in the new France. There's no room for pretensions. I, the simple son of a pastry chef, though a lawyer, still enjoy the smells of the kitchen and kneading the dough now and then."

He looked around the table, his eyes lighting on Maximin Isnard, Pierre Vergniaud, Marguerite-Élie Guadet, and Armand Gensonné. "I tip my hat to no one, Madame, nor do I expect such in return, but I make an exception in the case of these four." He bowed to each one in turn. "If only to hear their eloquence, you must end your self-imposed exile here in our beloved Bordeaux and venture to Paris. Their words have lifted the revolution from the mundane to a higher calling, a calling that we now carry to our borders and beyond! Down with the insurrectionists! Down with the enemies of France, whether they be within or without!

"With the National Convention bringing the criminals of August tenth to justice and the Committee of Vigilance with the teeth to bring our enemies to heel, we will return order to France! The priests will be punished. Those who stood against the events of June twentieth will taste our justice. Lafayette, whose desertion of his post topped a long list of villainies, will be prosecuted." Brissot's eyes glittered. "The royalist presses have been silenced and those who ran those vehicles of insurrection arrested. Finally, finally, our greatest triumph of all, Louis Capet and that woman are separated from their household and are incarcerated in the Temple prison!"

In his inebriated fervor, Brissot failed to notice Eugénie's expression of disgust and horror. She quickly schooled her features and murmured, "It appears from your words that the government has things well in hand."

"Yes, yes, Madame, and a new constitution is in the making to replace that other ill-conceived piece of business. Shortly, all things will be well under control."

"What of Monsieur Danton's role in the proceedings?" Eugénie asked innocently.

"Ah, yes, well, Danton does have his uses. Perhaps you've heard of some procedures that have been put into place. Monsieur Danton understands, as do we all, the necessity to 'confront and contain' and isn't squeamish about taking the steps that are called for. After all, it's clear that France must be protected from the threat of invasion by foreign troops, the émigrés, the political prisoners, the insurrectionists—all the saboteurs, in whatever guise they take. Danton is vigilant in this regard."

"You say the prisoners are a threat," Eugénie interjected mildly. "Pardon my naïveté, Monsieur, but how do they pose a threat?"

Brissot patted her hand. "There, there, it's nothing for you to trouble your head about, my dear. But, to answer your question, Danton said—and in this regard I concur with the Jacobin—that with the prisoners living in such close quarters, the potential for violent outbreaks is a real possibility. They must be watched, and watched closely. If a group should break into the prisons and kill some priests and political upstarts, so be it. The loss of a few lives will send a message to the survivors." He shrugged and flicked a piece of lint from his sleeve. "Eh, a few less mouths to feed."

I would hardly call half of all the prisoners, 80 percent at the Abbaye and the Carmelite, "a few lives"! Eugénie thought, but managed to maintain a bland expression.

"Did you hear," one of the guests said, addressing Brissot, "that *l'Autri-Chienne* fainted when they told her that her 'dear, dear friend,' Louise de Lamballe, had been executed? Pity that *l'Autri-Chienne* didn't see the head of her 'dear, dear friend' on a pike when they paraded it in front of her window at the Temple prison." The speaker was rewarded by approving grunts from around the table and a nod of agreement from Brissot.

Shocked at the man's words and his companions' response, Eugénie froze in her seat. *How did the queen endure the loss of her dearest friend? Thank God, I'd already heard about that poor woman's rape and mutilation! I don't know how I would have handled hearing it this way. What other horrific acts will be done in the name of the revolution?*

"Such talk is not fit for dining conversation or for our generous hostess's tender ears, my friend," Brissot chided his fellow Girondist in an uncharacteristic moment of sensitivity, "though a good day's work it was."

Eugénie rose from her chair, fighting to hold on to her composure. "*Messieurs,* if you will, coffee and cognac will be served in the salon."

When everyone was settled with his choice of beverage, Brissot turned the conversation to the drastic food shortages.

"The conditions worsen daily. Would that all growers were as productive as you, Madame!"

Eugénie dipped her head at the compliment. "We've been fortunate in our harvest," she demurred, wondering if this interminable evening would ever end.

"I beg to differ with you, Citizen Eugénie. It's more than simple good fortune. It's the care and handling of the land that's been passed down from generation to generation at this château. That, and the contribution of your stores throughout the countryside, makes you a heroine of our revolution. Madame, I salute you."

"Nothing more than anyone else would do in the same circumstances."

"Ah, Madame, your modesty becomes you as a daughter of the revolution, but again I must contradict you. The hoarding by many and the intentional manipulation of foodstuffs by others are legion. Those acts are criminal and will be punished. In addition, those who've indulged themselves and lived off the honest labor of others, with nary a thought for anything but their own pleasures, are now receiving their just deserts.

"We'll cleanse *La Patrie* of the parasites and maggots and sweep France clean as Ulysses cleansed the stables." Her guest was off and running again. "Our revolution bears much in common with the great labors of that ancient hero, and we, like him, will prevail! That I promise you!"

Pushing himself up from his chair, Brissot bent towards his

hostess. "We've presumed on your generous hospitality far too long. It's time we took our leave, but be assured, I'll waste no time informing the Assembly of your good work here, and advising the Deputies that this district, through your efforts, is a shining example of what our great revolution can bring to all of France." He raised his glass of cognac and turned to the room.

"*Mes amis,* let us raise our voices to salute Citizen Devereux and sip this fine libation in thanks for this evening and bid her *adieu.*" A chorus of *"À Citoyenne Devereux! Vive la France!"* resounded through the room.

A short time later, Eugénie stood in her bedchamber, staring at her reflection in the mirror, amazed that, except for the expression of naked horror in her eyes, she looked little changed by the events of the evening. She went over to the basin on her corner table and scrubbed her hands and face, wishing that she could as easily cleanse herself of the men's foulness, the stench of them that threatened to seep into her soul.

After a restless night and little sleep, Eugénie rose early. Before the rest of the household stirred, she was dressed and downstairs. She walked slowly along the gallery, pausing at each of the portraits of her ancestors. Her fingers trailed along the gilded frames as she looked into the face of each one. These men and women had contributed their talents, their resources, and sometimes their lives to this France, this country that they had loved. The weakness she had felt on awakening gave way to a feeling of strength as she traced each face.

She stopped briefly in the kitchen for bread and cheese, stuffing apples and carrots in her pockets for the horses. She grabbed a bottle of the Evian spring water from the shelf. She looked at it pensively. Funny, she thought, this was introduced in the same year the Bastille fell. Even in the midst of momentous events, the more mundane occur as well. She shrugged her shoulders and set off for the stables.

Her spirits lifted as she stopped at each stall to dole out the apples and carrots. She smiled as she heard Roan II whinny his welcome. She unlatched the door to his stall. As docilely as a lamb he followed her to the tack room. He waited patiently as she went inside and returned laden. She placed the paraphernalia in a heap on the ground and looked up at The Roan.

"You mighty beast," she said, flinging her arms around his neck, her cheek next to his. "How I love you!" The horse looked at her quizzically and pawed the ground. "I know, I know. I'm nothing but a silly woman. Here's a carrot for indulging me." The Roan crunched his reward as Eugénie quickly saddled him.

The hills were still shadowed with the waning night as they traversed the far pasture. One star after another blinked out as Eugénie watched the awakening sky. Apricot streaks, heralding the sun, bled into the edges of the horizon. The Roan slowed to a halt as he, too, looked to the East. Eugénie leaned back in the saddle and took a deep breath, filling her lungs with the sweet smell of the freshly mown hay. A peace swept through her and she felt renewed by the promise of the new day. She laughed. Infected by his mistress's mood, The Roan broke into a gallop, slowing only when they entered the forest at the far corner of the château property.

They made their way deeper and deeper into the dark woods. The thickets rustled with the movements of woodland creatures. A covey of quail scattered at their approach, protesting loudly and disappearing into the underbrush. Content in each other's company, horse and rider ambled further into the gloom. Eugénie noticed the first signs of approaching autumn. Here and there, squirrels scampered, collecting their winter store. She noticed the green foliage that in a month's time would be transformed into rich reds, yellows, and oranges, and, a short time later, gone, leaving stripped skeletons ready for their long winter's nap.

The air was warm on her cheek and a gentle breeze ruffled the curls at her neck. Ahead, through thinning trees, Eugénie saw a glen flooded with sunlight. They entered the natural clearing and Eugénie slid from the saddle. Masses of late-blooming wildflowers bordered a brook that bubbled along one side of the glade. Birds on the wing flickered through the light and shadow. "Oh, how beautiful," Eugénie breathed, looking around her as she led The Roan over to the creek. She watched the water cascading over the rocks and delighted in the fish that flashed beneath the surface. The Roan lowered his head and drank thirstily.

Feeling the sharp pangs of hunger, Eugénie reached into the saddlebags and pulled out the cheese, bread, and bottle of water. She took a long sip as she scanned the clearing. At the far edge, she saw what appeared to be the remains of a cooking fire. Curious, she walked over and kicked the charred logs. A poacher, no doubt, and, from the looks of it, recently gone. Ah, well, there's more than enough on this land for those who have little, but with winter coming... I'll send Jamie to find him. There's plenty of room in the village and work for willing hands.

Eugénie spread a blanket on the soft grass. Sitting cross-legged on it, she soon sated her appetite and quenched her thirst. She looked over and saw The Roan lazily munching grass at the creek's edge. *You're enjoying this respite, too, aren't you, fella?* Lying back, she cradled her head on her arms and closed her eyes, letting the warmth of the day seep into her. Time flowed by as she thought back over the recent months.

Eugénie sat up with a start. She had fallen asleep. She looked up to see dark, lowering clouds rolling rapidly across the sky. She shivered. Was it the sharp breeze that had suddenly come up? Or was it something else? The glen, which had looked so inviting a short while ago, seemed to close in on her. She felt a foreboding, a constriction in her chest.

Oh, Bridger, Bridger, where are you? Please, please come back soon. In the past, during the times we've been separated, I had the beauty and the joys of the world I lived in and loved to comfort me and to ease the pain of missing you. But there's no comfort in this world now, only the next nightmare and the next and the next, choking and smothering all that's fine and good, ripping my world apart. The beasts come at night, their eyes glowing, their fangs bared. I'm afraid. How can I stand against them to protect my people, this land, this country? Where did the dream go? When did it die?

When the first bolt of lightning cracked the sky, followed closely by a roll of thunder, she screamed and leaped to her feet. Quickly, she rolled up the blanket, jammed it in the saddlebag, and swung up onto The Roan's back. At her command, he whirled, raced through the clearing, and galloped into the woods. The rain began, coming down in sheets, blinding her.

Too late she saw the shadowy figure lurch into their path. Too late she saw the gleam of the blade in the dim light. But The Roan saw and The Roan understood. He trumpeted, his nostrils flaring. Rearing high, he took the slashing blows on his foreleg and chest. The attacker reached up to grab the stallion's rein, his other arm arching in a descending blow. The Roan danced to the side. In a lightning move, he reared again and the deadly hooves with 1,700 pounds of power behind them smashed into the would-be assassin's face. The assailant fell back and lay still. Blood pooled around the inert body. Sightless eyes stared up at nothing.

"*Oh, mon Dieu, mon Dieu!* What did that monster do to you?" Before Eugénie could clamber down from the saddle, The Roan whinnied and shook his head. He plunged down the path at a breakneck speed and headed for home, leaving a trail of blood in his wake.

XXXIII

Eugénie could feel The Roan's strength ebbing.

"We're almost there, we're almost there," she whispered. The stallion stumbled and went down on one knee. Eugénie slid from the saddle and gently checked the wounds. She choked back a sob. The blade had only grazed his foreleg, but the chest wound was deep and bleeding. The great horse raised his head to his mistress. The expression of trust in his eyes almost broke her heart.

"Come on, big fella. Up you go. You're not going to let a couple of nicks stop you, are you?" The Roan struggled to his feet. "Good boy! Good boy!" She stroked his cheek. "We're almost there." She took his reins, more for her own comfort than his need.

Slowly, they made their way across the last pasture through the torrential downpour.

"Just a little farther, a little farther," she coaxed. With flagging steps, breath laboring, he moved forward. "There's an extra portion of oats and fresh straw in your stall. Almost there, we're almost there."

As they struggled forward, she watched the stable buildings come nearer and nearer until finally they were through the gates.

"Charles! Jean! Come! *Vite, venez vite!*" At Eugénie's call, the grooms ran out of the stable, but pulled up short at the sight of the stallion covered with blood. "Quick, guide him into his stall. He's lost so much blood. Careful. Careful!"

Eugénie ran to Jeremy's room; gathered needles, thread, and the other implements she needed; and was back in The Roan's stall just as the grooms finished settling the great horse down. The chest wound, which had begun to clot, opened afresh and the metallic smell of blood mingled with the sweet smell of straw.

"There, there," she crooned, stroking him with one hand as she pressed a cloth against the wound to staunch the flow. "Jean, press the cloth against the center. I'll stitch back to it from both ends." With steady hands, she worked quickly, pulling the jagged skin together and stitching it into place with the thick surgical thread.

The Roan lay still, breathing shallowly, the twitch of muscle under her fingers the only sign of his pain. "I know, I know," she whispered.

She worked steadily, barely breathing, until the wound was completely closed. Only then did she allow herself the luxury of taking a deep breath. She rocked back on her heels and rubbed her forehead with a weary hand.

"Jean, Jeremy has a poultice recipe in his office. Take it to the kitchen and have one of the girls make it up. Have her soak some sugar lumps in it, as well. By the time you're back, I should be finished stitching and taping his foreleg." The groom nodded and was off like a shot.

"Charles, cleanse his leg while I get more thread."

Jean returned a short time later with the salve and the sugar lumps. Eugénie was sitting with the stallion's great head in her lap, stroking his forelock and talking to him softly. The horse was still, his eyes closed. She gave Jean a tired smile, as he knelt down next to her with the plate of sugar lumps and the poultice. Eugénie picked up three sugar lumps and held them against The Roan's lips.

"Here, fella, your favorites." The Roan's nostrils flared. He opened his eyes and lipped the treats into his mouth. The great jaws worked, crunching the lumps. "Good boy. Good boy." Eugénie gently lifted his head and slipped out from under him. "I'll just put this nice salve on you." She talked as she applied the paste to his chest. "Then I promise I'll leave you alone to rest. There, now, all done." The poultice in place, she fashioned a loose bandage to cover the wound, anchoring it around his legs and over his neck. "Well, if you aren't a picture." She laughed at him, leaning back to view her handiwork. With a show of his old spirit, The Roan rolled his eyes.

Eugénie stood and brushed off her trousers. Only then did she see the dark stains that covered her jacket and blouse.

"Jean, Charles, I think Jeremy would be proud of us. I'm going to go and get a bite to eat and change these clothes. While I'm gone, please replace as much of this straw as you can without disturbing him. I . . . " Suddenly she became aware of a low rumbling coming from the other stalls.

"What's that noise?" she exclaimed.

" 'Tis the horses, Mistress. Ever since you and The Roan walked into the stableyard, they've been making that sound. He's their leader. They smell his blood. Somehow, they can feel what he's feeling. They're afraid."

"Ah," Eugénie nodded. "I've heard horses making noises of encouragement when a mare's birthing, but this—I've never heard of anything like this. When you're finished here, you and the rest of the hands go to each stall and try to quiet them. Add a handful of oats to their feed. I'll make the rounds myself when I return."

As Eugénie emerged from the stableyard, she saw Marie running towards her down the path.

"*Mon Dieu!* Mistress, you're hurt!" she cried, seeing Eugénie's bloodstained clothes. "I just heard there'd been an accident! *Oh, mon Dieu!*"

"No, Marie, I'm not hurt." Eugénie sagged into her friend's arms. "It's The Roan." Leaning heavily on Marie, Eugénie walked slowly back to the château. As they reached the stairs, she stopped and covered her face with her hands.

"I've done everything I can do, everything. Oh, Marie, if he..."

"There, there," Marie soothed her. "What would The Roan think if he heard you say such a thing? Besides, you know he's too ornery to do anything but get better. Now, come along and let me draw you a nice, warm bath."

Marie sprinkled bath salts in the tub and stepped back as Eugénie slipped into the warm water and rested her head on the rim, closing her eyes.

"After you've had a nice soak, I'll tuck you into bed. On the morrow everything will look different."

"Oh, Marie, the bath feels like heaven, but," she said, sitting up and straightening her shoulders, "I'm sleeping in The Roan's stall until he recovers."

"You will not, Mistress. You'll sleep in your bed like any other reasonable human being. The nights are getting colder. What good will you be to that horse if you get sick?"

"Then," Eugénie retorted, "I'll just have to take plenty of blankets with me, won't I? No. No," she held up her hand when Marie started to speak, "that's the end of it. No more discussion." She paused, a look of distaste on her face. "As much as I'd like to leave that villain's corpse to the vultures, ask Jamie to collect the body and bury it, but somewhere off the château lands." She put her head back wearily and closed her eyes.

He found her there with the dawn light slanting through the stable door making a halo of her chestnut curls. She lay with her head cradled on her arms in her makeshift bed of blankets close to The Roan's belly. The stallion opened his eyes briefly at his silent approach. Bridger saw the pain in their depths, and something else. He stood quietly, looking down at the woman and her horse, willing the great champion to muster his strength. As if in answer, The Roan let out a long, shuddering breath. Eugénie moaned in her sleep and reached out to stroke his flank. The Roan quieted under his mistress's hand. Her hand stilled, then moved up the long body and stilled again. She stirred and opened her eyes.

"Ah, fella, the fever's come," she said softly, sitting up. "Worry not, we'll get you cooled down," she said brightly. "You just keep on doing your part and leave the rest to me. You'll be right as rain in no time." She stood up, rubbing the back of her neck. She looked down at The Roan, measuring his condition. She bent to pick up the water bucket and turned. The bucket clattered to the ground.

"Bridger? Bridger!" She threw herself into his arms and held on, fighting back tears, and fear and defeat.

He held her close, rocking her, wordlessly sending her his strength and courage. When she stepped back her face was calm and her eyes were clear.

"Oh, Bridger," she breathed.

"How...?" he began.

She shook her head, her finger to her lips, and turned back to The Roan, saying, "Fresh troops have arrived and high time, I say." She picked up the bucket. "Bridger, no point in your just standing around. The Roan needs fresh water for his toilette. If you would be so kind, sir." Joining in the charade, Bridger took the pail.

"At your service, Madame. 'Pears The Roan's been slacking off since I've been gone. No doubt Montross and I will have an easy time of it in our next head-to-head." Behind them, The Roan gave a weak snort.

It was a difficult job, but, with Bridger's help, Eugénie gave The Roan a rubdown with cool water laced with chamomile. She applied the liniment and a fresh poultice, and then bandaged the wounds. They sat with the stallion until he slipped off to sleep. Eugénie motioned to Bridger to follow her and they tiptoed out of the stall.

Hand in hand, they walked over to the low stone wall that fronted the yard. When he spanned her with his hands and lifted her up onto the wall, Bridger noticed she was lighter and her waist smaller than when he'd left.

Bracing on her hands, Eugénie leaned back, working out the kinks in her shoulders. She ran her fingers through her hair and let out a long sigh.

"What a picture I must make!"

"As pretty a picture as I'd ever hope to see." He smiled at her womanly vanity. Taking her hand, his face turned serious. "When did this happen? What..."

"Seven days ago, yesterday." And for seven days and seven nights you haven't left his side, Bridger thought. The Roan should be recovering by now, but the wound is festering... and the fever. There's infection.

"I fear the chest wound's infected," Eugénie said, plucking the thought from his mind. "He was healing nicely until three days ago when I saw the first signs of it and, now, this morning, the fever. I don't understand. He was doing so well."

Bridger pulled himself up on the wall beside her. "Tell me how it happened."

Eugénie bit her lip, forcing back the tears. She took a deep breath and looked away.

"Oh, Bridger, if The Roan hadn't acted so quickly," she said, burying her face in her hands. "He saved my life."

Bridger pulled her close and she burrowed her face into his shirtfront and allowed the tears to flow. "If he dies, how will I live with myself?"

"You will because that's what you have to do. Just as he, your champion and guardian, did what he had to do." Bridger waited until the sobs subsided. He stroked her head and said gently, "These may be more than simple wounds."

"What do you mean?" Eugénie asked, sitting up and shoving the hair back from her tear-streaked face.

"Since the beginning of time, man has found ingenious ways to kill. Poison."

"Poison?"

"Aye. Did you see any residue around the cuts?"

"No, I didn't see anything but blood. Blood everywhere. So much blood."

"Some poisons are fast acting, others slower, depending on the strength of the man or beast to withstand or overcome the agent. The bleeding may have cleansed away some of the poison, but the loss of so much blood weakened his system, making it harder for him to combat what remained." His voice trailed off, leaving unsaid what both of them knew. The appearance of the infection after the early signs of recovery did not bode well.

In spite of Eugénie's efforts, The Roan's fever soared. His coat darkened with sweat. Tirelessly, through that day and into the evening, Eugénie and Bridger covered the great horse with cool compresses and fed him herb-soaked sugar lumps. Night fell as they finished putting fresh dressings on the wounds. They turned, hearing footsteps, to see Marie approaching the stall. All day, she had been back and forth to the stables bringing food and replenishing liniments and bandages. This time, she arrived carrying a basket and blankets.

"Mistress, you and the captain haven't touched the food I've brought," she said, her eyes dark with worry. "Here are some of your favorites. They're piping hot. Please, you must eat something."

"Bless your heart, Marie," Eugénie said and smiled at her wearily. The thought of food turned her stomach, but for Marie's sake she made a show of digging into the basket. "Oh, Bridger, look, the tarts you love so," she cried, holding one out to him. Bridger took the offering and ate it with relish, as Eugénie bit into an apple. Bridger made short work of a capon leg, washing it down with wine that he drank straight from the bottle. Eugénie nibbled at this and that, but enjoyed her fair share of the wine.

Feeling more relaxed than she had in days, Eugénie finished off the bottle and wiped her mouth daintily. "Marie, please tell the kitchen how delicious their feast was. I can see that many hands took part in it."

"Everyone is so worried about The Roan." Marie hesitated, afraid to ask what was uppermost in her mind.

Eugénie read the question in her eyes. "By tomorrow, I'll be better able to tell how he's doing. The fever rises and falls. I've leeched the wounds and kept salve and clean bandages on them. It's in God's hands now." Just then, a shudder ran through the stallion. His legs spasmed, then he stilled and lay quiet once more. Marie looked around and cocked her head.

"It's eerie. I've never known the stables to be so silent."

"They're standing watch over him," Eugénie said softly. "Thank you for the blankets, Marie. The captain has traveled a long way and has not rested since he arrived. Bridger, go with Marie. I'll see you in the morning."

"That you will, and every minute in between," Bridger said tightly. "We'll stand watch together, as we did so long ago under far different circumstances." Her heart swelled with the memory of that long-ago night. He saw her silver eyes glow with it as she turned to him.

"Very well, then." Eugénie nodded and said to Marie, *"Merci, ma chère amie."* Marie bowed her head and slipped away.

Eugénie sat by The Roan's head and Bridger settled down beside her. They passed the long hours recalling the great horse's triumphs. Eugénie laughed, remembering his antics at the Whittingtons' auction, which had permanently bonded the woman and the stallion. They remembered how Bridger had found The Roan ragged and broken after the beatings he had suffered at the hands of Sam Brown and his ruffians, the horse's miraculous recovery, his subsequent voyage to France, his racing triumphs. Remembering Jeremy's early attachment to The Roan brought tears to Eugénie's eyes.

"Oh, Bridger, if only Jeremy were here I'm sure he'd know what to do."

"He could do no more than what you've done, my sweetheart. This way, he'll remember The Roan as he saw him last, proud and gallant, neck and neck at the finish of our three-way race." The Roan stirred under Eugénie's hand as if in agreement.

"The Roan, proud and gallant," she smiled, "the winner in every race he ran."

"I've been meaning to ask you," Bridger said. "Why did you stop the tradition of naming each of his progeny 'The Roan,' with the addition of the next Roman numeral?"

"Actually, The Roan put a stop to it. His last foal would have been The Roan XX. When I presented the newborn to him and pronounced his name, 'The Roan XX,' The Roan would have nothing of it. He shook his head, pawed the ground, and turned away from the colt. I tried everything, but every time I spoke of 'Roan XX,' he'd shake his head. Finally, I understood. It was the name. With a new time must come a new name. I chose Thistledown, in the true Scottish tradition." She smiled up at Bridger. "It was as close as I could come to *White Heather*. Jamie's delighted, as you might expect. The colt's remarkable, the best of The Roan line, surpassed only by his sire."

Bridger nodded. "There will never be one better." He laughed. "In charge to the end."

They dozed off.

As the dawn crept up over the hills and lightened the stall, the great champion stirred. Eugénie was instantly awake. She nudged Bridger, who turned towards her sleepily. Together, they watched The Roan gather himself and, with a mighty effort, rise to his feet. Eugénie's heart caught in her throat and tears sprang to her eyes. Bridger stood and drew her up beside him to stand together to honor the valiant horse that stood before them. The Roan stepped forward, graciously accepting their salute. Suspended in time, they acknowledged him one last time, knowing that the moment had come. They bade their farewells. One last nuzzle. One last stroke.

One last time, Eugénie slipped up on his back. The Roan strode out of his stall. Slowly, he circled the stableyard. He greeted each horse in turn as he passed each stall. Completing the circle, he returned to the front of his own. Eugénie understood. She slid down from his back. Taking Bridger's hand, she walked away from The Roan and into the middle of the yard. She stood there, looking up at the sky towards the rising sun.

After a few minutes, she turned and walked back. She entered the stall to see the stallion once more lying where he had lain for so many days and nights. Together, Eugénie and Bridger knelt beside him. He lifted his head and whinnied softly. She cupped her hands under his head, as she had done so many times. He gently lipped her fingers. She brought her face next to his. Moments passed. She felt the weight of his head sink into her hands. The Roan was gone.

XXXIV

The last days of September slipped by as the household mourned the loss of the great stallion. The Roan's stall was empty and would remain so. Eugénie spent an afternoon cleaning and waxing his tack and hanging each piece in place. She felt his spirit so acutely that she half expected to hear his familiar whinny. When she was finished, she took a solitary walk to the pasture where he had frolicked and raced with his herd. She saw in her mind's eye how he would single out his progeny one after another, a colt or a filly, and put the youngster through its paces to test for speed and stamina. His parental pride was apparent in each one's ability, but Eugénie knew that his favorite, by far, was Thistledown, who looked heartbreakingly like his father and shared the great one's heart and spirit.

Riding Thistledown up the long avenue towards the château, late one morning, Eugénie smiled across at Bridger, who was matching her pace on Montross. At that moment she felt the weight of her loss shift and lift off her heart. One day she would be reunited with The Roan and the other loved ones she had lost, but for now it was the living that needed her.

Bridger returned her smile. He had watched her struggle with her grief and had seen her spirit begin to rally. Now he saw the brightness in her silver gaze. She's come to terms with it, he thought, and she's ready to move on.

"Nothing like a ride in this crisp air to work up an appetite," Eugénie announced, flinging herself off the colt's back and handing the reins to the groom who had met them at the stable gate. "Over dinner, Jamie will report on the progress of my new project for the château." She ticked off on her fingers the ambitious plans she had undertaken as they walked from the stables to the château. Looking at her radiant face, Bridger's heart lifted. Yes, she's back. He picked her up and whirled her around, interrupting her in midsentence. Squealing, Eugénie hung on for dear life.

"Put me down! Put me down, you lout!"

"What'll you give me if I do?" Bridger laughed. He stopped twirling, but kept her in his arms.

"This," she answered, kissing him soundly on the mouth.

"Not enough, not nearly enough." He deepened the kiss as he let her slide down his body until her feet were once more on solid ground. Breathlessly, they stepped back from each other.

"And what was the reason for that?" Eugénie asked, looking up at the man who, even after so many years, could still melt her heart with a glance.

"You," he answered simply, "just you." He took her hand and they walked into the château.

"We have a grave situation facing us," Eugénie said, looking around the table at Marie, Jamie, and Bridger. She paused to take a forkful of roasted lamb and savored the flavors that mingled on her tongue. "The lawlessness in the countryside has reached epidemic proportions. Daily, I hear reports of houses being broken into and ransacked; of priests and royalist sympathizers being dragged from their beds in the middle of the night, imprisoned or, worse, executed, on the flimsiest of charges. These outrages aren't limited to the clergy and the royalists. The innocent and law-abiding are caught between progovernment and antigovernment factions. Even before things reached the present level of mayhem, I knew I couldn't stand by any longer and do nothing.

"So Jamie and I worked out a plan to transform the château into a haven—a sanctuary, if you will—for people who can no longer live safely in their homes or those who've been turned out of theirs, unable to meet the higher rents or pay the burdensome taxes. Jamie, will you please bring us up to date."

Jamie nodded and took a sip of the Bordeaux, smiling at its complexity and long finish. "Madame, if I may, I must call our attention to this '92 vintage that we're tasting for the first time, drawn this morning straight from the barrel. In my opinion and in the opinion of our winemaker, this '92 vintage will prove to be one of the greatest Bordeaux of all time." The others joined Jamie and sipped the deep-red wine, silently paying homage to its early promise of great character.

Ah, Jamie, Eugénie thought, thank you for reminding us of the blessings we still have in spite of the horrors that surround us.

"Now, the project," Jamie said, clearing his throat. "We're moving ahead on several fronts. The additional silos you requested are completed and are rapidly filling as the harvests come in. Additional blocks of housing are under way. Some are already finished. They're designed to house several families. Each has one large hall for day-to-day living, a separate space for communal cooking, and a second floor divided into bedchambers. Several families have arrived from the district and have settled in already. The able-bodied will join our people in the patrol system that we instituted after Monsieur Renaud's unfortunate end. The families and individuals who come to live here will contribute their skills and talents. I project that we'll reach completion by spring, early summer at the latest, because as more people move in we'll have that many more hands to assist us. It was a complex plan, Miss Eugénie. I admit I was skeptical, at first, but it's working out exactly as you predicted. When we're finished, the area the structures cover will be five times what was originally on the land."

Bridger raised his glass to toast the undertaking. "The scope takes my breath away, not to mention the generosity it represents. If I understand correctly, this installation will rival a large town, providing livelihoods and protection for its inhabitants."

Eugénie nodded, her eyes shining. "Oh, Jamie, I'm amazed at the progress you've made. It's nothing short of a miracle. Attend closely to the patrols. They must be vigilant. This countryside has become as dangerous as the streets of Paris, if not more so." Eugénie turned at the sound of footsteps, to see one of the messengers from Paris standing in the doorway.

"*Entrez, s'il vous plaît,*" she said, motioning the young man into the room.

"Jeremy sent me with urgent news," the messenger began. "As the king's valet..."

"What's this?" Bridger asked, turning to Eugénie. "Jeremy a valet?"

"Yes, you heard it right," Eugénie said with a laugh. "Danton, suspicious of every breath the king and queen take, thought to place Jeremy in their household as his spy. It works to our advantage. In addition to reporting on Danton's activities, Jeremy can now report firsthand on the welfare of the family."

"Ah, yes," Bridger said, "I heard on my journey here that the royal family had been imprisoned in the old Temple fortress."

"Their imprisonment is a prelude to I know not what, but I fear the worst," Eugénie said, distress clear in her eyes. "What news do you bring from Jeremy?" she asked, turning back to the messenger.

"He wanted you to know that the new governing body, the National Convention, is far more radical than the Legislative Assembly. A good fifty percent are lawyers. A large number are civil servants, and there are physicians, some patriotic clergy, journalists, writers, and pamphleteers. There are constant clashes amongst the Jacobins, the Girondins, and the independent Deputies."

"I would have thought that Brissot's Girondins and Robespierre's Jacobins would have much in common," Eugénie said.

"Maybe in some regards, Madame, but the word on the street is that the Girondists seek to direct the revolution along legal grounds with order prevailing, instead of the mob rule and hysteria that the Jacobins encourage. The struggle is over whether Paris or the outlying districts will control the revolution." The messenger paused and looked down.

"What is it?" Eugénie asked, alarmed by the man's hesitation.

"It's the king, Madame. The king is going to be put on trial."

Eugénie lurched forward, grasping the arms of her chair. "Put on trial! What crime is he being charged with?"

"The government found incriminating papers in his apartment at the Tuileries after the family was taken to the Temple. Jeremy says that more and more of the Deputies feel that removing the king from power is not enough, that he is a rallying point for the insurrectionists."

"Imprisoning him wouldn't eliminate that fear, either." She stopped as awareness crept into her mind. "Only his death would accomplish that," Eugénie said softly.

The messenger nodded. "That's the conclusion Jeremy reached, as well. He said to tell you he hasn't heard this expressed openly, only through whispered innuendos and insinuations."

Eugénie sat back and let out a long sigh. "What of the king? Is he aware of this?"

"No. According to Jeremy, the family is cut off from all information. The staff that attends the family is made up of spies for the government. Jeremy has told the family nothing, wishing them to have what peace they can, for as long as they can."

Shaking her head, Eugénie pressed her lips together, lost in thought. After a few moments, she said quietly, "Before you set off on your return trip, be sure to have some refreshment."

"*Merci*, Madame." Bowing, the messenger left the room.

"Those poor, poor people. To think it was always Louis's intention to raise the plight of the common man. Little did he know that it would come to this." She turned to Bridger. "Thank God you relayed the message to Robert Morris to move ahead building Azilum with all speed and to set in motion the plan to rescue the royal family."

As October passed into November, rarely did a day go by without a message arriving from Paris. Evidence against the king was mounting. Reports came, telling of the guards' rude treatment of the royal family, especially the king. Fearing that the queen might sew messages and smuggle them out of the prison, her embroidery was taken away. The king's razor was confiscated. When he refused to be shaved, it was returned, but he was closely watched while he shaved.

In a touching letter, Jeremy outlined the family's day. First thing in the morning, the family came together for prayers. After breakfasting as a family, the king and queen gave the children their lessons. Midday they spent in the gardens under close watch. At 2:00, without fail, they sat down for dinner, during which time their rooms were thoroughly searched, every day. Evenings were spent playing games and, before going to bed, the king read aloud to the family. After praying together, the family retired to their sleeping chambers.

It was snowing lightly on the morning that yet another messenger arrived at the château. Eugénie and Bridger were sharing a late breakfast and listening to Jamie and Marie's household reports when the young man walked into the small salon. Eugénie noticed at once that the usual spring was missing from the step of the now-familiar messenger. With a sense of foreboding, Eugénie took the letter from him.

"*Merci,* Jean-Jacques." The young man turned and left the

room. Eugénie opened the letter with trembling hands and began to read aloud.

"Hmmm, there's no salutation."

On December 11th the king presented himself to the National Convention. Dressed in an olive-green silk coat, he stood with quiet dignity until he was told he could take his seat. He appeared unaware of the insult. When President Bertrand Barère addressed him as Louis Capet, he interrupted and said, "I am not Louis Capet. My ancestors had that name, but I have never been called that."

The President ignored him and continued to read the indictment that accused Louis of deception and conspiracy. When asked for his response, Louis said he had done nothing illegal and casually dismissed the incriminating documents that had been confiscated from the family's apartment at the Tuileries.

I watched the proceedings from beginning to end and was struck by his regal bearing throughout. It was almost as if he'd distanced himself from the scene. The only lapse in his demeanor occurred when he was accused of "being responsible for shedding French blood." He angrily denied the charge and was clearly very upset, but quickly recovered his composure.

When we arrived back at the Temple prison, another hardship was visited on him. He was told by his gaolers that he would no longer have access to his wife and children.

Eugénie stopped reading, her eyes wide with shock. "Does their cruelty know no bounds!" She took a moment to collect herself and then continued to read.

They told him that he would be required to apply for any visits in the future.

The cruelties that have been heaped on this family have been monstrous, but nothing more cruel than this. The king looked at the men aghast. His face turned ashen. Somehow, I don't know how, he rallied himself and turned to me and asked quietly if I'd be so kind as to serve him a cup of coffee. Serve him coffee? It was all I could do not to go down on my knees and beg his forgiveness for all the atrocities of these vile monsters. Miss Eugénie, it was the hardest thing I've ever done to just stand there and not attack those men and tear them limb from limb. Instead, I served him a cup of coffee.

Once the guards withdrew, the king lapsed into silence, sipping his coffee and staring off. What a sad, sad place he's come to. I was about to excuse myself when he turned to me with a look of resolve on his face and said, "I will devote the days and nights allotted to me to craft my defense. I have excellent advocates, Jeremy — Monsieur Malesherbes, Monsieur Tronchet, and Monsieur Romain de Sèze, whom you may know, as he's from Bordeaux. No? Well, it's of no mind. His reputation for eloquence is of the first order. I'll base my case on my constitutional inviolability and stand on my conduct as a citizen king. Monsieur Malesherbes wishes to challenge the credentials of the court and point out that the Convention's role as both judge and jury is contrary to the codes of the revolution. That won't do at all. That would only anger and arouse them."

Even now, I shake my head, thinking about his ill-conceived strategy. They don't consider him a king, citizen or otherwise.

He asked that I request paper and quills from his guards. Even the simplest things he must beg for! By the end of that evening, as I readied him for bed, I was utterly exhausted. It's beyond my understanding how he bears up so well. Before I left him for the night, his last words were of you. He bade me to send you his warmest regards.

Eugénie looked up at Bridger, whose face reflected the same sorrow she felt. "It's come to this," she whispered, letting the letter slip from her fingers onto her lap. Reaching for a brighter note, she said, "But you can't tell from the tone of the letter whether or not Jeremy thinks the indictment can be proved at trial."

Bridger nodded. "The accusations are so broad: deception and conspiracy. Then again, the papers from the family's apartment that Louis shrugged off may substantiate his offenses. But do they need to substantiate them? It's well known that many have been convicted and executed on specious charges. But what's this growing sentiment against Louis that you spoke of? What's it based on?"

"Oh, Bridger, who knows? Maybe it's come from the need for a scapegoat, someone to blame for their misery," Eugénie replied, shaking her head. "Or maybe it's fostered by the gossip mongering of the press, the pamphleteers, who turn fiction into fact or print whatever comes into their heads with no regard for the truth, so long as it furthers their ends. The journalists, if you'd call them that, fabricate lies, anything to sell their papers, and the more outrageous the better.

"Now these purveyors of salacious fiction and lies sit in the National Convention and hold sway. Brissot, Marat, Robespierre, and so on and so on, they all have papers to broadcast their views and opinions. We can only hope that there's so much squabbling amongst the Deputies and fighting for influence and power amongst the factions that they won't be able to come to any agreement about the king's guilt or innocence. Granted," she sighed, "it's not much to hang our hopes on."

Later that afternoon, Eugénie and Bridger were strolling in the garden where the winter sun had erased all signs of the morning's snowfall.

"So far," Eugénie remarked, "the weather's been mild for this time of year, but I smell a change in the air." In spite of the warm sun, she shivered and pulled her cloak tighter around her. Bridger saw the movement and put his arm around her, pulling her close to his side.

"The expansion of the château is quite an undertaking."

"Indeed it is, but it may well prove to be the château's salvation. We must expand our support for those around us, for our own safety as well as theirs. The only weakness in the plan is how to manage such a vast community. But," she said, her face brightening, "the answer may have arrived on our doorstep, this very day."

"Oh?"

"A family named Champion arrived this morning, who are interested in moving onto the château property. There are two brothers, their wives, and six children. Jamie and I interviewed them. One brother is an accountant with a good head for numbers. The other is a builder. The wives have wide-ranging household skills, and their children have been taught to read and write and the beginnings of their parents' skills.

"Oh, Bridger, seeing them and talking to them has shown me that there are still good people left in this world. I'm especially pleased that Jacqueline falls right in the middle of the children's ages. I've always felt lonely for her. Certainly, there are other children here, but none with her schooling and the other opportunities that these children have grown up with."

Bridger looked sharply at her. "Really? You've never spoken of this."

"What would've been the point? Jacqueline had to take the hand she was dealt."

"Not a bad hand, all things considered," Bridger said mildly.

Eugénie smiled up at him. "No, not a bad hand, but this just makes it better. Bridger, these people are a godsend, in more ways than one. The two brothers can partner with Jamie in completing and overseeing the expanded château system, and the wives can help Marie manage the château and the other living accommodations. They'll be joining us for dinner and we'll discuss these arrangements together."

"What of their politics?"

"They were very forthright. To the extent that they hold political views, they're republican. But they've seen the present régime wipe out their hard work with taxes and levies and wish only to have safe homes in return for honest work. They'll be an invaluable addition to our community. Bridger, I can't tell you how I've worried about managing the growth of the château during the expansion and running it once it was finished. Oh, what a load off my mind this is!"

"What about the project in Pennsylvania? What if these people hear about it? Wouldn't that jeopardize everything you've worked for, and endanger you as well?"

"Other than Jamie and Marie, no one at the château knows anything about it. These are good, simple people. They've restored my faith in my fellow man. I doubt I'll be disappointed in them."

"I trust you won't, sweetheart. I've always marveled at your perceptiveness about people," he chuckled, hugging her close, "though you were a mite slow where I was concerned."

Eugénie gave him a sidelong glance. "Oh, Captain, I'd say I've more than made up for my early shortsightedness." She pulled his head down and planted a kiss on his smiling lips.

She laughed when he growled in her ear, "But there's always room for improvement, my sweet, always room for improvement."

By the beginning of Christmas week, the Champion families were settled into their new homes. Both Jamie and Marie reported to Eugénie that Claude and Bernard, Yvette and Suzanne had far exceeded their expectations. They moved easily into their new roles and had lightened the considerable burdens that Jamie and Marie had been carrying since the château expansion had begun.

The Christmas festivities got under way at dawn when bonfires were lit and the long-held tradition of the chatelaine welcoming her people into the château began, with the oldest person at the château leading the procession. Gifts were exchanged, followed by feasting and dancing. Eugénie whirled from one exuberant reveler to the next, until, gasping for breath, she heard the chimes striking midnight, signifying that it was time to hand out lighted candles and move into the courtyard for the Christmas caroling.

Every year, a choir of young boys and girls were chosen to lead the singing. The beauty of their young voices soared above the rest, bringing tears to the eyes of many. Eugénie looked out over the upturned faces of the people before her. My people, she thought, my family. The feeling of love that swept through her took her breath away.

"May God bless you and keep you," she whispered and then joined in the refrain of "Silent Night." As the last notes quivered on the night air, Eugénie raised her arms to her people.

"Joyeux Noël, mes amis. Joyeux Noël! Vive la France!"

XXXV

The château's people traditionally spent the day after Christmas with their families or visiting amongst themselves. Eugénie and her family, as she had come to think of the MacKenzies and Bridger, were enjoying a quiet supper, recounting some of the highlights of the Christmas Day's festivities.

"I know I say it every year, but this year's choir was the best yet," Eugénie exclaimed.

Marie smiled at her. "And every year, you're right."

"This year's was especially good because the Champions' voices are so beautiful," Jacqueline spoke up, pleased to single out her new friends.

Eugénie smiled affectionately at her godchild. What an extraordinary young woman she's becoming. The château chimes ringing at that moment startled everyone.

"Who could that be at this hour?" Eugénie asked, looking around. Marie rose quickly and went to see who was at the door. Only minutes later, she returned, followed by Captain Brion. He entered the room and bowed to Eugénie.

"Forgive the intrusion, Madame Devereux. I trust you had a *Joyeux Noël.*"

"Thank you, Captain, we certainly did, and I trust you did as well. May I offer you some refreshment?"

"A glass of wine, if I may."

Once the pleasantries had been carried out, Eugénie turned to the soldier. "What brings you out so late in the day?"

"Madame, I wouldn't have intruded on your privacy," he said in his usual stilted fashion, "but a message was relayed to me from Paris that I knew you'd wish to hear. The king went on trial before the Convention today. Romain de Sèze pled his case eloquently. The powerful defense and the king's dignified manner notwithstanding, the universal belief is that the verdict will be 'guilty.'"

A look of sadness crossed Eugénie's face. She thought for a minute and decided to keep Jeremy's information to herself. "What's next?" she asked. "Who'll determine his guilt or innocence, and if he's found guilty, what then?"

"As I understand it, there will be an oral vote by the Deputies. If he's found guilty, there's a difference of opinion between those who say the Convention should decide the sentence and those who say it should be decided by the will of the people. At this point, it's anybody's guess, milady. Now, I must thank you for your hospitality and be on my way. I still have much to attend to."

"Of course, Captain," Eugénie said, rising, "and thank you for coming all this way to tell me this news."

"*De rien,* Madame. It's little enough, after all you've done. I'll be forever in your debt." He started to leave, but turned back. "It's a fine thing you're doing here, expanding the château into a community for those in need." Blushing furiously, he bowed and left the room.

"*Mon Dieu,* it's done," Eugénie said, slowly sitting back down in her chair.

"For the sake of argument," Bridger said, "how could the king be prosecuted by the Convention since, as I understand it, the Constitution holds that he and the Convention are one and the same? It would be as if he were prosecuting himself. As if that weren't enough, the men who are trying him already expressed their opinion that he was guilty before the trial began. It's a complete miscarriage of justice."

"If you abide by the Constitution, none of it makes sense—none of it," Eugénie agreed. "But Bridger, these men play fast and loose with that document, referring to it and using it only when it supports their arguments and suits their purposes. They completely ignore it when it doesn't."

A steely look came into her eyes. "I wonder more and more what our revolution was for. Was it simply an excuse for ambitious individuals to grasp the reins of government for their own ends? We're living in a tyrannical state that's far worse than anything that existed under the monarchy. And does it provide order? Does it avail the citizenry of protection under the law, or safety in their homes? No. We're in a state of anarchy and lawlessness like we've never known. People live in fear in their homes—fear for themselves and for their families.

"Individual freedoms? What individual freedoms? *Liberté, Égalité, Fraternité!* A mockery! They exist for a self-chosen few, small pockets of special-interest groups who maintain their power using fear, imprisoning and executing at will those who stand against them, anyone who they perceive might pose a threat to them. So, I ask you, what's the difference between then and now?" She looked into the faces of Bridger, Marie, and Jamie, challenging them to refute her words. She was met with silence.

"Miss Eugénie," Jamie finally spoke, alarm in his voice, "these are dangerous words. If someone should..."

"Jamie," Eugénie interrupted him, "I will not be controlled by fear. I know, I know," she said with a sigh, silencing Bridger. "Caution. I'll be cautious. I'm not a fool, but I will speak frankly in the presence of those I love and trust." She shook her head and gazed out of the window. "I fear what history's verdict will be," she murmured.

Bringing her gaze back into the room, she said, "I've heard other distressing news. In their attempt to distance themselves from the monarchy, fearing guilt by association, even the enlightened Deputies are willing to go to any lengths to put the king aside. How did it come to this?"

"If the verdict is guilty, what do you think the sentence will be?" Jamie asked quietly.

Eugénie took a deep breath and slowly let it out. "Who can say? I do know that Monsieur Brissot has predicted every step the Convention has taken so far. Referring to Rousseau's belief in the will of the people, he's been adamant that the ultimate judgment must come from them. But I don't think he speaks for the majority. The Convention jealously guards its power. I doubt most of the Deputies will agree to turn the king's sentencing over to the people. Brissot also made it clear that, should the verdict be guilty and the sentencing be decided by the Deputies, the Girondins will vote for imprisonment or banishment, not execution."

Eugénie paused and rubbed her head. "I cannot believe we're sitting here contemplating the death of this well-intentioned, if ineffectual, man."

"But what's the alternative?" Bridger interjected. "How can he be allowed to live? He'd always be a rallying point for the dissidents, who're disenchanted with the status quo. He's caught in a vise and there's no way out."

The days dragged on as the nation held its collective breath. On January 15, 1793, the verdict was handed down by the Convention. Of the 749 Deputies, 693 voted guilty. With unseemly haste, the Convention met two days later to pass sentence. It was not the will of the people that determined the sentence of Louis XVI, but rather a voice vote by the Deputies of the Convention. Of the 721 Deputies present, 361 voted for his execution and 319 voted for his imprisonment and banishment. A majority was not necessary. The larger number determined the sentence.

Late on the dark wintry evening of January 21, Jamie accompanied a messenger into the library, where Eugénie and Bridger were sitting by the fire enjoying some port and cheese. With a heavy heart, Eugénie stood up and walked over to the young man, who appeared ready to drop from exhaustion.

"Madame Devereux, Henri Canton, at your service," he said, holding out an official-looking letter. She took the letter and turned it over, relieved to see Jeremy's familiar script.

"Jamie, please see that Monsieur Canton has refreshments and accommodations. He's ridden long and hard."

"I'll see to it, Mistress," Jamie replied quietly and escorted the messenger from the room.

Eugénie sank into her chair, turning the letter over and over as she stared into the fire that crackled on the grate. Bridger watched her silently, knowing that there was nothing he could say to soften the moment.

"This is it," she said.

Bracing herself, Eugénie broke the seal and began to read.

Madame Devereux,

I am writing to you at the behest of Monsieur Georges Danton to inform you of the last days of Louis Capet, inasmuch as you have shown yourself to be a revolutionary of the first order and a staunch supporter of the people in thought, word, and deed. In the last few months, since his arrival at the Temple, I have been in the service of Louis Capet as his valet. Louis Capet has exhibited a composed manner throughout the trial, the rendering of the verdict, and the sentencing. He speaks often of his deep concern for his family, from whom he has been separated throughout the proceedings. He appears to be at peace regarding his sentence, but has expressed that he wishes, with all his heart, to clear his name of the accusations brought against him.

In his correspondence, he forgives his enemies and says of Marie Antoinette that "I have never doubted her maternal tenderness." He says how sad it is that it has come to this after all that they have gone through together and asks for her forgiveness "for whatever vexations I may have caused her in the course of our union." He states his innocence time and time again.

On the evening of January 20th, representatives from the Convention came to see Louis Capet to read the final pronouncement. When the reading was finished, Louis Capet requested three days to prepare for his execution. They denied his request and restated that the execution would take place early the next day. He asked to see a priest and to have a last visit with his family. These two requests were granted.

That evening the family was reunited. It was clear that his wife and children knew nothing of what had taken place or what was to come. Louis drew them into his arms and told them the Convention's verdict and sentence. He exhibited extraordinary courage as he tried to console his family. As they were leaving, they beseeched him to let them see him one last time in the morning. Knowing it was a promise he could not keep, he promised to see them before he left, giving them that bit of peace during the night.

Before retiring, he spent his last hours in quiet contemplation. He roused himself finally and retrieved a small box from his bureau. As I watched, he pulled his wedding ring off his finger and put it on top of the box. Next, he removed the royal seal from his watch and stared at it for several minutes. Turning to me, he held out the ring and the box.

"Jeremy, would you be so kind as to see that my wife receives my wedding ring and this box, which is of no value to anyone but us, for it contains only clippings of hair from our family? Also, please see that my son receives the royal seal."

"I will see to it, sir."

"*Merci,* Jeremy," he said, adding softly, "Isn't it strange that after all the trappings and all the grandeur, finally life comes down to such little things?"

The following morning, Louis Capet rose early, made his confession, and was dressed and ready when his escorts arrived. He requested to have his hair cut in his chambers instead of on the scaffold. They denied his request, saying he did not deserve any special treatment. When Monsieur Santerre, the commander of the Garde Nationale, arrived, Louis Capet, in an almost impatient voice, gave his last command:

"*Allons!*"

Louis Capet traveled the two hours to the scaffold through silent streets cloaked in fog. The buildings along the way were shuttered by government order. The crowds that lined the streets were strangely quiet. Louis arrived at the scaffold and stepped down from the coach with admirable poise. He lost his composure when the executioner, Sanson, started to bind his hands and remove his coat. His priest whispered urgently to him and he drew himself up and ascended the steps to the platform. No expression crossed his face as Sanson cropped his hair.

He turned to speak to the crowd. Immediately, a deafening drumming commenced, drowning out his words. I was standing near enough to the scaffold to hear him proclaim his innocence, once more. After the execution, the body was taken to the Madeleine cemetery and buried there in a plain wooden coffin. And so ended the life of Louis Capet.

XXXVI

They came eager for salvage, dispatched by the government to strip Louis Capet's room. Like rats, they skittered across the floor, rushing hither and thither. Sweeping shelves clean of priceless books, they tore the volumes apart, seeking hidden treasure before flinging them onto the mounting pile in the center of the room. They ripped costly hangings from the walls, adding some to their stashes, discarding others. The tinkle of crystal shattering added to the din.

One of their number, his feral eyes gleaming, crossed to a simple table that was piled high with papers. Intent on his mission, he spared not a glance through the window behind the table. Even if he had looked, it was unlikely that he would have given a second's thought to the bleak courtyard below, the last vista of a fallen king. He rooted through the pile, balling the sheets and tossing them into the fireplace, where hungry flames lapped them up. Finding nothing, he impatiently scooped up the remainder of the papers. A pair of spectacles fell to the floor. He looked at them for a moment before crushing them under his heel.

In his haste, he would have missed it, had the delicate gold chain not slipped out and dangled in front of his eyes. Lips drawn back in a gap-toothed grin, he dropped the mountain of paper on the floor and threw himself down on his knees and pawed through the pile. There, buried in the papers, was a filigreed locket, encrusted with gems. He snatched it up. Thick fingers worked the closure, forcing it open. He stared at the dainty miniature. Did Louis Capet miss this Austrian bitch and her litter at the end? Furtively, he pocketed the locket. No matter, he's dead now.

A high cackle caused the scavengers to turn from their hunting to see a wardrobe with its doors flung open and one of their fellows dancing about, swishing an oversized undergarment back and forth. His companions hurled crude jests at both the clothing and the performer. Several hurried over to join in the fun. Quickly, they scrambled into elaborate costumes, parading and preening in ermines and silks, trailing cumbersome trains behind them. Some plopped plumed hats atop elaborately curled wigs on their heads. When one of them reached into a pocket and pulled out a gold watch and chain, the merriment ceased. In dead earnest, they fell on the clothing and ripped it to shreds searching for treasure.

On the other side of the room an armoire crashed to the floor, spewing forth heirloom linens and table and bed coverings, fragile porcelain, and all manner of gold and silver serving pieces. A free-for-all ensued, as the scavengers swarmed over the contents. Shunning the porcelain, they snatched up the silver and gold pieces and shoveled them into their rough drayage sacks.

In no time at all, the room was reduced to rubble, anything of value confiscated. Without a backward glance, they left as quickly as they had come, their bags of booty slung over their shoulders.

Others had come before the scavengers, some to mark a moment in history, some to retrieve a particular piece of art or furnishing for a government building. Some to gloat.

Dust motes danced in shafts of the late-afternoon sunlight as the doorknob turned slowly in the abandoned chamber. The door opened on silent hinges and the great Danton strode into the room. Even his hardened heart recoiled at the sight of the wanton destruction. He crouched down and sifted through fragments of priceless Sèvres and Meissen. He picked up a piece whose broken curve fit in the palm of his hand, admiring the partial idyllic scene portrayed in pastel colors. He slipped it into his pocket. He saw slashed paintings hanging drunkenly on the walls, torn window coverings, unidentifiable heaps of fabric strewn in every direction, an empty wardrobe, its contents in ribbons on the floor, a writing desk still standing on three legs, an armoire inlaid with mother-of-pearl and ebony lying on its side.

He walked slowly around the room, touching this and that. When he came to the stripped bedstead and looked down at the torn covers and hangings flung casually on the floor, he saw a nightcap dropped by a careless hand. He picked it up and looked at it for a long moment. Smoothing it with his hands, he placed it on the bed. He finished making his way around the room and ended back at the doorway. He looked once more at the nightcap lying on the empty bed, turned, and walked through the door, closing it softly behind him.

Eugénie opened a report from one of her Parisian agents and began to read his account of the king's execution. "The cheering of the crowd was deafening. Souvenir seekers bought pieces of his clothes and strands of his hair from Sanson, the executioner. Others dipped pieces of paper or handkerchiefs in his blood."

Disgusted, she put down that report and picked up another. She skimmed it briefly. "Oh, *mon Dieu,* is there no respect for the dead?" Marie's hands had stilled on her embroidery and Jamie moved closer to her and placed a protective arm around her shoulders.

"The king's room was ransacked, torn apart. Even his eyeglasses were smashed. All his beautiful things reduced to nothing."

"Dear heart," Bridger said, trying to find words of comfort. "They mean nothing to him now, and probably meant little to him then. From what you've told me, he was not a vain man and was little given to pomp and circumstance. He's free of them now. They can't hurt him any more."

"Oh, Bridger, it began with such bright promise. Such hope for a better tomorrow. But tomorrow never came."

"Come," he said gently. "Let's take a turn in the garden while there's still light."

The crunching of the gravel was the only sound as they walked slowly arm in arm, lost in their own thoughts. They passed the pond where Eugénie remembered laughing and cavorting with Germaine de Staël. How carefree we were then, she thought. She stopped and turned Bridger to face her.

"Bridger, it's time to take action," she said, looking up at him with resolve in her eyes. "It's past time. I can no longer languish here at the château, waiting for others to carry out what needs to be done."

"I'd hardly call your expansion project and your ambitious Pennsylvania undertaking 'languishing,'" Bridger said drily.

"Bridger," she said as if he had not spoken, "I've come to realize that I must go over there. The reports say the town is behind schedule. I must be there to add whatever aid I can to speed its completion. I must. Time is running out. With the king's death, how much longer will the queen be allowed to live? She is a lightning rod for every antigovernment malcontent, not to mention a rallying point for the allies."

"If they execute her, wouldn't that bring the European alliance down on their heads and escalate their current action against France?"

"Only a month past, I would have agreed with you," Eugénie said. "Your point is well taken, were reason to prevail, but blood lust wars with reason in this country and, at every turn, blood lust wins."

"How soon can you be prepared to go?" Bridger asked somberly.

Eugénie was silent for a moment, chewing on her lip. "It's the beginning of February. I'll stay for spring planting and to see the completion of the château's expansion. I'd say, midsummer at the latest."

"Dear one, I must leave once the winter winds have passed," Bridger said quietly. At her stricken look, he nodded, reading her thoughts. "I also," he murmured, taking her into his arms. "Each parting is worse than the one before. Don't fret, dearest. We'll make every day a lifetime between now and when I must go. I'll be back to see you safely across the Atlantic."

She pressed her body closer to his. "Oh, Bridger, how fortunate we've been to have these hours, these days, this time together. How rich you've made my life. If I'd never known you, known us..."

"But you have and you will, my sweet. Have no fear, I intend to be in your life for as long as there's breath in my body," he said, chuckling, trying to lighten her mood. "And I intend to be breathing for a very long time."

"I feel time is running out. That..."

"No, precious heart. Together, we'll wrest minutes, days, and years from the miserly hourglass. We'll drink together from life's cup. We have many adventures before us yet to share." As he spoke, snowflakes began to dust the ground. He looked up at the thick, quilted clouds in the dusk sky.

"And, unless I miss my guess, our next adventure is going to be very wet and very cold if we don't seek shelter and be quick about it." Eugénie grasped her skirts and took off up the path. Laughing, Bridger caught up with her and they raced towards the warmth of the château.

They burst into the salon to see Captain Brion standing in front of the fire warming his hands. Eugénie's cheeks were rosy from the chill, her eyes sparkling, as she came into the room, laughing up at Bridger, who was regaling her with one of his crew's misadventures. Lucky man, Captain Brion thought. Remembering his manners, he bowed to Eugénie.

"Captain, another report from Paris?" Eugénie asked, regaining her composure. *"Asseyez-vous, s'il vous plaît."* She settled into an armchair near the hearth and smoothed her skirts.

"*Merci,* Madame Devereux," he said, sitting in the chair facing her. "The report I bring isn't from Paris. I spoke to Monsieur MacKenzie about it when I arrived, but I felt it was necessary to inform you as well.

The sparkle left her eyes, replaced by alarm. "Captain?"

"You know the food riots have begun again in earnest," he said abruptly. When Eugénie nodded, he continued. "And with the riots, burning and plundering. The countryside is increasingly dangerous for anyone traveling about, most especially traveling alone. I've come to implore you not to travel by yourself and to arm yourself even within the château."

"Thank you, Captain, for your concern," she said, smiling warmly at him.

He looked away for a moment and then looked back at her, a deep flush creeping up his neck. "If I may be so blunt, Madame, it's no longer safe for you to remain here. It's not just the food riots that concern me. In spite of your generosity, in spite of your support for the revolution from the beginning, I repeat: You are not safe here. These marauders care not a whit for your politics or your largesse. They hate. They hate who you are and what you come from. And they covet what you have." His voice had intensified with each word. His chest heaved with the emotion behind his words. He rubbed his forehead with his hand, dropped it in his lap, and looked at her beseechingly. "Please, Madame, you must listen to me before it's too late." He pushed himself up from the chair and in his agitation began to pace the room.

"Captain Brion," Eugénie said, trying to calm him, "I cannot simply abandon my people and this place. I'll give serious thought to what you've said and I'll make my decision. But, I promise you, I'll not be dictated to by lawless bullies. We've lived on this land for generations and generations. We've survived through good times and bad. We've protected our people and our property. I will not be run off by fear and leave these people and this land defenseless. If I do decide to leave, it will only be—I repeat, only be—because my staying would endanger my people. Captain Brion, I appreciate your misgivings and I value your friendship." At her words, the captain's flush deepened. He mopped his brow with his handkerchief and walked over to her, bowed formally, and raised her hand to his lips.

"Madame Devereux," he said gravely, "I am at your service. If there is anything, anything at all, that you should ever need, if it's within my power to do, you have only to ask and it will be done. I implore you to give serious consideration to what I've said."

"I don't take your concerns lightly, Captain. I will double the patrol, at once. I'll travel armed and in company, and I'll inform my people to do likewise. As to the other, I will give it serious thought."

"Thank you, Madame. I'll see myself out." He turned on his heel and left the room.

When his footsteps had receded down the hallway, Eugénie turned to Bridger and exclaimed, "What a godsend! I was wondering how to avoid bringing suspicion on my departure. Now, with the captain's blessing and his escort, I can carry it out in an orderly and open fashion. Oh, Bridger, for the first time in months I feel a great weight has been lifted off me. I will travel to Pennsylvania and add my aid and efforts to completing Azilum while there's still time to save Marie Antoinette."

Bridger smiled at her and patted the seat beside him. "Come, sit with me." When she was snuggled against his shoulder, he took her hand. "First our conversation in the garden, and now this. I'd been struggling to find a way to broach the subject of your leaving France, at least for a while." He let out a long breath, shaking his head. "Traveling back and forth, as I have, I've seen the escalation of violence, the roving bands of brigands. After the poacher's attack," he said, his voice thickening with emotion, "I've become more and more afraid for you, here, at the château. I cannot express the relief I feel." He stroked her hand and cleared his throat. "Oh, Eugénie, my love." He cupped her face with his hands and gently kissed her.

XXXVII

The days of February scattered before the winds of March. Then harsh April storms swept through the valley, leaving in their wake a people further burdened with increased food shortages and onerous taxes. Gentle May's dazzling beauty arrived one morning to grace the battered countryside with her warmth and her abundant colors.

The severe winter and spring weather had slowed Eugénie's ambitious schedule, but she moved methodically forward. Each day the transformation of the château came closer and closer to completion. The château people worked hand in hand, shoulder to shoulder. Buildings rose out of the ground. Kitchen gardens were planted. The growing population of livestock grazed in newly fenced pastures. The Champions emerged as leaders, adding management duties to their other demanding work.

"I bless the day those two families arrived," Eugénie said after Marie told her of yet another example of the Champions' contribution to the community. The two women made their way down the aisles between the looms and spinning wheels. "How clever of Yvette Champion to suggest housing all these functions under one roof. It's so much more efficient. The women have each other for company, and the little ones have playmates. The dye vats were always clumsy in close quarters."

A lustrous cloth on a loom nearby caught Eugénie's eye. She watched as graceful fingers moved swiftly back and forth.

"Berthe, how beautiful!" Eugénie exclaimed.

The young girl looked up shyly and said, "*Merci,* Madame Devereux," and bent back down to her work.

"What a gift you have," Eugénie said, fingering the multicolored cloth and admiring its fine texture. Berthe looked up again, her eyes shining at the compliment.

"'Twas my mother's and my grandmother's before me. I learnt at their knees. But they never had a loom such as this. They'd be so proud if they knew I was here in this wonderful place, doing my small part to help." She ducked her head, blushing.

"Your work is no small part, Berthe. We're fortunate that you are here with us. It's a miracle that you survived the horrible disease that claimed your family this winter. I know they're looking down on you and sharing my thanksgiving that you and your special gift are safe and sound now, here with us."

"Oh, Madame, how will I ever thank you?" the young girl blurted.

Eugénie put her arm around the slender shoulders. "Dear child, it's not for you to thank me, but for all of us to be thankful that we're here together helping each other." Berthe's lip began to quiver. The young girl was clearly overcome by Eugénie's words.

"Berthe, don't forget," Marie said, "Jacqueline is expecting you to lend a hand with the young people's soirée on Friday."

Berthe brightened immediately at the prospect of helping her idol, Jacqueline.

"Oh, no, Ma'am, I won't forget! She's counting on me!"

"I know my daughter's a taskmaster. Be sure you make time for some dancing."

"Yes, Ma'am, yes, Ma'am, I'll be sure to do that!" Eugénie and Marie moved down the aisle, leaving the young girl humming happily over her loom.

The women emerged into the bedlam outside. They carefully picked their way through, sidestepping young boys pushing wheelbarrows and men balancing all manner of building materials on their shoulders. The shouting of the workers and the din of hammers were music to Eugénie's ears. As they approached the expanded kitchen building, they saw women setting up long tables and benches outside for the afternoon meal. Small children and dogs followed the parade of steaming dishes that marched out of the kitchen doorway.

"I don't want to get underfoot, but I have to see how the new arrangement's working," Eugénie said, ducking around the parade and entering the large building. A beehive of activity met her eyes. Fireplaces were roaring in the four corners. Pots of all sizes hung on iron rods, giving off delicious aromas. The droppings of fat from spitted lambs, pigs, and poultry hissed as they struck the flames. The women moved from station to station in a smooth minuet as they prepared the meal.

"It's working! It's really working!" Eugénie exclaimed. Marie smiled at her mistress's obvious delight. "From the beginning, I worried about the scale of the kitchen. It couldn't be too large or too small. Claude Champion is a genius! This is just right."

The chef rushed over to Eugénie. Kissing his fingertips, his eyes alight with pleasure, he cried, *"C'est magnifique! C'est magnifique!"*

Laughing, Eugénie grabbed his hands. "François, it is indeed." Her chef's approval was the ultimate tribute to Claude's design. François's early resistance to the plan for the kitchen had threatened to derail the project. Claude and Eugénie had persisted in spite of the chef's protests and threats to leave the château. Now, all was forgiven in the face of his exuberance and pride in the finished structure. François ushered the two women outside to one of the food-laden tables and personally served them the specialties of the day. He barely managed to eat a bite as he sat with them, raving about his new kingdom. Eugénie and Marie returned to the main house well fed and glowing from the morning's success.

Eugénie looked up from the book she was reading. A smile played on her lips as she watched Marie patiently showing Jacqueline a new stitch for her needlework and Jamie doggedly working on his ledgers. Her gaze shifted to the window. Dusk had fallen, signaling the end of another day. The months past had been long and exhausting. The summer solstice had come and gone, and the anniversary of the fall of the Bastille was rapidly approaching. The riots set off by the king's execution continued to plague the country, further undermining order and the rule of law. Some said this was Robespierre's intent, that he found it easier to hold sway in a state of anarchy. The guillotines worked tirelessly.

Eugénie knew that her days were running out. Soon, very

soon, she must bring her leaders together and prepare them for her departure. She would savor the precious moments at her beloved château during the days she had left.

Eugénie turned the page and resumed reading. Suddenly, a loud crash shattered the night. All four people in the room jumped to their feet and ran into the hallway. A brick lay on its side, surrounded by glass shards from the window above it. Looking through the gaping hole, they saw, to their horror, a mass of people surging into the courtyard. Eugénie could see some of her people in their midst bravely trying to hold the intruders back. Armed with poles, knives, and bricks, the mob was slowly inching forward.

"No!" Eugénie screamed. Snatching the pistol out of her pocket, she dashed to the front door and wrenched it open. Frozen, Jamie watched as, with terrifying courage, she flung herself into the night to meet her attackers.

A gunshot snapped him out of his paralysis. "Marie, keep Jacqueline safe!" he yelled over his shoulder and ran after Eugénie. He joined her in the center of the courtyard, where she stood tall, her smoking pistol aimed above the crowd. Surprised by the gunshot and her arrival, the mob stopped, but only briefly. Eyes hot with rage and hatred, the human wall began moving forward again.

"Halt!" Eugénie shouted. "I'll shoot the next man who takes a step."

The crowd froze. The man leading the mob glared around at his comrades. His voice rang out. "You afeared of a mere woman? Cowards! Out of my way! I'll take care of her!" As he lunged forward, the crack of the pistol sounded. He fell to the ground and a dark-red stain blossomed on his shirt. A growl went up from the crowd. Eugénie raised the pistol above their heads and fired again.

"I and my family before me have never turned a person in need away from our gates, but acts of intimidation will be met with harsh measures. I will not be threatened. If you have genuine needs, I will meet with your leaders and discuss them. If you come to attack and plunder, you will find no mercy here." As she was speaking, the expressions on the men's faces shifted and some had the decency to look shamefaced.

One of the more truculent men cursed and shook his fist in Eugénie's direction, yelling, "Ye're hoardin' what's rightfully ours! Open up your silos!" The man nearest to him poled him in the back and spat, "Shut up, you fool!"

Over the muttering of the crowd, a shout came from beyond the wall.

"Out of my way! Get out of my way!" The mob parted and Jeremy rode into view brandishing a whip. Those slow to move jumped quickly when the whip snapped against their backs. Quickly, the château's people surrounded the now-subdued crowd.

"Jeremy!" Eugénie cried, running towards him. The young man swung down from his saddle and looked closely at her.

"Miss Eugénie, if any of that scum laid a hand on you, point him out and I'll take him apart limb by limb!" Eugénie almost laughed at his fierce expression.

"I'm fine, Jeremy. Everyone's survived, little the worse for wear, except for that one, who paid a high price for his bravado," she said pointing at the slain man.

"Thank God," Jeremy said, letting out a long breath. "When I arrived in Bordeaux, I heard that a mob was marching in this direction led by a well-known instigator. I came as fast as I could." He looked over his shoulder at the corpse. "Looks like you did the district a service this night."

His eyes danced. "Appears to me, I could've saved myself and my horse the trouble of rushing back here. What's a couple hundred unruly ruffians against the two of you?"

"There was a moment there when it could've just as easily gone the other way," Eugénie said gravely. "Jamie, would you, Bernard, and Claude divide up the townspeople. Determine which ones should be turned over to Captain Brion and which should be chastised for their poor judgment. Make sure the latter group goes home with food for their families. Come, Jeremy, let's go inside and get you some refreshment."

"Mmmmmm, this is good," Jeremy said, eating the roasted pigeon with evident relish. "Since the king's execution, I haven't been able to force a bite of food down my throat. Being home, away from the madness of Paris, I feel like a human being again." Between mouthfuls, Jeremy brought Eugénie up to date. "The food shortages and rising prices are worse than ever. With so many people out of work, the mobs that prowl the streets are swelling daily. The law-abiding folk stay behind locked doors, fearing for their lives. They don't venture out unless absolutely necessary. Anyone abroad alone is immediately attacked and robbed, if not worse."

"Horrible! Horrible!" Eugénie whispered.

"It is that," Jeremy said grimly. "To his credit, Danton has taken some strong stands against his Jacobin comrades, Robespierre most especially. Danton is deeply concerned by the raging lawlessness that Robespierre appears to condone, saying that 'For a good cause, wrongdoing is virtuous.'"

Eugénie nodded. "Robespierre is quoting Syrus, an ancient Roman. What can that man be thinking? He's sanctioning violence!"

"It would seem so," Jeremy agreed. "For the same reason, Danton takes issue with Robespierre's position that 'the virtue of the common man' is paramount, saying it justifies any action, no matter how extreme. Lately, it seems to me, he disagrees with Robespierre at every turn."

"If I were Danton, I'd be wary of crossing swords with that one," Eugénie said tightly.

"To be sure," Jeremy said, nodding. "But whatever else is said about Danton, no one questions his courage or doubts that he will stop at nothing to protect France."

"Where do the other Jacobins stand? Is he alone in this?"

"For the most part, yes," he answered. "He's against the growing sentiment to put Marie Antoinette on trial, saying it would trigger a European invasion. He'd like to use the promise of her safety to negotiate with the Austrians. He also opposes the extreme economic policies that are supported by most of his comrades."

"I never thought I'd agree with that man, but everything you've mentioned makes sense to me. If his positions are as unpopular as you say, his power base must be close to nonexistent," Eugénie said.

"Unfortunately, that's true. His reasoning and common sense

used to carry the day, but no longer. And as he and others like him lose their influence in the Convention, the outlook for the queen becomes increasingly bleak."

Eugénie lowered her head, clenching her hands in her lap. Jeremy hesitated, not wanting to cause her more pain. Then, taking a deep breath, he said softly, "This past week, by order of the Convention, they took Louis-Charles away from her."

Eugénie's head shot up, eyes wide in shock. "What? They took her son? In God's name, why?"

"They're animals! They need no reason." His voice trembled with emotion. "Miss Eugénie," he said bleakly, "they put the poor little boy in the cell just below hers so she'd be sure to hear his pitiful sobs at all hours of the day and night."

"They are monsters!" Eugénie cried, shaken to the core. She looked away and closed her eyes. Only the ticking of the clock on the mantel disturbed the stillness of the room. "I had no idea things had gone so far," she finally said.

Turning back to Jeremy, she asked, "Are her precious Marie Thérèse and Elisabeth still with her?" Jeremy nodded. "Thank God for that. But for how long?"

"Events are moving fast, so fast." He stopped and shook his head. "It was just a day or so after that order that Danton called me to him and told me it was no longer safe for me to be associated with him. He thanked me for my service and, with some of his old gusto, clapped me on the back and wished me Godspeed. I wasted no time putting that godforsaken city behind me." He pressed his lips together. Looking into his eyes, Eugénie saw the boy in the eyes of the man. "Miss Eugénie, I am so glad to be home."

"So am I, Jeremy, so am I."

XXXVIII

Jeremy spent the next morning with Jamie familiarizing himself with the transformation of the château. They parted company at the stables—Jamie to prepare the household reports and Jeremy to revisit his realm. He lingered at The Roan's stall, touching each piece of the great stallion's tack. He turned, hearing footsteps, to see Eugénie coming across the stableyard. She quickly closed the distance between them and slipped her arm around his bowed shoulders.

"I knew I'd find you here. Many's the time I've come for the comfort his spirit gives me."

Jeremy turned his face into her shoulder and clung to her.

"Why, Miss Eugénie, why?" he asked, his voice breaking.

She stroked his back. "Oh, Jeremy, I don't know. I don't know. Only God knows why things happen the way they do. It's up to us to make the best of what we are and to try to meet triumphs and disasters, as He would have us do. I've often wondered why it is that we never question our good fortune, only our hardships."

Jeremy jerked away from her, his face streaming and his eyes hot with anger. "That's not good enough! Senseless, senseless brutality! Why?"

Eugénie grabbed his arms and shook him. "That's as good as we've got," she said fiercely. "Listen to me." She shook him again. "Not one monster, no, not tens of thousands of monsters can destroy what is good and pure and fine, unless we let them. The Roan ended his life exactly as he would have wished, doing the only thing he knew how to do—protecting what he loved. He was not a victim. He was a hero. Do not, with your anger, take away the gift he gave me—my life. My life is all the more precious to me because of his great sacrifice. Can you understand that, can you? Do you think it's been easy for me, for any of us, to see what's happening to this country, to watch those in power making a mockery of our revolution, to watch France being torn apart from within and invaded from without?"

Jeremy threw off her hands and turned away from her. She looked sadly at him and then stared off at some distant horizon that only she could see.

"After The Roan died," she said quietly, "I struggled as you are struggling now. What I'm about to tell you, I've not told another living soul. One day, I had what you might call a revelation. I've come to believe that The Roan represented the valiant spirit of the American people, and that he brought that spirit here to France. I believe that his courageous heart embodied the spirit that inspired that brave people to fight for their freedom and to institute a new social order, a social order that would stand as a shining example to all people, to reach for the stars, to believe that anything is possible.

"Yes, The Roan died brutally, but his spirit did not die. The nature of that spirit lives and will be the spark that'll rekindle the belief in the hearts of our countrymen that liberty, equality, and brotherhood one day can—and will—be the birthright of every man, woman, and child. The leaders, who've brought to pass the darkest hour in France's history, will themselves pass into darkness and France will return into the light. The blood of the ones who have fallen, and of those yet to fall, will soak into the earth and will come again in the future generations of France. If I didn't believe this, then The Roan did die senselessly and life is meaningless."

"I'm so ashamed," Jeremy said, his head bowed. "Can you forgive me?"

"Jeremy, Jeremy," Eugénie said, pulling him to her. "There's no shame in the pain you're feeling or in the way you express it. What you witnessed in Paris would have broken a lesser man and turned his heart to stone. When you cry for The Roan and rage at the fates, you're crying out against all the horrors of this world. The ultimate horror would be if you didn't and if every right-minded person in this country didn't.

"There's only shame if we spend our rage uselessly. Instead, we must channel it and turn it into a force for the good. The Roan's rage destroyed the evil poacher. Mine fueled the plan for the new château community.

"Jeremy, there's one last thing I want to tell you, and then we must go back and prepare for the afternoon's meeting. Come, let's go sit out in the sunshine." Taking his hand, Eugénie led him over to the stableyard wall. Jeremy lifted her up and boosted himself up beside her.

"From the minute you and that great horse laid eyes on each

other, those many years ago in Virginia, you were in each other's hearts," she began softly. "You and he grew into manhood together. These long months past, he missed you desperately. Not a day went by that he didn't find a way to pay a visit to your apartment here in the stables. He would simply make his way over to it and stand there." They looked over at the corner of the yard that housed Jeremy's room and office.

"Yes, not a day went by. Many a time, when I was out riding him, he'd prick up his ears and turn towards the North, as if he expected any minute to see you come riding over the brow of the hill, or he would look in that direction and whinny, calling out to you. But he never shirked his duties or pined for his friend. He had his work to do here, as you had yours to do in Paris. Somehow he knew that.

"It was your poultice that almost saved his life. But he knew, as I came to know, that he had finished what he had come to do. He brought the spirit of the new world to the old, with all its youthful courage and fearless optimism. As he smashed to death the mean-spiritedness that met us on the path that stormy night, so, too, will that same strength ultimately prevail over the cruel forces that would bring down the greatness that is France. He left us in body, but not in spirit. Now, in his memory, we must finish what we've come to do. We can do no less."

Their eyes met and held, sealing a pact between them. In the memory of the great stallion, they made a commitment to the future. Jeremy slipped down from the wall and turned to help Eugénie. Arm in arm, they walked back to the main house.

"There, I think we have it," Eugénie said later that afternoon. "Jamie, that's a splendid summary. We've achieved our objectives. Now for the next thing on my mind." She slowly panned the faces at the table—Jeremy, Jamie, and Marie, together with the Champions, Claude and Yvette, Bernard and Suzanne. The past and the future of the château, she thought.

"It's with mixed emotions that I make the following announcement. As of today, the management of Château de Beaumont will pass into the hands of the Champion families. During the next few weeks, Jamie, Marie, Jeremy, and I will train you to manage this property. You'll have the full stewardship of it and the powers needed to operate it until my return." The Champions looked at her with consternation on their faces.

"The stewardship of Château de Beaumont?"

"Until you return?"

"Where are you going?"

"I realize this must seem very sudden to you. It was never my purpose that it would come to this, but the events of last night made it clear to me that, in good conscience, I can no longer ignore the inevitable. As long as I remain, this château community will be a target for those who bear ill will towards members of the nobility. I'm the last of the great families that still live in this part of France. The rest have fled or have been executed.

"As much as I value my life," she smiled and then continued, "I come from stubborn stock and would stay to the last and meet death, if that were my destiny, standing here and defending what's mine. But I cannot and will not have on my conscience that any person in this community was harmed because of me."

Claude, supported by his brother and their wives, protested

vehemently and argued eloquently and pragmatically the reasons for her to stay. Seeing that he was making no headway, Claude finally said, "Madame Devereux, you are the heart and soul of this land. How can it survive if you take that away?"

Eugénie bowed her head. How could he know that he had just spoken the only words that could defeat her and the very words that assured her that he was the one person to whom she would entrust the Château de Beaumont?

"Claude, your words show me that you understand the nature of this place. I know that you and your families will protect and preserve it. I will return to this land and these people, but for now I place it and them in your hands. I'm meeting with Captain Brion tomorrow to inform him of the plans for my departure and of the château's new management."

She rose and walked over to the mahogany sideboard and poured a rare vintage Bordeaux into the eight goblets that she had set out earlier in the day. She took a moment to run her hand across the polished surface of the piece of furniture that had been standing in the same place for so many generations. Carrying the tray of glasses over to the table, she placed one in front of each person, resumed her seat, and raised her glass, saluting them.

"Now, if you will, please join me in a toast to this brave land and to the future. God bless us all."

XXXIX

Jeremy accompanied Eugénie into town for her scheduled meeting with Captain Brion. She was shocked at the number of armed guards that stood on every street corner and the expression of naked fear on the faces of the townspeople.

"None of the reports I received prepared me for this," she said under her breath to Jeremy.

The meeting was drawing to a close when a young soldier burst into the room, waving a sheet of paper.

"Captain, Captain!" He pulled up short when he saw that the captain had visitors.

"Yes, Lieutenant, what is it?" When the young man hesitated, the captain said impatiently, "You may speak in front of my guests. What is it?"

"A report from Paris, sir! There's been an abortive attempt to rescue Marie Antoinette!"

"What is it you say?" the captain exclaimed. Eugénie and Jeremy looked at each other and quickly glanced away.

Oh, dear God, Eugénie thought, the rescue effort failed! After all the careful preparation, this is the plan we thought would succeed. Well, we'll just have to be more effective next time.

"Yes, Captain," the soldier answered. "According to the report, this attempt was very carefully planned." The captain held out his hand for the report. The lieutenant handed him the papers, saluted, and left the room, closing the door behind him. After reading the report, Brion looked up at Eugénie.

"You, no doubt, have heard of the plots to rescue the queen in March and then again in June."

With an effort, Eugénie maintained a puzzled expression. "Only vaguely, Captain—something about an attempt to smuggle the queen and the children out of the Temple disguised in military dress."

"Yes, that one was supposed to take place in March. You have the gist of it. The plan was to rescue the whole family, but it never got under way."

"I know nothing of the one in June," Eugénie said, hoping her face did not give her away.

"Yes, well, it also came to nothing. The Baron de Batz..."

"Wasn't he the man who tried to save Louis on his way to the scaffold?"

"Yes, the same. Your information is very accurate," the captain said, looking at her closely. Eugénie kept her expression bland and he continued. "His plan was poorly conceived and came to nought. The difference between the plot in March and the one in June was that the latter plot meant only to rescue the queen, as was the case with this recent attempt."

"I can't imagine that she would agree to leave without the children."

The captain looked at her sharply. "You're correct, Madame. According to this report, her gaolers were found drugged and unconscious and a young man was discovered in her cell, according to a witness, trying to convince the queen to allow him to rescue her. If it weren't so upsetting, it would be ludicrous.

"You were a friend to her, weren't you?" he asked mildly.

"Yes, Captain, I was and still am. I've never thought the success of our revolution was threatened by the existence of the king and queen."

"Between us, Madame Devereux, I quite agree, but it's not wise for us to express such thoughts. I respect your honesty and am honored that you trust me with your views, but beware, for others would not hesitate to use them against you. Which brings us back to the purpose of your visit today. As you know, even before this report, I was in favor of your leaving France. Now, I'm all the more adamant, and the sooner the better. I'm glad that you've come to the same conclusion. I, myself, will lead your escort. What date do you propose for your departure?"

"We're presently in the middle of July. I should be prepared to leave mid-August."

"No sooner, Madame?" he said, dismayed.

"Captain Brion, it'll be difficult enough in only a month's time to complete my arrangements and prepare the people who'll take over the management of the château community. The date I've chosen will have to do," Eugénie replied firmly.

"Dear Madame, I hope you'll not come to regret this schedule. One last thing: All residences are now required to post a list on the front door, accounting for each person staying within."

"Whatever for?"

"Bordeaux, Toulon, Marseilles, and Lyon are aligned with the other federalist cities that believe that the governance of France would best be carried out by all of France, not by Paris alone. This puts these districts in direct opposition to the Parisian political factions. As you know, France is a war zone and we 'federalists' are considered by some to be as much of a threat to Paris as the foreign coalition is to all of France. The Parisian agents strike swiftly and harshly, even this far from Paris, and they're aided and abetted by local spies and informants. Hence, I beg of you not to tarry a moment longer than you absolutely must."

Eugénie's composure did not slip. She rose from her chair and gestured to Jeremy to do likewise. "Then, Captain, I've not a moment to spare. Thank you for your counsel and your assistance. If I can, I'll move up my departure date."

Brion stood and walked across the room and opened the door for her.

"Madame Devereux, it's my fondest wish that you will. I wouldn't want to see any harm come to you."

"I share that wish, Captain," Eugénie responded, her eyes twinkling.

"God go with you," Brion said, bowing as Eugénie and Jeremy passed through the doorway and down the hall.

Eugénie divided her time between visiting each family at the château to inform them of her imminent departure and making her preparations for the journey. She could barely keep her eyes open at the end of the day to read the messages and reports that continued to stream in, telling her, amongst other things, of the ongoing infamous night searches by the Parisian agents in nearby towns. She doubled the château patrol and watched daily for Bridger's return, fearing that even his daring and skill would be no match for the criminal elements that trolled the French ports.

One afternoon, as she, Marie, Yvette, and Suzanne were completing the inventories of the château's furnishings, Jeremy bounded up the stairs.

"Miss Eugénie, a horseman's approaching. Thistledown's saddled and waiting for you in the stableyard!"

Eugénie's eyes flew wide. "Bridger! Here, here, Marie," she said, thrusting her lists into her friend's hands. She whirled and peered into the nearest looking glass. "Oh, I'm a fright!" She dashed down the hall into her bedchamber, only to reappear seconds later in her dressiest riding habit, her hair secured on top of her head with an assortment of pins and combs. Without a glance at the others, who stood frozen where she had left them, she flew down the stairs.

The slam of the front door broke the spell. Jeremy and Marie grinned at each other and the Champion women looked as though an errant gale had just swept through.

"It's as though she's a mere maid and her swain has just come calling for the first time," Yvette said, smiling.

Eugénie galloped out of the stables, her heart leaping in her chest at the prospect of seeing Bridger again after so many long, hard months. She had barely topped the ridge when Bridger came racing towards her on Montross and pulled up alongside. Kicking her feet out of the stirrups, Eugénie flung herself from Thistledown's saddle, making a perfect landing on Bridger's lap. Montross reared and whinnied his protest. Laughing, Bridger reined in the horse and pulled Eugénie close against him, covering her face with kisses.

"I've been dreaming about this moment in all manner of ways, but never once did I imagine equine acrobatics. Precious heart, you never fail to amaze and delight me. After so long apart, let's not shortchange our first embrace." Cradling her in his arms, he slid to the ground. "Now," he growled and clasped her to him. The two horses looked indifferently around before lowering their heads to nibble some grass.

Bridger and Eugénie clung to each other as their lips traced and remembered the other's beloved face. Breathlessly, they stepped back.

"How do I ever leave you?" Bridger murmured.

"And how do I let you go?"

Bridger took her hand and kissed the palm. "We're deeply passionate about everything, you and I. When we're called away to the other obligations in our lives, it only heightens what we share when we return to each other." Eugénie closed her eyes and sighed, enjoying his closeness and the feel of his hair running through her fingers.

"No doubt, you're right, my love, but I do weary of those 'other obligations' sometimes." Opening her eyes and smiling up at him, she clapped her hands impatiently. "Come, you won't believe what we've accomplished since you left, and I can't wait to hear how you managed to evade the pirates that, I've heard, have all but closed our harbors."

"Ah, it's a story worth the telling," Bridger said, remounting

Montross and swinging her up in front of him. With Thistle-down trailing behind, they set off across the meadow and he regaled her with his exploits all the way back to the château.

The days passed at an alarming rate. At the suggestion of the Champions, it was decided that the main house be locked up and shuttered on the day of Eugénie's departure. Except for the pieces that Eugénie chose to take to America, all the valuables had been carefully stored away. The furnishings that were left in place had been covered with muslin and the elaborate draperies and priceless carpets put away under lock and key. The artwork had been the last. Each piece had been wrapped and placed in the solarium, which Eugénie thought was preferable to the moist cellar.

XL

Her footsteps echoed on the bare floors as she walked through the house. She visited each room, empty but for the ghostly, shrouded furniture. The late afternoon sun slanted through the bare windows and she cast her mind back to all the happy times the rooms had witnessed.

"And they will again," she vowed in a firm voice. She had chosen to spend these last moments in the house, alone with her thoughts, before she joined Bridger, Jeremy, and the MacKenzies at their cottage for dinner, spending the last night there before their departure the next day. She plucked the ring of keys from the pouch at her waist and made her way through the door to the cellar and down the steep steps. Singling out the key to the château's vast wine chambers, she unlocked the massive door and swung it open. Lighting the candle she had brought with her, she walked unerringly to the Bordeaux that had been laid down the year of her birth. She placed several bottles in the basket that hung from her wrist and returned to the doorway. She reached up to the ledge to the right of the door and took down the chalice that the head of the household traditionally used on celebratory or exceptional occasions. She twirled the stem, admiring again the ornately cut glass. She paused and read the family's motto on the crest: "NOBLESSE OBLIGE." She smiled, remembering when her father had explained its meaning to her so many years ago. "To whom much is given, much is expected—the obligation of the fortunate to care for the less fortunate." You'd be proud, Father.

Placing the chalice in the basket, Eugénie closed and locked the door behind her and made her way up the stairs. She passed through the doors that lined the back of the grand salon and sat down on a plaster bench on her terrace one last time. She looked out over the gardens that were flourishing in the mid-August sunshine. Her eyes lighted on the "Eugénies," her namesake roses. She never failed to be amazed at the profusion of their blossoms and the size of their blooms, dramatic in their range of colors from palest peach, to apricot, to salmon to vivid coral. Her gaze lifted to the vineyards beyond. She was comforted, knowing that in her absence the community would care for these gardens, these vineyards, this property as their own. For a long moment, she looked across her land, seeing not the toil it exacted, only its beauty.

She retraced her steps. At the front door, she turned to look back one last time. Then, straightening her shoulders, she opened the double doors, passed through them, and pulled them closed softly behind her, hearing the lock click into place.

When Eugénie arrived at the MacKenzies' cottage, a light supper was already laid out on the table. Uncorking one of the Bordeaux, they celebrated her birthday a day early, toasting both it and the journey they would begin the next morning. The moment was bittersweet. It had been decided that Jamie would stay back until he felt confident that the château was running smoothly. Afterwards, he would travel to Paris to help carry out the plan for the queen's rescue and then accompany her to America.

When the meal was over, they went to the courtyard where the château people had gathered to bid their chatelaine farewell. Eugénie raised her arms and a great cheer burst forth from the crowd. She saw some dabbing at their eyes and the dull ache in her chest deepened, but when she spoke, her voice rang out clear and true.

"We are a family!" she cried to the throng. Another cheer went up. "Tomorrow, we shall all embark on a new adventure under the best auspices." She pointed to the heavens where a silver sliver sailed against the dark sky. "A new moon, the moon of beginnings! This is not a time for sorrow, but of gladness. I leave you with a full heart, knowing that my family is strong and safe. You will be in my prayers and I will hold all of you in my heart until I return. May God keep you safe until we meet again." The crowd roared their love for their mistress, who, like her people before her, had protected and provided for them.

Eugénie stood on the steps to bid farewell to each member of the château family. She kissed each child, embraced each woman, and, in the custom that she had brought back from Virginia, shook each man's hand. When a man, woman, or child threatened to break down, she bolstered them up with a story that made them laugh. When the last cheek had been kissed, embrace given, and hand shaken, Eugénie returned with Bridger, Jeremy, and the MacKenzies to their home to snatch the few hours of sleep left before the early morning departure.

XLI

Escorted by Captain Brion and his soldiers, Eugénie, Bridger, Jeremy, Marie, and Jacqueline arrived at the port without incident. While Bridger's crew was loading the furnishings, baggage, and horses on his ship, *White Heather,* Eugénie stood on the dock bidding Captain Brion and his men good-bye and thanking them for the safe escort. The captain dismissed his men and turned to Eugénie.

"Madame Devereux, it has been an honor and a privilege to serve you," he said.

"Captain, I'm honored to have you as a friend," Eugénie said. At her words, the telltale crimson crept up his neck. "Until we meet again, Captain, may God go with you."

"And with you," he said, adding a whispered *"Comtesse."* Bowing, he pressed his lips to her hand, saluted, turned on his heel, and walked away.

They boarded at dawn and the strong tide soon carried them out to sea. Eugénie stood at the rail and looked back at the receding shoreline, bidding *adieu* to her country and her way of life.

"I'll return," she promised. "I will return." Bridger watched at a distance, his tanned hands on the helm, holding it true.

Later, as the setting sun bathed them in its golden light, his knuckles barely grazed her cheek before his hand cupped her chin and lifted it to gaze into her silver eyes. His heart stopped at the depth of sadness he saw there. As he watched, the silver shifted and stubborn pride broke the surface.

"I remember a time of us... only us," he said softly.

She smiled up at him, taking his hand. "I remember, too. That was then. This is now. All there will ever be is now." She looked down at their joined hands. "I know this. Only this."

XLII

AUGUST 1793
Paris — Conciergerie Prison

The ancient crone shuffled along with the others in that dim, damp place. Wailing, and shouted obscenities, filled the air. When she reached the gate of the tiny space, she stared at the prisoner within. Her rheumy eyes widened in shock. Her mouth gaped open. She let out a long, fetid breath. This wizened wretch was not the queen! They've made a mistake! Her mind screamed. There was nothing of the rosy-cheeked, laughing maid who had danced into her heart so many years ago. She had known her, waited on her, assisted her in childbirth. No! This shriveled drab was not she. Sunken eyes, slack skin, white skull visible between scraggly strands. No! The queen has gone to some other place. This empty shell is not she! The crone spat a brown stream through the bars, just missing tattered slippers, and stumbled forward, shoved by the next eager voyeur.

OCTOBER 16, 1793

"Rise and shine, widow Capet! Ye have guests today!" The guard watched with glee as his prisoner struggled to rise gracefully from the meager pallet that had long since lost its freshness. "Ain't ye the lucky one, havin' these spacious accommodations all to yerself. Selfish of ye, I'd say, knowin' the prison's filled to the gunnels with all yer stinkin', precious nobles and priests. But not fer long," he chuckled nastily, "not fer long. La Guillotine's waitin' fer ye, she'll be workin' overtime today!"

The words hurled at the woman went unheard and unattended. She had perfected the art of withdrawing into the memories of happier times. Her gaze did not see the filthy walls, nor did she smell the foul stench. She walled herself away, traveling through rooms of memories in her mind.

She saw a young, fresh-faced girl, hiding behind a marble column, giggling. She smiled and remembered. Suddenly the music of Wolfgang Amadeus Mozart burst into her head. She watched his nimble fingers dance over the keys, his eyes vivid with delight, his smile dazzling as he struck the last chord. She saw him lift his arms, acknowledging the thunderous applause that met his spontaneous composition. She watched him slide down from the bench and skip over to her, pulling her from her chair and turning her to face him. Grinning, he gave her a broad wink. Her diminutive curtsy answered his deep bow. They clasped hands and he pirouetted gracefully, pulling her along behind him, as he scooted off on his little-boy legs down the long hallway to play their favorite game of hide-and-seek.

She giggled, knowing that he would find her and kiss her and vow to her his eternal love.

Had her frivolous, willful nature, her wanton self-indulgence, her overweening pride justified a punishment of this magnitude? Had they not taken from her all that they could take—her palaces and carriages, her jewels and gowns, her friends, her husband, her babies, her freedom—leaving only the breath in her body? When would they snatch away even that and send her to oblivion, to a place where they could take no more?

"I was a queen, and you took away my crown;
a wife, and you killed my husband;
a mother, and you deprived me of my children.
My blood alone remains:
Take it, but do not make me suffer long."

—Marie Antoinette,
speaking before the tribunal at her trial, October 1793

"I finish by observing that I was only the wife of Louis XVI
and I had to conform to his wishes."

—Marie Antoinette's summation at her trial
after two fifteen-hour-long days of questioning by the tribunal

"I have seen all, I have heard all, I have forgotten all."

—Marie Antoinette, 1793

Appendix

Dear Reader, often the weaving of the fictitious and the factual in a historical novel blurs the lines between what is real and what is the product of the author's imagination. I am including below a list of the fictitious characters and places marked with a star (★) and the historical figures and places in the novel so that you can distinguish between the two.

There may well have been a château similar to Château de Beaumont in the Bordeaux valley at that time, but, to my knowledge, such a place did not exist any more than did Eugénie Devereux, the countess who resided there. Bridger Goodrich, however, was an actual American shipper who became a privateer under the British flag during the American Revolution and eventually married and settled in Bermuda. His involvement with Eugénie is fictional.

The cafés of the Palais-Royal that are mentioned, as well as the colonnade itself, were famous gathering places. The relentless course of events that propelled the revolution down its circuitous dark path—including the lavish regimental banquet at the Palace of Versailles, the "women's march" on Versailles, and the royal family's doomed flight from Paris, to mention just a few—are historically accurate.

Many of the people, places, and events recounted in the novel may be familiar to you because of recent films, books, and articles about Marie Antoinette, the French Revolution, and the France of that period, but, speaking for myself (and probably many of you), the name "Azilum" was unknown until I stumbled upon it in an obscure periodical. One of the articles in that periodical described how a group of Americans led by Robert Morris joined a group of French nobility to carry out an ambitious plan: to rescue Marie Antoinette from her prison in France and spirit her across the Atlantic to a town built expressly for her on the bank of the Susquehanna River in Pennsylvania—a town named Azilum. The guillotine put an end to that bold plan. Little remains today of the town except a few ruins that stand as a testament to a group of courageous men who, though revolutionaries themselves, sought to save the last symbol of the *ancien régime*.

PEOPLE

Lambert-Sigisbert and Nicolas-Sébastien Adam, sculptor brothers

Mercy d'Argenteau, Austrian ambassador to France

★Comte d'Armagnac, Eugénie's late husband

Comte Charles d'Artois, Louis XVI's brother

Captain Aristide Aubert du Petit Thouars

Antoine Barnave, a leader of the Feuillants

Rose Bertin, Marie Antoinette's dressmaker

André Brevost

★Captain Brion

Jacques Pierre Brissot, a Girondist

Charles Bue Boulogne

Charles Alexandre de Calonne, Minister of Finance

Marquis de Condorcet, Marie Jean Antoine Nicolas Caritat

★The Champion family: Claude and Bernard, Yvette and Suzanne

Isaac René Guy le Chapelier
★Baron Henri and Baroness Lisbeth Conti
Georges Danton
★John Darby, a criminal from America
Jacques-Louis David, painter
Camille Desmoulins
★Eugénie Devereux, Comtesse de Beaumont
Peter Duponceau
Adrien Duport
Elisabeth, sister of Louis XVI
Axel Fersen
Jeanne Louise Henrietta Genet Campan
Armand Gensonné
Étienne (Stephen) Girard
Captain Bridger Goodrich
Marguerite-Élie Guadet
Henri-Maximin Isnard
Lucien Isnard, Mirabeau's protégé
★Jeremy, Eugénie's Master of the Horse
Marquis Gilbert de Lafayette
Princesse Louise de Lamballe
Alexandre Lambeth
Bernard-René de Launay, Governor of the Bastille
Emperor Leopold of Austria, brother of Marie Antoinette
King Louis XVI
★The MacKenzie family: Jamie, Marie, and Jacqueline
Le Duc and Madame de Maille
Stanislas Mailliard
Queen Marie Antoinette

Queen Marie Thérèse, wife of Louis XIV

Anne-Josèphe Theroigne de Mericourt

Comte de Mirabeau, Honoré Gabriel Riqueti

Jacques Necker, Minister of Finance

John Nicholson

General Louis de Noailles

Duchesse Louise Marie Adélaïde d'Orléans

Jérôme Pétion

★Marcel Renaud, official in Bordeaux

Jean-Baptiste Réveillon

Maximilien Robespierre

Pierre Louis Roederer, Procureur-Général

Jean-Jacques Rousseau

Charles-Henri Sanson, executioner

Jean-Baptiste Sauce, acting mayor of Varennes

Romain de Sèze

Abbé Emmanuel Joseph Sieyès

Baroness Germaine de Staël, daughter of Finance Minister Necker

★Amelia Stanton

Charles Talleyrand

Antoine Omer Talon

Lucy de la Tour du Pin

Marquise Louise de Tourzel

Pierre Vergniaud

Abbé Vermond, Marie Antoinette's personal advisor

★Randolph Whittington

LOSS OF INNOCENCE

PLACES

Azilum
Bordeaux valley
Café de Foy
Châlons
★Château de Beaumont
Clermont
The Hamlet at Versailles
The Hôtel de Ville
Montmédy
The Palais-Royal
Pont de Somme-Vesle
Porte Saint-Martin
Saint-Antoine
Saint-Cloud
Saint-Marcel district, Paris
Sainte-Menehoulde
Salon de l'Oeuil de Boeuf, a chamber in the king's apartment
Salon Doré in Versailles
Varennes
Vincennes

More praise for *A Time for Treason:*
A Novel of the American Revolution,
Anne Walther's earlier novel
about Eugénie Devereux and Bridger Goodrich,
set in Virginia and Bermuda
on the eve of the War of Independence

"Walther effectively describes the Gunpowder Theft of 1775, in which Eugénie helps conspire to steal gunpowder from the Bermudian governor.... Patrick Henry's 'Give me liberty, or give me death' speech, brushes with Martha Washington and Thomas Jefferson, and painstaking details of colonial life . . . add historical color."

—*Publishers Weekly*

"With verve, *A Time for Treason* tells the story of Comtesse Eugénie Devereux de Beaumont's adventures in colonial Virginia and on the island of Bermuda.... A banquet of compelling detail and romance."

—J. S. Holliday, historian, author of
Rush for Riches: Gold Fever and the Making of California
(Oakland Museum of California and
University of California Press)

"Based on an act of treason involving Bermuda, the Colonies, and England, the novel is a blend of du Maurier's atmospheric romanticism and thoroughly researched historic fact.... [Walther] feels the passion and drama of the Revolution, sees its bright colors, and she wants to share, to instruct, and to give us a wild ride we won't forget."

—Ann Seymour, Fashionlines:
The E-Magazine for the Elegant Edge

"The author weaves a complicated plot, combining real and fictional characters in an engrossing tale of love, treachery, bravery and passion."

—Merla Zellerbach
Nob Hill Gazette, San Francisco

Critical acclaim
for Anne Walther's book
Divorce Hangover:
A Successful Strategy to End
the Emotional Aftermath of Divorce

"A step-by-step path to mental equilibrium, *Divorce Hangover* touts positive thinking, self-reliance, conflict resolution and a determined effort to create financial and emotional independence."

—*Atlanta Journal-Constitution*

"Liberating...."

—*Dallas Morning News*

"*Divorce Hangover* is filled with excellent advice and workbook exercises that every divorced person will find truly helpful. It is a very readable, caring book that demonstrates clearly and concisely how you can dispel the divorce hangover demons from your life."

—Mel Krantzler, Ph.D.
Director of the Creative Divorce,
Love and Marriage Counseling Center

"Many books have been written...about divorce..., but what's been needed . . . is something really worthwhile on 'after divorce.' Now we've got one and a good one. *Divorce Hangover* is it.... We desperately need the practical, valuable, down-to-earth and human advice that Anne Walther doles out.

—Melvin M. Belli
Attorney

"Anne Walther describes in this book a devastating syndrome that she aptly designates 'divorce hangover.' . . . [She delineates] the possible causes and all the symptoms of this chronic illness, . . . [and] presents in a simple but magisterial manner precisely the steps one can take either to avoid or to rid oneself of this emotionally crippling disorder. This book may well be one of the monumental psychological books of this decade. Certainly it should be on the 'must read' list not only of men and women already suffering from 'divorce hangover' but also by those who may be contemplating divorce."

—Meyer Friedman, M.D.
Mount Zion Medical Center,
University of California, San Francisco

"An eminently practical approach that is *'guaranteed to work.'* "

—*Rochester Times-Union*

"There's a lot of help out there for divorced people in the way of books...[but] the best book I've seen in a long time is *Divorce Hangover*."

—*Star* (Tarrytown, NY)

Companion book to *Divorce Hangover*
is Walther's book
Not Damaged Goods:
A Successful Strategy for Children of Divorce
from Infancy to Adulthood

This book offers children of all ages the ability to

- recognize and work through the issues that confront them at the time of their parents' divorce

- understand and deal with these issues as the children mature

- anticipate and resolve the challenges they will face in the future

Walther understands that divorce affects the entire life span of children. In this book, she gives children the tools to handle their circumstances, so that they do not live their lives as "damaged goods." Her professional practice and lifetime experience have created this successful strategy for children of divorce.

Stories written expressly for a particular age group are followed by exercises and questions that guide readers through their specific situation. Serving as a communication bridge for children and parents, the book gives parents a tool to understand the feelings and issues confronting their children during the divorce and afterward. This book and *Divorce Hangover* offer the entire family a way to resolve the emotional baggage of divorce and move successfully into the future.